QUEST FOR THE SECRET KEEPER

ALSO BY VICTORIA LAURIE

Oracles of Delphi Keep

The Curse of Deadman's Forest

ORACLES OF DELPHI KEEP

QUEST FOR THE SECRET KEEPER

VICTORIA LAURIE

DELACORTE PRESS

Text copyright © 2012 by Victoria Laurie
Jacket art copyright © 2012 by Antonio Javier Caparo

All rights reserved. Published in the United States by Delacorte Press, an imprint of Random House Children's Books, a division of Random House, Inc., New York.

Delacorte Press is a registered trademark and the colophon is a trademark of Random House, Inc.

Visit us on the Web! randomhouse.com/kids
Educators and librarians, for a variety of teaching tools,
visit us at randomhouse.com/teachers

Library of Congress Cataloging-in-Publication Data
Laurie, Victoria.
   Oracles of Delphi Keep : quest for the secret keeper / Victoria Laurie. — 1st ed.
      p. cm.
   Summary: In 1940, when Delphi Keep is taken over by the Royal Navy as a communications outpost, Ian, Theo, and Carl dread being evacuated to the earl's winter residence where they will no longer be protected, but are even more concerned about deciphering the third prophecy and identifying the Secret Keeper.
ISBN 978-0-385-73861-3 (hc) — ISBN 978-0-375-89560-9 (ebook)
[1. Orphanages—Fiction. 2. Space and time—Fiction. 3. Gorgons (Greek mythology)—Fiction. 4. Dover (England)—History—20th century—Fiction. 5. Great Britain—History—1936–1945—Fiction. 6. Morocco—History—20th century—Fiction.] I. Title.
   PZ7.L372792Oqm 2012   [Fic]—dc23   2011029517

The text of this book is set in 12-point Goudy.
Book design by Vikki Sheatsley
Printed in the United States of America
10 9 8 7 6 5 4 3 2 1
First Edition

For my grandparents
Carl and Ruth

AN OATH SWORN

A hidden cave, Morocco 1232 BC

General Adrastus Augustus of Lixus tugged hard on the large sack filled with gold, silver, and other treasure he'd managed to snatch away from the Carthaginians currently looting his city. Sweat ran into the creases of his brow as he pulled the last of his massive fortune into the mouth of a cave, relieved to have snuck right past the Carthaginian guards posted at the harbor.

His vessel was tucked into a small lagoon not far away, and the general had already determined that he would wait until nightfall, in a few hours or so, to load the treasure onto his boat and sail away, with no one the wiser.

The general had discovered this small cavern after first arriving on the beaches of Morocco when he was a boy, during the time his father had ruled the great city of Lixus. He remembered climbing the large rock wall down the beach only to discover this hidden cove and, at the opposite end, another rock formation.

Curious, he'd come to this side and found the small and

1

somewhat shallow cave with the most astonishing secret: in the back wall of the cave was a skeleton, set into the rock as if somehow the very stone had formed around it. How the bones had become encased in solid rock was a mystery he'd long wondered about; what truly fascinated him was that they were clearly human. As he knew the bones to be a secret—no one had ever mentioned them, and bones encased in stone would be something worth talking about in Lixus—he thought this the perfect place to hide his wealth until that evening.

With a final tug he lugged the last sack close to the seven others he had already laid at the foot of the bones, and sat down to wipe his brow. It was while he was catching his breath that something quite extraordinary happened: as if by magic, the wall that held the skeleton disappeared, and the bones that had been entrapped by it clattered to the ground at his feet.

"By Zeus!" Adrastus exclaimed, jumping up in utter amazement. But he was even more astonished when he saw that on the other side of where the wall had been stood a beautiful woman with her arms crossed over her chest, and eyes that seemed to pierce his soul.

For a long moment he stood gaping at her, and it wasn't until she lowered her arms and bent over slightly that he realized the woman was gravely injured. Blood seeped through a wound in her side, and she shook with the effort to maintain her posture.

"My lady!" Adrastus gasped, leaping forward to catch

her as her legs gave out and she fell into his arms. "What wickedness has befallen you?"

But the lady did not answer him. Instead, her trembling fingers pulled off two large bronze cuffs that adorned her wrists, and she pushed them into his chest. "These belonged to my husband, Iyoclease," she said, her voice barely stronger than a whisper. "And now they belong to you, General Adrastus of Lixus."

Adrastus eyed her closely. He was quite certain he had never seen her before, because he would have remembered a lady so lovely. Still, as he lifted her in his arms and gently eased her over to one of his sacks of treasure so that she could lean against it, he asked, "Have we met before, my lady?"

The woman coughed and a small bit of blood appeared on her hand when she covered her mouth. "No, General, but in the next few hours before my death, we shall know each other quite well."

Adrastus removed his cloak and covered her. "I must find you a healer," he said, thinking perhaps the lady's condition was making her a bit delirious. "You have lost much blood, my lady. If you are brave enough to sit here for a bit, I shall go in search of a healer immediately."

But the woman only clasped his arm tightly and said, "Please, General, do not waste what little time I have left with such a noble but fruitless cause. You must sit with me and I must tell you a tale and then I will ask something of you, something of the greatest importance."

3

The general had no intention of allowing the beautiful creature to fade away when he was certain he could find a healer. He was about to gently protest and pry her hands off his arm if need be when she said to him, "My name is Laodamia of Phoenicia. I am an Oracle of Delphi and I have seen the way of things, General Adrastus. I know that you will grant me this wish, so perhaps you will agree to listen and allow me to get to my tale?"

The general gasped anew. "My lady," he said, "you do not wish to imply that you are *the* Laodamia of Phoenicia? The greatest Delphian Oracle the world has ever known?"

The pale features of the lady's countenance lifted in a sardonic smile. "Yes, General, I *do* mean to imply that very thing."

Adrastus looked at the place where the wall had been and back at the woman before him. He remembered a coin given to him by his mother for good luck. It had been engraved with the great Oracle's face, and he could clearly see the resemblance to the beauty on his coin, but his mind was having difficulty believing what his eyes beheld. "But, my lady, how can this *be?*"

Again the woman pushed the bronze cuffs at him. "Here," she said. "Take them, General. They are key to opening the portal at will. Use them to help you on your journey, and to help the United find each other."

Adrastus stared down at the cuffs, still reluctant to take them, but Laodamia would not give up until he had donned them. To his surprise, they fit perfectly.

"When you want the portal to open, merely cross your arms over your chest and think of the next place you must go. The portal will act as both guide and protector. You will need it to act as such in order to stay alive, General. And do not take these words lightly, my friend, for they will mean the difference between the salvation of mankind and its utter annihilation."

Laodamia was breathing heavily, and Adrastus could see now that her wound was mortal; how she found the strength to speak at all was quite beyond him.

Yet speak she did. She spoke of things nearly beyond his ability to understand, but he took in every word with rapt attention, and then, when the day had grown long and she was finished, she said this to him: "So you see, my champion—for that is what you will be to me, Adrastus of Lixus—I and the United desperately need you to carry out a mission. Momentarily, my protégée and dearest friend, Adria, shall be arriving. . . ."

At that very moment Adrastus could hear the faint *clop, clop, clop* of hoofbeats approaching from the far end of the newly enlarged cave.

"She will need some of your silver, my friend," Laodamia added, "to fashion the boxes which I have requested of her, but which could not be made until now. She is also bringing the prophecies to be stored in the treasure boxes, which she has kept hidden for me in her father's home."

"Prophecies?" Adrastus asked, anxious to learn everything before the great Oracle's strength gave out.

Laodamia offered him a weak nod. "Yes. Prophecies which will likely make no sense to you, my dear general, but which are of the greatest importance to the One and the United."

Adrastus remembered from her tale who this One was, and he hoped he would have a chance someday to meet this greatest Oracle of all.

"The contents of these prophecies are to be kept secret. *No one* can know of them. You must be my Secret Keeper, and swear an oath to me that you shall deliver the boxes to their proper hiding places and *never* allow them to pass into the hands of our enemies."

Outside, the sound of hoofbeats drew even closer. "I swear, my lady," Adrastus said, taking her hand formally, bowing his head, and placing his free fist across his chest. "On my life, I swear my allegiance to you and this cause. I shall be your Secret Keeper."

When he looked up again, Laodamia's pale face was stained with falling tears. "Thank you, General," she said, "and forgive me for what I am about to say to you. . . ."

At that moment the hoofbeats outside came to a stop. "Mia!" a woman's voice called.

But Laodamia did not answer; instead, she held Adrastus's gaze and said, "There will come a day, shortly after you pass through a bright green door on your way to hiding the final box, when you shall be tempted to betray your oath to me. I cannot tell you why; this is what I have foreseen. The full consequences of that betrayal are beyond my sight, but know this: they would be disastrous. So I will only ask that you weigh your decision carefully, bearing in mind what I have said to you here today."

"*Mia!*" the other woman's voice exclaimed, and Adrastus looked up to see another incredibly beautiful woman standing over them, holding several scrolls in her arms.

Laodamia regarded her visitor with calm dignity. "Adria," she said, "meet your future husband, General Adrastus of Lixus."

General Adrastus thought he had been shocked as much as he could be until he heard the Oracle utter those words. "*Future husband?*" he and Adria said in unison.

The Oracle took a ragged breath and a tiny smile formed on her pale lips. "Yes," she said. "I have foreseen it, and it will be a most happy union, I can assure you."

Adria dropped to her knees and set the scrolls aside. "By Zeus, Mia!" she exclaimed as she took in the condition of her mistress. "Forget such talk and tell me, what has happened to you?"

But Laodamia ignored her and pulled the cloak about her more tightly, concealing her wound from her protégée. "Adria, I am fine. You do not need to worry about me." She then turned again to Adrastus. "I beg of you another promise, General."

Adrastus could see the light dimming in the great Oracle's eyes, and he felt a deep pang in his heart at the thought of her death. He knew her from legend, of course, but now that he had sat with her for a time, he found he was oddly heartbroken by the thought of losing her after even so brief an encounter. "Anything," he told her, wanting her final moments to be spent in peace. If there was something he could do, another promise to make or oath to take, he would do it.

Laodamia held his hand and closed her eyes. "I wish for my funeral pyre to be lit on this ·beach," she said. "Do it when the night is upon you, then take your treasure and the first box Adria crafts, which will contain my second prophecy, to a cave in the foothills of the mountains. The journey there will be long and arduous, but you will escape notice. I have foreseen it, so go there with confidence. Your treasure will be quite safe hidden deep in the cave you choose, but mark the route as I have instructed you, so that those who need to find the Star you wear about your neck, and the box, will see the way.

"When you return, Adria will have finished the rest of the boxes and I will have been reduced to ash. Bury my remains next to those of my beloved, then take Adria with you through the portal to begin hiding the rest of the boxes."

Adrastus opened his mouth to protest the last bit, and he noticed that Adria was about to do the same, but at that moment Laodamia's eyes flew open and she looked at each of them sternly. "Vow this to me!"

Adrastus looked at Adria and something passed between them. The general couldn't have explained what it was, but he suspected it was the first hint of a deeper bond to come. Still, he lowered his gaze and considered for a long while what the Oracle was asking of him. He had accepted the earlier vow because the city he had loved and was bound by oath to protect was in his enemies' hands. There was nothing left for him there, and he could hardly return to Greece; the shame of losing Lixus to the Carthaginians would be too great.

Being the Oracle's Secret Keeper was just the cause he needed, and her faith in him seemed so absolute that he found his spirits lifted and his purpose renewed by accepting the charge. He also felt no pangs about leaving his treasure behind for a time. If the greatest Oracle the world had ever known had stated that it would be safe, then he believed it with absolute certainty. He could always return to retrieve it, and with the cuffs to open the portal any time he commanded, he could move his treasure freely anywhere he chose after his mission was complete.

But bringing along this woman, Adria, well, that was another matter entirely. She was beautiful, of that there was no question, but would she become a burden to him? Not only that, but Laodamia had said they would actually marry! Even though his faith in the Oracle was absolute, this one prediction he chose not to accept.

Adrastus of Lixus was a bachelor at heart, and he had *no* plans to marry anyone. Ever.

But did the Oracle need to know that? Laodamia was not asking him to marry the woman now; she was merely asking him to bring Adria along. And that was a charge he felt he could accept, especially when he remembered that the cuffs would allow him to open the portal at will. If she became too much of a burden, he would simply open the stone wall and push the woman through.

With a sigh, the general resigned himself. "I vow this to you, mistress," Adrastus finally said, and he heard Adria say the same words at the same time, which he found quite remarkable.

When next he looked at the great Oracle of Delphi, her eyes were still open but no longer stern, a beautiful smile was held across her lips, and the life within her was gone.

A GRAVE PREDICTION

A graveyard outside Dover, England, May 1940

Ian Wigby stood rigidly at the foot of a grave with bitterness in his heart. This wasn't his first visit to the grave site, and he knew it would not be his last.

He'd come here on several occasions over the past eight months, each time finding himself holding the same angry stance.

It was the inscription on the tombstone that most upset him, because it reminded him how close he'd come to having his most earnest questions answered.

HERE LIES ERROL WALLACE
A GENTLE GARDENER
29 DECEMBER, 1866–20 AUGUST, 1939

Footsteps behind Ian caused him to turn. "Thought I'd find you here," said a smiling young man with white-blond hair and a tall, thin frame.

Ian sighed and unclenched his fists. "Hello, Carl," he said.

His best mate came to stand next to him and stare down at the neatly tended grave. "Waiting for those bones to talk again, eh?"

Ian allowed himself a small smile. "Wish that they could," he said. "It's just so blasted frustrating."

Carl nodded knowingly. "We missed having a chat with him by less than a month."

Ian's heart felt heavy with regret. "And I had the sundial the whole time, Carl," he told his friend, using the same words he'd uttered nearly a dozen times since finding the grave. "If only I'd thought to use it sooner!"

The late Errol Wallace was the only person Ian knew of who had ever met the woman who had given birth to him.

Ian's mother had handed him over as a newborn to the gentle gardener before she'd disappeared behind the wall of the portal, taking her reason for abandoning him and her identity with her.

Ian had heard the story secondhand from the Earl of Kent, who was his patriarch and the overseer of the large orphanage, Delphi Keep, where baby Ian had been taken in. Any further detail about that fateful encounter between Mr. Wallace and Ian's mother had been taken with the gardener to his grave, and so ended any hope Ian had of ever finding his mother, and any inkling of where he'd come from.

The knowledge left a well of bitterness within him

that he found difficult to reconcile, and hence he often found himself here, standing over the gardener's grave, stiff and angry at the hand fate had dealt him.

But Carl's support always helped temper his mood. With a sigh Ian said, "Is the last group ready to leave?"

Carl nodded. "Thought you might like to come back to the keep and say your farewells."

Ian's mood turned gloomier. Eight months previous, Germany had invaded Poland; and England, France, and the others in the European alliance had declared war on Germany and its allies. The battles in those eight months had been quite fierce, and both aerial and nautical invasion were constant threats, given the strength of the German armed forces. Children under the age of sixteen from all the port cities across England were being evacuated to safer, more rural areas to live with foster families or other relations, and most of the orphans of Delphi Keep were gradually being moved to farms and homes within Kent's interior.

The last six orphans, aside from Ian and his band of special friends, were being relocated to Dartford that very morning.

Reluctantly he turned away from the grave site. "Let's see them off, then," he said.

The young men hurried out of the graveyard and trotted along the road in the direction of the village proper.

As they neared their home in Dover, the road grew more congested with traffic, clogged mostly by military lorries and marching soldiers.

A few of the military vehicles had bright red crosses on them. "Looks like another shipment of wounded have come in," Carl remarked.

Ian eyed the lorries grimly. News from the front hadn't been good. The allies were taking a heavy beating from German and Italian forces, and every day more and more troops were coming back with terrible injuries.

As a port city, Dover had grown quite rapidly into a military outpost, and many of the larger buildings had already been converted to offices and quarters for the armed forces. The earl himself had offered the east wing of Castle Dover as lodgings for some of the higher-ranking officers, and Delphi Keep was being converted to a hospital now that most of the children had been sent into England's interior.

So much change was taking place all around him that Ian was having difficulty keeping up. "When we get back, mate, you might want to have a talk with Theo," Carl said, interrupting his thoughts.

"Why?"

"She's worried about you."

Ian smiled. Theo was the closest person in the world to him, even closer than Carl. Theo, however, was Ian's baby sister, even though he knew they weren't related. She had come to the keep on a terribly stormy night when Ian was five and Theo was two, and Ian had been put in charge of naming her and looking after her. He'd taken that charge quite seriously, although the roles had often been reversed and Theo made sure to look after *him*.

Theo was a very special young lady. She was twelve years old, and well on her way to being forty—or so Madam Dimbleby liked to jest. Extremely mature for her age, Theo was also gifted in a way that many adults had a difficult time accepting, until they'd been around her long enough to see with their own eyes what she could do.

Ian's little sister was an Oracle, gifted with the ability of sight. She knew things about people that she should not, and she often saw things that had yet to happen.

So when Carl said that Theo was worried about him, Ian paid attention. "What's she saying?" he asked.

"She didn't give me the details," Carl said. "She simply said that she wanted to speak with you because she was terribly worried."

Ian thought on that for a moment. "Are you sure she wasn't referring to Madam Dimbleby?"

Theo had quietly told him and Carl that she'd had a most distressing vision about their headmistress. She felt strongly something terrible was going to happen to her. "I've seen a grave, Ian," she'd whispered. "And I know it's a grave for our headmistress!"

"Are you certain it's Madam Dimbleby?" he'd pressed. After all, Delphi Keep had two headmistresses: Madam Dimbleby and her cousin, Madam Scargill.

Theo's face had become pensive. "I believe so," she'd said. "What I mean is that when I look at Madam Dimbleby, all I can sense is some terrible violence that I'm certain she'll suffer!"

So without telling the lovely older woman a thing

about Theo's grave prediction, the three of them had taken turns keeping an eye on Madam Dimbleby as she'd both orchestrated the relocation of Delphi Keep's orphans and assisted with the many wounded soldiers now filling the space at the keep.

The task of keeping a watchful eye on her was not an easy one, as Madam Dimbleby was a woman with energy to spare. Keeping track of her meant keeping close to her, which further meant making themselves available to the many tasks she charged them with as she bustled through her busy schedule.

She'd thought they'd all been most helpful, however, and Ian admitted to himself she'd also been running them quite ragged.

"I suppose once we say our farewells to the others, we can find Theo and relieve her of the duty of watching Madam Dimbleby," he said to Carl.

Carl sighed dramatically. "That woman will be the death of me." But Ian saw that he wore a mischievous smile.

It began to rain then and Ian and Carl quickened their pace. At one point they had to wait to cross the street until a large uncovered vehicle passed. Carl slapped Ian's arm excitedly. "Look!" he said, pointing. "Germans!"

Ian peered at the passing lorry and noted that it did contain a group of about a dozen men in German uniform, sitting with their hands bound and wearing miserable expressions.

"I bet they were the ones captured from that German U-boat!"

The day before, word had spread that a German U-boat, skulking its way through the channel, had had a severe mechanical malfunction, which had forced it to surface within several hundred feet of a British patrol ship.

What had been most shocking of all, however, was that the German command aboard the ship had rigged the boat with explosives and sunk it rather than allowing the advanced submarine technology to fall into enemy hands. Most aboard had been drowned when the U-boat sank, but several men had been pulled out of the water and captured. Ian knew they would be brought to Dover for interrogation by the admiral in charge of these waters, although Ian doubted they'd give anything up.

"It looks like they're being taken to Castle Dover," Ian remarked.

Carl became even more excited. "Let's try to get a closer look at them!"

Ian was about to protest; after all, the year before, he'd had several very close and nearly fatal encounters with the enemy. But Carl had already started running after the lorry carrying the Germans. Ian had no choice but to chase after him.

Given the heavy traffic along the road, Ian and Carl had no trouble keeping up with the prisoners all the way to the castle.

As they drew closer, they could see that the lorry containing the Germans had pulled to a stop right next to a small bus, which several orphans from Delphi Keep were being loaded onto. Ian was relieved to see that Madam

Dimbleby was assisting the children. If she was there, then Theo must be close by.

Ian and Carl, quite out of breath by then, shuffled over to stand near Madam Dimbleby, who was a bit teary as she helped the children. "There you go, Jasper," she said, guiding one young boy with a slight limp up the steps of the bus. "There's room in the back for you."

Carl's chest was pumping hard, but he still managed to ask the headmistress if both he and Ian could go aboard to say their farewells.

"Yes, yes," said Madam Dimbleby. "But hurry along. They've got a bit of a drive ahead of them to Dartford."

Carl dashed onto the bus, but Ian held back. "Madam, is Theo about?" he asked.

"She's inside, Ian," Madam Dimbleby said gently, but with a small shake of her head. "Theo's been sticking to my apron strings so much recently that I felt we both needed a bit of a break from each other. I've sent her to help find some spare sheets for the soldiers at the keep. She's upstairs right now rummaging through the earl's extra linens."

Ian smiled, thanked his headmistress, and boarded the bus, which he noticed was stuffy with stale air. Several children were attempting to open the windows, but the bus was old and the windows wouldn't give way easily. Ian hurried to the back to assist a girl of about seven, named Margaret, with her window. He worked the latches with one hand while tugging on the pane with the other. After a loud squeaky protest, the window gave way.

As the cooler air rushed in, Ian overheard a soldier out-side ordering the German prisoners to disembark from the lorry. He then overheard one of the Germans say, "What does the English pig want us to do?"

"He is ordering us down, Commander," another man said in reply.

Ian looked with narrowed eyes at the Germans and toyed with the pouch about his neck, which held a very special stone of magical properties. The stone—part of a gem once known as the Star of Lixus—was made of pure opal, and it allowed the bearer to understand and speak any language ever spoken as if it were the bearer's very own tongue.

Ian's eyes traveled to the British soldier unloading the Germans from the lorry. And Ian noticed that only when the soldier moved his gun threateningly did the Germans obey.

"Do what he says, men," said the German commander with a sneer. "We will have our opportunity soon enough."

"What are you staring at?" asked someone right behind Ian, causing him to jump.

Ian turned to see the boy named Jasper holding a roll of extra clothing and blinking up at him with large brown eyes. "Nothing," Ian assured him, and moved out of the way so that Jasper might take his seat next to Margaret. The pair were siblings and had come to the orphanage after losing both their parents to consumption.

Carl, meanwhile, was jovially making his rounds, saying

goodbye to all the occupants on the bus. Ian marveled at how easily Carl made friends and how so many of the children genuinely seemed to like him.

As all the passengers got settled, Ian moved to lower a few more windows. Each time, his eyes returned to the German soldiers being herded off the lorry, and he noticed that several were whispering among themselves.

At that moment, Admiral Ramsey—a man Ian had come to admire greatly—exited the front door of Castle Dover along with his personal assistant and a few other high-ranking soldiers. Seeing Madam Dimbleby, the admiral nodded and began to walk to her. Theo had suggested to Ian that the admiral was rather fond of their headmistress, and judging by the way Madam Dimbleby blushed every time the admiral was near, Ian tended to believe her.

From the bus, Ian could see that the appearance of the admiral captured the German commander's increasing attention. Rather boldly and loudly, the commander turned to one of the British soldiers guarding him and asked, "Do you speak German? Can you understand what I'm saying to you?"

The soldier seemed to understand at least that much, because he shook his head. "No," he said.

"Do any of you soldiers speak German?" For emphasis the commander pointed to all the men guarding his group of prisoners.

Again the British soldier shook his head. "We'll have a translator here soon," he said, not looking as if he especially cared if the commander understood him.

But Ian could tell that the German commander did

understand the soldier, and a twisted grin lit on his features. When the admiral had drawn a bit closer to their bus, he saw the German commander look round at his men. "When I give the order, as one we will move for their guns. Take down the admiral first, and shoot as many of the others as you can," he told them.

Ian's heart dropped to his feet and he bolted for the front of the bus. "They're going to shoot the admiral!" he yelled at the top of his lungs, lunging for the steps. "It's a trap! It's a trap!"

As he emerged from the bus, several astonished faces stared in absolute shock at him—including that of Admiral Ramsey, who was now standing a few feet away next to Madam Dimbleby. "You speak German?" he gasped as Ian stopped dead in his tracks.

In an instant, Ian realized that he was speaking the last language he had heard, and as his eyes darted to the German prisoners, he realized his mistake, as they too were looking at him with a bit of astonishment.

Even before he had a chance to react and explain himself, however, a terrible cry rang out from inside the castle, and on the second floor Theo's pale face appeared in a window and she screamed, "*Iiiiaaaan! Nooooooooooooooo!*"

Ian barely had the presence of mind to register what happened next. The German commander shouted, "Now!" and all together the prisoners rushed forward and overtook their British guards. A wrestling match ensued; the German prisoners attempted to secure the weapons from the overwrought soldiers, now fighting for their very lives.

From around the castle, other British soldiers began dashing forward to assist their fallen comrades, and the children on the bus screamed in panic and fear.

Out of the melee emerged the German commander, wielding a knife he'd managed to secure from one of the fallen soldiers. Wearing a crazed look in his eyes, he held the knife aloft and forced his way out of the tangled mess, heading straight for the admiral.

Ian lunged at the admiral, tackling him to get him out of the way before the German commander could stab him. Because Ian had shoved the admiral, the German's mark was off and the knife connected with the side of the bus. Ian still had a grip on the admiral's military jacket, and as the German came at them again, Ian grabbed the older man and heaved him around, up the stairs of the bus and safely out of range of the knife.

When he turned, he stared right into the commander's eyes, which were slits of rage. Again he heard Theo scream his name, and the sound was so wrought with fear and anguish that he reflexively turned his head to her.

Movement he saw out the corner of his eye caused him to snap back, and he realized the commander was now charging straight at him, the knife aloft. Ian closed his eyes, waiting for the steel blade to strike his chest, when he himself was shoved violently aside and a horrible scream pierced the chaotic sounds of shouting men and angry curses.

Something heavy landed right on top of him, and he

crashed to the ground. A shot rang out, and then another, and another, until finally, everything went quiet.

Ian opened his eyes slowly, aware that the thing that had hit him was a person. His right arm felt wet and he looked at it. With a great deal of shock, he found it covered in blood.

Then it seemed that there was a rush of people all around, and he heard someone panting heavily and whimpering in pain. Belatedly, he realized that his headmistress was sprawled on the ground with him, and as he was pulled out from underneath her, he saw that the knife that had been meant for him had instead been sunk deep into her chest.

"No!" he cried, scrambling onto his knees and scooting over to cradle her head. "Oh, Madam! What's happened to you?"

Madam Dimbleby's face was very, very pale, and her lips were turning blue. A gurgling sound came from her chest every time she attempted to breathe, and there was nothing but agony in her eyes as she stared straight ahead without focusing on anything.

Shoving his way over to kneel beside Ian, Admiral Ramsey sucked in a breath when he took in Madam's condition, then lifted his chin and shouted, *"Medic!"*

Ian felt on the verge of panic; clearly the woman who had been like a mother to him was barely clinging to life. He scooted as close to her as he could, wriggling out of his coat to lay it gently under her head. "Oh, ma'am!" he whispered, feeling the agony of guilt. "Why, ma'am? *Why* did you do such a foolish thing?"

Madam's hand came up and gripped Ian's arm weakly. "Ian!" she choked just as a soldier wearing a large red cross appeared from the gathering crowd to crouch down next to them. "Send for Gertrude!"

Madam Dimbleby was referring to her cousin, Gertrude Scargill, the other headmistress at Delphi Keep. Ian's head snapped in the direction of the old keep, at least a kilometer away, and he wondered with despair if he could make it back with Madam Scargill in time. He knew Madam Dimbleby's injury was quite grave; if the bleeding wasn't stopped very soon, she would likely die. Ian was torn between staying with her and doing as she bid, but one more look into her eyes convinced him he must succeed in this errand for her.

He'd gotten no farther than a few hundred meters when he saw a figure emerge right next to him. Ian started a bit when he realized someone was matching him stride for stride, but he quickly realized it was Carl. "Ian!" Carl gasped as he came up alongside him. "Wait!"

With great reluctance Ian slowed his pace and snapped, "I've got to fetch Madam Scargill!"

Carl reached out and firmly took hold of Ian's upper arm, yanking him to a rough halt. "Let me!" he said between pants. "I'm faster over distances than you! You've got to go for Eva! Theo says she and Jaaved went into the village to mail a letter."

With a jolt Ian realized that only Eva might be able to help Madam Dimbleby.

Eva was one of the special orphans who had been allowed to stay behind at Delphi Keep. She had come through the portal from Poland on the eve of the war with Germany, and like Theo, she also had a very special gift—that of a healer.

As a healer Eva was incredibly powerful, and she had in fact already saved several lives—Carl's included. "Right!" Ian agreed, already turning away from the path to the keep. "You bring Madam Scargill and I'll go for Eva!"

Ian had to bypass the small patch of woods, which housed the secret entrance to the portal, but he hardly gave this a second thought, so intent was he on finding Eva as quickly as possible.

And it was perhaps because his mind was so focused that he completely missed the sounds of running footsteps and the large figure moving through the brush, until he ran right into it.

A LOST WARRIOR

Ian went sprawling to the ground, where he lay for a moment, discombobulated. He had no idea what he'd just run into, but it felt like he'd gone headlong into a solid brick wall.

When he was able to pick his head up, he realized he wasn't far off the mark. Blinking furiously to clear his vision, he saw a very tall and fierce-looking warrior standing over him, wearing, of all things, a leather skirt, a brass breastplate, and a cone-shaped helmet.

The warrior appeared both startled and quite angry. "You there!" he shouted at Ian, pointing his long bronze sword directly at Ian's chest. "Up with you!"

Ian scrambled to his feet, flustered by the man's sudden appearance. He was so flustered, in fact, that he found it hard to form words—especially when the soldier stuck the point of his sword into Ian's chest. "Where is this place?" the soldier demanded, his eyes darting quickly to the side to take in his surroundings.

"Er . . . ," said Ian. "Dover, sir."

The soldier blinked at him, as if he'd never heard the name Dover before, and Ian couldn't help wondering, given the soldier's dress and abrupt appearance, if the man had perhaps come through the magical portal hidden just beyond the trees. "Dober?" he said, his tongue working to say it correctly, and failing.

Ian wasn't about to correct the man, especially since he had such an urgent mission to complete. "If you please, sir," he said quickly, "I'm on a terribly important errand. I truly must be off!"

The soldier didn't lower his sword. Instead, with his free hand he removed his helmet, and he glared hard at Ian.

Seeing the man free from his helmet caused Ian to suck in a slight breath. The soldier looked familiar in a way that sent goose bumps along Ian's arms. He was tall and broad shouldered, with a straight nose, a square jaw, light blond hair, and ice-blue eyes. Ian knew he'd seen this man before, but he couldn't for the life of him place where. There was also the possibility that—given the man's period attire—he might be involved with the prophecy. Still, as much as Ian wanted to question the soldier, he didn't have time, because every moment he spent standing there was a moment Madam Dimbleby's condition was worsening.

Ian shifted on his feet, wondering what to do. The soldier regarded the movement and said, "I do not know this place, Dober, and I seem to have lost my way. You may get back to your errand when you have led me back to my soldiers."

Ian looked anxiously to the woods again. "Please, sir!"

he cried, desperate to get to Eva. "You *must* let me go! My headmistress has been horribly wounded and I must see to getting her a healer!"

The soldier's eyes softened a fraction. "What is this headmist you are speaking of?"

Ian clenched his fists in frustration. "My head*mistress*," he clarified, knowing that the Star of Lixus was allowing him to speak in whatever tongue the soldier was speaking; however, it wouldn't translate those words coming out of Ian's mouth that were not found in the soldier's vocabulary. "My headmistress, Madam Dimbleby, the woman who has looked after me since birth. She's been stabbed in the chest, and if I don't leave at once to bring back a healer, she will very likely die!"

The soldier frowned. "Where is this healer you speak of?"

Ian pointed to the village, visible just beyond the downs of Castle Dover. "There."

The soldier lowered his sword. "Go, then."

Ian could hardly believe it. The soldier was letting him go! Still, he knew that after he found Eva, he'd need to come back and either help or question the soldier. Knowing the portal, he thought it wasn't likely that the soldier was there by accident. In fact, it was far more likely that his appearance had something to do with the prophecy. "If you'll wait in those woods for me," Ian said, pointing to the patch of forest by the castle wall, "I promise I'll return and help you after I've seen to getting the healer."

The soldier nodded. "I understand," he said. "Now be off lest your headmist perish."

Ian raced along to the village, his eyes searching for any sign of Eva, when an idea occurred to him. Reaching into the pocket of his trousers, he retrieved a magical instrument in the form of a sundial, left to him by the great Oracle Laodamia. He had to pause in a doorway and take a few breaths before he could say, "Please show me where Eva is!"

Immediately the dull surface of the dial shone brightly, as if it had just received a polish, and a dark shadow that had nothing at all to do with the angle of the sun appeared.

The magical instrument responded to the sound of a voice asking the location of anything or anyone. So long as the object was a physical thing, the sundial would work like a compass, pointing to the object's location until that object was found. Once that happened, the dial would again go blank, casting no shadow no matter how bright the sun.

Ian glanced in the direction the shadow was pointing, and raced off again. He wound his way through the crowd of villagers and soldiers and finally managed to spot Eva half a block down.

"Eva!" he shouted. "Eva, come quickly! Madam's been hurt and we need you straightaway!"

Two women nearby looked sharply at Ian, and he overheard one of them say, "What the devil did that boy just say?"

"I've no idea!" exclaimed the other. "He sounds as if he's speaking in a foreign tongue."

Ian blanched. Of course he had. The last language he'd heard was something other than English—though he was hard-pressed to say exactly what tongue he'd been speaking. Still, Eva did turn around and Ian knew she could understand him, because she too was wearing a piece of the Star, which Jaaved had given to her the year before.

Beside her was Jaaved, another one of the special orphans of Delphi Keep and the boy responsible for finding the Star in the first place. As the pair raced down the block toward Ian, he doubled over, attempting to get as much air into his lungs as he could before he'd be forced to run again.

"What's happened?" Eva asked.

Ian eyed the pedestrians around them. He couldn't tell what language they were speaking to each other—the Star had a way of jumbling things—so he pulled both Eva and Jaaved close and said in a rush, "Madam Dimbleby has been stabbed by a German prisoner at Castle Dover, and her life is hanging by a thread!"

Eva gasped and gripped Ian's arm tightly. "Take me to her!"

Ian nodded and was about to race off with his companions when Jaaved took Eva's hand and said, "Let me, Ian. I can take her to the castle. You're still out of breath."

"I'll catch up," he promised. "Madam is right outside the front entrance, unless she's been moved inside. If anyone bars you from seeing her, find the earl and he'll insist on getting you close to her."

Jaaved nodded and tugged on Eva's hand. The pair flew down the street, running as fast as they could. With a pang, Ian thought about poor Madam Dimbleby and hoped desperately that they'd make it to her in time.

After catching his breath, Ian began to trot down the street himself, weaving in and out of the traffic, growing frustrated when it seemed that the already crowded streets were becoming even more congested.

The village clock gonged four times, and Ian realized that another ship of soldiers had likely come into port in the past half hour, which was the reason the village was suddenly full of people.

He worried that Jaaved and Eva—who were somewhere up ahead—would be caught in the swell and further de-layed in reaching Madam Dimbleby. It was all Ian could do not to shove his way forcefully through the crowd, and he settled for pushing firmly against the throng while grinding his teeth and clenching his fists.

He finally freed himself from the congested streets and set off across the downs, running again as fast as he could. He made sure to travel back the way he'd come, as he had to keep his promise to the soldier and find out what he was doing so far out of his own time. Also, if the portal was in-deed open, Ian wondered if it had opened for him. The last prophecy had suggested that it would open to a land he would resist. Maybe that land was the one from which the soldier had stepped.

Making his way to the spot where he'd found the soldier, Ian soon determined that the man was nowhere about. For a moment he considered abandoning the man and running back to the castle to see what had happened to Madame Dimbleby, but just then Carl came hurrying along the path.

"There you are!" his best friend said when he saw him.

"How is Madam?" Ian said right away.

"Eva's with her," Carl told him, stopping to clutch at his side like he had a stitch from running. "And Madam Scargill is there too."

Ian sighed with relief. "She's still alive, then?" he asked almost tentatively.

Carl nodded, but his face was grim. "She's in terrible shape, Ian. Eva is giving it her best, but her abilities have been weakened by all the healing she's been giving to the wounded soldiers."

Since the war had begun and injured soldiers had been arriving in Dover, Eva had volunteered to assist Dr. Lineberry—the village's lone physician, who'd been recruited to help the other navy doctors with the overflow of wounded. Eva never revealed her abilities to the soldiers she sat with, but almost all of them had made remarkable recoveries.

While it was a wonderful thing for Eva to lend her healing gift to the wounded, only those closest to Eva understood its cost on her own robust health. Over the past few months she'd become overly fatigued, and very thin, causing Carl—who was quite sweet on her—to dote on her like a lovesick puppy.

Even with Carl's attentions and affections, Eva was so worn out of late that she'd been ordered only the day before by Dr. Lineberry to take time off to rest, but Ian had seen her sneaking around the beds that morning, checking on a few of the patients.

He was now terribly worried that even she would not have the strength to heal Madam Dimbleby. "Is there anything we can do?" he asked Carl.

His friend shook his head. "No. Except wait for word."

Ian again eyed the patch of forest. "When I went looking for Eva, I saw a soldier here," he told his friend.

"A soldier?"

"Not one of ours and not one of the Germans," Ian told him, edging close to the path that led toward the portal. "I think he might have had something to do with the prophecy."

Carl cocked his head. "Why do you think that?"

"Because of the way he was dressed," Ian explained. "And because he was wearing a helmet exactly like the one we found by that skeleton in the portal wall."

Carl's eyes went wide. "He came through the portal?"

"I think so."

Carl looked around. "Well, where is he, then?"

"I had to leave him here while I went for Eva. I don't know where he's gone off to."

Carl marched toward the woods. "He's probably gone back the way he came, Ian," he said reasonably.

Ian followed him and soon they came to the stone steps that led down to the portal. After descending the stairs, they were about to pass through the large iron gate that guarded the entrance to the tunnel and the portal when the very man they were looking for stepped in front of them, his sword drawn. "Oh, it's you," said the soldier when he saw Ian.

Carl gave a yelp and backed up several stairs. The soldier considered him. "Who is this?"

"He's a friend," Ian explained quickly. "Just like me." The soldier's gaze remained doubtful. "Is the portal wall closed, then?" Ian asked, making his voice light and friendly.

"I don't understand this magic," the soldier said, waving his free hand behind him. "I came back down the stairs, saw Calais in the distance, and just as I was calling out to him, a stone wall appeared, locking me here in this tunnel."

Ian turned over that name in his head. "Calais," he repeated softly. Where had he heard that name before?

But the soldier eyed him suspiciously. "I should not have mentioned him to you," he said. "The wall is obviously the work of a sorcerer, and it is well known that once a sorcerer knows the birth name of someone, they gain power over them."

Carl made a sort of strangled laughing sound. "Sorcerer?" he said. "What? Like Magus the Black?"

At this the soldier's head snapped toward Carl. "You know the sorcerer Magus the Black?"

Carl pumped his head enthusiastically. "We know him and his sisters, Caphiera, Atroposa, and Lachestia, all too well, I'm afraid."

The soldier pointed his sword at Carl. "Is Magus your master, then?"

Ian and Carl both shook their heads vigorously. "No, sir!" they said together. "We hate Magus and his three

34

sisters!" Ian added. "They've been trying to kill us for over two years, in fact!"

The soldier's eyes flashed with recognition. He lowered the sword and considered both Ian and Carl. "Are you . . . Ian?" the soldier asked him, and to Ian's ears his name sounded like Eye-an.

Ian smiled. He must have heard Carl say his name and gotten the pronunciation wrong. "I'm Ian," he answered, but said it correctly.

The soldier removed his helmet and tucked it under his arm. "Eeee-an," he repeated with a nod.

Carl laughed but quickly ducked his chin when the soldier's steely gaze settled on him. "And you?" the soldier asked, his tone a bit stiff.

"Carl," Ian's friend said promptly. "Carl Lawson."

"I am . . . ," the soldier began, but seemed to catch himself, as if he was wondering whether revealing his name was a good idea. At last he said, "I am Argos."

"It's nice to meet you," Ian said, only then realizing what a serious predicament the soldier was in. He pointed down the length of the tunnel. "I'm afraid you're stuck here with us for a little while."

The soldier turned and considered the blackness behind him. "You must tell me where, and what period I'm in," he said.

Ian's brow shot up. "You know you're in a different time?" he asked.

"I have heard of a magical gateway to another place and time. It is a thing of myth in my land, but someone I

35

know well believes in its existence so much that I tend not to doubt her."

Ian's mind leapt with an idea. "Could you by any chance be speaking of the Oracle Laodamia?"

Argos's eyes softened. "I am indeed," he said. "She is a great and noble lady and one of my dearest friends."

"You *know* Laodamia?" Carl gasped.

The soldier pointed his thumb at Carl. "Does he not hear well?"

Ian smiled. "We have a great deal to share with you," he said. And on the steps he explained all that had happened to them in the past two years, including the discovery of the prophecies, and how they had yet to act on any part of the third scroll from Laodamia's treasure box. Ian even fished out his copy for the soldier to inspect, but Argos couldn't read it, which Ian realized was because it was written in English. Ian read it aloud to the soldier, the piece of the Star allowing him easily to translate it into Phoenician, and while the soldier listened intently, Ian hoped something within the lines would spark a connection for the man.

The first of you shall be the last
When champion steps out from the past
To corner you with sword and might
Do not tempt him with a fight!
Win him to you; win his heart
For he will serve you till you part
With his coming, time is near

Travel soon to save your dear
One with name of open water
Perfect tribute to her father
He will join another realm
As duty calls you to the helm
Cross the water, save two souls
Learn from me within these scrolls
While you search for safe way home
You will visit man of stone
Heed this warning, know it well
Listen not, and find you fell
Ian Wigby must not drink!
Potion poisoned with dark ink
Face the foe with all your courage
Save yourself, and fight the urge
Force the choice upon another
He will save his loyal brother
See the next one of your crew
Boy of noble heart proved true
Four now serve the greater cause
But first at portal you will pause
The land I fear you dread to go
Will open now, and cause you woe
Steadfast though your hearts may be
Here you risk what's kept you free
Quest for Keeper must begin!
Though the odds at hand are slim
Find my champion deep within
Land that makes your heart grow dim

At your side strides next of kin
Save the Keeper from the wind
Ice will kill him if she can
All is part of evil plan
In the midst of all this doom
Find the fifth within the room
He is foe of greatest threat
Leave him, though, and soon regret
For he will fight on side of others
And you will lose your loyal brothers
So heed me here and listen close
Need your enemy with you most
Bring the fifth back through the door
Leave behind the raging war
Seer, Seeker, Healer true
Metal Master will come too
Thinker's heart will not be yours
But time will change the final course
Will you win or will you lose?
The answer lies in whom you choose.

"Well, that first part's clearly about you, Mr. Argos," Carl said, pointing to the very first lines of the prophecy.

"Who is Meester?" the soldier asked Ian, eyeing Carl as if he were a bit daft.

"Uh," Ian said, not knowing how to explain that to the Phoenician soldier. "It's what we say when talking to someone older than us."

Argos scratched his head. "You all have very odd customs," he said.

Ian turned to Carl. "Maybe we should just call him Argos from now on?"

Carl shrugged as if it made no difference to him, and tapped the paper again. "You'll have to agree that these lines are about him, though, right, Ian?"

Ian nodded and noticed that the soldier held a faraway look in his eyes. For a long time the man was silent, likely mulling over all that Ian and Carl had told him, but at last he said, "I am to assist you with your quest. The Oracle has foretold it, and as her servant, I am bound by oath to obey."

Ian pointed to the closed wall of the portal. "I think that's the reason it opened for you. I don't know what you're supposed to do here, but it's clear—given these first few lines of the prophecy—that we'll need you."

Argos also looked to the end of the tunnel, and Ian felt a pang at the sadness and worry etched in the features of the man. "I will do as the prophecy instructs and hope that if I see your quest through, I will be allowed to go back to my home in Phoenicia."

"That's all well and good," Carl said, motioning at the man's clothes, "but how are we ever going to explain you to everyone else?"

Ian blanched. Carl was right. Argos would stick out like a sore thumb, and in these dire times any stranger out of uniform in the village was looked at with suspicion. "We'll need to find you some proper clothes," Ian said, lifting the small pouch from around his neck and handing it to the soldier. "And you'll need to wear that," he added.

Argos considered the pouch before taking it, and opened it up to peer inside. Tipping out the small bit of opal into his hand, he said, "A beautiful jewel, but what need have I to wear such a thing?"

"It's from the Star of Lixus," Ian explained. "It will allow you to understand any language. You'll be able to communicate with anyone if you wear it."

Argos put the opal back in the pouch and looped it over his head. "If you say so," he said.

"He'll have to stay here until we can get him some proper clothes," Carl said.

"We'll have to inform the earl," Ian said. "He'll know how best to handle Argos's appearance."

Ian felt uneasy about leaving Argos alone, but the soldier assured them that he would stay put. "You have given me a great deal to consider, Ian and Carl Lawson. I will stay and sort out everything you have told me, and wait for you to return."

With that, the two trotted quickly up the stairs and were on their way.

Once they'd reached the edge of the wood, they saw Jaaved jogging in the direction of the village. Ian called to him, and the Moroccan boy spun on his heel and hurried back. "I was looking for you two."

"Is there news?" Ian asked, his heart pounding with dread.

Jaaved shook his head. "No. I was sitting with Theo

and she said to go looking for you. She said she couldn't put her finger on it, but she thought you might need another bit of the Star."

Jaaved raised a small pouch identical to the one Ian had given Argos, and Ian took it, marveling at Theo's keen ability.

"Thank you," he said. He knew he should share with Jaaved the story of the soldier's appearance, but not wanting to tell it twice, he asked, "Have you seen the earl?"

"I expect he's back at the castle," Jaaved said. "We're all waiting on word from the surgeon about Madam Dimbleby."

"Let's be off, then!" Carl said impatiently. "The longer we wait here, the more time we waste."

When they finally reached the front of the castle, they found a mass of soldiers queuing up to go through the main doors to report for duty. These were the same soldiers who'd just arrived in Dover, Ian assumed.

Searching the grounds, he saw Theo standing at the far eastern entrance, looking about as if she expected to see them at any moment. Ian called to her and she flew toward him.

When she reached him, she hugged him so fiercely that he had difficulty breathing. A small sob escaped her and she pulled her head back to regard him. "I saw him stab you," she said hoarsely. "Just before the German prisoners attacked, I had a terrible vision of that dreadful man stabbing you to death!"

Ian was quick to shake his head. "No, Theo," he said.

"I'm right as rain. Madam Dimbleby took the blade. It never even nicked me."

Theo considered him and said, "You've brought news." Ian wondered how much her intuition was telling her about the appearance of Argos.

"Yes," he said. "But the earl will need to hear it too. Have you seen him?"

Theo opened her mouth to reply, but before she even had a chance, a green motorcar filled with military police pulled to an abrupt stop next to them, and the men quickly surrounded Ian, Theo, Carl, and Jaaved. "Ian Wigby?" one of the grim-faced men asked.

"Yes?"

"Come with us."

The order was direct and allowed no room for argument. Ian knew in an instant he was in terrible trouble, but he couldn't for the life of him imagine for what.

"Why should he come with you?" Carl demanded, stepping protectively closer to Ian.

But the military police gave no reply. Instead, one of the officers shoved Carl aside and Ian was forcefully grabbed underneath each arm and pushed unwillingly into the awaiting vehicle. "Oy!" Carl shouted as the door slammed and Ian was wedged between two soldiers. "What's he done? Where are you taking him?"

But no one answered him, and as the driver depressed the gas, Ian had a chance to see Theo's features crease with worry.

He was driven only a short distance, to the west wing of

the castle, and he wondered why the soldiers hadn't merely walked over to escort him to that entrance.

Once clear of the vehicle, he was again held fast under each arm and marched into the entrance, which was guarded by another soldier, who saluted as the military police passed by.

After the group gained access to the building, Ian was walked briskly down a hallway and through a door then ordered to stand with his arms outstretched. He did so without complaint until one of the soldiers began to search his pockets, pulling out all the contents to inspect them and laying them on a nearby table. "Those are my things!" Ian cried, but the soldier paid him no mind. Instead, he continued with his search, pulling out Ian's sundial and his map of the many tunnels that ran under Dover. When the soldier unfolded his map and inspected the drawing, Ian attempted to swipe it from him but was roughly cuffed by the other guard and told to keep still.

Ian glowered at the soldier when he pocketed the map and motioned to the other soldier to leave. Without a word the two men left the room and shut the door with a hard slam. Almost immediately after, Ian heard the sound of a key being inserted into the lock on the other side and the click as he was firmly shut in.

Ian frowned and kicked the leg of the table. They had no right to take his map from him. Still, he decided that it was a good thing they'd left his sundial at least.

Glumly he walked to the chair on the other side of the table and sat down.

To distract himself he looked all about the room, which, except for the table and chair, was empty. It also held a small window, and Ian eyed it to see if he could fit through and escape. He had no idea why he was being treated like a criminal, but he knew he didn't particularly feel obliged to find out. The window, however, was far too small and he sighed as he bleakly surveyed the rest of his surroundings.

He knew that just down the corridor was the earl's study, which the man still retained for his private usage, although he allowed His Majesty's armed services to use much of the rest of this side of the castle as they saw fit.

In this room, however, there was nothing to amuse Ian and he quickly grew bored. Later, when he'd concluded by the shadows creeping along the wall that he'd been in the room for several hours, the door opened abruptly and in stepped his military police escort. "Come with us," said one of the men.

Ian got to his feet and moved obediently to stand again between his escorts, who, fortunately, did not hold him gruffly under the arms as they had before. The small party marched through the door and turned left, heading in the direction of the earl's study. Ian was surprised by this, because he knew the earl would not like it if he learned that a member of the military was utilizing his personal study.

Then again, perhaps the earl had recently obliged them the full use of this wing.

The soldiers led him directly up to the earl's study door before halting. The man to his right gave two hard knocks, and from inside Ian heard someone bark, "Enter!"

The door was pushed open and Ian was shoved a bit roughly through by the soldier on his left. When he had a moment to take in the people in the room, he was more than a little shocked.

Sitting commandingly behind his desk was the earl himself, looking slightly fatigued and largely concerned. Standing to his right was Admiral Ramsey, and on the left, surrounded by more military police, was the German commander, who was now sporting two black eyes, a large cut above one brow, and a fat lip, to boot.

Ian sucked in a breath when he took in the commander, and he was even more unsettled when he realized that the German's coat was smeared with blood. Madam Dimbleby's blood.

Anger flooded Ian from head to toe. His hands curled into fists and he glared hard at the German, who stared sullenly back through his swollen eyes and spat at Ian. "You traitor!" the German growled. "I know your accent is too perfect for you to be English! You are German and you betray the Reich!"

Ian couldn't help himself and in a flash he lost all control. He lurched forward in an effort to attack the commander but was caught and held firmly in check by his own guards. "Liar!" he shouted at the prisoner, rage coursing through him. "If Madam Dimbleby dies, I'll not rest until I see you hang for it!"

The earl stood so abruptly that he knocked his chair back and it fell over. The noise startled Ian and jerked his attention to the earl. Trembling with a rush of adrenaline,

45

Ian looked up at his patriarch, who was eyeing him with such anger that Ian quickly deflated and reined in his emotions. "I'm terribly sorry," he said to the earl, whose lips were compressed to form a very thin line.

"Speak English, lad," the earl said curtly.

Ian's eyes bulged. He quickly realized that the bit of the Star he wore had caused him to speak in the prisoner's tongue, and now he had his first inkling of why he was here, surrounded by guards. Ian cleared his throat. "I'm terribly sorry, my lord," he said, bowing his head and dropping his eyes to the floor.

"You see, Hastings?" the admiral snapped, even as he motioned impatiently for the guards surrounding the German prisoner to take him and exit the study. "He gives himself away! This young man of yours is clearly a German spy!"

Ian had looked up at the commander as the man was being roughly taken out of the room, but his head snapped to the admiral when he heard the accusation. "I'm not a spy!" Ian protested.

One quick look from the earl made him shut his mouth tightly. "The lad speaks a bit of German, Peers," his patriarch said calmly as he reached over to right his chair and take his seat again. "Several of my orphans speak it, in fact, as I insisted that their schoolmasters give them lessons in German, French, and Latin well before the war broke out. Knowing how to speak the enemy's language hardly makes the young man a spy."

But the admiral didn't look convinced. "Oh, I speak a

bit of German myself, Hastings, and I heard him," he said to the earl. "I heard that boy shout to the German commander to stab me!"

Ian shook his head vehemently, wanting with all his might to explain to the admiral that he hadn't shouted for the commander to attack. He'd shouted a warning. Unfortunately, Ian now knew that he'd shouted that warning in German.

The earl regarded Ian for a long moment, and Ian thought the earl might be considering how much to explain to the admiral about Ian's ease with the German language and how much to keep secret.

Theo, Jaaved, Eva, Carl, and Ian had all been warned by the earl not to reveal anything about Laodamia or the quest they had embarked on to anyone outside Delphi Keep, lest it invite too much interest or suspicion.

Finally, however, the earl said, "Ian, tell the admiral what happened leading up to the prisoners' attack and what you heard the Germans say."

Ian noted the slight warning in the earl's eyes, and he understood perfectly that he needed to stick to the story— that his schoolmasters had taught him to speak German— and not mention the Star. He took a breath, then explained. "I was on the bus, my lord, seeing the last group from Delphi Keep off, and the bus was terribly stuffy, you see, so I opened a few of the windows. That's when I overheard the commander telling the other prisoners to attack on his signal. He told them to go for our soldiers' guns and kill as many of us as they could.

"He also specifically mentioned killing you, Admiral Ramsey, and in my panic and haste to warn you, I forgot to speak English. My mind was so focused on interpreting what the Germans were saying that it didn't switch back over to my native tongue until too late."

The admiral regarded him shrewdly. "Your native tongue," he said simply. "Might that actually *be* German, lad?"

Ian's jaw fell open, but before he had a chance to defend himself, the admiral pressed his point by saying, "You could easily pass for a German citizen, with your light hair and blue eyes and tall build. You are tall for your age, are you not, Mr. Wigby?"

"Peers," the earl warned quietly. "You are far too suspicious for your own good. Ian Wigby has been at my orphanage since he was a babe no older than a day."

The admiral's eyes cut to the earl. "And yet my men have discovered this map on his person! The young man carries a map of secret tunnels and passageways that would allow our enemies to catch us unawares!" For emphasis, the admiral removed Ian's folded map from his inside pocket and tossed it rudely onto the earl's desk.

Ian grimaced and barely resisted the urge to surge forward and grab the map. Only the earl's calm demeanor held him back.

Picking up the map, the earl unfolded it and considered Ian's sketches of the many tunnels that ran underneath the grounds all along the White Cliffs of Dover. Ian knew the earl had seen his map before—he himself had shown it to his patriarch—but at the moment he seemed to study it as if he had never laid eyes on it.

Looking up at Ian, the earl then said, "Well done, Master Wigby. I see that your devotion to the project I assigned to you has in fact been thoroughly documented."

Ian blinked furiously at the earl before he caught the quick wink the earl sent him. "Thank you, my lord," he said, although he hardly knew what for.

"What are you talking about?" snapped the admiral, clearly forgetting that he was addressing an earl.

But Lord Hastings Arbuthnot hardly seemed to notice Admiral Ramsey's impropriety. Instead, he chuckled as if he held some inside joke, and regarded the admiral merrily. "As I know that Ian greatly enjoys exploring the many caves and tunnels that are part of the landscape near my castle, I asked him many months ago to begin sketching out a map of the underground tunnels leading out from Castle Dover so that I might offer you and your men a safe place should the worst happen and the Germans invade our coast. This map is rather crude, but nearly complete, am I right, Ian?"

Ian nodded vigorously. "Yes, my lord. I was almost finished searching through all the tunnels. There are quite a few, as you can see, and I had planned to make you a much neater master map to give to the admiral by week's end."

The earl smiled at him and nodded, clearly pleased with his answer. "You see, Peers? Ian had nothing but the best of intentions."

"Best of intentions?" the admiral repeated, shaking his

head as if he seriously doubted that. The admiral then took a different turn and said, "I understand that the lad was visited by a couple from Austria who wished to adopt him, and they had a private meeting with him. Perhaps you could explain to me, Hastings, how a young man of unknown origins came to have a private meeting with enemies of the crown?"

Ian's mouth fell open again. The admiral was twisting events to fit his theory that Ian was a spy, and the thought so offended him that he could hardly contain himself.

The earl, however, gave Ian a small shake of his head, to warn him against a sudden outburst, before he stood up to face the admiral. "The Austrian couple appeared on the doorstep of Delphi Keep some two years ago to make inquiries into the adoption of two of my orphans. They were very specific in their request to adopt two older children, as they claimed not to have the patience to care for babes.

"The couple then proceeded to have brief interviews with at least a dozen of my orphans, which is a common practice when an interested couple wishes to adopt any child over the age of three. As I suggested, these interviews took place two years previous, which I must also note was well before the war began. And further, they chose not to adopt Ian, but instead took home another young lad and a girl."

The earl paused then to gauge the admiral's reaction to his argument, and after noting that Admiral Ramsey was clearly still suspicious, the earl sighed and added, "My dear friend Peers, you have known me since primary school. Our mothers were also quite close; can you not take the word of an old friend as voucher for the lad's loyalty to king and crown?"

Admiral Ramsey considered the earl a while. Finally, he gave a long, tired sigh himself and nodded. "Very well, Hastings," he said rather reluctantly, and motioned for the guards at Ian's side to step back.

Ian felt a wave of relief when the soldiers moved back to the door and stood at ease. "Thank you, Admiral," he said. When the admiral did not look at him, Ian felt the need to say more. "Sir, may I just say that I would never, *ever* put you or Madam Dimbleby in harm's way. In fact, I would never put anyone I know or have great affection for in danger. My loyalty is, as the earl suggests, to His Majesty and England as long as I live."

The admiral's eyes finally swiveled to him, and he gave one curt nod.

The earl folded up the map and, waving it at Ian, urged him to step forward to the desk. "Here, lad," he said gently. "Take your sketch of the tunnels and turn it into a map the admiral will find useful."

Ian nodded and attempted to take the map, but the earl held fast and looked Ian straight in the eye. "That section in the middle, however, the one with the old stairwell leading down to the tunnel within the woods?"

Ian was startled that the earl had brought up the tunnel leading to the portal. "Yes, my lord?"

"Do not include it in your map for the admiral, as it leads nowhere and I'm certain it is quite unstable. I

51

wouldn't want the soldiers to risk being trapped or killed in a cave-in."

"Ah," said Ian with a nod. "Yes, my lord. I understand completely, and I shall leave it off the new map."

He then attempted to smile at the admiral, to show him there were no hard feelings, but the older man simply glowered at him as if he was yet unconvinced of his allegiance.

Free to go, Ian would have fled the study straightaway; however, he remembered Madam Dimbleby. Clearing his throat, he asked, "My lord, can you tell me how the headmistress is?"

The earl winced as if he'd been physically hurt, and instead of answering Ian, he looked up at the admiral, who crossed his arms and stared out the window without saying a word.

Ian's heart thumped in his chest as he imagined what no one would tell him—that Eva had been too late to save Madam. "No," he whispered, his voice choked with emotion. "Please tell me she hasn't . . . !" He couldn't even finish the sentence.

"She lives," growled the admiral without turning to look at him.

Ian's shoulders sagged with relief. "Thank heavens," he whispered. "May I see her?" he asked the earl.

But his patriarch shook his head sadly, leaned across his desk, and said, "Lad, I'm afraid Maggie's condition is most grave. She was taken back to the keep, where the naval surgeon did all he could for her, but the outlook is not good, I'm afraid. He doesn't know if she'll last the night."

Ian took the news like a blow to the chest, and it was all he could do to inhale a ragged breath. He placed a hand on the desk to support himself and it was a long time before he could speak. "Eva?" he asked meekly.

The earl's eyes darted to the admiral—who was still staring out the window—before looking back at him. "She is at Madam's bedside. Perhaps you should go to your sister, who is also at the keep, and see if there has been any sign of improvement. I shall be along to check on you and the others after I've concluded a few additional affairs with the admiral."

Ian's lower lip was trembling as the full weight of the news hit him. He couldn't trust himself to speak another word, and he certainly couldn't tell the earl about Argos with the admiral standing there, so he merely nodded and hurried from the room.

GRIM NEWS

With a bit of trouble, Ian managed to get back to his room at the top of the keep. He'd had to wind his way through the many cots set up in every available nook and cranny of the old structure—each waiting to receive an injured soldier.

Only one room now held patients, and that was the schoolroom behind the castle, which had the largest open space to accommodate them. For now, many of the cots stood empty, but Ian had a feeling they wouldn't be empty for long.

He started his search in the schoolroom, his eyes going out of habit to the spot where his old desk used to sit. Madam Dimbleby was not in that room, although Ian searched the rows and faces of everyone there.

He considered that after her surgery, she might have been moved to her own room, but when he went to the west end of the keep, he found that room empty.

Ian would have pulled out his sundial to find his friends, but the keep was too crowded for him to do that discreetly. Instinctively, he trudged up the steps, past his old room, and down the hall to the doorway that led to the east tower.

He turned the knob and pulled—but the door was stuck fast. This often happened, when the resident ghost of Delphi Keep—a cantankerous spirit who haunted the east tower almost exclusively—locked trespassers either in or out, depending on which side of the door they happened to be on.

With a tired sigh Ian leaned his head against the wood paneling. "Please, ghost?" he said. "It's been a right awful day, and I'd just like to find Carl and Theo."

There was a click and then the door pressed hard enough against Ian's head that he stood back. With a loud creak it opened all the way. "Thank you," he said, and hurried up the stairs. As he made his way up, he heard the door close behind him. Before he even crested the landing, he heard voices.

"Who's there?" asked one.

"It's me, Carl," he said, hurrying up the last few steps.

"Ian!" Theo shouted, jumping off the cot that served as Ian's bed and hurrying to his side. Throwing her arms around him again, she asked, "You all right?"

He nodded and gave a small smile to Jaaved and Carl, who were looking at him with concern. But he then realized who else was in the room and his mouth fell open a bit. "Good eve, Ian," Argos said, nodding to him from Ian's cot. He was now dressed in thin trousers and an old green shirt. Ian recognized the clothes as belonging to Landis, their groundskeeper.

"I pinched 'em from the laundry downstairs," Carl confessed.

Argos scratched at the fabric. "How do you people wear such coverings?" he asked.

"You'll get used to it," Carl assured him.

"So all of you know?" Ian asked Jaaved and Theo. They both nodded. "Have you had a chance to tell the earl?" Ian asked Carl, wondering if the earl already knew but hadn't wanted to let on in front of the admiral.

"No. He's been locked up in that room with Admiral Ramsey all afternoon," Carl replied. "We were waiting to see if perhaps you'd had a chance to tell him."

Ian told them that he hadn't, and then he explained why he'd been dragged off by the military police. He ended by telling them that he'd finally been let go to come see about Madam Dimbleby, and he noted their somber faces.

"She's been moved into the girls' dormitory," said Theo, her voice no louder than a whisper. "The doctor wanted her kept in a quiet place, away from the noise of the rest of the hospital. Madam Scargill is there along with Eva." Ian felt his hopes lift a bit until Theo added, "She's doing her very best to help Madam, but . . ."

Theo's voice trailed off and Ian's chest tightened with fear. "But what?"

"Eva doesn't know if she has it in her to save Madam Dimbleby, Ian," Carl said, his voice choked with emotion.

"She's so worn out from healing all the soldiers who've come through that she says there's precious left for her to give to Madam."

Ian's eyes darted to the floor and no one spoke for several minutes. Beside him, he could hear Theo sniffling, and he knew he should attempt to comfort her, but he was so upset by the prospect of losing the only mother figure he'd ever known that he found he could barely breathe.

Theo must have sensed this, because she placed her hand in his and leaned against him, which sparked a question Ian had for her. "Theo?"

"Yes?"

Ian hesitated. The question he had to ask was a difficult one, and he wondered if he could even utter the words, but Theo's vision from a few days before about a grave site prepared for their headmistress greatly distressed him. "Do you really see her passing?"

He could feel the eyes of Carl and Jaaved on him, and he knew he'd asked the one question they couldn't. Theo took a long time to answer him. "Sometimes, the future is not so certain, Ian," she said softly. "On very rare occasions, my visions contain two outcomes, and I have no idea which will actually take place."

Ian understood that to mean that Theo had seen both Madam's recovery and her passing, and the uncertainty only caused him further turmoil. He stood up then and moved to the window, opening it to allow the cool evening air to come in.

In the distance he saw a bright yellow automobile turn

off the road and begin to make its way down the gravel drive. Behind him Theo said, "The earl is coming."

"Should we go down to meet him?" Ian asked without turning around.

"No," said Theo. "He'll come to us."

Theo was correct, because a short time later the door below opened, and up the stairs came the earl. He looked rather surprised to find them all seated quietly, and his expression was even more surprised when he took in Argos. "Good evening," he said to the soldier. "I don't believe we've had the pleasure of an introduction."

Ian and Carl both stood and began to tell the earl who the soldier was and, more importantly, where he'd come from.

"The portal?" the earl said, blinking at the revelation. "So the prophecy has begun," he said, sitting down heavily on a nearby stool.

"It has," Theo said definitively. "The first few lines of the prophecy clearly talk about Argos's arrival."

The earl sighed. "It has been an eventful day," he said, his eyes pinched and tired as he looked at a yellow bit of paper in his hand.

Theo pointed to it and said, "Is there news, my lord?"

The earl nodded dully. "Yes, although I'm afraid it's some rather troubling news."

"About the war?" asked Carl.

The earl closed his eyes and inhaled deeply, then let the air out slowly before folding the paper back into a neat little square. "In a way, Carl," he said. "I've received a telegram from my associates in British intelligence. As you know, I have been assisting with the intelligence gathering from my sources overseas. Some of my dear friends from abroad have been risking their lives to gather useful information through their connections in Berlin.

"A fortnight ago, one of my associates traveled to Antwerp, attempting to sway the Belgium forces loyal to King Leopold to give up their vow of neutrality and declare war against the Germans—"

"But Belgium is all but lost!" Ian exclaimed, interrupting the earl. Rumors abounded that King Leopold was about to declare a surrender to the Germans, and most of the soldiers flooding their port the past few days were from Belgium. In fact, nearly all the injured in the schoolroom below had fought along the Belgium-France border.

The earl regarded Ian soberly. "Yes, Ian, and my associates at British intelligence suggest that King Leopold will declare his surrender the day after tomorrow."

"But what about your friend?" Jaaved asked.

Ian glanced at him and noticed the worry creasing the young Moroccan's face. Theo stared intently at the floor for a moment before letting out a small gasp, and immediately she began to cry. "Monsieur Lafitte!" she whispered, and covered her face with her hands.

Ian hardly knew what to do. He didn't know what Monsieur Lafitte had to do with this tale . . . and then it struck him like another blow to the chest. He looked up at the earl and asked, "Your friend in Antwerp. It's Monsieur Lafitte?"

The earl nodded gravely. "Yes," he said. "I'm afraid so."

Carl pointed to the yellow telegram still clutched in the earl's hand. "But you've had word from him, right, my lord? He's hiding somewhere, I'd wager, and he wanted you to know he's safe. Is that right?"

The earl considered the folded piece of paper in his hand. "No, Carl, I'm afraid not. This telegram was sent by Leopold's most trusted aide, a man named Antoine, who traveled with Monsieur Lafitte to Belgium. Antoine has escaped the German guard by way of a fishing vessel, which took him to Norway. He was able to wire me from there. My dear friend Leo was betrayed by the very men he hoped to trust in the Belgium royal court, and was turned over as an Ally spy to the Germans three days past."

Ian gasped. Monsieur Lafitte had shown them all considerable kindness a year before, and his daughter, Océanne, was someone Ian had great affection for.

"What do you think's happened to him?" Carl asked, clearly shaken by the news.

Theo began to cry in earnest, and Argos got up to go sit next to her and hold her hand. Ian gave the soldier a grateful smile and turned his attention back to the earl, whose distress was etched into every line on his distraught face. "I'm afraid I have no way of knowing," the earl said somberly. "But the Germans are not known for their leniency or mercy when it comes to suspected spies."

"But Monsieur Lafitte will surely talk his way out of it," Carl insisted.

The earl got up and moved to look out the window. "It

is a very bad sign that Leo has not been heard from in several days," he said. "Antoine believes my dear friend is already dead."

Ian couldn't process that. Monsieur Lafitte had been a jolly, affable fellow. How could he be gone?

"And if it is the case that it is too late to save my friend," the earl added, his voice hoarse with emotion, "then Madame Lafitte and Océanne are in very grave danger indeed."

"Were they with Monsieur in Belgium?" Ian asked, his heart pounding with renewed fear.

The earl turned from the window and looked again to the telegram. "No," he said, and Ian felt a flicker of relief. "Leo had moved them to a secret location in Paris. He told me that he would send word to me of their location should he suspect he might be discovered by the Germans and the worst happen, but that telegram has not arrived. I know that Leo would have sent it if he could, and I can only imagine that if he did send word of their location it was intercepted by the Germans and they may very well know exactly where to find Madame and Océanne."

"But France is still holding the line!" Carl exclaimed, his own emotions getting the best of him. "They'll be safe in Paris as long as the Allies keep the Germans at the Belgium border."

The earl turned back to the window, which had a beautiful view of the sea. It was growing dark outside, but Ian thought the earl might still be able to see the ships coming one by one into the port.

"The Allies are pulling out of France," the earl said. There'd been no formal announcement yet, but the massive gathering of their troops on Dover's shores told them of the certainty that Churchill had ordered them to return to England. "It's only a matter of time before all of France falls."

Carl was on his feet now, pacing back and forth in near panic. "We've got to find them!" he said. "My lord, we've got to get to Paris and rescue Madame and Océanne!"

The earl turned back to look at Carl and there was such sadness in his eyes that Ian had to look away. "It's impossible, Carl," the earl said. "We've no way of locating Madame Lafitte and her daughter, and France is far too dangerous a place for us to linger while we look."

All of a sudden Theo lifted her tearstained face to meet Ian's eyes. He knew immediately that she was thinking the same thing he was. "The prophecy," she mouthed.

Ian fished it out of his pocket and hurried over to the earl. "My lord," he said in a rush. "I believe we *must* go in search of Madame and Océanne! And I believe that Argos's appearance signifies that very thing!"

Ian pointed to the second set of verses within the prophecy, even reciting them aloud to prove his point.

" 'With his coming, time is near; travel soon to save your dear. One with name of open water, perfect tribute to her father. He will join another realm, as duty calls you to the helm. Cross the water, save two souls, learn from me within these scrolls.' "

"Ian's right," Theo said. "My lord, we *must* go in search of Océanne and Madame Lafitte!"

Before answering, the earl lifted the paper containing the translated prophecy from Ian's hands and read it for himself. He paused only once, to look up at Argos, still seated next to Theo, holding her hand and trying to take it all in.

Finally, the earl passed the prophecy back to Ian and crossed his arms over his chest. "It will be a very harrowing journey," he told them. "The admiral has instructed all commercial and luxury vessels not to leave port, as there have been a few German U-boat sightings of late."

"We'll have to risk it," Ian said firmly. "My lord, we cannot leave the Lafittes to the Germans!"

The earl nodded. "I agree, Ian. Especially not as it now appears to be critical to fulfilling Laodamia's prophecy." He then eyed Argos again uncertainly. "And what of our guest?" he asked.

Theo answered right away. "He must come," she said firmly. "Otherwise, he wouldn't be in the prophecy above the rescue of the Lafittes. He must have some purpose to fulfill with us in France."

The earl addressed his next question to Argos. "Will you journey with us across the water, my good man?"

"Of course," Argos said easily. "I'm perfectly comfortable on the water."

"Then it's settled," Ian said. "Shall we leave in the morning?"

The earl pulled at his beard. "There are many details to work out first, Ian. And supplies to be gathered." Ian looked at his patriarch expectantly. "And I gather by that look on your face, my good young man, that you expect to work out much of that this evening?"

"No time like the present," Ian replied with a grateful smile.

The earl grunted. "Very well. Why don't you four and our dear guest, Mr. . . . er . . . Argos, accompany me back to Castle Dover and we can at the very least get him some clothing that fits him a bit better, hmmm?"

THE WITCH'S DILEMMA

An alley in the city of Versailles, France, the same day.

A haggard-looking woman dressed in little more than rags shuffled quickly down the smelly cobblestones to her flat. In her gnarled hand she clutched a train ticket, and she cursed herself anew while she hurried along, anxious to pack and be on her way. The ticket had come at a dreadfully high price and had used up almost all her savings, but she'd not argued with the collector, lest he would deny her the passage she so desperately needed.

All about her, people were rushing to pack and flee the city. The Germans were heading straight for Paris—of that there was no doubt—and those close to the capital city were certain to be caught up in the net of French defeat.

She'd heard that Germans had no stomach for those who were different, and the Witch of Versailles was *most definitely* different.

With a sigh of relief the witch reached her front door and inserted her key, mumbling reproachfully to herself as she stepped across the threshold, leaving the door open to make as hasty a departure as possible.

She'd seen this coming. Many a night she'd peered into her crystal and seen the certainty of France's downfall, but the thought was so unfathomable that she had doubted the visions and convinced herself that it was only her fear reflected in the fissures of the crystal.

Soon the streets would be overrun with German invaders, and those who did not fit the Führer's idea of what a "proper" citizen should look like were certain to find no safe haven within the newly occupied land.

The witch had heard rumors of what the Nazis were capable of. Her own visions had confirmed that they could commit unspeakable acts of torture and inhumanity. She'd seen things in her crystal ball that had frightened her straight down to her toes, and the Witch of Versailles wasn't easily frightened.

At least she had a plan, she reasoned as she gathered various odds and ends. She had a niece in Bayonne, and the witch thought that if that small city was not far enough south for her to disappear into, then she could easily slip over the border into Spain. She spoke a bit of Spanish; perhaps it wouldn't be so terrible.

The witch moved quickly and efficiently about her humble home, tucking her meager belongings into a small satchel. She paused to look for the silk scarf she wrapped her crystal in, and noticed it on her small table in the corner. A gust of wind entered the flat and blew the scarf out of her reach. Muttering to herself, the witch bent to re-trieve it, but another gust sent it scuttling under the cot.

It was then that the woman realized she was no longer alone in her tiny flat. Jerking up, she whirled around and faced the open door. The temperature within the room—which had been nice and cozy a moment earlier—plummeted, and the witch began to shiver, and not just from cold.

Standing in the alley were two of the most frightful creatures the witch had ever had the displeasure of meet-ing. Caphiera the Cold and her sister Atroposa the Terrible hovered in her doorway.

"Good evening, mistresses," she said with a deep bow to the two sorceresses stepping over her threshold.

"Witch," said Caphiera, adjusting the dark sunglasses she wore. The witch didn't know for sure why Caphiera wore the glasses, but she suspected it was because of the ef-fect the sorceress's eyes had on those who got caught gazing into them—something the witch was careful to avoid.

In fact, the witch thought it wise not to stare too long at either sorceress, as the view was most distressing.

Caphiera the Cold was quite tall—at least six feet, pos-sibly an inch or two more. She had blue-tinged skin and elongated limbs adorned in fine, expensive textiles. Her fingers were long and talonlike, and her face was the most frightful of all. White hair tipped with icicles capped a long countenance with high cheekbones, an exaggerated nose, and full blue lips. Behind those lips were two rows of sharply pointed teeth, exposed fully when Caphiera smiled wickedly—which was often.

The witch worked to control her shivers and focused on the other sorceress—whom, by comparison, was nearly a beauty. Atroposa was shorter than her sister, but not by much. Her limbs were also long and reedlike, and adorned in rags, which, along with her hair, fluttered unceasingly about her. Her skin was so pale it appeared diaphanous, and her face was unremarkable except for her long tendrils of translucent locks and the two hollow eyes that stared out hauntingly at the witch.

"Going somewhere?" asked Atroposa in a voice that moaned like the wind on a cold lonely night.

The witch attempted a smile and failed. "Off for a visit with my niece, mistress," she explained, hoping these two would not cause her to be late to the station.

Caphiera crossed her arms and looked about the flat distastefully. "We have need of your services, witch." Her icy tone brokered no arguments.

"Of course!" the witch agreed, and shuffled over to the table with two chairs. Taking her seat, she retrieved her crystal and its stand from her satchel, placing them on the table. "What is it you wish to know, mistresses?"

Atroposa stepped forward, and the witch felt the bite of the cold wind. "Our brother is missing," she said. "We wish to know what has become of him."

The witch was surprised. She'd made the acquaintance of Magus the Black only the year before, when he was searching for his third sister. The witch had helped him then, and he'd shown his appreciation by being most generous with a few gold coins. "You search for the sorcerer Magus?" she asked.

"Yes," said Caphiera, still standing near the open door.

The witch rubbed her cold hands together and peered down into her crystal. "I see him," she said after a moment. Dread filled her heart when she realized what had happened to the great sorcerer. "He is deep belowground. He has been captured and is being held prisoner in a small dark room of four stone slabs, infused with magic. This magic is poison to him and I fear his strength is draining slowly away."

The witch was tempted to look up at the two sorceresses to gauge their reaction, but she decided it would only distract her, so she continued to tell them what she saw. "This prison is your sister's doing. It seems as if they've had a terrible fight, and even now she stands guard over him in the ground just beyond the walls of the prison."

The witch did look up at this point, and she saw that Caphiera and Atroposa were exchanging knowing looks. "He has bungled things again," said Caphiera with a sneer. "As I was certain he would."

"We must make haste to rescue him," said Atroposa. "Lachestia will surely kill him if we do not intervene."

But Caphiera was unmoved. "Why should we risk our own lives to save our incompetent brother?" she snapped. "Lachestia has always been unbalanced, and Magus knew of her mental condition well before he went in search of her. It's no wonder, given her incredible power and unpredictable nature, that Magus got himself in trouble. I say that if he wasn't clever enough to keep himself out of danger, then he should suffer the consequences."

Atroposa opened her mouth to speak again, but Caphiera cut her off. "We have another mission which must take precedence, my sister!"

After a moment's hesitation, Atroposa reluctantly nodded and turned back to the witch. "We wish to know of the Secret Keeper," she moaned.

The witch now remembered that the last time these two had visited her was to inquire after the mysterious man called the Secret Keeper, and again the witch wondered what secrets he might be keeping. She peered back into her crystal and saw a tall man powerfully built with broad shoulders and arms corded with muscle. He had dark curly hair and deep brown eyes; everything about him was quite striking, in fact. "He is somewhere in the South of France, mistresses, but soon he will be very close indeed," said the witch.

Caphiera stepped nearer to the table and the temperature around the witch dipped several more degrees. "Where is he going?"

The witch's teeth began to chatter. "Paris," she told them, hoping the pair would soon be satisfied and depart. "He is coming to the capital to hide something. . . ."

"What?" asked Atroposa.

The witch closed her lids and concentrated on the image forming in her mind's eye. "A small box," she said. "Made of silver."

When the witch opened her eyes, Caphiera was smiling wickedly, exposing those frightening teeth. "When will he arrive?"

"Within a week, I believe."

"What part of Paris will he venture to?" Atroposa pressed. "The city is very large and we will need to find his location before the Germans arrive and begin meddling in our plans."

The witch frowned. The images floating in her mind were quickly becoming jumbled. "I cannot see his destination clearly," she complained. "It seems he is working to conceal himself and his mission."

The witch knew immediately that her answer did not please the sorceresses. "When will it become clear to you?" Caphiera asked, her tone frigid.

The witch blinked and focused again on her crystal. "He will be near a green door," she said at last, allowing a small sigh of relief.

But again she could tell that her answer hardly satisfied her guests. "Paris is full of green doors!" bellowed Atroposa. "How can we possibly find which green door the Keeper will visit?"

The witch concentrated as hard as she could on the slippery man in question. But try as she might, she could not decide which section of the city he would be headed toward, and then, as if he was aware that he was being watched by an unseen presence, the Keeper darted straight out of her vision. "I'm sorry, mistresses," she said wearily. "He is gone from my sight." But then something else within

71

the ball caught the witch's attention. "You are not the only ones searching for this man," she said. "A group of children search for him too. And a woman. Separate from the children, but with a close connection to this Secret Keeper all the same."

Caphiera and Atroposa exchanged meaningful looks. "You say the Keeper will appear in Paris within the week?" Caphiera asked.

The witch nodded vigorously. Of that she was certain.

"Then I trust that it will not be too much of an inconvenience for you to postpone your visit to your niece," the sorceress said easily.

The witch caught herself before a protest could leave her throat. She knew that to refuse either of these women would surely lead to death. Still, she couldn't help attempting to argue a little. "Kind mistresses," she began. "Surely I would only be a burden to your quest? An old woman like me would slow you down. And both of you are certainly clever enough to discover the Secret Keeper on your own. My second sight confirms it!"

But Caphiera was far too intelligent to fall for the guise. "You will accompany us, witch, and when you locate the Keeper, be grateful that we will allow you to live."

The witch thought of something just then, part of a vision she'd already had in fact. She pretended to give a small gasp as she peered into her crystal. "Oh, my!" she said.

"What is it?" Atroposa demanded.

The witch made a bit of a show of looking alarmed. "It's the Germans, mistresses! They will invade Paris on the day the Keeper arrives! Oh, I fear for both of you if the Germans should encounter such powerful women! What they would try to do to you! The horror!" And with that the witch fell out of her chair and onto the floor, pretending to faint from the awful image.

"What's happened to her?" she heard Atroposa moan.

Caphiera's silver boots clinked loudly on the cement floor as the sorceress approached. In the next instant the witch was kicked soundly in the stomach, and she gave a sharp cry as the air was thrust right out of her. "I thought she might be faking," Caphiera snapped.

The witch rolled onto her knees and worked to pump the air back into her lungs, all the while silently cursing herself for not getting to the train station ten minutes sooner.

"When she recovers," said Caphiera to her sister, moving over to lift the witch's crystal ball from its pedestal, "bring her along."

A few moments later—well before the witch had recovered her normal breathing pattern—her arm was gripped as if by a vise and she was dragged from the flat, leaving all her other possessions behind.

A DREADFUL NIGHT

As the party walked across the downs toward Castle Dover—the earl having left his motorcar at the keep because they couldn't all fit in it and Argos had eyed the thing as if it were a small monster—Ian took in the earl's posture. He had seen how weary the earl had been of late; he had so much to worry about with the news from the front lines always seeming to be terrible. Their forces were in full retreat at present, and Ian knew the earl was especially worried about an invasion from the sea.

To top all that, the earl's dear headmistress was clinging to life, and the earl had just learned that another close friend had recently been taken captive by the enemy.

Ian couldn't fathom what kind of a toll that took on a man, but he suspected it was great. Beside him Theo let out a gasp, spinning round to stare at the keep, which, Ian could see over his shoulder, was aglow with soft lights from the inside.

"Theo?" Ian said, knowing she was having one of her visions.

But Theo seemed not to hear him. Instead, she let out a bloodcurdling scream, cried out, *"Madam!"* and dashed off down the hill, running as fast as her feet could carry her.

Ian was too stunned to understand fully what had just happened, and a moment later he felt Carl's hand on his arm. "It must be Madam Dimbleby!" Carl said.

Ian closed his eyes and whispered, "No!" as a terrible ache settled firmly into his chest. He opened his eyes, ready to go chasing after Theo to offer her comfort, when a faint buzzing sound came to his ears. The noise was so odd that it caused them all to pause and look about.

"What *is* that?" Carl said, his chin slightly tilted as he searched the dark sky.

Ian realized that the noise was indeed coming from above. It sounded like a very large hornets' nest getting closer and closer. "Look, there!" Jaaved said, pointing at the horizon just offshore.

"What?" Ian asked, his voice now raised above the din.

"Those dark shadows!" Jaaved said. "I think they're planes!"

"Good heavens!" the earl exclaimed. "Everyone! Get down!"

No sooner had the earl spoken than a whistle pierced the night sky, and seconds later an earth-shattering explosion sounded down by the harbor.

Ian was pulled roughly to the ground by the earl just

as a second whistling and explosion sounded, and then another and another. Ian could barely think past his own fear and the events taking place around him.

But then his eye happened to catch a glimpse of white moving across the downs and he jumped to his feet and shouted, *"Theo!"* He burst into a run as if his own life depended on it, and it wasn't long before he was gaining on her. *"Theo, stop!"* he shouted, but either she could not hear him above the noise from the planes or she was ignoring him completely.

A whistling noise pulled his attention skyward again just as an alarm was sounded down at the wharf, echoing across the downs too late to do any good.

Another bomb went off, lighting up the night sky with fire, and Ian twisted his head, knowing it had come from behind him. He gasped when he realized the bomb had hit Castle Dover, and the sight so shocked him that he tripped over his own two feet and went sprawling to the ground. For a moment he lost all orientation, and then the shadows overhead seemed to be right on top of him.

"Oh, noooooooooooo!" Ian cried just as another explosion blew more of the wharf apart.

Adding to the cacophony were screams and shouts of panic. Ian scrambled to his feet but he was now shaking from head to toe. Another blast to his right lit up the area all around him, and with no small amount of horror, he realized the Nazis were dropping their bombs everywhere from the harbor to Castle Dover. At any second, they would strike the keep!

As if she were immune to the chaos and horror around her, Theo continued her mad dash across the downs, her small figure vulnerable to the murderous horde above her. Ian set off after her again, but this time, he didn't bother shouting; he knew his voice could never rise above the noise. Instead, he put every ounce of energy into reaching Theo.

And then, as if things weren't bad enough, small explosions sounded just to his right, and clumps of grass and dirt flew up into his face and against his clothing. He knew that at least one of the pilots had seen him and was loosing his machine gun on him. The shock of being shot at was enough to cause Ian to lose his footing yet again, and he crashed to the ground, covering his head and trying in vain to make himself disappear.

More gunfire erupted, but in the chaos, Ian couldn't tell where it was aimed, and he shivered all over, waiting to feel the bite of the bullets—but none came.

And then something tumbled to the ground beside him, and he heard Carl's cries. "Ian! *Ian!* Are you hit?"

Ian lifted his chin and stared at Carl. "I'm all right!" he shouted, staggering to his feet. Desperately he searched the dark terrain for any sign of Theo.

Finally, he spotted her, facedown on the ground, and after crying out her name with such force that he felt a searing pain in the back of his throat, Ian raced to reach her. At last he got to her still form, dropping to his knees a few feet from her, unable to touch her for fear he'd know for certain that she was gone. His chest heaved, and his fists clenched, and an anger so keen that he thought he'd never feel anything else formed inside him.

The planes were moving off now as sirens continued their mournful wail, but Ian paid the departing planes no attention. "Ian!" he heard Carl gasp as his friend approached and sank down beside him. But Ian couldn't even acknowledge him. He was focused on Theo, willing her to move.

To his utter amazement, a moment later she did. First her head lifted, and she looked about; then, pushing up onto her knees, she looked behind her. Ian's shoulders sagged with relief and he reached forward to gather her close. "Thank heavens," he whispered hoarsely.

In the next instant Theo was sobbing so hard he thought she'd pass out. Ian hugged her fiercely and patted her back. "There, there," he whispered, unable to get his injured voice to a higher volume. "You're safe, Theo. Everything's all right."

"No!" she wailed, lifting her tearstained and dirty face to his. "Everything's *not* all right!"

At first Ian misunderstood and pulled her slightly away to look her over carefully. "Are you hurt?"

Theo shook her head vigorously. "No," she said, pushing her face back into his shirt. "It's not me. It's Madam Scargill!"

Ian was thoroughly confused, and he made an attempt to lift her chin with his fingers and wipe at the mud and tears on Theo's face, as if that could clear up his confusion too. And then something flickered behind his sister, and he knew.

"Gaw," said Carl, who'd moved up next to him and obviously hadn't understood what Theo had said. "I hope no one was in there."

Just a hundred meters away, a small section of Delphi Keep was on fire, and Ian knew it to be the headmistresses' study. The bombs had miraculously missed the keep overall, save for that one section, which was now completely engulfed in flames.

Men with buckets, shovels, and wet sheets darted about, doing their best to extinguish the flames, but none of it would be in time, and Ian closed his eyes to think about the poor woman who'd helped raise him since he was one day old.

As long as he'd known her, Madam Scargill had been sharp and curt and had avoided showing him much kindness, but overall she'd been a good woman, and she'd always had the children's best interests at heart.

"Theo," Ian whispered. "Are you sure?"

Theo closed her eyes and wept and wept, managing a tiny nod. "I . . . I . . . had a vision of her in her study just . . . just as the bombs fell, and . . . I tried to get there in time!" she wailed. "But . . . but I couldn't! Oh, Ian, I couldn't warn her to get out in time!"

Ian hugged the poor girl to him again and met Carl's curious gaze. "Madam Scargill," he mouthed.

Carl gasped and got to his feet immediately, dashing off to help the men fight the flames.

Ian would have joined him, but he didn't think his legs could support him just yet. Soon after that, footsteps approached, and Ian turned his head to see Argos, his eyes large and wary, as he made his way over to Ian and Theo.

"Is she well?" he asked, squatting down and placing a gentle hand on the top of Theo's head.

Ian nodded.

"And you?"

"Fine, thank you, sir."

Argos sighed and sat down next to them. "Your patriarch has gone to his home," he said.

Ian looked over his shoulder and saw Castle Dover alight with flames. His stomach contracted at the thought of the many people who could at that moment be trapped within its walls, injured or dead, and he decided he had to help. Looking earnestly at Argos, he asked, "Would you watch over Theo?"

"You are off to lend aid?"

Ian nodded again.

Argos held open his arms. "Give her to me. I will protect her with my life."

The soldier's pledge filled Ian with a renewed sense of warmth for the man. He didn't know much about Argos, but what he knew he liked immensely.

"You'll need to take her back to the portal tunnel," Ian told him, carefully handing Theo over. "Without a uniform you'd be tagged as a stranger here, which would make people immediately suspicious of you. Especially after all of this."

Argos nodded and got to his feet, gently cradling Theo in his arms. "I will keep her safe," he said, turning away and leaving Ian alone to contemplate whether to go to Delphi Keep or Castle Dover.

The flames at Delphi were nearly out now, and with a great deal of relief, he could just make out the figures of Eva and Jaaved, helping Carl fill buckets of water from the outside pump. The fire at Castle Dover looked far from over, and Ian knew where he was needed most.

Ian then pointed his weary body to the castle and hurried away.

SAD GOODBYES

The funeral for Madam Scargill was held three days later in the drizzling rain. Hers was one of a dozen burials being held in the small village after the German air raid, and the residents of Dover were numb with both sadness and fear, but they all turned out to attend the funeral of the late headmistress.

With a pang, Ian felt the absence of Madam's beloved cousin, who was still far too fragile from her knife wound to attend the funeral. The earl himself had delivered the horrible news to Madam Dimbleby when Dr. Lineberry was certain she could survive the shock.

Still, the cries of her anguish could be heard for many hours that day, and Ian wished over and over that there was something he could do to take a bit of Madam's pain away. But there was nothing for it. Her cousin, who had been like a sister to her, was gone.

Ian himself still found it hard to believe. Madam Scargill had been such a force of nature that the world seemed a bit muted in her absence. Looking round at the crowd hovering by her black lacquered coffin, he could tell he was not alone in his thinking.

The earl gave the eulogy, which was a touching tribute to the woman who'd spent twenty years in his employ. Ian tried not to stare at the burns on the earl's hands, or at the way he winced when he stepped to the podium. He'd received a terrible scrape from falling timber while fighting the flames at his home.

Castle Dover had suffered greatly from the fire. A third of its rooms were beyond repair, and still the earl had managed to find the time to write such lovely words about Madam Scargill.

Ian found he admired the earl all the more.

"She was a right good old bird," whispered Carl as the coffin was slowly lowered out of view.

Ian agreed but thought twice about commenting. His voice had suffered a terrible strain when he'd screamed on the slope after Theo, and every time he talked, his throat burned. Dr. Lineberry had advised him against speaking for the next few days, but he'd cheated now and again.

Next to him, Theo squeezed his hand and sniffled. "If only I'd got to her in time," she said. "If only I'd realized that the funeral I saw wasn't for Madam Dimbleby, but for Madam Scargill!"

Eva, who was standing on the other side of Theo, draped an arm about her. "Theo," she said gently, "it's not your fault. Your visions come to you in pieces and parts, and sometimes there is no way of knowing who they will involve."

Ian was grateful to have Eva with them. Even though the poor girl was herself in a rather fragile state after having helped Madam Dimbleby just enough to make it through the night after her surgery and recover, Eva still offered Theo her powers of comfort and healing. As Ian looked on, he could see Theo's terrible sadness and guilt lift a bit.

Carl put in his thoughts as well. "You did all you could, Theo, and you nearly got yourself killed in the process. It was a miracle that machine gun didn't finish you off!"

Ian closed his eyes against the painful memory of watching Theo fall amid the hail of gunfire. He would never forget it.

"Why do they not burn the body?" Ian heard a voice ask. He opened his eyes to see Argos bending low to ask Jaaved. In the days since the bombs had fallen, Jaaved had taken to helping Argos acclimate to his surroundings, making sure that Argos did nothing unusual enough to provoke any suspicions.

The Moroccan boy shrugged. "They don't burn their dead here," he explained. "Instead, they put them in a box and bury the box."

Ian wondered if Jaaved was reminded of his grandfather's funeral pyre, and he felt another pang when he thought about the wonderful elderly man who'd befriended them in Morocco. He had tried to save them from fierce tribal warriors, only to lose his life for his efforts.

Then the services were over, and people began to move away so that Madam Scargill's final resting place could be properly covered with dirt.

Ian saw Landis, the keep's groundskeeper, wipe his eyes and don his cap before shuffling away without speaking to anyone.

Their own group moved off too, with Ian leading them away from the cemetery to the main road. Argos and Jaaved were deep in discussion, and Ian thought it fitting that the soldier was being shown the way of things by the only other soul in Dover who'd never seen a motorcar before coming to England and had to learn all about the modern world after coming from his own rather humble origins.

As they moved along the road, Ian lost himself in melancholy thoughts but was soon aware of the loud horn of a car. Still holding tight to Theo, Ian stepped closer to the edge of the lane, thinking the driver wanted them to move over, but in the next moment the car pulled up next to them and someone rolled down the window. "I say!" cried a familiar and welcome voice. "But you lot are looking a bit dreary!"

"Mr. Goodwyn!" Theo shouted, pulling out of Ian's grasp and hurrying to the side of the car.

Thatcher Goodwyn, their friend and schoolmaster, beamed out from the interior, looking dapper in his military uniform. He and his twin brother, Perry, had joined the military shortly after England had declared war. Perry was deeply entrenched in military intelligence and was often called away to London, but his brother was usually stationed at Dover as an aide to Admiral Ramsey.

Ian remembered when he saw his schoolmaster that Thatcher had been dispatched to Plymouth for the past several days and likely had no idea what had happened to Madam Scargill.

"Why the sad faces?" Thatcher asked, looking round at their group.

And then he took in their clothing; they were dressed in their Sunday best, and with their proximity to the cemetery, he seemed to put it all together. "Oh, heavens," he said, his jovial smile vanishing. "Who have we lost?"

"Madam Scargill, sir," Carl answered. "She was killed in the air raid."

Thatcher's visage became pale. "That can't be!" he gasped, but one look at their faces told him the truth of it. "Why, that's terrible!" he said before taking note of the drizzling rain. "Come, come," he said, opening the passenger door. "Let me drive you back to the keep at least."

Theo hurried round to the door and got in, followed by Eva and Carl, but Argos held back and so did Jaaved. Thatcher noticed the muscular man in their midst and said, "Oh, hello. I don't believe we've met. I'm Thatcher Goodwyn."

Argos eyed Thatcher's motorcar doubtfully. "I'm Argos."

Thatcher's face registered confusion. Ian said, "There's a great deal we should explain, sir."

"Well, then, by all means, get in and tell me!" Thatcher insisted. "We'll go to my home, where we'll have some privacy."

Ian attempted to smile reassuringly at Argos. "The motorcar won't hurt you," he said. "I promise. It's a bit like riding in a covered carriage."

"But where are the horses?" Argos asked, his eyes still wary.

"This kind of carriage doesn't need horses," he explained patiently.

"It runs on magic?" Argos asked.

Ian scratched his head, trying to decide what answer might satisfy the warrior. "In a way," he said. "But it's a type of magic that everyone can use."

When Argos made no move to get into the car, Ian took him by the arm and said, "I promise, you won't mind it a bit."

Ian discovered quickly just how wrong he was. Argos gripped the back of the seat so tightly his knuckles were white, and it was all Ian and Jaaved could do to keep him from leaping from the motorcar during the short trip to Thatcher's home.

"Is everything all right?" their schoolmaster asked, looking a bit nervously in the rearview mirror.

"Fine, sir!" Jaaved told him. "Our friend has just never been in a motorcar before."

"Never been in a . . . ?" Thatcher repeated as if he was having trouble keeping up with the conversation.

"We've a lot to explain, sir," Theo reminded him.

Once the seven of them were out of the motorcar and inside Thatcher's small home, Argos seemed to relax again. "Would everyone like a spot of tea?" their schoolmaster asked.

"I would like wine," said Argos.

Thatcher smiled politely at him, and again it appeared

as if what Argos had said took a moment to register in his mind. "Er . . . but it's ten o'clock in the morning, my good man."

"What is ten o'clock?" asked Argos innocently.

Thatcher looked at Ian as if he needed help translating. Keeping his voice to a whisper, Ian said, "Sir, Argos isn't from England."

Thatcher's brow rose. "Oh?" he said, looking merrily back at Argos. "Where are you from, exactly?"

"Phoenicia."

Thatcher's brow furrowed. "Greece?"

"Yes."

"Well, you're a long way from home, my good man!" Thatcher said as everyone looked at him expectantly. "How did you manage to find your way to Dover?"

"I walked."

Thatcher blinked rapidly. Then he seemed to make the connection, and he eyed Ian, directing his next question at him. "Through the portal?" he asked, his voice no louder than a whisper

Ian—and everyone else at the table—nodded.

"From where, again?"

"Phoenicia," Theo said, repeating what Argos had already told him. "And from the time of Laodamia."

Thatcher's mouth now hung open and he stared in disbelief at the stranger at his table. "But . . . but . . . but . . . ," he stammered. "You look, and you sound, so . . . so . . . so . . . *normal!*"

"The earl's loaned him some clothes," Carl explained. "And Ian's loaned him his bit of the Star."

Thatcher sat back in his chair and swiped a hand through his hair, obviously struggling with the news of the stranger's origins. After a moment, he got up and loaded the stove with wood, lit it, then set a kettle on for tea. When he next took his seat, he seemed to have composed himself. "You knew Laodamia?"

Argos smiled. "I *know* her well," he said. "And you will forgive me, sir, but to me, she is still very much alive."

Thatcher shook his head and closed his eyes. "Right," he said, holding up a hand in apology. "Quite right. Forgive me. You must be most anxious to get back to your home, I'd imagine."

Argos's smile turned melancholy. "Oh, I am, Thatcher. I am. But these young people have shown me Laodamia's prophecy, which says that the portal will not open again until we venture across the sea to rescue an ocean."

Thatcher blinked rapidly again and turned his attention back to Ian, looking most confused. In any other circumstance, Ian would have laughed, but the past few days had sucked the humor right out of him. So he explained to his schoolmaster how the earl's dear friend had been captured and likely killed by the Germans in Belgium, leaving his wife and daughter, Océanne, trapped and unaware of his fate back in Paris.

He then pulled the translated version of Laodamia's prophecy out of his pocket and read it through for Thatcher.

"My, my," said the schoolmaster when he was finished. "It does seem as if she is being quite specific this time, doesn't it?"

"It does," Ian agreed. "And I don't believe we have much time to waste. King Leopold surrendered to the Germans this morning."

Ian had heard the news buzzing on the lips of most of the funeral attendees. Everyone speculated that it was only a matter of days before the Nazis broke through the French lines, especially with the full retreat of British soldiers on the move. Ian could feel the anxious knot in his stomach tighten at the prospect of having the Germans so close to his homeland, and it tightened even more when he thought of them marching into Paris and discovering Madame Lafitte and Océanne. He shuddered to think what might become of them at the hands of the Germans.

"How are you planning to get to Paris?" Thatcher asked next.

"We're sailing," Theo told him, revealing the plans they'd finalized only the day before. "On the earl's yacht. We're to leave tomorrow before dawn and sail to Boulogne."

Thatcher frowned. "The earl's yacht will make a large target if you get caught behind enemy lines, Theo."

"That's why we have a plan," Ian told him. "Jaaved and Argos will helm the ship from Boulogne farther down the coast to Le Havre, where the earl has a good friend who will make sure to keep his boat safe. Then Jaaved and Argos will meet us in Paris at the . . ."

Ian couldn't remember the name of the fountains, so he looked to Jaaved, who smiled and said, "Fontaines de la Concorde."

"Yes, the Fontaines de la Concorde," Ian repeated, attempting to commit it to memory.

"Why aren't Jaaved and Argos staying with the earl's yacht?" Thatcher asked. "What I mean is France could be overrun in a matter of days, my friends, and it might be safer for both of them if they stay with the earl's yacht and wait for you."

"No," said Theo with that faraway look in her eyes. "They *must* come to Paris. It's very important, in fact."

"Why, Theo?" Thatcher asked.

Theo's look grew pensive, and she focused on her schoolmaster's face. "I've no idea, Mr. Goodwyn, but I do know it's terribly important."

Thatcher nodded, satisfied with her answer, and Ian marveled at how much trust Theo's word had among the adults who knew her well. "Has the earl gained permission from the admiral to launch his boat tomorrow?"

All boats coming into and leaving Dover port were now required to gain permission from the office of the admiral. It was the only way to control the heavy wharf traffic and ensure that those boats coming in weren't filled with spies or saboteurs.

Ian frowned. "Not yet, sir. The admiral's a bit suspicious of the earl's intentions these days, and I'm afraid I'm the cause of it."

Thatcher's brow creased with an unspoken question,

and Ian had to explain the events surrounding poor Madam Dimbleby. "My heavens!" Thatcher exclaimed when he heard the news about the kindly headmistress. "Is she recovering?"

"Yes," Eva told him. "She will live, but there's nothing I can do to mend her broken heart over the loss of her cousin. That will take time, I'm afraid."

Thatcher laced his fingers together and looked at each of the people, gathered round the table. "Leave your port pass to me," he said. "I will make sure it is granted and that you have a clear path out to the channel. You'll likely be required to leave very early indeed, so be ready."

Everyone at the table breathed a huge sigh of relief and thanked the schoolmaster.

Thatcher got up from the table then, carrying his teacup and saucer to the sink, and everyone seemed to take that as a sign that it was time to leave. He offered to drive them, but the dispirited group voted to walk instead. Ian knew he'd welcome the exercise, even if the weather was still foul. They gave their farewells to the kind Mr. Goodwyn and struck out in the rain again.

Carl and Ian ended up walking together not far behind Jaaved and Argos, who were in the lead and obviously anxious to get back to the keep. Eva and Theo were walking together behind Carl and Ian. It was slow going through the rain and mud-lined streets, which were quite crowded given the weather.

During their walk home, Carl asked, "Ian? What do you

think about that part where Laodamia is talking about you not drinking the potion?"

Ian squirmed in his Sunday blazer. "I think she's talking about the vial from the box," he said. The last silver treasure box they'd acquired had contained the prophecy and a small vial of black viscous liquid, not anything Ian could imagine himself ever wanting to ingest.

"Why do you think she's warning you not to drink it?" Carl said, as if reading Ian's mind.

"Dunno," Ian said with a shrug. "You'd have to put a gun to my head to make me swallow that inky swill. It's at least three thousand years old, and poisonous."

"Well, someone's going to drink it down," Carl said, and Ian heard the nervous tension in his voice. "I just hope it's not me."

At this Ian openly laughed. "I don't think you'll have to worry about it, Carl. You know it's poison, so there'd be no reason for you to have a taste."

"You're bringing it along, though, aren't you?" Carl asked.

Ian's momentary good humor dimmed. "Yes," he said. Ian had considered leaving the vial behind, but he wasn't certain that the prophecy intended for him to leave it in Dover. The mention of the poisonous liquid was tucked too close to the lines describing the rescue of Madame Lafitte and Océanne, and he couldn't risk not having it at hand if it was needed.

They were nearing the end of the village, and Ian

noticed the traffic increasing significantly. More and more wounded were arriving every day, and by the sight of them, things along the front lines seemed dire indeed. "Ian!" he heard Theo shout from far behind, and he turned just in time to see Theo's small frame waving frantically at him.

He and Carl raced toward her, only to discover Eva lying on the ground next to an unconscious man, bleeding from a wound in his side. "Eva saw this man was trying to hide his wounds!" Theo said. "She picked him right out and led him over here to help him, but when she laid her hands on him, she went gray and sank to the ground. He fainted right after she did!"

Carl rushed around to Eva's head and lifted it off the grimy streets. Several people stopped and asked if they needed assistance, and Ian said, "Yes! Someone please send for Dr. Lineberry!"

Ian removed his blazer and handed it to Carl, who wrapped it around Eva's shoulders. Carl's own face went pale with worry while he held the poor girl. Looking about, he said, "We've got to get her out of this rain." He gently eased her farther into his arms and with Ian's help was able to lift her from the ground.

"Someone look after the soldier!" Ian called to the gathering pedestrians while he followed Carl, who was walking awkwardly with Eva toward the nearest shop. The shopkeeper inside saw them coming and hurried to open the door. "What's happened to the poor girl?" asked Mr. Ferguson, one of two bakers in the village.

"She's fainted," Ian said. "Is there somewhere clean and dry he can set her down?"

"Yes, yes!" replied Mr. Ferguson. "I have a cot in the back!"

Ian and Carl followed the kindly baker to the back of the shop, where Carl set Eva down and smoothed back her wet hair. "Carl?" she said, her eyes fluttering.

The corners of Ian's mouth quirked. His best friend certainly had a way with the girls. "I'm right here," Carl whispered to her. "And we've sent for Dr. Lineberry."

"Here," said the baker, shoving a glass of water at them. "Get her to drink that."

Ian thanked the man and held the glass while Carl propped up Eva's head so that she could take a few sips. "I'm better," she said, but her pasty white complexion begged to differ.

"When was the last time you had a proper meal, Eva?" Carl asked.

Ian then noticed how very thin the girl had become of late. He knew she'd been taking her meals in the room where Madam Dimbleby was recovering, but he wondered how much she was eating.

Eva feebly brushed a lock of hair out of her eyes, her head wobbling slightly on her neck. "I don't recall," she said.

Mr. Ferguson made a tsking sound and hurried off again. He was back in a moment with a thick slice of bread coated in sweet butter. "Eat," he ordered. Ian's mouth watered. Butter was very hard to come by these days, as much was being rationed for the war effort.

Eva stared hungrily at the offering. "I didn't bring any money, Mr. Ferguson," she confessed.

"Doesn't matter," he said, pushing the bread more firmly at her. "Consider it my treat."

Eva took the bread and began to take slow and careful bites. "You've been doing too much," Carl chided quietly when the baker went back to tend his shop.

Eva lowered the bread and stared at her lap. "They all need me, Carl," she said. "I can feel their suffering, and that pulls on me each night, insisting that I heal them."

Ian eyed Eva more closely now. He noticed the dark circles running under her eyes and again took in her gaunt appearance. With a bit of shock, he realized that having Eva stay so close to the wounded soldiers was slowly killing her.

And that was an awful realization, because one of the only safe places for Eva, as a member of the United, was Delphi Keep. It had been built on a ring of magical monoliths, which had the power to protect Theo, Eva, and Jaaved from the likes of Magus and his evil sisters. If Eva left the place that was draining the life from her, would she be hunted down by one of the sorcerers and killed anyway?

But Ian did not share this with Eva or Carl, because he knew that given the choice, she would stay at the keep to be near both Carl and the wounded soldiers who needed her so desperately.

Dr. Lineberry arrived and Ian and Carl moved away from Eva's cot to allow him to look her over. The young men ventured into the front of the shop to give them some privacy and they were both surprised to find the earl standing with Theo, looking terribly worried.

"How is she?" the earl asked.

"She's awake and talking," Ian said, hoping to reassure them all. "Dr. Lineberry is looking her over now, but, my lord, I think we should consider moving Eva out of the keep."

Ian took note of the raised eyebrows from both the earl and Carl, but Theo was nodding vigorously. "Yes, indeed," she said. "The poor thing will eventually waste away to nothing if someone doesn't intervene and separate her from all those wounded men."

The earl eyed Theo and motioned for all of them to walk to a quiet corner of the shop where they could have a bit of privacy. "How can we possibly keep Eva safe if she's away from the orphanage, Theo?"

"Send her to your aunt, my lord. I'm sure that Lady Arbuthnot wouldn't mind. And your aunt will surely be able to detect when danger may be approaching. She'll keep her well and safe, my lord, I'm sure of it."

"So she's not coming with us to France?" Carl said, and Ian noticed that Carl's face was still concerned. He knew that Carl didn't much care for the idea of being separated from his sweetheart. The sticky part was that Océanne also had affection for Carl, and Ian's best friend had yet to write to Océanne that his own heart was now fully committed to Eva.

"Absolutely not!" said Theo, as if she were in charge of the whole operation. "The poor girl will never last a day.

97

What she needs is a bit of rest and some convalescence. And now that Madam Dimbleby is well on her way to recovering, I believe you should also send her to Lady Arbuthnot's, my lord. She and Eva can return to good health together."

The corners of the earl's mouth quirked. "Would you allow me, Theo, to ask my kind aunt if she has room for company on such short notice? Or should I merely ship them off this very evening to arrive unannounced on her doorstep?"

Theo blushed slightly but her tone never wavered. "Of course you should ask her, my lord, but she'll say yes. I know it. And there is no need to worry over the time it will take to send a telegram. Lady Arbuthnot will be waiting for you at Castle Dover when you return. My senses tell me that she's not at all happy about missing the early train from London, which caused her in turn to miss Madam Scargill's funeral. I believe she'll be most anxious to make up for it by graciously accepting Eva and Madam Dimbleby into her home."

Theo, as usual, was spot on target. Eva was taken by the earl back to Castle Dover so that the wounded soldiers would not be a constant source of strain for her, and Ian, Carl, and Theo went along for company. When they all arrived, the good Lady Arbuthnot was waiting for them in the front hall. "Hastings!" she said in her radiantly rich voice as she swept over to her nephew and wrapped him in her arms. That day the lady was wearing an abundance of emerald-green taffeta and a matching hat with a giant ostrich feather. "Oh, I'm so terribly sorry for your loss!" she exclaimed. She then backed away from her rather embarrassed nephew but still held tightly to his arms. "I missed the morning train," she said gravely, as if confessing her sins. "I woke up at the proper time and knew I had to make haste, but I ignored my own intuition and was caught on the street by dear Lady Ballentine. Do you know her son, Bartholomew?"

"I do, Auntie, but—"

"He's just returned from the front," Lady Arbuthnot continued, ignoring the earl's efforts to speak. "And it's even more dreadful than we suspected! I've had the most awful visions lately, Hastings!" she exclaimed. "I've seen that dreadful man, Adolf Hitler, marching under the Eiffel Tower!"

Ian felt his stomach contract. Like Theo, Lady Arbuthnot was an extremely gifted seer, and if she saw the German Führer marching through the streets of Paris, then Ian had little doubt that it would happen.

"How soon?" he said, then remembered his manners. "I mean, how soon do you see that, my lady?"

Lady Arbuthnot turned her attention to him, only then noticing that he and the others were also there. "Ian!" she said, leaving her nephew and rushing over to give him a hug. "Oh, my lad! How big you are!"

Ian felt the air squeezed out of him and was relieved when she left him for Carl and then for Theo, who was quite close to the earl's aunt.

"My heavens, Theo!" Lady Arbuthnot said after she'd let Theo go and stood back to have a look at her. "But you are becoming quite the young lady!"

"Thank you," Theo said with a curtsy. "But I'm wondering if you could answer Ian's question for us, as you're far better with dates than I am. When do you see the Führer marching on Paris?"

Lady Arbuthnot placed a hand to her head and closed her eyes. "Late June," she said. "The twenty-second or twenty-third, I believe."

Ian breathed a small sigh of relief. That was almost a full month away. That would give them plenty of time to find Madame Lafitte and Océanne.

"But France will fall to the Germans much sooner than that," the lady continued. "I give it a week, in fact."

Ian felt his heart plummet, and barely caught the narrow-eyed squint Lady Arbuthnot was now focusing on her nephew. "Hastings," she said. "Why do I see your yacht making its way to the French shores?"

Ian, Carl, and Theo returned to the keep shortly after tea. The earl hadn't needed to explain things to his aunt nearly as much as Ian had expected, and Lady Arbuthnot wholly agreed that if Laodamia had written their rescue attempt in the prophecy, then that was exactly what they must do. "I do not relish the idea of you and the children putting yourselves in harm's way, but it must be important to the quest if Laodamia has written about it. No, you must go, Hastings. And keep your wits about you and the children close. I do see Madame Lafitte and her daughter being found, but the path before you is fraught with danger. So please be careful. And Eva of course will come to stay with me while you are all away. I also must insist that you allow me to invite the lovely Madam Dimbleby to my flat for the duration of her recovery, the poor dear. To have gone through such suffering these last few days! I shall make special arrangements for her to travel in my own railcar, where she will be well tended on the trip to London."

Ian couldn't help smiling at the smug look on Theo's face when Lady Arbuthnot said all that, but Carl looked depressed about leaving Eva behind, and that made Ian a bit less amused.

As they were taking their leave, Thatcher came into the parlor and handed the earl his port pass. "You'll have to leave before the next shipment arrives from France," he said. "Four a.m."

The earl took the pass and thanked Thatcher. He then looked at Ian and said, "We'll meet here at half past three, Ian. Make sure everyone is packed and ready to depart, and please, tell Jaaved to get some rest tonight. Even though he has assured me that he has piloted many a boat in his own land and that he is a most capable sailor, I've much to teach him about the rigging and navigation to Le Havre."

When they arrived back at the keep, they were all astonished by the number of wounded soldiers now filling the dozens and dozens of cots in the front half of the orphanage. Nurses and doctors hurried about and the keep no longer looked or seemed like a home for children; it seemed like a full-fledged hospital. As they made their way through the throng to the stairs, they were all shocked when they nearly bumped right into Madam Dimbleby.

"Madam!" Ian gasped when he saw her. "You're up and about!"

The frail woman offered him the faintest of smiles. "Dr. Lineberry insisted I attempt a few paces today," she said weakly. "I agreed, but I'm still quite angry at him for not allowing me to attend Gertie's funeral." Madam began to tear up at the mention of her cousin, and Ian took her hand and lent her some support. "There, there," he said gently, motioning to Theo and Carl to go on up ahead of him. "Let's walk you back to your bed, shall we? And I'll personally tell the good doctor that you followed his instructions to the letter."

But when Ian had led the way back to Madam's room, he discovered it filling up quickly with the wounded. "Oh, my," said Madam Dimbleby, pulling her robe closer about her.

Ian grimaced. These men certainly needed the space, but this was, after all, Madam Dimbleby's room. He nearly put his foot down, but then he thought of the kind Lady Arbuthnot's invitation and he decided there was no better time than the present.

Slowly and carefully he worked the headmistress over to a chair near the door, told her he'd be back straight-away, and dashed out to find Landis. Once he'd told the groundskeeper his predicament, Landis agreed to get out his bicycle and make haste to Castle Dover.

Within a half hour a car from the earl's fleet had arrived

and Ian was helping the frail woman into the motorcar with a small satchel of her belongings. "Eva will be with you to keep you company at Lady Arbuthnot's," he told her. "And don't worry about us. We'll be well enough."

Ian's throat tightened when he saw Madam's lower lip tremble. She looked up at him with sad eyes. "Was the funeral beautiful, Ian?"

Ian swallowed past the large lump in his throat. "It was indeed, ma'am. Madam Scargill would have been most pleased."

He stepped away then and closed the door, wishing never to see that look on Madam Dimbleby's face again.

ACROSS THE WATER TO SAVE TWO SOULS

Ian felt as if he had just closed his eyes when he was shaken awake. "Ian?"

Ian opened his lids to find Argos peering down at him. "Are you awake?"

Ian nodded groggily and sat up, yawning. Argos was attempting to quietly wake Carl, but Ian knew he wouldn't have much luck. Carl was a deep and sound sleeper. "You'll need to hold his nose," Ian whispered. "It's the only way to wake him."

Argos looked doubtfully at him and continued to gently shake Carl, who, in turn, continued to slumber. Finally, Ian got up, walked over to his friend's cot, and held his nose between his fingers. Carl jerked awake within three seconds. "What's happening?" he gasped, and Jaaved woke up with a start too.

"It's time to go," Ian told them, returning to his cot to get dressed.

After putting on his clothes, he hurried down the stairs

and knocked on what used to be the nursery door. Theo opened it, looking sleepy. "Is it time?"

"Yes," he said. "We'll need to hurry if we're to make it to the castle in the next twenty minutes." Theo nodded while yawning and closed her door. Ian then went back up the tower steps to check his satchel and make sure he had everything.

"Do you have the sundial?" Carl whispered.

"Yes," Ian said.

"Prophecy?"

"Yes."

"Vial?"

Ian sighed, his patience low. "Yes, Carl, I have all of it. Worry about your own things, would you?"

Carl said nothing for a few moments, but then he asked, "Some nibbles for the boat?"

"You won't want to eat on the boat, Carl," Jaaved told him, pointing to the window. "It's quite windy out this morning. The channel's going to be very rough."

"If you're implying that I might get seasick, I can assure you I won't," Carl said stubbornly. Then he turned to Ian and said, "Really, Ian, did you get us some nibbles for the trip?"

Outside, it was still very dark, and Ian made sure to pack an extra sweater, because out on the water it was likely to be chilly.

Once they were all certain they had everything they needed—save Carl's nibbles, of course—they made their way down the spiral staircase, pausing to collect Theo, and continued down the main stairs on tiptoe.

Luck was with them, and they managed to leave the keep without waking a single injured soldier.

Without speaking, the group hurried along the dark road to Castle Dover, and Ian could see the earl waiting for them on the front steps. "Good morning," he said to them quietly.

"Good morning, my lord," they all answered.

"Are we ready for our voyage?"

As one they nodded, and the earl motioned for them to follow him. Winding their way through the earl's residence in a somewhat circuitous path, they avoided the sections of the castle that either had been ruined by fire or were currently occupied by soldiers. Eventually, they found their way to the back of the castle and out into the earl's garden.

Ian winced when he realized that much of the earl's beloved hedge maze had been burned to a crisp, but the earl hardly seemed to glance at it as they walked to the back garden gate.

Ian felt a tinge of déjá vu; the last time he'd gone through the garden gate in the wee hours of the morning, he'd been running for his life from one of Magus the Black's hellhounds. He'd barely escaped, and his arm still held the scar from the bite that awful creature had inflicted on him.

He attempted to put the memory out of his mind and moved silently with the others down the winding path, past the small patch of woods where the portal was hidden, to the road leading to the harbor.

They arrived at the earl's boat shortly thereafter, and the earl lowered the ladder so that they could all climb aboard. Ian marveled at the beauty of the earl's ship as he helped Theo up the rungs.

Once they were aboard, there wasn't much for Ian, Theo, and Carl to do, save concentrate very hard on not being sick and look out for any signs of trouble, of course.

Luck was on their side that day, because they reached Boulogne in just a few hours, the earl's vessel being a swift one. Theo walked on shaking legs over to the ladder, and Ian carefully lowered her to the deck. He and Carl waited with her while the earl spoke to Argos and Jaaved about their course to Le Havre. "If the Germans break through the French line, they will march the bulk of their forces straight for Paris. This means it will take them time to secure the coastline and all the major ports, but Boulogne is too close to the front line to leave the vessel unattended. This is why you must travel farther south and seek safe harbor in Le Havre. When you dock, leave the ship in the hands of my dear friend Monsieur LaBlanc, the harbormaster. If the Germans reach his harbor, he will know how to hide the boat's origins.

"From there you must make your way to Paris. Jaaved, do you have the map of France I gave to you?"

"Yes, my lord," Jaaved answered immediately, reaching into the fold of his coat and pulling out the map to show the earl.

"Excellent. I have marked the map with the safest route, and as your French is perfect and Argos here wears the Star, you should be fine. But with your darker skin, Jaaved, you must be very careful about attracting unwanted attention. If you do encounter the enemy, do exactly as they say and speak only in French. Give them no reason to suspect you or where you come from, do you understand?"

Jaaved pumped his head up and down and Argos said, "We will not call attention to ourselves, Hastings. We will find you at the Fontaines de la Concorde as soon as we can."

The earl nodded but his expression was troubled. He looked at Theo, whose color was finally returning, and asked, "Theo, are you quite positive that Jaaved and Argos need join us in Paris? I feel it will be much safer for them to remain with my yacht in Le Havre and await our arrival."

Theo said, "They *must* join us, my lord. It's imperative, although I can't quite explain why."

The earl sighed. "Very well. I trust your intuition, Theo." Turning back to Jaaved and Argos, he asked them again if they felt comfortable with managing the boat's rigging and such, and they both assured him they did. It was then time to say goodbye and wish them bon voyage.

The earl's yacht set off again, and the four of them watched as it sailed out of port, weaving between the many fishing and military vessels rushing out. When the yacht was a mere speck on the horizon, the earl motioned for them to come along, and off they went through the crowded streets, making their way to the train station.

The small city of Boulogne was teeming with people, and Ian was amazed that most of those who crowded the streets were soldiers from his own homeland. He knew that Prime Minister Churchill had ordered the vast army stationed in France to pull out and retreat to England, but Ian could hardly believe it was happening until he saw it up close.

Everyone in the streets was gloomy; no one wanted to believe the Germans were capable of taking France. However, the evidence was all around them.

If France did in fact fall, what would that mean for England? Ian wondered. He knew the earl's thoughts were equally pensive, because he could see his patriarch's eyes darting here and there as if he was calculating the number of departing soldiers.

It proved quite difficult to obtain a rail pass, as most of the tickets for the day had already been purchased. It seemed that while the port was full of departing British soldiers, the train stations were filled with fleeing French citizens.

From the snatches of conversation happening around Ian, he knew that all those leaving the area wanted to put as much distance between themselves and the invading Germans as possible.

The sad expressions and tearful goodbyes of those around him were heartbreaking and Ian had to work at keeping himself detached.

The earl was finally able to secure them passage to Paris later that afternoon, and while they waited, Ian stared mindlessly at the crowds and Carl and Theo played a game of cards.

They asked if he wanted to join, but his heart wasn't in it. Instead, he settled for surveying the people around him. While he was in this state of observance, he happened to catch sight of something familiar.

Stepping onto an outgoing train across the platform was a very tall man with broad shoulders, thick curly hair, and a long cloak. As the man took hold of the rail to step up onto the train, Ian spotted a gleaming bronze cuff wrapped round the man's wrist.

At first, Ian's mind was slow to make the connection, and he stood up from his seated position to get a better look at the stranger boarding the train. Focusing on the man, he took several paces forward and watched the stranger take the final step aboard. The conductor then blew the warning whistle and the train began its slow chug out of the station. Ian hurried forward just as recognition burst into his mind, and he shouted, "General Adrastus!"

The man in the doorway of the departing train jerked, whirling around, and their eyes met. Ian knew he wasn't wrong; Adrastus of Lixus stared at him in shock for three heartbeats and then the train had moved on and he was lost to Ian's sight.

"Ian?" he heard the earl say.

Ian stared at the back end of the train, straining to see if Adrastus had perhaps gotten off and was coming back to meet him. But the longer he waited, the more the crowds closed in for the next train, and Ian could not see any sign of the general.

"Ian?" he heard the earl repeat, and he finally tore his eyes away and looked to the earl.

"Sorry," he said when he noticed the earl, Carl, and Theo all looking up at him curiously.

"You all right?" Theo asked.

Ian nodded. "I saw him," he said. "General Adrastus. He was boarding the train that just left here."

The earl turned to read the overhead sign displaying what trains were leaving which platforms. "He's headed south," he said. "Along with the rest of northern France."

"Perhaps he's on his way to Paris too?" Theo said.

Ian looked back at the platform, searching the crowd once again. He had met the general only once, a year earlier, when he and Carl had nearly been killed by one of Magus's servants. The general had saved their lives, but once he knew who Ian and Carl were, he'd made haste to leave their company.

The mystery of Adrastus of Lixus was something that teased away at Ian's brain, especially as he knew the prophecy had instructed him to find the general—for what specific reason he hadn't yet determined, but to know he'd been so close to the man and yet so far frustrated Ian greatly.

With a tired sigh he pulled his eyes away and went back to sit next to Carl and Theo. "We can only hope that we'll meet him in Paris," he said. "Laodamia has told us that we need to find him, so it's obviously important that we do."

"We can use the sundial!" Carl said.

Ian brightened. He reached into his trouser pocket to pull out the sundial, then he studied the dull surface and knew it was just the thing to help him locate the general. "Excellent idea, Carl. And we can also use it to help us locate Océanne and Madame Lafitte as well."

The earl reached out and squeezed Ian's shoulder. "Best to tuck that instrument away for now," he whispered while looking pointedly at the crowds and the nearby strangers subtly eyeing the trinket in Ian's hand. "We'll make use of it later when we have some privacy, all right, Ian?"

Ian hurried to tuck the ancient magical relic away. "Right," he said. "Apologies, my lord."

They waited several more hours for their own train to arrive, and when it finally did, Ian felt weary to the bone. Dusk had fallen, and although they'd eaten a bit of bread and cheese midafternoon, they were all still quite hungry.

When they were seated in their berth, Carl—who was in a foul mood—grumbled, "I told you to make sure to bring some nibbles along."

The earl chuckled. "We'll see about your stomach in Paris, Master Lawson. In the meantime, attempt to get some rest. We'll be in the capital soon."

Tired as he was, Ian didn't feel he could sleep. He was far too restless and worried about finding Océanne and Madame Lafitte. Still, he reasoned that the sundial would make their search go much faster, as all they had to do was ask the dial to point the way, then follow the shadow until it led them straight to the mother and daughter.

Once they had discovered Madame and Océanne, they could use the dial to help them locate the general, then scurry back across the channel to England.

Ian should have felt at ease once he'd determined to use the sundial; however, he knew that Laodamia's quests were never easy, and something was likely to come along and disrupt even the most well-thought-out plan.

This troubled him greatly, because try as he might, he could not find the flaw. Surely the sundial would work for them when he asked it to find the Lafittes, wouldn't it?

Ian took out the dial and decided to test it. "Where is Theo's set of jacks?"

The tarnished face of the sundial changed immediately to burnished bronze and a shadow appeared, pointing across the aisle to Theo's satchel, which was tucked into the overhead bin. Ian smiled. The dial was working perfectly. There was no need to worry.

With another sigh he leaned back against the gently rocking cushion of the train seat and settled in for a good long nap.

A PLAN GONE AWRY

They arrived in Paris midevening, and the earl was quite motivated to find them a place to take their supper, as Carl's stomach gurgled loudly from the moment they stepped off the train.

They found a quaint little eatery near the River Seine and enjoyed the rich food and the hum of the city about them.

Their meal would have been perfect, in fact, if not for the constant snatches of conversation they overheard about the approach of the German army while the British quickly abandoned the French shores.

Many a Parisian felt betrayed by their allies, and after a bit, Ian found his appetite had all but left him. When the earl asked if he was all right, he leaned in and whispered, "How can we leave them to fend for themselves, my lord?"

The earl sat back in his chair and surveyed the surrounding tables as more of the talk reached their ears. The earl's shoulders drooped a bit; then he too leaned in and answered Ian. "It is certainly not without tremendous regret, Ian, that we must leave our friends in their hour of greatest need, but the German forces are far mightier than anyone imagined. We must retreat for now to ensure that we do not also fall to the Nazis."

Ian looked down at his plate, his morale dropping to a new low. "I feel terrible for them," he said. "They're about to be overrun by the enemy, and there's nothing we can do to help them."

"Not now, perhaps," the earl agreed. "But England shall never back down, lad. We shall fight to the end, of that I'm sure."

Ian was not consoled by the earl's words. He said nothing more, just pushed his food about his plate moodily and didn't participate in the dinner conversation. After a bit, he noticed that Theo too had fallen silent, and when at last he looked up, he saw that she was holding tightly to her crystal, her eyes holding that faraway cast.

"Theo?" he asked.

Between Theo's fingers Ian caught sight of a bright pink glow, which was turning quickly to red. "Something is terribly wrong," she whispered.

All eyes were immediately on her. "What is it?" the earl asked.

Theo shook her head, her eyes still unfocused. "We're in danger, my lord," she said. "We must leave at once and find somewhere to hide."

Without questioning her further, the earl motioned for the waiter to bring him the bill, and after he laid down a few francs, they were off again. "Our hotel is just across the river," he said, walking quickly and with purpose across a cobblestone bridge.

Ian carried his satchel and Theo's, as he wanted her free to focus on what danger was approaching them. But she said nothing as they walked; she merely pressed them with her quick steps to move faster to the hotel.

Once they had entered the building, Ian expected her fearful look to ebb, but she continued to hold her crystal nervously and start at any nearby noise. "Theo," Ian said, setting their satchels down while the earl approached the front desk to secure their rooms. "What is it?"

There were tears in Theo's eyes, and Ian knew that whatever it was had Theo scared half to death. "I'm not sure, Ian," she whispered. "But something is out there and I feel as if it's hunting us."

Goose pimples lined Ian's arms and he looked to the door, expecting at any moment for a hellhound to burst through and attack them. He couldn't imagine the beasts would enter the middle of Paris, but he knew that frightened look on Theo's face all too well, and almost always the hellhounds were to blame for it.

Ian turned to Carl and said, "Wait with her here."

"Where're you going?" Carl asked, but Ian didn't answer him. Instead, he turned and hurried to the door of the hotel.

Peering out the glass window, he surveyed the crowd for any signs of panic or cries of help. He knew the beasts would cause a disturbance if they were close, and he hoped he'd have enough time to get Theo to safety if he could simply determine from which direction they were likely to come.

The crowd outside, however, remained fairly calm, and the only anxiety he read on their faces likely had to do with the impending German invasion. Cautiously, Ian pushed through the door and walked out onto the street. A gust of wind brought a sudden and dramatic chill to him. He wiped his face and felt something odd on it. Looking at his fingers, he realized there was frost on them.

Another chill took hold of him, but this one ran straight up his spine. Quick as a flash, he darted back into the hotel and ran directly to Carl and Theo. The earl was just leaving the clerk at the desk, and Ian wasted no time explaining; he merely took hold of their bags and hurried over to the earl. "The sorceresses!" he hissed, fear taking hold of his insides.

The earl did not ask him to explain; instead, he reached out for Theo's hand and motioned for Carl and Ian to follow him. They all but ran to the lift and darted inside just as the doors were closing. "Second floor," the earl said to the lift attendant.

They rode the short way in silence, and with a *bing*, the doors opened, and they dashed out. "We shall hide in our rooms," the earl told them, eyeing a key and the sign posted on a nearby wall indicating which rooms were where. "This way!" he said, hurrying down the corridor.

Ian glanced at Theo's pendant as it bounced against her throat while she trotted next to the earl. The crystal had gone from bright red to radiant pink, and he hoped that meant the sorceresses were moving away from them.

When they got to their appointed rooms, the earl opened a door and ushered them inside. "In here for now," he said.

Ian saw that he was entering a suite, in harmonious tones of green and pink. He dropped the satchels and took charge of Theo, leading her to a nearby settee and sitting her down. "Is it better?" he asked, noticing that the crystal about her neck was still bright.

Her eyes focused on him. "A bit," she said, "but I can feel them, Ian, and I fear they're quite close."

Behind him, Ian heard the sound of a window being opened. He also heard Carl whisper, "Gaw, blimey!"

Ian turned his head to see that his friend was at the window, peering down at the streets below. Carl then took several steps back from the window, his expression terrified.

The window faced another building, lending them a terrible view, but from what must have been an alley down below, they clearly heard voices echoing up the brick and mortar to them.

"I tell you, mistresses," said the first voice, "I can sense that a magical instrument of great power is right now being employed!"

"Describe it, witch!" said a second voice, which Ian would recognize anywhere.

"Caphiera," he said so softly he doubted anyone else had heard it.

There was a pause, and then the first voice—a

woman's—said, "It is small and made of metal, but its size and composition belie its magical powers."

"What need have we of magical instruments!" howled another voice, and Ian shivered. Atroposa was with her sister on the streets below. "We've this green door to find, which will reveal the Secret Keeper!"

"I sense that this magical instrument will be put to use against you, mistresses," said the first voice. "That is why I mention it now and, unfortunately, distract you from our purpose."

Ian sucked in a breath at the same time Carl did. They looked at each other in astonishment before Ian flew into action. Tugging at his clothing with trembling fingers, he pulled out the sundial, its surface still shining brightly and a shadow pointing across the room.

In the next instant Carl was by his side, whispering, "Turn it off, Ian! Turn it off!"

But Ian was so shaken by the appearance of the sorceresses just outside their hotel that all rational thought had left him. For the life of him he couldn't think how to make the shadow disappear.

"Ian!" the earl said into his ear as he too stepped close to him. "Get it to stop pointing!"

Ian stared blankly first at Carl, then at the earl. His mind was frozen, and the more he tried to think of a way to make the sundial stop pointing, the more he couldn't think at all.

"What did you ask it to find?" Carl whispered, bouncing from foot to foot as he shook his hands anxiously. "Oh, no, Ian! You didn't ask it to find Océanne, did you?"

"It is them!" shrieked another voice, hollow and haunting. "The Oracles are nearby, Sister! They must be using one of Laodamia's trinkets!"

"Ian!" Theo said, her voice soft but urgent. "Answer the question! *What* did you ask the sundial to find?"

Ian blinked and his mind cleared. Without saying a word, he bolted forward to the pile of satchels near the door and pulled up Theo's.

From outside he heard Caphiera say, "Lead us to this magical instrument, witch, and we shall fill your pockets with gold!"

Ian tore at the latches of Theo's satchel, his fingers trembling so hard it was difficult to get them to cooperate. "Your jacks!" he whispered when she came over to him. "Where are they?"

Theo's fingers weren't shaking nearly as much as Ian's, and she tugged the satchel away from him and rummaged around inside until she pulled up a small sack that jingled in her hands.

Immediately the sundial's burnished surface became dull and lifeless. Ian stared at it, his chest heaving from the quick breaths coming into and out of his lungs. Outside, there was a slight shriek and the first voice they'd heard cursed loudly.

"What is it, witch?" Caphiera asked.

"It's gone!" she said. "The magical vibrations have ended!"

"They've stopped using the trinket?" moaned Atroposa.

"Yes," said the witch, and she cursed again. "I cannot sense where it is now."

For a long moment nothing stirred and no one spoke. Ian had no idea what was happening out in the alleyway, but he suspected the sorceresses were assessing the buildings they were standing between, and perhaps wondering if the young Oracles they were after might be inside.

The earl, who'd been standing next to Carl, left his side and approached the window slowly and cautiously. Keeping well out of sight, he eyed the alley, and Ian knew that he spied the sisters, because he could see the earl's jaw clench and his lips press together.

"We will search the buildings," said Caphiera, and Ian closed his eyes and thought, *Oh, no!*

"We'll start with this one," she added, and then only her heavily steeled footfalls could be heard slowly fading away.

Ian opened his eyes then and stared about at his companions. "Quickly," the earl said, already hurrying to the door, his own satchel in his hand. "They have gone to the building next door first. We must put as much distance between us and them as we can!"

At the door, the earl paused and turned to Ian. "Whatever you do, Ian," he warned, "do *not* ask that sundial to find anything more until we are safely out of Paris. Do you understand?"

Ian gulped. "Yes, my lord," he said, realizing that his plan to find Océanne had quickly thwarted.

With that, they were once again on the move.

That night they stayed in a small inn on the outskirts of Paris. Ian was so exhausted by the time he was finally able to lay his head on his pillow that he hardly cared if the sorceresses were still searching for them. He fell asleep almost as soon as he'd closed his eyes, and did not wake until near dawn, when he sat bolt upright after having a terrible dream. Awake, he found the earl sitting in a chair next to the window, peering out into the night.

"My lord?" Ian said, wondering if the earl had been there all night.

Without taking his eyes from the window, the earl said, "It's all right, lad. Go back to sleep."

Ian didn't argue, but going back to sleep seemed impossible. He lay there alone with his thoughts while Carl snored loudly next to him and Theo tossed and turned on the opposite bed. He still felt terrible for nearly getting them killed by being so careless with the sundial, and he wondered who the other woman with the sorceresses had been.

They'd called her witch, but he wondered if in fact she was a witch. One thing was for certain, however: they couldn't use the sundial to help locate Océanne and her mother, which left them at a clear disadvantage. How were they ever to find them?

At last, rays of sunlight began to peek into the room and Ian sat up again. One look at the earl's drawn features and he knew the poor man had most certainly been awake and kept watch the whole night.

"If you'd like to sleep a bit, my lord, I'd be happy to take over the watch for you."

The earl turned to him. "Thank you, Ian," he said. "But we will not be here long enough for me to rest."

The earl then got up from his chair and stretched tiredly. Carl stirred next to Ian, and he nudged him with his elbow. "Carl," he said. "Wake up."

Carl groaned grumpily and tugged at his clothing. They'd all slept in their clothes, in case they needed to make another hasty exit. "I'm still tired," he complained.

Across the room, Theo sat up, rubbing her eyes. "Is it time to leave?" she asked.

"Yes," the earl told them. "I think it best that we move along."

Travel weary and grumpy from their troubles, the four left the inn and made their way by metro across Paris to the opposite side. Here the earl led them to a set of offices, where he told them to wait outside but to come in immediately and fetch him if any sign of the sorceresses appeared. He returned shortly, looking quite pleased with himself.

"My lord," Carl said the moment the earl appeared. "Might we have a bit of breakfast soon?"

"Yes, Carl," the earl said. "But first we shall need to get settled. This way, please."

They followed the earl for three blocks, until they came to a row of tall flats facing a street lined with shops. The earl paused in the middle of the street and eyed a bit of paper and then the flat they were standing in front of.

"Here we are," he said, climbing the steps. Ian, Theo, and Carl followed.

"Where are we?" Carl asked.

"These are our lodgings while we're in Paris," the earl replied.

"You've rented us a flat?" Ian said.

The earl inserted a key into the main door's lock. "Yes, Ian," he said, pushing open the door and allowing them all to troop inside. "It occurred to me that Caphiera and Atroposa would likely search every hotel and inn until they eventually found us, so I thought it best not to lodge longer than last night in one. I've rented us a flat on the top floor, and my hope is that you three can remain hidden here while I attempt to locate Madame Lafitte and her daughter."

They began to climb the stairs then, all three of them trudging up slowly. "We're not going to help you search for them?" Theo asked the earl.

"No, Theo," he told her. "I will make as many inquiries as I can with my associates here in Paris who may know of their whereabouts, but you three are to remain hidden here."

"But what about Jaaved and Argos?" Carl asked. "Who's going to meet them at the Fontaines de la Concorde?"

The earl paused midstep and turned to Carl as if he'd completely forgotten about Jaaved and the man from the portal. "It will take them a few days to arrive from Le Havre," he said after a moment's thought. "If we have not discovered Madame and Océanne by then, I shall send you boys out once a day to the fountains to see if Argos and

Jaaved have arrived while I continue to search for the Lafittes."

"What about me?" Theo asked, obviously injured at having been left out.

The earl looked first at Ian, then at Theo. "I think it best that you remain hidden here, Theo."

"But why, my lord?" she asked, her face pouty and frustrated.

"Because the cause cannot lose you, Theo," he said softly. "You are the One, remember?"

Ian looked pointedly at Theo, willing her not to argue. The One from Laodamia's prophecies was the most powerful Oracle of all and would gather all the other United to her to battle Demogorgon's evil forces. If Theo was lost, then they would all be doomed.

Still, this did not appear to ease her foul mood. Ian thought he heard her mutter something about that being silly, but even Theo wasn't brazen enough to argue with the earl.

They reached the top floor of the four-story building and the earl opened their flat to them. Ian and Carl rushed in, anxious to explore their surroundings.

The flat was quite charming, open and spacious, with a delightful view of the city. Ian made his way to the terrace, which overlooked the street below. Directly across from them, he could see the row of shops, and one in particular caught his attention, due to the bright green door with the large brass knocker attached to it.

Ian squinted to see more detail, but he couldn't determine what sort of shop it was, and there didn't appear to be a sign over the shop like the ones over its neighbors'.

He would have thought that quite odd had Carl not rushed to his side and pointed to the shop next to the one with the green door. "Look, Ian! A bakery! Let's see if the earl will let us get a bite to eat, shall we?"

When they went to ask the earl, however, they discovered him slumped in a chair in the sitting room, fast asleep. "Don't wake him!" Theo quietly cautioned. She was busy covering him with a throw.

"We were going to see about breakfast," Carl told her. "There's a bakery just across the street."

"Then go see about breakfast, Carl," Theo replied, bending to untie the earl's shoes.

Ian smiled. Theo was forever proving herself a grown-up. He nudged Carl and off they went, promising to return with something for her.

He and Carl raced down the stairs and over to the bakery, where they purchased several loaves of bread and some breakfast croissants, which were still warm and were buttery and delicious.

Nibbling on their wares, they went out of the bakery, and Ian had a chance to observe the neighboring shop up close.

As he'd observed from the balcony of their new flat, there was no sign or lettering on the front of the shop to indicate what it was. It also appeared to be abandoned by its owner, because a fair amount of dirt and litter had collected just in front of the door.

"What is it?" Carl asked when he noticed that Ian had stopped to inspect the shop.

"Nothing," Ian said, leaning in to peer through the lone window, which revealed only an empty large room. "Just having a look inside."

"What do you see?"

Ian squinted into the gloom. The room was a good size, and it was bare. The far wall, however, held his attention, but he couldn't fathom why. There was nothing unusual about it other than it didn't appear to have been plastered over like the other three walls; the stone was left bare.

"Ian," Carl said impatiently, jiggling the door handle, which sounded like it was locked tight. "What do you see?"

Ian pulled his head back. "Not a thing. The shop's abandoned."

Carl looked up and down the row of bustling businesses surrounding the shop. "Odd that no one's thought to open it back up again," he said. "These other shops seem to do a right good business."

Ian shrugged.

Still, as they walked back across the street to their flat, Ian couldn't help glancing a time or two over his shoulder to peer at the green door again. Something about it continued to tug at him.

The rest of the day passed without incident. There was a radio in the flat, and while the earl slept, Ian, Carl, and

Theo sat around it, listening to the grim news from the front lines. The Germans were pummeling the remaining French forces, and it appeared it was only a matter of time before France would give way.

Late in the afternoon the earl woke with a start, and seemed to be in a terribly foul mood after discovering that he'd slept the day away without making a single inquiry. "I shall have to double my efforts to find Madame and Océanne tomorrow," he said. "I will leave early in the morning, and I must insist that you three keep to the flat except at mealtime. I'll leave you with some francs for food, but please don't wander far from here."

They all agreed and Ian hoped the earl would be successful straightaway so that they could return to England as soon as possible.

The earl, however, was not successful the next day. Nor the next. Nor even the next.

On the morning of the fourth day, when Ian thought he'd go mad with boredom, the earl took him aside just before leaving and said, "I think it's best if you and Carl go to the fountains today to see if Jaaved and Argos have made their way to Paris, Ian." He then handed Ian a hand-drawn map and added, "I've drawn the location of the Fontaines de la Concorde on this map. Follow the arrows, and stay no longer than an hour or two."

Ian nodded. "Very well, my lord. We'll go at noon."

The earl smiled, gave his shoulder a squeeze, and headed out the door.

At the appointed time, Ian gathered Carl and told

Theo to stay in the flat until they returned. "We'll bring you back some sweets, all right?" he said when she stood moodily by the door.

"But what about lunch?" she asked.

Ian looked across the sitting room to the balcony and the bright sunny day outside. He took a few francs out of his pocket, gave them to her, and said, "I'm sure it will be all right if you only venture out to the shops across the way. If you could also bring us back enough bread for supper, I'm sure the earl would be grateful."

Theo sighed, but she took the money and went out to sit on the balcony. Ian felt bad for her, as at least he and Carl weren't going to be cooped up in the flat another day with nothing but dire news on the radio to occupy their time.

He very nearly suggested breaking the earl's rule and bringing Theo with them, but he knew that wouldn't be the smart thing to do. She'd be much safer here.

"Are we going, mate?" Carl asked him, pulling Ian's thoughts away from Theo.

"Yes," he said quickly, hurrying through the open door.

The young men reached the street and trotted down its length, working their way steadily along the earl's map toward the fountains.

They discovered that they were several blocks away from the Place de la Concorde, where the fountains were located, but the earl's map was easy enough to follow. Ian spotted them from some distance, in fact, and they ran the rest of the way, only to find the square brimming with grim-faced pedestrians hurrying through the streets.

No one, it seemed, was interested in stopping to gaze at the marvelous fountains, save Ian and Carl. "They're worried about the war," Carl said.

Ian sat on the brim of one of the fountains. "I wish the earl would find Madame Lafitte and Océanne," he said.

"He will," Carl said confidently. Ian knew he had absolute faith in the earl.

Ian nodded, but his heart felt sick with worry. "I wish we could help. If only I could ask the sundial to point the way to Madame Lafitte and Océanne!"

Then a terrible thought struck him, and he patted his pockets anxiously until he felt the small point of the sundial's tip. "What is it?" Carl asked, looking at him with concern.

Ian closed his eyes and swallowed hard, knowing he'd just made a most grievous mistake. The sundial responded to any question asked aloud about the location of something as long as the person asking the question was also holding the dial. Pulling the relic out of his pocket, he peered at it with half-closed lids, willing its surface to still be tarnished and dull.

Instead, the surface gleamed in the sunlight, save for one thin shadow pointing directly east.

Carl gasped, and Ian looked up at him, filled with regret. "Ian!" Carl said. "What have you done?"

"I didn't mean to!" Ian said anxiously. "I only realized that I had the sundial in my pocket after I'd wished out loud to find the Lafittes!"

Carl's head snapped to the bustling crowd around them. "Well, make it stop!" he said, his voice rising in pitch.

"I can't!" Ian told him. He knew there was no way to turn off the magic until the lost item in question was discovered.

Carl focused his attention back on Ian. "Ask it to find something else!" he suggested.

"Like what?"

Carl swiveled his head, looking for anything to name. His eyes peered into the fountain and he said, "Ask it to find you a franc!"

Ian did, and immediately the surface of the dial lit up with nearly a dozen small shadows pointing in a semicircle around the surface. Ian let out a curse and nearly dropped the instrument. "Carl! What have you made me do?"

Carl pointed to the fountain. "It's pointing to the coins in the fountain!" he said. He took the sundial out of Ian's palm while kicking off his shoes, then boldly stepped right into the water and began picking up the coins. Ian also kicked off his shoes and joined Carl, and soon the boys were soaking wet, but every time they lifted a coin, one of the shadows disappeared.

Ian spotted several people walking past looking at them with disapproval, and he knew it was only a matter of time before a policeman was notified and came to investigate. "Quickly, quickly!" Ian said, picking up as many coins as he could get his hands on, all the while willing more of the shadows to disappear.

"You there!" they heard when only two of the shadows remained. "Stop this instant and get out of the fountain!"

Ian glanced up to see a French officer with his hands on his hips yelling at them. "Yes, sir!" he said, reaching for the only coin left in the fountain.

"Why is there still a shadow?" Carl whispered when Ian had snagged it.

Ian began moving with his cache of coins to the edge of the fountain and noticed that the policeman was walking over to them too. Ian looked down. The shadow was still pointing due east, and with great dread he realized that the sundial had not forgotten to point the way to the Lafittes.

Still, Ian had bigger issues at the moment. The French officer approaching them looked mad enough to cart them off to jail if Ian didn't think quickly. Before the officer could even open his mouth, Ian thrust his cache of coins at him and said, "We're terribly sorry, sir. We were just having a bit of a lark, and we realize we've been awfully inconsiderate."

The policeman took the wet coins, albeit with irritation because they were dripping all over his uniform, and Ian nudged Carl to give up his portion too. Carl did, and quick as a flash they were out of the water, snatching up their shoes and making a hasty getaway. "Just a moment!" the officer warned.

But Ian didn't wait. He bolted out of the square in his stocking feet, carrying his shoes and hoping Carl would follow suit.

Behind him he heard a sharp, piercing whistle and knew the officer was calling for others to chase them down, so Ian snaked his way through the bustling streets to a side street well off the square.

To his immense relief, Carl came up right behind him, panting heavily and wearing a huge grin. "That was bloomin' marvelous!"

Ian leveled a look at him. "Might I remind you that we still have the issue of the sundial to deal with?"

Carl's smile faded, but only slightly. "Is it still pointing to a franc?" he asked.

"No," Ian said, unclenching his palm and showing Carl the surface of the relic. "It's pointing to the Lafittes, and I don't know how to get it to stop."

Carl eyed him curiously. "Really?" he said. "Well, I do."

"How?"

"We'll simply locate Océanne and her mother and the dial will stop pointing."

Ian blinked. He'd been so concerned that the dial was sending out waves of magical energy, which might attract the sorceresses to them, that he hadn't even focused on the fact that the dial was able to lead them directly to Océanne and her mother.

"Come on," he said, squishing his soggy feet into his shoes. "We'll have to be quick about it and keep alert for the sorceresses."

Carl caught him by the arm just as Ian was turning to dash down the alley. "What if we see the sorceresses coming before we find the Lafittes?"

Ian pressed his lips together, hating what he was about to suggest, but knowing it would be the only choice left if it came to that. "We'll have to toss the dial," he said. "I'll throw it as far away from us as I can, and we'll have to make a run for it."

Carl appeared shocked by Ian's suggestion that they quit one of their most prized magical possessions, but soon he nodded and the young men set off again.

A COLD CALCULATION

Caphiera the Cold paced the floor of the abandoned steel mill, mumbling curses and curling her long fingers into fists. "They are after the Keeper!" she snarled as her sister stood nearby, the rags that made up her clothing blowing in her own wind.

"Of course they are, Sister," Atroposa agreed.

Caphiera stopped her pacing and stared hard at the witch, sitting huddled in her cloak, blue with cold while frost formed on her crystal ball. "Can you see them?" the sorceress screeched, making the witch jump.

"No, mistress," she admitted meekly. "I can sense that they are still in Paris, but until they use their magical instrument again, I am hard-pressed to locate them."

Caphiera spat irritably on the ground, a nub of ice forming where her spittle landed. "Intolerable!" she snapped. Turning to Atroposa, she said, "We *must* find them, Sister, before they reach the Keeper!"

"Yes, Caphiera," said her sister. "And we shall. They will use the instrument soon enough."

Caphiera spun away in irritation from Atroposa. How could she remain so calm? They were about to give a report to their father, and Caphiera feared his reaction, but perhaps if she worded their status carefully, he would allow them a few more days?

"Light the fire," she said to Atroposa.

Her sister walked over to the large stone hearth in the center of the mill and lit a long match, which nearly blew out as she lowered it to the wood they'd made the witch gather.

Atroposa then stood back and blew softly in the direction of the kindling, and soon a roaring fire was blazing. Caphiera took several steps away from it—the heat being most disagreeable to her—as they all waited in silence while the wood crackled and burned, filling the large space with a sweltering warmth.

Before long there was an insufferable noise like grating boulders and crushing rocks, and it filled the room until, finally, a deep voice said, "My daughters . . ."

Caphiera bowed low, as did her sister, then held her pose until her father spoke directly to her. "What news have you to tell me?"

"We are here in Paris, Sire," Caphiera said. "We are searching for the Keeper and we feel he is very close."

More sounds of boulders churning echoed out from the hearth. "I had expected you to find him by now, Caphiera."

The sorceress tamped down the nervous tension those

words inspired, and pointed to the witch, who was still sitting in front of her crystal, staring terrified at the hearth. "We have a seer at our disposal who is helping us locate the Keeper," she said, hoping her voice sounded confident. The grating sound, however, was a key that her sire, Demogorgon, was not satisfied with that answer, and Caphiera was near panic. She knew what would happen if her father grew too impatient, and already she could feel the tingling along her skin, which she knew would quickly turn into a burning sensation.

She looked at her sister and saw that the constant wind about Atroposa was beginning to fade, and her clothing whipped less frantically. In fact, it was now blowing gently, as if lulled by a soft breeze.

"The children we seek are also here in Paris, Sire! We know they are nearby, in fact," Caphiera said in a rush.

The tingling along her arms stopped. "You have seen them?"

"The witch has," Caphiera said, pointing to the woman at the table. "She has seen them and is helping us to hunt them along with the Keeper."

"Where are they now?" said the voice, and Caphiera felt another tickle of fear creep along her backbone. Demogorgon did not seem to be addressing her or her sister, but the witch, and Demogorgon never addressed a mortal.

She turned her attention to the woman across the room, who still appeared to be paralyzed with fear. "*Answer, witch!*" she shouted, willing the woman not to say anything stupid.

The woman jumped, then looked back down at her crystal as sweat ran into the creases of her brow and dripped down the sides of her face. Caphiera felt another few seconds tick by, and that tingling sensation crept along her skin again. Her father was quickly running out of patience. She was about to shout at the witch again when the woman leapt to her feet and said, "I have seen them, mistresses! They are at the fountains!"

"Which fountains?" Caphiera asked quickly, ready to pounce on any new information to offer her sire.

The witch stared hard again at her crystal. "I believe they are at the Fontaines de la Concorde! I went there once when I was a little girl, and I would recognize them anywhere."

"You're sure?" Atroposa asked, and Caphiera glared hard at her, wanting very much to slap her sister.

But to her relief the witch nodded vigorously and said, "Yes. And they have employed the magical instrument again. I believe if we leave now, I can lead you straight to them!"

Caphiera whirled back to the hearth, eager for her father to release them so they could be on their way. For a long moment, however, he did not. At last the roaring flames simmered and he said, "Go, my daughters. Use the witch. Kill the children. Bring the Keeper to me, alive if you can."

Caphiera bowed low, attempting to suppress the smile creeping along her lips. They had escaped the wrath of their father for another day. "Thank you, Sire," she said, then stood to turn away.

Just as she'd taken a step, however, Demogorgon called her back. "Caphiera," he said.

She stiffened. "Yes, Sire?"

"After you bring me the Keeper, you and Atroposa will go to the aid of your brother. Lachestia keeps him in a prison of her making, and my patience with her is at an end. Find and release Magus, kill Lachestia, and await my return."

Caphiera's sly smile returned. "As you wish, Sire. As you wish."

A PERILOUS MISSION

Ian and Carl ran through the streets of Paris, dodging motorcars, lorries, pedestrians, bicycles, and horse-drawn carts. All the while Ian kept a close eye on the sundial as it led them block after block farther east. "How far do you think they are?" Carl asked, his breathing labored as he worked to keep up with Ian.

Ian shrugged. "I hope it's not too far," he said, eyeing the sky worriedly, thinking about how he'd told Theo they'd be gone only an hour or two.

"If we don't find them by nightfall, we'll have to hide the sundial and go back to the flat," he said, knowing that eventually Theo would become so worried that she'd go looking for them, which would put her in danger too.

At the next intersection he and Carl paused, waiting for the traffic to part, when Ian heard what sounded like a rumble of thunder. He glanced again at the sky, which was crystal clear, without a cloud in it.

"Did you hear that?" Carl asked just as the last motor-car moved out of their way.

Ian nodded, focusing again on the sundial, which was pointing him left down a quiet street filled with flats. "There must be a storm coming," he said. He was used to the weather in Dover changing unexpectedly.

Another rumble sounded, and then another and another in quick succession. Carl, who'd been trotting along beside him, stopped abruptly. Ian looked back to see his friend staring off in the opposite direction, and Ian had no choice but to stop as well. "It's this way," he said impatiently.

But Carl seemed to be ignoring him, and to add to Ian's frustration, the rumble of thunder was growing closer. They'd be drenched soon if they didn't hurry. "Carl!" he snapped, but when his friend finally turned to look at him, Ian could see the fear in his eyes. "What is it?"

"That's not thunder, Ian," he said.

Ian blinked just as another round of loud rumbles drifted to his ears, but oddly, the ground under his feet rumbled too. And then he knew, and a terrible foreboding came over him. "Bombs!" he gasped, his voice no louder than a whisper.

Carl turned away from the oncoming torrent, dashing straight for Ian and catching him by the shirt collar. "Run!" he yelled. "Ian, run!"

Ian and Carl raced down the street, looking anywhere to find shelter. Behind them the thunderous noise was joined by sirens, and Ian knew that the city was being attacked by the German Luftwaffe.

He and Carl darted this way and that, running up steps to the flats and pulling on the doors, but all of them were locked. It seemed there was no place to hide, and what was worse, there was no one about on this quiet street to aid them.

"Where do we go?" Carl shouted just as the sound of an approaching plane rose above the explosions, coming closer and closer.

Ian turned his head this way and that, looking for a doorway or overhang where they might huddle, but he was so panicked his eyes found nothing suitable. He was about to tell Carl to duck in the stairwell of one of the buildings across the way when an explosion at the back end of the street sent both of them to the pavement.

Ian covered his head with his arms as another explosion shattered one of the flats they'd passed after first turning down the street. Ian could feel small particles of debris sprinkling his back and hair. He knew he was screaming, but he couldn't hear his own voice above the battery of noise. Getting to his feet, he reached behind him, grabbed Carl by the collar, and pulled him up and along the sidewalk, searching for someplace to hide from the falling debris, but the pair quickly tumbled to the ground again after another bomb exploded nearby.

When the rain of debris stopped, Ian lifted his chin and saw that poor Carl had a large cut on the side of his head, which began to bleed.

Ian shook Carl's shoulder, but his friend only lay there,

limp and lifeless. *"Carl!"* Ian screamed, afraid the injury was much worse than it appeared.

Carl showed no signs of recovering himself. Ian got to his knees and lifted him by the shoulders. Ducking low, he pulled Carl along, desperate to find shelter.

Another explosion was so near it caused a percussion that sent Ian tumbling to the ground for a third time. He landed on his backside with a hard thud, and it was a moment before he could collect his wits.

Coughing and choking on the mixture of dust and smoke, Ian attempted to regain his footing, still terribly worried about Carl. However, as he was struggling to do that, a hand gripped his arm firmly and jerked him up.

The cloaked figure who'd grabbed him then moved over to Carl, lifted him under the shoulders, and pulled him into a nearby doorway.

Ian blinked, wiping at the soot and dust stinging his eyes. The ringing in his ears wouldn't allow him to think straight. A moment later he felt someone take hold of his hand and pull him toward the same doorway.

He followed numbly along and managed to keep his feet underneath him even when another building just down the street was shattered by yet more bombs.

Once inside the doorway, Ian stumbled, belatedly realizing there were stairs leading down. The cloaked stranger prevented him from tumbling, but just barely. He was all but blind within the darkened stairwell, and his free hand gripped the railing tightly.

Finally, he reached the bottom and leaned against the

wall, attempting to collect himself. Unable to hear much of anything above the distant barrage of bombs and the ringing in his ears, he felt something brush past him, and a moment later the dark was illuminated by the strike of a match. He coughed several times to clear his lungs as the stranger lit a lantern. By its light Ian could see that Carl was lying nearby, bleeding badly from the head.

Ian moved to help him, but the cloaked stranger shot out an arm to bar him from doing so, and then the stranger pointed to the floor. Ian was to take a seat.

Obediently, Ian slid down the wall to sit and coughed several more times. His lungs felt thick and heavy, and his eyes burned. As he squinted at poor Carl, he felt terribly guilty.

He wished he'd remembered that he'd been carrying the sundial when he asked to locate Océanne and her mother. If only he'd kept his thoughts to himself, he and Carl would be back at the flat with Theo . . .

"*Oh, no!*" Ian shouted, jumping immediately to his feet. He'd left Theo all alone on the fourth story of a building in the heart of Paris! What if their flat had been bombed? What if she'd been injured . . . or worse!

Ian would have run straight to the stairs if he hadn't been stopped again by the stranger, who latched fiercely on to his arm. "No!" the stranger shouted directly into his ear. "You will not go out onto the street yet!"

Ian realized two things at once. The first was that the stranger was a woman; the second, that he could now hear her above the ringing in his ears.

Still, thoughts of Theo being trapped and defenseless in their flat fueled his panic. "My sister is in terrible danger!" he said desperately. "You must let me go!"

But the cloaked woman would not release him. Instead, she pulled him away from the stairs and pointed firmly to the ground. "Sit!" she ordered. "You can do nothing for her until the bombs stop."

With great dismay Ian listened to the thunderous booms still echoing from above. He knew it was suicide to go dashing through the streets of Paris as it was being bombed, but that didn't stop him from worrying about Theo. He was nearly beside himself with fear.

Nearby, Carl moaned, and Ian's attentions were diverted temporarily to his injured friend. "What's happened?" Carl said, attempting to lift his hand up to the large cut on his head.

"Stay still," said the woman.

She got to her feet then and regarded Ian, who could barely make out her features within the folds of the cloak. "I must get water and a fresh cloth for your friend's wound," she told him. "You must promise to stay here."

Ian was so dismayed he didn't have the ability to reply. Instead, he merely nodded.

The woman moved away from them, down a long corridor and beyond the ray of light from the lantern.

Carl opened his eyes, squinting through his lids with a pained expression on his face. "Where are we?"

"Belowground," Ian told him.

"How'd we get here?"

"A woman helped us."

"What woman?"

Ian shrugged. "Dunno. You were hit on the head by some rubble and knocked out, and a woman came and helped get you here."

Carl looked about. "Where'd she go?"

"To get you some water and cloth for your head."

Neither of them said a word for a time after that, but then Carl seemed to read Ian's troubled mind. "Theo," he whispered.

Ian balled his hands into fists. He was angry at himself for leaving her behind. "I should have listened to my instincts," he said. "I nearly invited her with us but then I remembered what the earl had said, that she would be safe at the flat, so I left her there."

Carl coughed and rubbed his watery eyes. "She might be perfectly safe, Ian," he said. "And being with us hasn't proven itself to be free of trouble, you know."

Ian knew his friend was right but he couldn't let go of the guilt for leaving Theo on her own. "How's your head?" he asked, changing the subject.

"It bloody well hurts."

"What can I do?"

Carl tipped his head back against the brick. "Stop feeling so responsible for things you have no control over. If Theo's crystal had told her she'd be in danger, don't you think she would've mentioned it?"

Ian hadn't considered that. "She didn't say that we'd be in danger either, did she, Carl?"

Carl sighed. "When *haven't* we been in danger, Ian?"

The cloaked stranger returned shortly thereafter, carrying a small bowl of water, several torn strips of cloth, and a second lantern. She sat down in front of Carl and wiped his hair from his temple to have a look at his wound. "Glad to see you're awake," she said.

"Thank you," Carl said.

"We're quite fortunate you came along when you did," Ian said to her.

"I was racing home to get to my flat and out of danger when I practically tripped over the two of you in the street."

"You live here, ma'am?"

The hooded figure dipped a cloth in the bowl of water and wrung it out before answering him. "I live down that corridor," she said.

Ian watched her as the hood of her cloak fell away to reveal the lovely face of a beautiful middle-aged woman. With great care she dabbed at Carl's wound, and as she lifted her hand, Ian could see a thin bronze cuff hugging her wrist.

It reminded him slightly of the ones General Adrastus wore, and he was surprised to realize that in the four days they'd been in Paris, this was the first time he'd thought of the general since spying him on the train in Boulogne.

He wondered at the coincidence, especially when the woman wrung out the cloth again and Ian saw a second cuff on her other hand. "You see something you like, young man?" she asked, and Ian started. Her voice was slightly deeper than most women's, and there was a hint of a foreign accent there too.

"I'm sorry," he said. "It's just that I've seen cuffs like the ones you're wearing before."

The woman's hands stopped wringing the cloth and she looked sharply at him. "Where?"

Ian was taken aback by her tone, and the question was more a demand than an inquiry.

It was Carl who answered. "Oh," he said, looking at the woman's jewelry. "They're just like the general's."

The kind stranger sucked in her breath, gazing at Carl. "The general?" she repeated. "What do you know of the general, boy?"

Carl must have realized that her attention had become acute and perhaps he shouldn't have mentioned that. "I'm sorry, but I'm feeling very dizzy," he said, leaning his head back against the wall and closing his eyes.

Their savior frowned and laid the cloth gently over Carl's forehead before swiveling to face Ian. She did not say a word, but her expression and arms folded across her chest demanded explanation.

"We met a man last year in Spain named General Adrastus," he told her, feeling nervous under her glare. "He wore two bronze cuffs just like yours. One on each wrist."

To Ian's surprise the woman closed her eyes and sighed with relief. "How did you meet him?" she asked softly.

Ian had a sense that the woman meant the general no harm, and wondered if the cuffs each of them wore meant that they were related. "He saved our lives," he explained. "Carl and I were being chased by someone very bad, and this man helped us. He prevented us from being harmed, in fact."

The woman's eyes snapped open again. "This man who saved you," she said to them, dabbing again at Carl's wound. "Will you describe him for me?"

Carl opened his eyes and gave Ian a warning look, but Ian shrugged. What had they to lose, really? "He was very tall, and appeared quite strong. He had black curly hair and a beard and an accent like yours, but not quite so pronounced."

The woman nodded, and Ian thought she looked sad. "Yes, that is my general," she said.

Carl was staring at the woman, apparently fascinated. "Who are you?" he asked boldly.

"I am his wife," she told him simply. "My name is Adria."

Ian and Carl exchanged looks. "It couldn't be," Carl said, knowing immediately what Ian was thinking.

"Couldn't be what?" asked Adria.

Ian shifted uncomfortably. "I believe we've heard of you," he said.

Adria appeared surprised. "Heard of me?" She laughed, separating the strips of cloth she'd brought along to bandage Carl's head. "However could you have heard of *me*?"

"You were one of Laodamia's attendants, were you not?" Carl asked. "The one who crafted the silver boxes for her prophecies?"

Adria's hands froze. It was a moment before she spoke, and when she did, her tone was sharp, almost accusing. "How do you know of Laodamia and the boxes?"

Ian waved his hand wearily to get her attention. "Allow me to introduce myself," he said. "I'm Ian Wigby, and my sister is named Theo."

Adria stared at him with incredulity and it was another several seconds before she could speak again. "By the gods," she whispered when she'd found her voice. "Is it really you, then?"

Ian nodded.

"How many treasure boxes have you collected?"

"Three so far," he said. "We're working through the prophecy of the third box."

"And the Oracles?" she asked.

"Well," Ian said, "we have Theo, our Seer; Jaaved, our Seeker; and Eva, our Healer."

Adria let out a long relieved breath. "Laodamia would be quite proud," she told him. "You've done well, Ian. She was right to choose you."

"I've a question," Carl said into the silence that followed.

Adria seemed to struggle to tear her eyes away from Ian. "Yes?"

"How is it that you came to know General Adrastus? Wasn't he born something like a thousand years after you?"

Adria's features softened into something of a smile. "As you are by now aware, the portal makes even a thousand years immaterial."

Carl nodded. "So, where is the general?" he asked, squinting down the passage into the dark.

Adria moved closer to Carl and wrapped a long piece of cloth around his head. He flinched a bit but otherwise held still. When she was done, Adria said, "I don't know."

Ian was confused. "You don't know what?"

"Where my husband is," she clarified.

"How long have you two been separated?" Ian asked.

Adria shrugged. "Again, the portal makes time immaterial. I have been searching for him for what feels like many long years, but I cannot be certain."

"You've been going in and out of the portal?" Ian said, his eyes wide with amazement.

"Yes."

"But why aren't you two together, then?" Carl asked. "I mean, how did you become separated in the first place?"

Adria stood and collected her bowl of water and the bits of cloth that remained after Carl's bandaging, and said, "It's a long story. One that I do not yet know I can share with you."

Ian frowned. "Why not?"

"Because there are things in your world that have yet to take place, Ian, which may affect the past. The more you know, the more you could alter both the future and the past. I must consider carefully what to tell you."

"Do you hear that?" Carl asked abruptly.

Ian listened, grateful that the ringing in his ears had finally subsided. "I don't hear anything."

"Which is what he means," Adria said. "The bombs have stopped."

Ian got to his feet and stared up the stairwell. "We've got to go back to Theo," he told her.

"Yes," she agreed. "I'll accompany you, but first let me take this back to my room and gather a few things."

Adria hurried down the dark hallway as Ian helped Carl get to his feet. Carl swayed a bit as he stood. "You all right?" Ian asked him.

"Slightly banged up but otherwise fine," Carl assured him. Ian was hardly convinced, and decided to keep a close watch on his friend.

Adria returned with a small bundle of belongings, and after she took up her lantern and motioned to Ian to bring the other, they made their way to the steps.

As they climbed the stairs, the air became thicker, clogged with dust and smoke, and all three of them were coughing and squinting into the murk when they eventually pushed their way into the open.

Out on the street the air was not quite so thick, but the shock of what they saw made them all gasp anew.

Nothing about their surroundings looked even remotely familiar. Most of the buildings on the street were demolished, and several of those remaining were on fire.

Their building had miraculously been spared a direct hit, but all the windows were blown out, and the face of it was scarred and pockmarked from flying debris.

A piano sat in the middle of the street, almost completely intact, while all around it were strewn bits of furniture, broken glass, and torn fabric. The patch of sidewalk where they stood seemed to be the only area not completely covered with debris. And just down the cluttered way, Ian saw the figure of a man, lying facedown.

Ian's stomach lurched, and reflexively he took a step in the man's direction, but Adria's arm shot out and she said, "Wait! I will go and see to him. You two stay here."

Before he could protest, she was hurrying away. "Do you think he's alive?" Carl asked.

Ian stared at the man with dread in his heart. "No."

A moment later his fears were confirmed. Adria bent down, pulled up on the man's shoulder, then quickly laid him back down. Standing, she looked back at Ian and Carl and shook her head.

Ian tore his eyes away from the figure in the street and stared round again, his heart now hammering hard. All he could think of was Theo and how impossible it would be for her to live through something like this. If the building where they'd been staying had been hit, how would he ever find her amid the rubble? How could she possibly survive?

And then Carl brought up something he hadn't even thought of. "Do you think the earl's all right?"

"I've no idea," Ian admitted, feeling even more distressed now that he'd been reminded of the earl.

Adria joined them again, her face rigid and grim. "I fear that if we stay here, we will be recruited for the rescue efforts," she said. "As much as these people need our help, we must honor your quest and see to your sister's safety."

Ian nodded dully. He hated to turn his back on anyone

nearby who might need his help, but there was far too much at stake for them to be delayed in returning to Theo.

He was just about to take a step away when Carl reached out for his arm and whispered, "Océanne!"

Ian's heart dropped again. Quickly, he dug into his pocket and let out a relieved sigh when his hand touched the familiar disk. Pulling it out, he observed the dial; the shadow across its surface was the only thing marring the otherwise bright face of the bronze relic.

Adria stepped close to them. "The sundial!" she said, staring at it with obvious affection. "What have you asked it to locate?"

"Our friends," Ian said quickly while he tried to sort through whom to go to first. "Madame Lafitte and her daughter, Océanne."

Adria looked at him quizzically. "How did you lose track of them?"

"Monsieur Lafitte was captured in Belgium," Carl said. "He was named as a spy and Theo suspects he's been killed. His wife and daughter have been in hiding here in Paris, and if it weren't for Laodamia's prophecy, we might not be here searching for them at all."

Adria's eyes became large. "The prophecy?"

Ian sighed impatiently. They were standing about, wasting time. "The Oracle told us to cross the sea to save two souls, one of which had the name of open water."

Adria's face shone with understanding. "Océanne," she

said. Then she looked again at the surface of the dial. "It's pointing but a short distance away."

"How can you tell that?" Ian asked her, wondering how she could possibly gauge the distance.

Adria pointed to the surface of the dial. "See how fat the shadow is? The closer the thing you're searching for is, the fatter the shadow becomes."

Carl turned to Ian and asked, "Who do we go to first?"

But Ian couldn't decide. He felt torn in half by the weight of the decision. It was Adria who helped him determine the answer. "What does your heart say, Ian?"

"My heart?"

She nodded. "It will help you determine the answer if you ask it. Who must we get to first?"

Ian closed his eyes and remembered what Theo had told him just a few months before. She'd said that when he found himself with a difficult decision to make, he should simply close his eyes, focus on the question, and feel the answer come to him around his middle. "You'll know with your belly button," she'd said with a giggle. "The right way will feel light and ticklish around your middle."

Using her technique, Ian was surprised by what his middle was telling him. "Océanne," he said firmly, and opened his eyes. "We must find her and Madame Lafitte first."

Adria offered him a small smile. "This way, then," she said, heading in the direction of the pulsing shadow.

They set off in what Ian thought was the general

direction from which they'd come. It was nearly impossible to tell, because the air was thick with dark smoke, obscuring the horizon and making it difficult to decipher which way was which.

Carl and Ian followed close behind Adria.

Along the way, and to distract himself from the terrible sights all around, Ian revealed to Adria that they'd had a close encounter with the two sorceresses Caphiera and Atroposa at the hotel when they'd first arrived in Paris. "There's a woman with them who seems to be able to track the sundial when it's pointing at something," Ian said nervously.

"A woman?" Adria asked.

"They called her a witch," Carl said helpfully. "But I think she might be a seer, like Theo. She can sense when we've employed the sundial."

Adria looked sharply at Ian, as if to ask him why he'd done such a foolish thing in light of the witch's ability.

"It was an accident," Ian said, feeling foolish.

Adria didn't comment; she merely quickened her pace, ignoring the pleas for help, which seemed to come from everywhere. The cries from those in the streets and trapped in the rubble pulled hard at Ian, and judging by Carl's expression, they wore on him too. At one point, Carl asked Adria how she could stand to ignore the suffering all around her. "I have seen far worse," she said simply. "Adrastus and I have traveled through the portal time and time again, and always there is suffering and death. It is what feeds the underworld god, after all."

"Is he responsible for all of this, then?" Carl asked her, waving his hand at the destruction all around.

"You mean the war with the Germans?" she asked. Carl nodded. "No," she told him with a sad smile. "Man is responsible for his own suffering. But there is a far greater cost than just human lives, which is something these men like Adolf Hitler never consider. Demogorgon has been waiting and watching while we humans have spread our seed and now blanket the earth. He has known that eventually, there would be so many people that an evil, power-hungry ruler like this German Führer would start a global war, one in which there was so much death and misery and destruction that Demogorgon's power would reach new heights. If enough misery and death is created, then the god down below may indeed break free from the underworld, and as long as Magus, Caphiera, Atroposa, and Lachestia are here to assist him, there is nothing any of us can do to stop it. Well, except for you and the others, of course."

"But how are we to stop him, exactly?" Ian asked.

Adria looked at him sideways. "Collect the seven Oracles of the United, Ian, and the way will be made clear to you."

"But what if we fail?" Ian pressed. "What if we can't find all seven?"

Adria stopped and looked at him directly. "Then every man, woman, and child on this earth is doomed."

Carl made a face. "Glad to know we're not under any pressure," he muttered.

Adria ignored him and pointed to a large building with only minor damage across the street. "Your dial's shadow points to there, Ian, correct?"

Ian glanced down at the dial, then up again, and a wave of relief washed over him. "They're in there," he said.

Without discussing their quest any further, Ian trudged through the debris-covered street to the front door of the building. He raised his hand to push open the door when a strong force shoved into him and a yelp sounded from behind.

"Quickly!" Adria's hushed voice said into his ear. Ian realized their companion had pushed both him and Carl through the main door and was at that moment moving them as fast as possible down the hallway.

"My neck!" Carl protested, and Adria hissed at him.

"Shhh! Say not another word!"

Ian obediently allowed himself to be propelled through the front foyer and down the first-story hallway all the way to the back. They stopped in front of the door to a flat. Adria let go of Ian and Carl, turned the handle, which opened with ease, and pulled them both into the flat. No sooner had she gained them passage and shut the door behind them than she held out her hand and demanded that Ian give her the sundial.

Reluctant to let it go, Ian hesitated.

"Quickly!" Adria insisted.

Ian gave her the dial and Adria held it in her hands, closing her eyes and whispering to it. A moment later she opened her hands and the dial was blank and tarnished again. Adria sighed in relief. "Tuck that away," she said, handing the relic back to Ian and still speaking softly. "And do not ask it to find *anything*, do you understand?"

"What's going on?" Carl asked impatiently.

Adria turned toward the door and stared out the peep-hole. "There is evil afoot," she told them. "The sorceresses are near."

Ian felt his blood go cold. "How do you know?"

Adria moved away from the door. "I know," she told him. For emphasis she pointed to the back of the flat and crooked her finger as if to suggest they follow her. Ian and Carl did, and she led them through the parlor to the kitchen area. Above the sink was a window overlooking the garden, and out in the yard Ian saw dust and pieces of debris being tossed about—as if a sudden wind had blown in and was causing great chaos. Even the trees were sway-ing to and fro.

If that weren't eerie enough, ice crystals began to form at the edges of the window, and when Ian placed his finger on the pane, he could feel the cold seeping in.

"Where are they?" he whispered, trying hard not to tremble.

Adria was watching the yard intently. "Near," she whis-pered back. "Very near."

She then pointed them back the way they'd come and the three of them huddled in a corner of the flat, waiting with bated breath. At one point Ian distinctly heard the sound of metal heels clicking on the tile floor out in the hallway. He remembered the steel-tipped boots Caphiera had worn when she'd trapped them in the portal tunnel two years previous, and he shivered anew.

Minutes ticked by and Ian and Carl both watched Adria, waiting for her to let go her tense posture and alert them that the sorceresses had gone, but for a very, very long time, Laodamia's attendant held perfectly still.

Ian hoped that if he was correct and Océanne was in the building, she would remain safe inside and not attempt to come out, lest she encounter one of the dreaded sorceresses. He tried not to think about what Caphiera had done to another boy from their orphanage two years previous when he'd had the great misfortune to stare directly into her eyes and been turned to solid ice.

Finally, as the light in the room began to dim, Adria got to her feet and motioned for the two of them to follow.

As they stepped out into the hallway, they saw some wary figures coming up the main stairs. It seemed the building's occupants had been hiding in the basement until it was clear the air raid had passed.

Ian moved ahead of Carl and Adria, anxious to watch the grim-faced Parisians hurry up to their flats. He couldn't say with certainty that he believed they were in the right building for the Lafittes, but his heart pounded with anticipation all the same as one by one the residents shuffled up the steps. And then, as one older gentleman stepped aside, Ian saw her. Océanne. She looked weary and pale and frightened, but still as lovely as Ian had remembered her. Her chin lifted in his direction and her expression changed to one of amazement.

Ian closed the distance to her. "Hello, Océanne," he said shyly, thinking that she had grown even more beautiful in the year since he'd last seen her.

"*Ian Wigby?*" she gasped.

"We've come to rescue you," he said before he realized how silly that must sound. In the next moment he had the most horrific thought about how terrible he must look, covered in soot and grime and dirt from head to toe.

Océanne, however, was still staring at him in disbelief. "Is Carl with you?" she finally asked, and Ian felt his heart sag a bit.

"Hello," Carl said, walking down the hall to join Ian.

Océanne took one look at Carl before flinging herself into his arms, hugging him fiercely. "Carl!" she cried. "Oh, Carl!"

Ian stepped back, his shoulders slumping and the joy of seeing her evaporating. He happened to catch Adria's eye then, and there was such sympathy in the way she looked at him that Ian felt embarrassed and ashamed.

"Océanne?" they all heard from just down the stairs. And then Madame Lafitte crested the landing and gasped. "Good heavens! Whatever are you two doing here?"

Carl was patting Océanne on the back awkwardly. The girl was still clinging to him as if he were a life vest and she were out to sea. "We've come from England, ma'am," he said. "The earl brought us here to search for you. Your husband sent a note begging for our assistance."

Océanne let go of Carl abruptly. "Papa?" she asked. "But where is he?"

Carl and Ian exchanged looks. Clearly Océanne did not know that her father had likely been murdered. "Detained," Ian said after a moment.

Madame Lafitte studied him carefully. "By whom?" she asked pointedly.

"Madame," said Adria, coming to their rescue. "I fear that we have much to explain, but first I must alert you that we are in terrible danger at present and must make haste to leave this building at once."

Both Madame Lafitte's and Océanne's expressions turned fearful. "Will there be another air raid?" Océanne asked timidly.

"Perhaps," said Adria. "But there is even more danger afoot. How quickly can you pack a few belongings and be ready to travel?"

Madame Lafitte looked quite taken aback. "I shall go nowhere without my husband," she said. "Leo insisted we wait here for his return, and with Paris now in ruins, I'll not have him come here to find us gone and assume the very worst!"

"We'll send word," Ian said quickly. "Madame, we've come here with the earl himself. Your husband, Monsieur Lafitte, begged the earl to find you and take you back to England where he knew you'd be safe. He can't get back to Paris at present, you see, and he's terribly worried about your well-being."

Madame Lafitte eyed Ian for several long moments, her hands wringing together nervously. Finally, she seemed to relent. "Very well, Ian. Let us get our things together. We haven't been upstairs since the bombs began. Is it dreadful outside?"

"Yes," Adria told her honestly. "You should bring some sensible clothing and good shoes, Madame. The way back is littered and treacherous."

Océanne's mother took her by the hand and they moved to the staircase. Ian and Carl waited patiently by the front door, but Adria seemed ready to be off. She often anxiously focused her attention on the stairs, as if willing Océanne and her mother to hurry, and Ian wondered how she knew the sorceresses were close.

As if reading his mind, she told him, "If you focus, Ian, you can sense the sisters too."

Ian frowned. *How?* he wondered. His eyes met Carl's and his friend shrugged. Ian stared at the door, then closed his eyes, waiting for something to tell him that the sorceresses were near.

"Feel with your mind," Adria said encouragingly. "Extend your thoughts outward, away from yourself."

Ian's brow furrowed. He had no idea what Adria was going on about. *This is rubbish!* he thought. *Absolute rubbish!* As he was about to give up, however, the strangest feeling came to him. It was as if a part of him extended itself to encounter something thick and heavy in the atmosphere, which also left a bitter taste in his mouth.

He was astonished by the sensation. And as he focused on the disquieting feeling, an image appeared in his mind's eye. Well, not quite an image. Just the impression of a cold and dangerous presence alongside an equally dangerous but slightly more tempestuous one. Without knowing how he knew, Ian could tell that Caphiera and Atroposa were somewhere across the street, hidden and watching the front of the building carefully. Ian was both fascinated and repulsed at the same time.

"What's he doing?"

Ian's eyes snapped open to stare directly into Océanne's, which were bright blue and quite beautiful and were looking at him curiously. "Nothing!" he said quickly. "Shall we be off, then?"

Both Océanne and her mother carried small bundles held tightly to their chests and each wore traveling clothes, with a sweater draped across her shoulders.

"This way," Adria coaxed, and the party moved down the hallway to the rear exit out the door and on their way to find Theo.

A SEARCH FOR THE EARL

The closer Ian and his companions drew to their flat, the more littered and ravaged the streets appeared, and the more crowded. From all corners of the city, sirens could be heard as ambulances carried away the injured, blankets were laid over the dead, and every available Parisian citizen worked to pull the trapped from the rubble or helped firefighters contain the dozens, if not hundreds, of fires.

The air grew thicker with smoke as well, and it was soon difficult to breathe. Madame Lafitte had graciously handed Ian and Carl two of her spare kerchiefs to cover their noses and mouths, and Océanne used her own. Even with the layer of cloth over his nose and mouth, Ian still found it quite hard to breathe.

Only Adria seemed immune to the effects of the smoke. She needed no kerchief or cloth, but covered her mouth simply with her hand.

Finally, Adria turned a corner and Ian saw that the

street was the one that held the building of their flat, although the street was hardly recognizable now. Many of the buildings along the road had been hit directly by bombs, and Ian's stomach squeezed as he searched ahead for any glimpse of Theo or the flat.

"Blimey!" Carl whispered, moving up to walk next to Ian. The destruction in this section of the city was particularly bad.

Behind them they heard Océanne gasp and give a small whimper. Ian looked over his shoulder and found her turning away from a body with a sheet thrown over it lying in the middle of the street. Ahead, there were several more.

Ian's heart began to pound hard. He felt as if he were walking through his own personal nightmare, and the more they walked, the more he found himself on the verge of panic.

Carl saw it first. Ian had been staring at the half-standing buildings, most with large gaping holes in them, others with whole corners demolished, their rubble spilling into the street. He didn't realize until Carl grabbed his arm and halted that the building with the most destruction was theirs.

"*Oh, no!*" Carl whispered.

Ian stared at the pile of rubble, comprehension dawning slowly as he took in the head of the lion that had once stood proudly outside their set of flats. The statue had been blown to bits, save for the head, which had been tossed into the street where Ian's party had all come to stand.

Ian moved the kerchief away from his mouth and stared with horror at the four-story building, which had been reduced to one and a half stories. A hand, lifeless and blue, was sticking out of the rubble.

Ian turned away and his stomach heaved. He'd had nothing to eat since breakfast, so there was nothing much for him to give up, but still his stomach convulsed.

He sank to his knees then, feeling so stunned and lost and dreadful all at the same time that his mind felt ill equipped to process the whole of it.

Distantly, he became aware of Océanne crouching down next to him, speaking words he could barely hear. He felt paralyzed. Perhaps if he held perfectly still, Theo would be all right, and she would come to him and tell him that she hadn't been in the building when it collapsed. That her crystal had warned her in time and she'd fled to safety.

And then Ian raised his eyes to look about him. Everywhere he looked, there was destruction. It seemed no building had been spared . . . save one.

Across the street, the bakery where they'd purchased their breakfast rolls that very morning was nothing but rubble, and the market where they'd purchased their staples had also been blown to smithereens, but the abandoned shop with the green door stood completely unharmed.

As if in a dream, Ian got to his feet, his eyes pinned to that door. He staggered forward, hearing Carl and Océanne call his name, but he ignored them. Intent on his target, never taking his eyes off it, he weaved his way through the crowd.

As he drew closer, his heart hammered so hard he felt it would burst through his chest. And then his hand rested on the door handle and he turned it and was not at all surprised when it opened.

The interior was dark; only a bit of light from the street made its way inside. But someone was huddled there; of that he was certain, because as he'd opened the door, he'd heard a small gasp. "Ian!" shouted a shaky voice from inside. "Oh, Ian!"

A slight weight crashed into him and Theo was hugging him fiercely. "Thank heavens," he whispered, holding on to her for dear life.

The others gathered around but it was a moment before Ian felt able to release her. He fought back his emotion, not wanting to cry in front of Océanne, of all people!

But Theo had no such reservations. She openly wept and hugged first Ian, then Carl, then Océanne and her mother, and even though they had not yet been introduced, she hugged Adria as well. "I've been *so* terribly worried about you!" she finally said to them all.

"We felt the same way about you," Carl told her. "When we saw the flat, we thought the worst."

Theo's eyes pinched as she looked across the way. "It happened so quickly I barely had a chance to escape. One moment I was reading in the parlor, and the next I had the most urgent feeling that I should leave the flat and move downstairs. To be perfectly honest, I had no idea why, but I obeyed my instincts."

"But how did you know to come here?" Ian asked her, marveling that she'd chosen the one building on the street that had sustained no damage.

"I don't really know, Ian," she admitted. "I simply got to the foyer and felt that I must quickly move outside. I wanted to resist the impulse, you know, because of the earl's instructions, but when I looked out the window at the green door, it seemed to call out to me. I felt I couldn't ignore it, so I came here to have a look and just as I arrived, I heard the planes! I don't even think I thought through what to do next. My hand automatically reached for the door handle and it opened."

"It was locked just the other day," Carl remarked.

Theo nodded. "I assumed it would be too, but when I tried the handle, it was unlocked, as if it were inviting me to find shelter here. So I came in and hurried to the back. Just as I got down and covered my head, the first bombs exploded!"

Ian's heart gave a pang when he thought about Theo trapped in this small shop alone, listening to a rain of destruction. She must have been terrified.

He was about to tell her how sorry he was for insisting that she stay behind when he noticed Adria staring at the green door intently. She then ran her hand along some letters carved into the wood, with an expression that Ian could only describe as wonder. Curiously, Ian squinted at the letters and found that they were written in some foreign tongue. "Can you read them?" he asked her.

"Yes," she said.

Carl and Ian exchanged surprised looks. "What do they say?" Ian asked.

"They invoke a powerful magic," she told him. "They mark the entrance to a portal."

Ian gasped. "A portal? You mean a way back to England?"

Adria shrugged. "Possibly," she said. "Or to other lands."

Theo had all but recovered from her terrible fright. "The sorceresses said they were looking for the Keeper by the green door. They must have been talking about this door, Ian!" she said.

Adria appeared quite surprised by that. "Where did you learn this?" she asked.

Ian explained that he'd learned it when they'd had the near miss with the sorceresses at the hotel.

Adria stepped back from the door and moved inside the small shop, lined with empty shelves now covered in dust.

While she inspected the shop, Theo turned to Ian and asked, "Who *is* she?"

"Her name is Adria, Theo. She was Laodamia's attendant and the craftsman of our treasure boxes."

Theo's eyes grew large with wonder, and Ian smiled. He then added, "And she's now married to General Adrastus."

"Pardon me," said Madame Lafitte, and they all turned to her. "But might I ask where the earl is?"

Ian blinked. He'd nearly forgotten about the earl. Turning to Theo, he asked, "Have you seen him?"

Theo shook her head and bit her lip. "I haven't."

Madame turned to the rubble that had been their flat, and her hand flew to her mouth. "Oh, my!" she whispered.

Theo quickly said, "I don't believe the earl went back into the flat before the bombs struck, Madame. I didn't pass him on my way here and had only just arrived when I heard the first planes."

"And he has not come back here to look for you?" Carl asked.

"No. I've been watching, though," she said, pointing to the shop's lone window, which, remarkably, still held its glass intact. "When it grew dark, of course, I could no longer see the individual faces passing by. However, it has only been fully dark for a short while."

Ian stepped out of the shop and onto the street. He stared up and down the way, searching for the earl's face among the few pedestrians, but there was no sign of him. "He'd try to come back here," Carl said. "If he weren't hurt himself, he'd attempt to make his way back to the flat."

A knot of anxiety formed in Ian's stomach. Where could the earl be? "We should look for him," he said to Carl.

Madame Lafitte was now quite concerned. "But where was he at the time of the air raid?" she asked pointedly.

"Looking for you, ma'am," Ian told her. "For the past several days, the earl has been looking for you and Océ-anne."

"But I've not seen Hastings since last year," she insisted. "He's not come round to our flat even once."

"He didn't know where to look," Ian assured her.

"Didn't my husband tell him where we'd be?" she pressed.

Ian thought carefully about what to say to Madame Lafitte. He knew that it was not his place to tell her that her husband had likely been murdered; that was a job for the earl. "I believe," he said, "that the telegram your husband sent to the earl was incomplete, Madame. It left off the number and street where you were staying, and only listed Paris for your location. The earl has been making inquiries through friends and acquaintances here in Paris since we arrived."

Océanne was staring hard at Ian, and he shifted his weight from foot to foot uncomfortably. "Where did you say my father was when he sent the telegram?"

Ian found himself at a loss—he couldn't lie to Océanne. It was Carl who saved him from the uncomfortable moment when he said, "We only heard from the earl that Monsieur Lafitte was detained, Océanne. We have no idea where he is."

Madame Lafitte's hand fluttered nervously around the pearls at her throat, but she forced a smile when Océanne looked up at her. "I'm sure he's quite well," she said to her daughter. "But we must focus on finding the earl at the moment, so that he can tell us more about where your father is."

Theo stepped out into the street. Ian went to stand by her and took her hand, still incredibly relieved to find her both alive and well. "I'm terribly worried about the earl, Ian," she whispered so that the others wouldn't hear.

Ian knew what that likely meant and the destruction all around him added to his own fears. "Can you sense him, Theo?"

Theo nodded and closed her eyes. "I can. I know that

he still lives, but there is also a desperate feeling to his energy. I believe he's in a great deal of pain."

The knot of anxiety in Ian's stomach tightened. "He's injured?"

Theo nodded. "Yes. I'm certain of it. He needs help immediately."

"We've got to go to him," Ian said, pulling the sundial from his pocket.

No sooner had he freed the small relic than a hand tightened about his wrist and a sharp voice said, "No!"

Startled to his toes, Ian looked up to see Adria gripping his arm and staring at him fiercely. "You will draw the sorceresses to you!" she hissed. "And they must *not* discover this place, Ian." For emphasis, Adria's eyes swiveled to the green door.

Ian wrenched his arm from her grasp and glared hard at her. At the moment, the door was the least of his worries. "The earl is injured and needs our help, ma'am. I will use whatever means necessary to locate him as quickly as possible."

Adria eyed the sundial moodily. She seemed on the verge of doing something drastic, so Ian closed his hand around the object and held it tightly to his chest. If she planned on taking it, she'd have to fight him to do it. Ian knew it was their only hope of finding the earl in time to help or even save him.

"We can take it away from here before we ask it to find the earl," Carl suggested, obviously overhearing their conversation. "With any luck, we'll be able to draw the sorceresses far away from this place."

Adria glared at Carl, clearly not at all pleased with his suggestion. "And then Caphiera and Atroposa will hunt you two down."

But Ian was resolute. He would never find the earl in all this wreckage if he didn't use the sundial—of that he was certain—and Theo's conviction that the earl was injured only fueled his determination to find the earl quickly. "We'll be careful," he assured Adria.

Adria turned away from him dismissively, her anger palpable, and she strode into the shop without a backward glance. Ian sighed, suddenly feeling very tired.

Placing his hands on Theo's shoulders, he said, "Carl and I will work our way west before we use the dial. The sorceresses are on the east side of the city, so with any luck, we'll be able to use the dial to find the earl's location before they find us."

Theo looked worried. "I should come along," she said to him. "Perhaps I can use my own abilities to help you locate the earl without the sundial."

But Ian shook his head. "The shop is guarded by a powerful magic, Theo. You'll be safest here with Adria to help guard you, and we'll need someone to look after Océanne and Madame Lafitte."

Theo continued to look worriedly at Ian, but she didn't argue. "Very well," she said with a sigh. "But please, hurry back, would you?"

He smiled and ruffled her hair. "We'll do our best," he assured her.

Ian then motioned to Carl, who took up the lantern Adria had loaned them. "Leave that," Ian told him. "We have your pocket torch." Carl had brought out his torch as the hour grew late on their way back to Theo.

But Carl shook his head. "We can save the batteries if we bring this."

Ian considered that to be a very smart suggestion. "All right," he said, and they waved to Theo, Océanne, and Madame Lafitte before setting off.

Their journey was difficult, as both of them were exhausted and also very hungry. They'd had almost nothing to eat in the past twenty-four hours, and Ian found his grumbling stomach to be quite a distraction. But then they passed an overturned bread cart and he and Carl snatched up several rolls after quickly leaving a few francs for the absent vendor.

Finally, the young men arrived in a neighborhood where only two buildings had been struck and felt it far enough away from the green door to use the sundial. The streets by then were deserted, but here at least the lamplights were lit.

Ian moved underneath one and pulled out the sundial but hesitated. "What're you waiting for?" Carl finally asked as Ian simply stared at the dial's face.

"I'm worried about using it," he admitted.

"We have no choice, mate," Carl told him. "It's got to be done."

Ian inhaled and exhaled slowly. He then eyed the streets up and down and attempted to use his own powers of awareness to sense the sorceresses. He was surprised to discover that he felt them—but very distantly. He looked in the direction from which he thought their energy radiated. It was coming from the same area where the Lafittes' flat was. With some hope, Ian crossed his fingers that they were still there waiting outside the flat, because that was a good distance away from where he and Carl were now standing. He could only hope that the earl was not to be found in the same direction. Ian then had another idea and closed his eyes again, wondering if he might use his own powers of location to find the earl, and thus not need to open the sundial's magic. But when he attempted it, he could feel only a tiny thread of energy, with no distinct location. All his anxiety about the condition of the earl returned, and he made up his mind not to waste another moment on indecision. "Sundial," he said, "please point the way to Hastings Arbuthnot, the Earl of Kent."

In a flash the dull, tarnished surface of the dial vanished and a burnished, shiny surface replaced it. One faint shadow formed at the twelve o'clock position. "He's north of here," Ian said, looking in the direction the dial was pointing.

"Let's be off, then," Carl told him. "We'll have to hurry if we're going to avoid the sorceresses."

Ian and Carl began running down the street, leaping

over fallen debris, frustrated when they were slowed by large piles of bricks that had spilled into the road, blocking their way forward.

On one of their treks over a mound of rubble, Ian sliced his knee open on a shard of glass, but he could hardly stop and tend to it.

After a bit, they reached a section of road that was impassable. The air raid had destroyed two buildings across from each other, which had littered the street with a mountain of debris, completely obscuring the road ahead.

"We'll have to go around," he told Carl, motioning with his finger to the left, down a street that ran perpendicular.

Carl appeared uncertain. "There's a load of debris down there, Ian," he said, coming to stand next to him. The street Ian had suggested was also filled with rubble.

"It'd be harder to climb that," Ian countered, pointing to the huge mound of rubble in front of them. "We have no choice but to try and get around the block as best we can."

That section of the city appeared deserted; no one was about to give them directions for an alternate path and that made the area all the more disquieting.

Tripping all along the way, Ian reached out with his senses to feel the sorceresses and realized they were much closer now. Somehow they'd moved even more swiftly than he'd counted on.

"They're coming," he told Carl as the pair continued to struggle through the rubble.

"You can sense them?"

"Yes. Adria showed me how back at Océanne's flat."

"How far away are they?"

Ian shrugged. "Perhaps a kilometer or two." He had no real idea how he knew their proximity, but when he said that, he felt it was correct.

"We've got to find the earl quickly or turn off the sundial."

Ian stopped abruptly and stared in shock at Carl. "You know I can't, Carl," he said. "I have no way to turn it off other than to find the earl."

Carl had stopped too. "Then what did Adria say to get it to stop pointing to Océanne and her mother?"

Ian shrugged. "I have no idea."

"Blimey!" Carl growled before collecting himself again. "We've got to find the earl immediately!"

Ian and Carl took up their dash through the debris again and rounded the corner. Here the roadway was clear, but again it was deserted. Panting for air, Carl said, "What's the sundial say now?"

Ian took it out of his pocket while Carl held the lantern near it, and he was quite surprised to discover that the earl appeared to be behind them. The dial was now pointing to the six o'clock position. At once, Ian and Carl turned to look over their shoulders at the massively damaged block where the German bombs had caused so much devastation. Not a single building still stood, and some were unrecognizable. Carl gasped. "Ian! Do you think the earl's somewhere in *there*?"

Ian stared at the ruins, dread creeping into his heart. If

the earl had been in one of those buildings, how could he have possibly survived?

Another inspection of the dial, however, indicated that the shadow was still pointing to the rubble. "Come on!" he cried, and dashed down the street.

The friends had made it nearly halfway down when the dial's shadow suddenly shifted to the three o'clock position. Ian paused and looked about. To his left was a building, which had once been a series of flats; he could tell because much of the face of the building had been destroyed, exposing the inside floors like a dollhouse. "My lord!" Ian shouted as he leapt over a broken chair.

Carl hurried to his side and they scrambled up and over the debris to the first floor. "My lord Hastings Arbuthnot! Can you hear us?"

Something sounded nearby and Ian stopped in his tracks to listen. He had no idea if he'd just heard the earl responding to his calls or his imagination was playing tricks on him, so he turned to Carl and asked, "Did you hear that?"

Carl shook his head. "Lord Arbuthnot!" he called. "It's Carl Lawson! Are you here, my lord?"

Again Ian detected a slight noise coming from the same direction, as the sundial's shadow now pointed to the two o'clock position. "This way!" Ian cried, and hurried into the structure. He made his way past broken furniture, crumbling walls, and bits of glass.

The young men entered a hallway within one of the flats and continued down its length to a door leading to the inside corridor. Ian turned the handle and pushed, but the door was jammed against something in the hallway beyond. "Carl!" he said. "Bring your lantern over the dial again!"

Carl brought the lantern close and Ian inspected the surface. It was pointing directly to the area beyond the door, the shadow much thicker now and pulsing. Ian turned to the crack he'd managed to create when he'd attempted to open the door, and called out to the earl again.

This time he clearly heard a voice; weak and shaking, it said, "I'm here, lad."

Ian's heart began to race. "He's on the other side!" he said, pushing at the door with all his might.

Carl joined him and they threw their shoulders against the wood again and again, but the door wouldn't budge.

"We'll have to try one of the other flats!" Carl said, panting and rubbing his shoulder.

Ian nodded, but before he turned away, he put his face to the crack again and said, "My lord, we're just going round to another flat. We'll be along in a moment."

Ian motioned for Carl to hold the lantern up toward the top of the doorframe, and he could see that a beam from the floor above had dropped down and was blocking all the doors into the hallway.

"What if we made our way upstairs to the second story and went down the inside stairwell?" Carl suggested.

Ian felt supremely anxious. He could sense the sorceresses coming ever closer, and he knew that if he didn't find the earl's exact location quickly, the dial would continue to act as a beacon, drawing Caphiera and Atroposa directly to them.

Getting up to the second floor would be tricky and time consuming, and he briefly wondered if there were any other options, but his mind was so filled with worry that he found it hard to think. "Yes, yes!" he said at last. "Let's hurry, Carl!"

The pair dashed back the way they'd come to inspect the face of the building. Carl pointed his torch up the side of the structure, inspecting the broken facade for footholds, and found a section where the rebar was exposed, creating a makeshift ladder of sorts.

Ian hurried over to it. Slinging his arm through the handle on the lantern, he slowly began to climb up and had to twist awkwardly toward the top to grab hold of the floor of the second story, but he made purchase at last and scrambled to his feet. He could see that he'd entered the master bedroom of the owner, and had to push aside the door to the wardrobe, blown clean off its hinges, making room for Carl, who was also scrambling up the rebar.

Carl crested the landing with a grunt, nearly toppling over amid the wreckage, and Ian had to lurch forward to catch his friend, but the momentum carried them both sideways and into the door of the wardrobe. It clanged Carl on the head and he winced, hissing sharply through his teeth.

"You all right?" Ian asked him.

Carl shoved the door aside. "Fine," he said. "Let's find the earl." The pair wasted no more time, making their way through the flat to the door leading to the outside corridor. When they opened it, they both gasped.

The floor of the hallway had a terrible crack leading down the entire length and it sagged in the middle as if the entire building had been squeezed. The resulting pressure had forced the floor to fold in by several inches.

"Do you think it's safe?" Carl whispered, looking skeptically at the floor.

Ian gulped. "No. But what choice do we have? The sorceresses are on their way to us, and we can't turn off the dial's magic until we reach the earl. I don't believe there's any other way to get to him."

Ian eased one foot out of the flat and onto the hallway floor. As gingerly as he could, he slowly put more and more of his weight on that foot, testing the strength of the floor.

It held.

Fortunately, the flat they'd chosen to climb up to was very close to the inside stairwell—just two doors down, in fact.

Inch by inch Ian moved along the side, holding his breath for most of the way. Behind him, Carl pointed his torch in Ian's direction to add light to the shadows the lantern created. Ian was most grateful that Carl had remembered to bring that torch.

Finally, he made the landing for the stairwell and turned back to face Carl. "Throw me your torch!" he called.

Carl tossed it to him and Ian pointed it for Carl while his friend made his way—much more quickly—across the sloping floor.

When he reached Ian, they both breathed a sigh of relief and hurried down the stairs.

"My lord!" Ian called. "Are you here?"

"Ian!" a faint voice cried. "I'm in here!"

Ian quickened his pace, scrambling through the debris cluttered hallway, tripping in his haste to get to the earl. Carl barely prevented Ian from crashing to the floor and somehow they both managed to find their way to the earl.

When Carl's beam focused on their patriarch, it was all Ian could do not to cry out at the sight. The earl was in a terrible state, pinned to the floor by a large section of wall, which covered his legs and much of his torso, leaving the earl barely able to gasp for air.

The poor man's face was pale and bloody. His nose looked broken, one eye was swollen, and his lips were blue. He also seemed to be in no small amount of pain. Ian didn't hesitate to move to one side of the wall while motioning to Carl to grab the other side. "We've got to lift this off him!"

Carl gripped his side securely and gave a nod to Ian. The pair heaved with all their might and the wall moved, but just barely. "Carl!" Ian said, his voice strained. "I'll hold it up while you pull the earl free!"

Carl hesitated. "I've got it!" Ian assured him, feeling his knees start to wobble and his arms shake. *Hurry!*

Carl let go of his end and Ian groaned anew with the effort to keep the wall up high enough for Carl to ease the earl out.

He watched with gritted teeth while Carl bent low and took the earl by the shoulders, but as he was pulling him out, the earl gave a sudden shout of pain, and Carl stopped.

"Pull me free, Carl! Just do it!" gasped the earl.

Carl lifted the earl again, his face set with determination, and he heaved backward. The earl cried out again and Ian lost his grip. The wall crashed down with a thud as Ian fell backward, knocking his head against a brick.

Ian lay there for a moment, trying to collect his thoughts, and was soon squinting in the dim light, seeing Carl hovering over the earl.

"He's free," Carl said. "But he's blacked out."

Ian got unsteadily to his feet. Leaning against the wall for support, he went over to see for himself. With tremendous relief he saw the color had returned to the earl's lips and face now that he was able to take full breaths. "We must get him to hospital immediately!"

"How, Ian?" Carl said desperately.

Ian looked up and down the hallway, searching for an idea. Nothing came to mind, so he made a decision, which he didn't like, but it was the only obvious choice left to them. "I'll have to bring back help," he said. "Will you wait here with the earl?"

Carl didn't look at all happy with that idea, but he finally shrugged. "I suppose it's the only way," he said. "Yes, I'll wait here. But see if you can find us some water, Ian. If the earl wakes up, I'll need to try and get him to drink something."

Ian nodded. "Wait here with the earl. I'll be right back."

Ian left the lantern with Carl, taking the torch and

making his way back down the hallway. Squeezing in through one of the flats right next to where they'd found the earl, Ian took two steps and stopped dead in his tracks. In an instant he was so shocked and so frightened that he stopped breathing.

Lowering the beam of the torch a fraction, he saw it glint off the metal object at his feet, and it was a very long moment before he found the courage to inhale.

He stepped slowly and carefully away, mindful not to disturb anything in the room as he left.

Once he was back in the hallway again, he paused to catch his breath and heard Carl say, "Did you find the water?"

Ian swallowed the large lump in his throat and looked toward his friend. Carl's face was illuminated by the lantern, and for a moment or two Ian debated whether to tell him what he'd found.

"Ian?" Carl said. "What's the matter, mate?"

In reply, Ian held his finger to his lips and said, "Shhh!"

Carl's brow furrowed. "What is it?" he whispered loudly.

Ian moved slowly and steadily back down the hall to Carl and the earl. He noticed that Carl had managed to find a torn but otherwise intact cushion to place under the earl's head, and he also saw that the earl's eyes were open and staring up at him.

Crouching down beside the pair, Ian leaned in and said, "There's an unexploded bomb in the flat next door."

Even in the dim light, Carl's face went starkly pale. He made a sound much like a sharp squeak, then clamped his hand over his mouth as if the noise might set off an explosion.

The earl's breath wheezed in and out, but even in his dreadful condition, he still managed to lift his hand to grip Ian's arm and gasp, "Get . . . out!"

Ian nodded. He fully intended to get as far away from that ruined building as possible. "We'll have to make a stretcher," he told Carl. "I can't leave you here with the earl while that bomb's next door."

Carl's eyes were wide and staring hard at Ian, but eventually he took his hand away from his mouth and whispered, "Right."

The earl still had hold of Ian's arm, however, and he inhaled a shaky breath and said, "No! You . . . Carl . . . out now! Leave . . . me!"

Ian looked kindly down at the earl. "I'm terribly sorry, my lord, but in this instance, I shall have to ignore that order." With that, he gently pried the earl's fingers from his arm and motioned to Carl. "Leave the lantern so the earl has some light," he instructed.

Before turning away, he looked again at the earl. "We'll be back, my lord. I promise."

A DARING ESCAPE

Ian and Carl tiptoed down the corridor. Ian had his sights set on the wooden planks they'd had to clear out of the way in the stairwell, but Carl had a better idea. "There was that door to the wardrobe in the upstairs flat, Ian," he whispered when Ian began to hand him the planks. "The one that hit me on the head. I believe it's strong enough and wide enough to support the earl, and light enough for the two of us to carry him between us."

Ian eyed the rest of the stairs up. He hated to go up to that rickety floor again, but they had little choice. The planks in front of them weren't wide enough and were far too long. "Very well," he said, but put his hand on Carl's chest when his friend attempted to move up the stairs. "I'll go," Ian told him.

"You'll need help," Carl insisted stubbornly.

Ian shook his head vehemently. "That floor's too unstable. If something happens to me up there, then you'll

187

need to get help for the earl. We can't risk the both of us being injured and unable to save him."

Carl glared at him. "Then I should be the one to go up," he insisted. "You're the Guardian, remember? The Guardian who must protect the One? The prophecy says that you can't die, Ian, or we'll lose Theo and we'll all be doomed."

Ian felt torn by Carl's words. He knew that going back upstairs was terribly dangerous; how could he let his friend face it instead of him? But Carl was right. There was an extra prophecy they were aware of that had suggested that if he, the Guardian, died, then the One—Theo—would quickly follow. He knew that he needed to stay alive to protect her from the dreaded four sorcerers.

In the end, Ian decided that he would risk it. Carl was always stepping in to volunteer for the more dangerous missions, and Ian knew that someday his luck would run out. "No, mate," he said, placing a hand on Carl's shoulder. "I'll go."

Not wanting to argue any longer, Ian hurried up the stairs with barely a backward glance.

Sweat dripped from his temples and inched its ticklish way down his back while he crept along. Finally, he made it to the flat and tiptoed through the hallway to the place where he and Carl had clambered up the side. He picked up the wardrobe door, which was surprisingly light, and turned to make his way back to Carl when a sound from below stopped him.

He thought he heard voices in the distance, and a wave of relief flooded through him. He could ask them for help!

Ian squinted into the dark street, attempting to gauge where the voices were coming from. After a moment, he determined that the people speaking were on the other side of a large pile of rubble, just out of sight. He set down the wardrobe door and the torch and cupped his hands around his mouth, ready to shout out to the strangers, when he felt a cold prickle on his skin.

Lowering his hands, he looked down at his bare forearm, lined with goose pimples. And then a voice, sharp and clear, reached his ears. "Which way, witch?"

"Somewhere over there, mistress!"

"Are you certain?" asked another voice, this one like a low moan.

"Yes, yes! The magical instrument is quiet again, but I know it came from somewhere down that street."

Ian clicked off the light of the torch and felt his mouth go dry. Very carefully and quietly, he took up the wardrobe door again and ducked down the hallway and into the main corridor.

Tucking the torch into his pocket, he held the door in front of him and, on his tiptoes, eased along the side of the wall, moving far faster than he had earlier, and in the dark, no less. He heard the floor groan and felt it vibrate but he dared not stop or even slow down.

"I was about to go looking for you," his friend said when he reached him.

Ian was panting and soaked with sweat. "We've got to hurry!" he whispered. "The sorceresses are here!"

Carl's eyes grew large, but he didn't say a word.

Ian decided not to tell the earl about the approaching danger, and focused on getting him out of the hallway as quickly as he could. "My lord," he whispered, "Carl and I will need to move you onto the stretcher, and we must do it quickly. We'll go carefully, but as there is a bomb in the room next door, if you could try to be very quiet, that might be best."

The earl nodded. "I understand, Ian."

Ian moved the door of the wardrobe alongside the earl, and together with Carl, he managed to slide the door under the man without a terrible amount of fuss.

Once the earl was safely in the middle of their make-shift stretcher, Ian asked, "You all right, my lord?"

The earl's face was a mask of agony. He was gritting his teeth, and beads of sweat had formed on his forehead. After a moment, he was able to nod. "Yes," he whispered, although his face had grown paler still and his breathing sounded a bit thick and liquid. Ian locked eyes with Carl. They had to get the earl out and to someone who could help him immediately.

"I'll take the front," Carl said, moving to the head of the door.

Ian placed the lantern at the earl's side and asked him if he felt able to hold on to it. "Yes," the earl said, moving his feeble fingers to hold the lantern still.

To have said that it was a difficult task, moving the earl through a dark hallway littered with debris while thoughts of a nearby bomb pulled at their psyches and the two sorceresses closed in, would have been to understate their pre-dicament immensely. Once they'd made it to the stairwell, Ian motioned to Carl to set the makeshift stretcher down and they took a very brief rest. Ian pulled Carl to the side, and the pair thought through their options. "How are we going to get him out of here?" Carl asked.

Ian's eyes roved to the main entrance, which was com-pletely blocked by debris. There was no sense taking him out the front anyway; Caphiera and Atroposa were out there. He looked next to his left and studied the doors of all the flats. He knew he'd never get them open because of the sloping ceiling. Finally, with few options left to them, Ian pointed up.

Bending down, he said to the earl, "My lord, I'm terri-bly sorry, but we will have to move you up the stairs."

"Can't get the front entrance open?" the earl asked, his eyes moving to the door, which was so close by.

Ian looked at Carl. He was hesitant to share the addi-tional danger they were in, and he thought the earl was already in terrible distress, but Carl nodded, as if confirm-ing that Ian should tell the earl the whole of it. "The sor-ceresses are outside," he said. "We need to move up the stairs and find a place to hide."

The earl's eyes widened. "The sundial?"

"I had to use it to locate you, my lord. I believe that was enough for the sisters to find us."

Carl glanced worriedly at the door. "Ian!" he whispered urgently. "We've got to move!"

Ian went to the earl's head and bent down to lift the cot. Just as he and Carl had hoisted the earl, there came a great cackle from outside. "I know you're here!" said Caphiera in a voice that chilled him to the bone. "We've sensed your whereabouts, Guardian! There is no escaping our keen eyes. Come out and we might spare your life!"

Ian froze, daring not even to breathe, but a push from Carl at the other end of the stretcher pulled him from his terrified thoughts and he began to shuffle backward up the stairs.

"Guardian!" moaned Atroposa. "Come out, come out, wherever you are!"

"Quickly!" Carl urged as Ian struggled to keep their makeshift stretcher as steady as possible while climbing the stairs backward.

After a few more steps, they reached the second-floor landing. Ian was panting very hard, and his arms were aching with strain. He took one look at the floor, however, and motioned up to the next story. Carl, who was also breathing hard, nodded and they continued on silently.

After reaching the third story, Ian was immensely relived to find the floor, for the most part, flat and even. It appeared able to withstand their combined weight. "Let's set him down for a moment and see if we can't find a place to hide," he said.

Lowering the earl as carefully as they could, Ian and Carl ran down the hallway, trying all the doors as they went along. One door was slightly ajar and Ian almost cried out in triumph. But as he swung the door open, he nearly fell straight through a huge hole in the floor, which allowed him to look a full two stories below. A small bit of mortar set free by his feet fell all the way down, clinking onto something made of metal. Ian held his breath and closed his eyes, waiting for the explosion he was certain would come.

Carl gripped him by the shoulder, and Ian could feel the tension in his friend's hand. But after a few seconds' pause, Ian realized that the bomb wasn't going to explode, and he stepped carefully away from the door.

Swallowing hard, he motioned for Carl to try the remaining doors. All of them were locked tight. They had made it to the other end of the building with no small amount of frustration when Ian tapped Carl's shoulder and pointed to a window just opposite them.

The entire pane of glass had shattered to the floor, leaving the window wide open. Through it, Ian could see another building, close to the one they were in, of identical shape and size.

Peering out, Ian gauged that the distance between the two buildings was perhaps six to seven feet, which was close, but not quite close enough.

There was no way out of the building they were in—Ian was certain of that—but perhaps there was a way out of the building next door?

"Guardian!" Caphiera screeched. "I know you are here!"

With no small amount of horror, Ian and Carl heard her near the front of the first-story entrance. "We'll have to try and get across!" Carl said.

Ian squinted down into the alleyway below. It looked very far away. "How?" he asked simply.

Carl's eyes lit with an idea. "The planks of wood in the stairwell!" he said. "They'll be long enough!"

Ian looked to the stretcher where the earl lay. The task seemed impossible, and they were running out of time. Below, Ian could already hear the sorceresses pushing on the door they had abandoned in their flight up the stairs.

And Carl didn't seem to want to wait for Ian to make up his mind. Dashing down the hallway, he ran for the stairwell. Ian had no choice but to follow him and hope they found enough sturdy planks to hold both their weight and the earl's.

Racing quickly and quietly down the stairs, Ian found Carl on the landing with the planks, scrambling to carry as many as possible. Most of them were quite long, and Ian helped him get them angled up into the stairwell.

Behind them there was a sudden crash, and dust and debris blew into the first floor, coating the area inside the stairwell.

Ian tried his best to keep moving up, but the stairwell was very dark, and they had only Carl's torchlight to work with.

"Guardian!"

The noise buffeted into the building, bouncing off the walls and echoing to every corner. Ian tensed, certain that the noise would be enough to set off the explosive, but he didn't slow down as he and Carl flew up the stairs.

Reaching the third floor, the boys stretched the planks out between them and raced down the corridor. They paused only to insert the wood onto the sill of the window and slide the planks across. Ian laid two on top of each other, giving them as much strength in the middle as possible, and Carl motioned to him, once they were in place, to retrieve the earl.

The boys sprinted back down the corridor, but no sooner had they lifted the earl than they heard the clank of metal on the stone of the floor somewhere below. "They are nearby, mistresses!" a third voice shrieked. "I can hear someone afoot and I sense that they are somewhere upstairs!"

"Quickly!" Carl whispered.

Ian needed no added encouragement. "You first, mate!"

Carl's face suggested he wanted to argue. Whoever went last would be the most at risk of being caught by the sorceresses, so Ian grabbed Carl by the collar and roughly shoved him to the window. "No arguments!" he hissed. "Now get across and pull the earl from your end!"

Carl handed Ian the torch and climbed up on the sill. He then moved over the top of the wardrobe door, making sure to step carefully around the earl until he had a firm purchase on the bare planks. Carl lowered himself to his hands and knees, crawling forward with haste. Ian made sure the earl's stretcher and the planks were well anchored on his end and he watched with a pounding heart as Carl inched his way to safety.

"Ian!" gasped the earl.

"Yes?" Ian replied impatiently. He didn't want anything to distract him from making sure Carl made it across.

"Leave me."

"No."

"Listen to me, young man," the earl said, attempting to sound stern. "You've no time! Follow behind Carl and get to safety. The sorceresses might not bother with me if you're away. And perhaps I can even slow them down."

And just like that, Ian had a brilliant idea.

Well, either brilliant or completely mad. The outcome would determine its merit, he decided.

The moment Carl reached the opposite windowsill, Ian pushed the earl forward to the middle of the planks, straining with the effort. "Don't move!" he whispered harshly when he saw the earl stir. Ian managed to get the earl to the three-quarter mark, far enough for Carl to reach the other end and pull him the rest of the way, then Ian pushed himself onto the windowsill and reached out to grab the lantern off the wardrobe. In its place he dropped the torch, and called, "Carl! Get him through the window as quickly as you can! I'll be back, but don't wait for me!"

Ian didn't explain further; he turned and bolted back down the corridor, stopping in front of the partially opened door to the flat with the gaping hole in the floor. "Aha!" cackled an evil voice. "I *knew* we'd discover you!"

Ian forced himself to stare down at the sorceress's silver boots. He knew better than to look her in the eye.

"Sister!" Caphiera called. "Our Guardian is attempting to flee into one of the flats on the third floor."

A cool wind floated up the stairwell to Ian, but he held his position even as every fiber in his body insisted he run away as fast as he could.

Someone else stepped up beside Caphiera, but it wasn't Atroposa. "I have done well, mistress?" asked the newcomer.

"Yes, witch," said Caphiera. "Now fetch the lad and bring him here, won't you?"

The figure next to Caphiera began to move down the hallway toward Ian. This was quite troubling, as he'd hoped that Caphiera or her sister or even both of them would attempt to capture him, but he supposed there was nothing for it; he was too deep into the thick of it to back out now.

"Where is he?" moaned Atroposa from the stairwell.

"Here, Sister," Caphiera said smugly. "Come see."

Ian waited, watching the hemline of a raggedy-looking skirt swish down the hallway. He dared not look up to see who was coming to fetch him, because he couldn't be certain the woman didn't have powers of her own.

But the witch seemed to catch something in his face, because she halted abruptly when she was only ten feet away. "The young man is up to something," she remarked.

"Bah!" Caphiera said. "Bring him here, witch!"

"No," the ugly woman said stubbornly. "Mistress, he means a trick of some kind."

Caphiera's impatience was palpable, and the air around Ian became noticeably colder. "Sister!" she barked. "Send a gust of wind to knock the boy over, won't you?"

Ian knew the waiting was at an end, and without another moment's hesitation he dropped the lantern into the hole, then whirled around and bolted back toward the window. An incredibly powerful gust·of wind came whipping down the hallway, blowing him off his feet and sending him hurtling down several more meters.

"*Ian!*" Carl shouted as Ian lay on the ground, his head pounding and his thoughts in utter disarray.

"There!" said Caphiera behind him. "You see, witch? The boy has been subdued. Fetch him for us."

Ian tried to get to his feet, but he failed on his first attempt. Behind him the witch was approaching quickly, but abruptly she stopped again. "He has started a fire," she said, looking uneasily at the open door where Ian had dropped the lantern.

"'Tis of no consequence!" Caphiera yelled. "We will be far away before it becomes an issue!"

But Ian knew better. Using every bit of energy he had, he pulled himself up to the sill and attempted to focus on Carl's urgent expression. "Leap for it, mate!" Carl cried, and Ian realized that all the planks had been knocked to the ground below.

"He means to jump from the window!" Caphiera cried, and an instant later a sharp dagger of ice burrowed into the wood right next to his hand. "Stay where you are or the next one will be buried in your back!"

Ian froze halfway in and halfway out of the window. Carl was frantically waving at him to make the leap as the witch's footfalls came again, this time more quickly.

Ian waited until she was almost upon him before he leaned forward and leapt out the window, reaching out frantically for the other sill. As he leapt, an explosion filled the night with a tremendous *BOOM*, and before Ian could fully register what was happening, he slammed into the opposite building and would have fallen to his death were it not for Carl, reaching out to clutch his shoulders.

Hearing a torrent of noises, Ian suspected that the second-floor corridor had given way and caused the third story to fall down too.

Carl didn't even pause to observe the disintegrating building; he pulled Ian the rest of the way in, and the pair lay on the ground, panting and spent.

But soon the air was too choked with smoke and dust for them to remain there, and they both staggered to their feet, taking up their positions around the earl's stretcher. As Ian bent low to take up his end, he realized his leg was bleeding badly. He knew he'd have to ignore it for now; the earl was in far worse shape.

With some difficulty Ian and Carl made it down the stairs of the flat next door, and Ian found that this building had an exit to the opposite side of the block as well. Motioning to Carl with his head, he indicated the left-side exit, and with a great deal of effort and straining muscles, the young men carried the Earl of Kent out of the ruins and into the relative safety of the darkened streets.

There, they both collapsed, and Ian knew he didn't possess the strength to carry the earl one more step.

To his immense relief, as he lay panting and exhausted, he saw several Parisians running toward him, one leading a horse drawn cart. When the small crowd gathered round to help them, Ian knew he and Carl had done all they could to see the earl to safety.

ENCOUNTER AT THE GREEN DOOR

The earl spent the next few days in a makeshift hospital. He suffered from three broken ribs, a concussion, and a broken arm but otherwise appeared to be in remarkably good shape, given his ordeal.

Ian's leg had also been tended to—it had required a dozen stitches—and other than a few additional scrapes, cuts, and bruises, both he and Carl were in excellent condition.

As for Caphiera, Atroposa, and the witch, Carl was quite certain they had perished in the explosion, but Ian held some doubt. He was convinced that he could still sense their evilness somewhere within the city.

At present, however, the question of the sorceresses' survival was the least of their worries. They had taken refuge in the shop with the green door but had yet to hear from, or locate, Jaaved and Argos. Ian and Carl continued to make their way to the fountains each day and the two young men debated using the sundial.

On the third day of their vigil at the fountains, Theo and Adria brought them a bite to eat. "Is there any sign of them?" Theo asked.

"No," said Carl, taking an apple and half a loaf of French bread from her. "I'd like Ian to use the dial, but he's worried the sorceresses will come looking again."

"Do you really believe they survived the blast?" Theo asked Ian.

Ian opened his mouth to tell her he couldn't be sure but he thought so, when Adria cut in and said, "They've survived much worse, Theo. It's quite likely they came through."

Ian frowned. He wanted to leave the city the moment the earl was well enough to travel, but if Jaaved and Argos did not arrive, then what would they do? The city was filled with rumors that the Germans were quickly approaching Paris and France was as good as defeated.

All seemed bleak, in fact, and Ian stared down at his own apple, suddenly not hungry. And that was when he heard his name being called. Snapping his head in the direction of the voice, he blinked in the bright light of the day, only to see Jaaved dashing across the square toward him, waving his arms and looking quite happy.

"Jaaved!" Theo shouted, running off to greet the Moroccan boy.

Ian and Carl exchanged happy looks, but then Carl's brow furrowed. "Where's Argos?"

Ian searched the crowded streets where Jaaved had appeared and was now making his way toward him with Theo.

Then, just as he was becoming anxious, he saw the soldier from the portal. "There!" he said, pointing with an excited laugh, relieved down to his toes that both of them had made it.

But in the next instant, Ian's arm was gripped tightly. "By the gods!" Adria said, looking as if she were seeing a ghost. "Iyoclease!" she gasped. Then, more loudly, *"Iyoclease!"*

Ian's jaw dropped. He and Carl exchanged looks again and together they said, "Iyoclease?"

But Adria was in motion, running at the soldier with her arms outstretched. The man they'd known as Argos turned to the voice calling out to him, and a look of shock came over him when he caught sight of her. It was quickly transformed into the brightest of smiles as he opened his arms wide to catch her and swing her up in a fierce embrace.

"How did you get here?" they both asked at the same time, and Iyoclease explained first. "Calais and I went hunting for two deserters. I thought I heard a noise coming from a cave and went in to investigate, I found a set of stairs and they led me to a wood I did not recognize. At the wood's edge, I found Ian, and Carl Lawson."

Iyoclease gestured to them and Ian could hardly believe that the real Iyoclease of Delphi was standing before him.

Adria was scrutinizing the soldier. "Yes," she said. "I remember now. Laodamia was quite lost without you."

Iyoclease eyed her as if she'd said something incomprehensible, and then he studied her intently. "Adria," he said. "You seem to have gained some years . . . how is this possible?"

"The portal," Adria told him. "The same as you, my friend, although I have been traveling through it for quite some time and I have aged accordingly."

"I believe you have much to tell me," Iyoclease said.

"But why did you say your name was Argos?" Carl said, looking more than a little put off at having been lied to.

Adria looked at her friend curiously. "You gave them the name of your father?"

Iyoclease nodded. "I am sorry about that, Carl. I was worried at first when you said that a sorcerer was trying to kill you both. I feared that if Magus or his sisters discovered who I really was, it might put you all in even greater danger."

Adria put a hand to her mouth, as if the idea horrified her. After a moment, she said, "You were wise, my friend. Of course they would know who you are, and what you mean to the quest. As long as you're here, our mission is vulnerable, which is why I cannot fathom why the portal opened to you in the first place."

"He's part of the third prophecy," Theo told her. "Near the beginning, in fact, his appearance is foretold."

Ian took out his worn copy of the prophecy and showed it to her, pointing to the lines, which clearly indicated Iyoclease's arrival. Adria nodded but her expression remained troubled and she addressed the warrior again. "I feel it best that you not linger in this time, my friend. The consequences of your discovery by the sorceresses would be far too great to risk. We must see to getting you back as soon as possible. There is a portal door not far from here."

"But we're not done with the prophecy yet," Carl protested. "There's still more sections to work through."

"No," said Theo, with that faraway look in her eyes. "I believe Adria may be right. Perhaps that's the reason we were to bring him along to France, Carl. So that he could assist us as far as this, then return home."

"I feel I've done nothing of significance," Iyoclease told her.

"Oh, I think you've done a splendid job seeing that the boat made it safely to the harbor, and you brought Jaaved back to us. That isn't insignificant at all," Theo assured him.

Adria was surveying the crowd around them, her forehead creased with worry. "We should leave this open area," she said to them, turning away and taking Iyoclease's hand while motioning to the others to leave the square.

When they were safely back at the small camp in the shop with the green door, Ian found a note from Madame Lafitte and Océanne. They had gone to visit the earl and would be back soon. It was a fortunate circumstance, because it allowed Adria to speak freely and without a great deal of added explanation.

"You came through the portal," Adria told Iyoclease when they were seated in a circle.

"Yes," Iyoclease said. "That much I have gathered."

"I too ventured past the wall," she explained. "But it was much later, nearly half a year after your de—" Adria caught herself and her hand moved to cover her mouth. Iyoclease was looking sharply at her.

"My what?" he pressed, but even Ian knew what she'd nearly revealed.

"Nothing," Adria told him. "Just know that it was later. I came at the request of Mia, who sent me on a quest to hide her most treasured prophecies. She commissioned me to create several silver boxes, and recruited a general from Lixus to hide them for the Oracles to discover."

"Lixus?" Iyoclease asked her. "What is this place?"

Adria smiled. "A city far from Greece," she told him gently.

"Who is this general?"

"His name is Adrastus," she said. "He is my husband."

Iyoclease's eyes widened. "Your *husband*? But what of Calais?"

Adria looked down at her hands, folded in her lap. "I married Adrastus after . . . ," she said, leaving her sentence unfinished.

Iyoclease got to his feet and began to pace the small room. Ian could tell he was struggling with all that Adria was telling him, and he knew the soldier was a very intelligent man. He'd picked up on the subtext, Ian was certain. "You must tell me how to go back," Iyoclease said.

"You must go back through the portal," Adria told him. Her gaze ventured to the far wall meaningfully and Iyoclease stopped his pacing and considered the stone. "How does it open?"

Adria held up her hands to show him her cuffs. "If the portal had already been opened by my husband, I could use these to send you back. But this is a dormant wall and I cannot open it."

Ian and Carl leaned forward and looked with interest at Adria's cuffs. She smiled and held them up again so they could see them better. Ian again noted that they were identical to the ones worn by Adrastus except that Adria's pair were much thinner. "They are from the same cuffs my husband wears," she told them. "It's through the cuffs that Adrastus controls the portals. When I initially went through the portal with him to hide the first box, we didn't get on so well. I was afraid he would leave me behind, so to ensure that I could follow after him, I took a thin layer from the top of the cuffs while he was sleeping. He woke to find them secure to my wrists and I thought for certain he would be angry with me, but he merely laughed and told me he would have done the same if our roles had been reversed."

"How is it that the cuffs control the portal?" Theo asked.

"No one knows," Adria told her. "But Adrastus and I believe it has something to do with the markings on them. Only Adrastus's cuffs will open a portal door and his also allow him to choose the time and place he wishes to select. It took us years and years to discover that. My cuffs will also open the door to any portal entrance I find, but only if my husband has already traveled through it."

Ian knew Adria might attempt to dodge his next question, but he wanted to know, so he said, "But how and why did you two become separated?"

Adria looked again at her hands, still folded in her lap.

"It is because of this portal," she told him bluntly. "This doorway is the last one we've needed to find, and we knew, after discovering all the others, that we could not discover it together."

"But why?" asked Theo.

Adria sighed. "When my mistress Laodamia charged us with our quest, she told my husband and me that one of us would betray the other and place the Oracles in terrible danger. She said this would occur at the time we discovered the final portal, marked by a green door. She warned me that if she was correct and it was Adrastus who betrayed the cause, then the course of his actions would cause my own death. She added that I must not allow the final box to fall into the wrong hands; the prophecy within must be protected at all costs."

Ian was confused. Adrastus had spent many years hiding the boxes and protecting their locations, not to mention that he'd also saved Ian's life in Spain; why would he suddenly betray all his efforts and freely give the last of the boxes over to the enemy?

He asked Adria as much. "I cannot fathom it," she told him. "My husband is the greatest man I have ever known, pure of heart and intention, and to think that he would betray me and the cause is incomprehensible to me. That is why we are separated. Adrastus has always feared this final prediction. So one night several years ago, just after we'd hidden the second-to-last box and we both knew there was only one portal left to discover, he left me."

Beside Ian, Theo gasped. "He left you? But why?"

Tears formed in Adria's eyes but she blinked them away. "He wrote me a note telling me that in order to ensure Laodamia's words did not happen as predicted, we must separate. He would go on to hide the final box alone and I must stay away."

"But you haven't stayed away," Carl pointed out.

Adria shook her head sadly. "No, Carl. I have not. I swore an oath to Laodamia that I would watch over the boxes and ensure the general did not betray us, and I will not stop looking for him until I have finished my quest."

But Ian had another concern. "Mistress Adria, you say that you've hidden all the boxes save for one, but we've only managed to locate three so far. Have we failed already?"

The woman smiled kindly at him. "No, Ian. You have not. And although Adrastus carries with him the last box to be hidden, it is not the last in the sequence to be discovered. We hid them out of order, you see. So it is the last box for us, but likely the fourth or the fifth one for you."

Ian was shocked by that revelation. "You mean you don't know what order we're supposed to find them?"

"No," said Adria. "I only know the order we were to hide them, and only because when Laodamia gave me the scrolls with her prophecies, she left explicit instructions for which scroll was to be placed in which box and in what sequence they would need to be hidden. The box we hid before this one was located in a cave close to your keep."

"That was the first box we found!" said Theo.

Adria nodded. "Yes, child. I gathered as much."

"So where are the other boxes?" asked Carl.

"I cannot tell you that."

"Why not?" he pressed.

"Because part of your destiny lies in the discovery of each box on your own. To tell you where the boxes are hidden would likely jeopardize your quest, and I'll not have that."

Ian noticed that Theo was toying with her crystal necklace. "So we should wait here for Adrastus to come and attempt to use the portal to hide the last box?"

Adria eyed Iyoclease, who was listening very carefully to their discussion. "Yes and no," she said. "Iyoclease *must* be sent back to his own time in Greece. His appearance here and my own memory of him tell me that he must have slipped through the portal to the present time. It also means that we'll find a way to send him back."

The flood of relief clearly showed on Iyoclease's face. "Thank you, Adria," he said to her.

But her expression was somewhat melancholy. "We will wait here for my husband and he will open the portal to let you return. We will then hide the final box."

"But what about us?" Jaaved asked.

"You must also return to your home. The portal near your keep will eventually open and lead you to the next box and all will be in sequence once again."

"We can't leave without the earl," Ian told her, just as a flurry of noise erupted outside. A shout made its way into their shelter.

"We've surrendered!" came the anguished cry. "The Germans have conquered France!"

Ian felt a well of remorse knock the breath right out of him. "Oh, no!" whispered Theo.

Adria turned to Ian, her expression sober. "You and your party must flee Paris before the Germans arrive."

"But the earl!" he protested.

"Leave it to me," she said, and hurried out the door.

Adria arrived back with the earl leaning heavily on her. Océanne and Madame Lafitte were arguing with her that the earl should have been left where he was at the hospital.

Upon seeing their patriarch, Ian and Carl rushed forward to take the grave-looking man from her and ease him over to a mattress they had wrestled from the wreckage of their flat.

Their patriarch's complexion was gray and he seemed much thinner than he'd been only a few days earlier. He lay back on the mattress with a sigh, and Theo brought forward a blanket to cover him.

Behind him, Adria said, "Enough!" in a voice that brokered no argument. Madame Lafitte and Océanne fell silent at once, but the tension in the shop remained. "The first place the Germans will go will be the hospitals," Adria said into the silence that followed. "They'll be looking for wounded soldiers and rounding them up. They will also be making a record of everyone there, and I hardly think the Earl of Kent would escape their notice."

Madame Lafitte hurried over to the earl's side and tucked the blanket around him. "Even so," she said. "He should not be moved for several more days!"

Adria eyed the earl and then all of them one by one. Ian agreed with Madame Lafitte. It was clear that the earl was still too weak and too injured to attempt to leave Paris. "We'll stay here until he's better," he told Adria. "We'll hide until he's well enough to travel and then we'll sneak out of Paris."

With a long sigh Adria nodded. "Very well, Ian," she said. "We'll wait until he's better."

It didn't take long for the Germans to arrive. Ian and Carl saw them first, when they went to collect some food for the group. The Germans paraded through the capital of France as if they'd always owned it, and the sight was enough to crush Ian's spirit.

Once the Germans began patrolling the streets, Adria hardly allowed them out of doors, reasoning that it was only a matter of time before the Germans began looking for subverts and people whom they felt were a threat to their cause.

"Your travel documents were lost during the air raid," she said to Ian, Carl, and Theo, "which will not make them suspect you initially, but they will want you to replace your identification papers with the French government immediately. As you have no former proof of your identity within the official record books here in France, you will all be identified as potential spies and turned over to the German authorities at once."

Ian felt their situation was quite desperate and without much hope—especially for the earl. If the Germans discovered that he was the Earl of Kent, well, Ian couldn't imagine what the Nazis would do to his beloved patriarch.

All around the city, large red flags with black crooked crosses were hung. Rumors abounded that Adolf Hitler himself would be making an appearance, and Ian shivered at the thought of having the hated Führer so close by.

Each time he and Carl went out for food and supplies, Ian could see the intense anxiety on the local civilian faces. Everywhere he looked he found the haunted eyes and anxious posture of Parisians who were terrified of the Germans crawling all over their homeland.

He had heard the rumors of German brutality in the other cities they had conquered, and he shivered at the thought of it continuing here.

Two days after the Nazis paraded down the Champs-Élysées, Ian and Carl came back to the shop after an early-morning food run to find the earl lying on his mattress and Madame Lafitte busy fussing over him, attempting to get the earl to drink some soup. "Hastings," she said with a laugh, "it does not taste like day-old smelly stockings!"

"I beg your pardon, my lady, but it smells exactly like them," replied the earl with a grin.

When the earl saw them in the doorway, he quickly cleared his throat and sat up with a grunt. "Hello," he said. "What news have you to share?"

"The streets are overrun with Germans," Ian said. "They're everywhere, my lord."

Behind him the door opened and Adria stepped through too. "The city is surrounded," she announced.

Madame Lafitte lost all hint of merriment and turned starkly pale. "Oh, my," she whispered. "How will Leopold ever get back to us?"

The earl had not yet shared the news that her husband had been captured by the Germans in Belgium, and he'd strictly forbidden Ian, Carl, Theo, and Jaaved from saying anything about it. "We must find a way out of the city," he said gravely.

"I know of a way out," Adria said confidently. "There are tunnels that run under Paris. Ancient tunnels which have dozens of unseen exit points, well away from the major roadways where the Germans are likely to look for anyone attempting to escape notice."

"Are you well enough to travel?" Theo asked the earl. Ian could see that his color had returned, and although he was still in some amount of pain and a bit weaker than before, his condition had greatly improved in just a few short days.

"Almost ready, Theo," he assured her. "I'll be quite well enough in a day or two. As long as Madame Lafitte doesn't force this awful concoction on me."

Madame Lafitte's smile returned a bit. "Oh, Hastings. You exasperating man!"

"When should we leave?" Carl asked, looking to Adria again.

Adria eyed the earl carefully, as if assessing his condition. "As soon as the earl is ready to travel," she said. "I will lead your group through the tunnels at midnight and leave you at the edge of the city. If you travel by night and stay away from the main roads, you should be able to reach Le Havre. If your boat is swift and you leave the harbor under the cover of darkness, you will likely escape detection."

At that moment Iyoclease and Jaaved came into the shop. Ian realized belatedly that they had not been there when he and the others had returned.

"We've been scouting the city," Jaaved told them. "The German guard is everywhere, and they're putting up posters announcing a nightly curfew and requiring all French citizens to report to the German registration stations to have their identification papers recorded. Anyone caught without proper identification after Friday will be brought before a tribunal and imprisoned."

"It is as I suspected," Adria told them. "We must get you out of the city tomorrow."

POTION POISONED WITH
DARK INK

The next morning, as Ian and Carl were returning from the market with enough food and supplies to see them to Le Havre, Theo came dashing over to them. "Thank heavens you're back!" she said, waiting only as long as it took for Ian to set his sack of food down to throw her arms around him.

Ian smiled and ruffled her hair. "It's a bit tricky with so many Germans about, but we managed, Theo."

When he looked at the other faces in the room, however, he knew immediately that all was not well. "What's happened?" he asked to no one in particular.

"The earl has come down with a fever," Madame Lafitte said.

"I'm fine," the earl said, his voice weak and strained. And then he began to cough and his whole face flushed red. He clutched at his ribs and Ian knew he must be in terrible pain.

They all waited for the spasm to pass, and when it did,

the earl was left spent and wheezing. "He needs medicine," Adria said. "There is an apothecary not far from here. I will go."

But Ian stepped in front of her, knowing he should be the one to take the risk. "Let me," he said. "Tell me where it is and what to get and I'll go." Adria eyed him with surprise, so Ian explained, "We can't risk anything happening to you, Mistress Adria. You're the only one who can lead the others out of the city. If something happened to you, we'd not last the day."

"We can't lose you either, Ian," Carl said, stepping up to volunteer. "I'll go."

Ian knew it was just like his friend to step into the face of danger and take the risk from everyone else.

"All right," Adria said. Moving over to her satchel, she retrieved a scrap of paper and scribbled both a map and the address of the apothecary along with the name of the medicine to get. "Pierre will know exactly what to give you," she said. "And give him a few of these for his trouble."

Adria dropped three small gold coins into Carl's hand and he stared at them in wonder. "Gaw," he said. "All that for the medicine?"

Adria smiled at him. "No, young man, all that to seal his lips about who came to visit and what they were asking for."

Carl tucked the coins into his pocket and moved to the door. When he went outside, however, Theo looked urgently at Ian and whispered, "Go with him!"

Ian was puzzled. "You think he won't find it?"

Theo's fingers went to her crystal. "He'll need you," was all she said.

Ian knew enough about Theo's gift not to question it, so he put his cap back on and hurried out the door. "Carl! Wait for me!"

The friends traveled stealthily through the city, using alleyways and side streets as much as possible. They reached the apothecary without incident and waited for two patrons to leave before going inside. "Are you Pierre?" Carl asked the weathered-looking man behind the counter.

"Yes," he said. "Who are you?"

"We're friends of Adria," Carl told him, fishing the paper from his pocket. "Mistress Adria said you'd know what this is?" For emphasis he pointed to the word scribbled across the top of the paper.

Pierre's eyebrows rose. "Someone have a fever and a cough?"

"Yes, monsieur," Carl said.

"This is an expensive request," Pierre observed, looking shrewdly at Carl as if wondering if the young man could afford it. Carl took out his three gold coins and displayed them to Pierre. "Mistress Adria said she is more than happy to pay for your cooperation."

Ian had to hand it to his friend. The meaning in Carl's choice of words was clear and Pierre nodded and quickly got to the task of preparing the medicine. Once he was finished, he folded the fine powder into a paper envelope and handed it to Carl in exchange for the gold. "You will need to make a tea of this," he said. "Use three teaspoons every four hours until the fever breaks and the cough subsides."

"Thank you," Carl said, tucking the envelope under his cap.

He and Ian then left the shop and traveled along the same path they had taken coming. Along the way they encountered no difficulty, and Ian began to wonder why Theo had insisted he go along. Carl seemed quite capable of returning with the earl's medicine, but no sooner had he finished that thought than the young men rounded a corner and walked right into a pair of German soldiers.

"Bah!" yelled one of the men. "Stupid boys!" Then he paused and spoke in halting words as he probably thought through the French translation. "Why don't you watch where you're going?"

Ian and Carl both backed up quickly. "We're terribly sorry," Ian said in a rush, raising his hands to show they'd meant no harm.

"Where are you off to?" demanded the other soldier.

"We're returning to our orphanage," Carl told him. "Our headmistress sent us on an errand and we were just returning."

"What errand?" asked the second soldier, an evil glint in his eye.

Ian gulped. He could sense that they were in terrible danger, but if they could simply keep their wits about them, he and Carl might be able to talk their way out of it. "We're retrieving some medicine," he said in a rush. "One of the orphans has come down with fever and a cough, and our headmistress is worried it will spread to the other children. In fact," Ian added, forcing a slight cough, "I do believe I myself might be coming down with it."

Carl caught on quickly and raised his own hand to his forehead. "My brow feels awfully warm," he said. "Might not want to get too close to us, sirs. We could be contagious."

The first soldier narrowed his eyes at them as if he was on to their ruse. "Show us this medicine," he demanded.

Ian looked at Carl. He knew that if they showed the soldiers the medicine, they risked having it confiscated. Thinking quickly, he pulled Laodamia's small vial of black liquid out of his pocket and wiggled it for the soldiers. If they took the poison and left them alone, then he'd be quite glad for it.

To his surprise, however, the second soldier crossed his arms and said, "Drink it."

Ian stared at him. "Excuse me?"

"Drink the vial," the soldier ordered, drawing his gun and pointing it at Ian so there could be no misunderstanding.

"But it's for the other orphan!" Carl protested. "If he drinks it, there'll be none left for the poor girl who is quite ill."

The soldier pulled back the hammer on the gun, his eyes never leaving Ian's. "You will have to get more, then," he said. "After you are made well by taking your medicine."

Ian's mind raced with the possible outcomes. Laodamia had predicted that if he drank the potion, he would die. If he didn't drink the vial, the German soldier would certainly shoot him. It seemed he would die either way.

As he worked the stopper from the vial, he could only hope that death by poison was at least fast and relatively painless.

He was about to raise the vial to his lips when Carl reached over and snatched it away from him. "My fever is higher than yours!" he said angrily. "I should drink the medicine first!"

Ian stared at him in shock and tried to grab back the vial. "Carl!" he shouted. "Don't!"

But it was too late. In one very fast move, Carl raised the vial and sucked down the liquid. Once he'd finished, he shook his head and said, "Blach! That was awful!"

Ian could see the inky black residue on Carl's tongue and he waited for signs of the poison to appear. He didn't have long to wait. As the soldiers began to laugh cruelly at what they'd forced Carl to do, Ian's best friend swayed on his feet.

Ian reached over just as the one soldier holstered his gun, slapping his companion on the back. The two walked away still laughing. "Carl!" Ian whispered urgently, reaching out to catch him when his knees buckled and he crashed into Ian.

"Are they gone?" Carl mumbled, his face growing paler by the second.

"*Why?*" Ian asked him desperately. "Oh, Carl! Why did you drink it?"

Carl's head lolled back on his neck and his cap fell off.

"Had to be done, Ian," he said. "'Ian Wigby must not drink, potion poisoned with dark ink.'"

Ian bit his lip and felt an awful terror sweeping through him. He well knew the prophecy too. "'Force the choice upon another, he will save his loyal brother.'"

Carl nodded dully. "Right," he said. "You're my brother, mate. Through and through." And those were the very last words he spoke before his lips turned blue and he stopped breathing altogether.

Ian held Carl and searched the street with wide pan-icked eyes, looking for anyone who might help him. No one was on the quiet street so near to the block that had been all but completely destroyed. The shop was merely two blocks away, so Ian grabbed Carl's cap with the earl's medi-cine, tucked it into his coat pocket, and with the speed and strength reserved for desperate moments, lifted Carl's limp and lifeless body onto his shoulders and began to run.

He was heavily weighed down, but his feet still pounded quickly over the pavement. Rounding the corner to the block where the green door was, he cried out desperately for help and a moment later saw Adria dash out of the shop and hasten down to meet him. "What's happened?" she asked, helping Ian ease Carl off his shoulders.

Theo came hurrying up to them as well, along with Océanne, Iyoclease, and Madame Lafitte.

Ian could barely speak, he was so overcome with grief, panic, and exertion. "The . . . vial!" he said. "He drank the vial!"

Theo sank to her knees and clasped both hands to her chest. "The one from Laodamia's treasure box?"

Ian nodded, staring forlornly at Carl, willing him to take a breath. "A German soldier ordered me to drink it, and I was going to, but Carl grabbed the vial and drank it instead!"

Océanne began to cry. "Carl!" she wailed, clutching at his hand before turning to Adria. "Can you help him?"

Ian looked at the Phoenician woman too. Perhaps she would know what had been in the vial and could suggest an antidote? He already knew where the apothecary was, and he was quite certain he could run very, very fast there and back.

But Adria was gazing at Carl with a bit of an odd look. "There is nothing to do for him," she said simply.

Ian was so choked with emotion that his next words were hoarse. "Please!" he cried. "You can't let him die!"

Adria's head lifted and she eyed the streets around them. "Come," she said. "We must move him into the shop, away from prying eyes."

Ian swallowed hard and allowed Iyoclease to lift his friend and carry him into the shop. He laid Carl down on one of the mattresses. Carl still had not taken a single breath, and Ian laid his head on Carl's chest, hoping for a miracle and the sound of Carl's heartbeat.

To his immense surprise he heard one lone *bah-bump* and felt a tiny rise to Carl's rib cage. He sat back and stared. "There's still some life in him!"

Adria came forward with a ladle of water. "Drink," she ordered.

Ian almost rudely pushed it away. He didn't care about his own thirst when his friend was lying so perilously close to death. But Adria's expression was firm, so Ian reluctantly took the ladle. As he was sipping it, he saw another tiny lift to Carl's chest.

Theo must have seen it too, because she placed her hand over Carl's rib cage and said, "He's not lost."

"No," Adria agreed. "But right now he is somewhere very far away." She then did something curious. She moved outside and came back with a set of iron numbers, which had marked one of the addresses on the now ruined street. After placing these near Carl's head, she sat back and watched the iron numbers for several moments without comment.

"Pardon me," Ian said with a hint of irritation in his voice, "but might I ask what those are for?"

Her reply was cryptic. "You'll see soon enough."

Just then they heard a voice from the corner of the room ask, "What's happened to Carl?" Ian turned to see the earl looking weak and sickly but staring with focused attention at them all.

"He has taken the Metal Master potion," said Adria.

"Metal Master potion?" Ian repeated.

Adria nodded. "It is the rarest substance on earth," she told him, "the very last vial of which was placed in the treasure box personally by me three millennia ago."

"What is it?" Theo asked. "Is it truly poisonous?"

"If swallowed, it is nearly always fatal," Adria assured her, and Ian's heart sank. "Only one in ten thousand souls are strong enough to withstand the effects," she added. "But if you are of the right nature, and have the strength to endure it, when you wake up, you will be able to make metal out of its raw materials and craft it into anything you can imagine."

Ian stared at her in utter confusion. "I don't understand."

Adria stood again and stepped over to the door to retrieve a small plank of wood with several exposed nails sticking through the other side. She held the wood out for them to see, then held her palm underneath the pointed ends of the nails. One by one they slid through the wood, dropping delicately into her hand. She then folded her fingers around the nails, and when she opened her palm again, they had been mashed together into a ball.

Casting aside the plank, Adria began to mold the clump of metal like wet clay, her artisan fingers skillfully manipulating the iron into the figure of a horse. When she was done, she handed this to Océanne, who was still overcome by Carl's condition. "Here, young lady," she said gently. "This will give you hope."

Océanne took the figurine cautiously and gasped when her fingers touched it. "It's solid metal!" she said.

Theo reached out and stroked the figurine. "It's warm but no longer malleable," she said. "How is that possible?"

"The silver boxes," Ian whispered. "You were more than just a craftsman. You took the potion yourself, didn't you?"

"Yes, Ian," she confirmed. "When I was a little older than Carl, I was given it by the woman who preceded Laodamia as the great Oracle of Phoenicia. She told me then they had waited hundreds of years for someone like me, and ordered me to drink a vial of the liquid.

"I lived in a state of unconsciousness for two days, but when I awoke, I had skills and abilities that defied all logic."

"Ian," Theo said to him. "Remember what the prophecy said? 'See the next one of your crew, one of noble heart proved true.'"

Ian's eyes fell to Carl again. No one had ever had a truer heart than Carl; of that he was certain. "He looks barely alive," he said to Adria. He was still terribly worried that Carl would not survive the poisonous effects of the potion. "How will he last two days in this state?"

"He will," Adria assured him. "Laodamia has foretold it and thus it will be so."

"What can we do for him while we wait?" Madame Lafitte asked.

"Keep him warm and quiet," Adria told her. "And watch for signs that he is working through the potion."

"What signs?" Theo asked.

Adria nodded to Carl. "Watch the air around him."

Ian did, and as he watched, he would have sworn that the atmosphere near Carl's body shimmered slightly. Adria then pointed to the numbers on the floor next to Carl's head. "Touch them," she said to Theo.

Theo moved to the numbers and lifted one into her hand. "It's warm!" she exclaimed.

But Ian wondered if perhaps the numbers had been in the sun before Adria had brought them inside. He didn't feel he could be so hopeful just yet.

The earl looked as if he was about to speak, but he began coughing instead. Ian remembered the medicine and pulled out Carl's cap and the envelope from the apothecary. "For the earl," he said, handing it to Adria.

She nodded and got to work preparing the earl's tea while Ian sat right next to Carl, laying the cap near his head and waiting for his friend to return to them.

ESCAPE

Océanne stayed right by Carl's side for most of the next two days. Ian thought he should hardly regret such devotion, given that his friend had saved his life by drinking the vial.

Still, those familiar pangs of jealousy found their way to his heart, and he struggled mightily when he saw how Océanne held firmly to Carl's hand and whispered, "Please, Carl! Please come back to me!"

Ian wanted Carl back as well, but he also wanted Océanne's affections.

He was able to distract himself by focusing on the metal numbers, which seemed to melt and change shape before his very eyes. Crude figures would replace blobs of metal, and as the forty-eight hours progressed, even those crude figures took on clearer shapes.

At one point Theo held up what had formerly been two number twos and exclaimed, "He's made a heart!"

Océanne clasped Carl's hand and wept with relief as

Ian attempted to swallow the large lump caught in his throat.

On the morning of the second day of their vigil, Carl's breathing had almost returned to normal. He was now taking one full breath for every three of Ian's. Adria had told them that his breathing would gradually become more regular and that, the gods willing, he would wake up very soon, and she assured them that his dexterity with metal would begin to accelerate. To demonstrate that, she placed two of the blobs of metal in his hands, and sure enough, his fingers began to work at them like those of a dreaming sculptor. Before long, his friend had crafted what looked like a duck or a swan, and then a dog . . . or perhaps a turtle. Their moods brightened as they all debated which.

The earl seemed to be in much better health as well, and was being administered to very diligently by the kindly Madame Lafitte.

Their plans to escape the city had been delayed to the following evening, when, Adria declared, both the earl and Carl would be well enough for the journey. Until then, Theo was keeping a watchful eye on the door and seemed nervous and fidgety. "What is it?" Ian asked her after watching her hold her breath when two pedestrians walked past the window of their shop.

Theo sighed. "I fear there is danger all around us," she said.

Ian thought that was rather obvious. "It is, Theo," he said. "There are enemy soldiers everywhere in this blasted city."

Theo didn't look at him but simply stared out the small window as if waiting for someone to approach and threaten them.

Ian felt bad for having been so curt with her. "We'll be off by tomorrow night," he assured her. "And with all the destroyed buildings, there isn't much traffic down this street. No reason for those soldiers to become suspicious of us yet."

Theo nodded, but her eyes betrayed her fear.

The next day Carl began to climb slowly out of his slumber, which was a welcome relief to everyone. While they were busy packing their supplies, preparing for the journey at midnight, Carl's eyelids began to flutter and his body gave small twitches, but most encouragingly of all, his breathing had returned to its normal rhythm.

"Look!" said Océanne when Carl moved his hand to his head.

"Eva?" he asked groggily. "Is that you?"

Océanne let go a tiny gasp, her face stricken.

Ian felt terribly sorry for her; she'd had no idea that Carl was sweet on someone else. "It's *Océanne*," he said quickly, going to kneel beside them.

But Carl still appeared to have trouble coming fully awake. "My lovely Eva," he sighed. "I made you a heart out of clay. . . ."

Océanne backed away from Carl as if he were a leper. "He's delusional," Ian said quickly, attempting to catch her hand.

But she pulled it back from him and glared accusingly. "*Who* is Eva?" she demanded.

Ian looked to Theo, and he was thankful that she came over to sit next to Océanne and explain what Carl should have told her long before then. "Carl cares for you very much," Theo said gently. "But not long ago, his heart was swayed by a very special girl in our orphanage. Her name is Eva, and, Océanne, I promise that when you meet her, you'll like her."

Tears welled in Océanne's eyes and she turned away from them to go sit in the corner by her mother.

Madame Lafitte had heard all of their conversation, of course, and Ian felt acutely ashamed by her look of disapproval. "One of you should have told her," she said quietly.

Ian stared down at the ground. "I'm terribly sorry, Madame."

Carl took that most inopportune moment to cry out, "Eva? Where are you?"

Ian wanted to thump him but Theo hurried to take his hand in hers. "There, there, Carl. Lie still."

Within the next few hours, they all heard the clock on a nearby church chime twelve times. Adria rose to her feet and motioned for the rest of them to follow but held up her hand to Iyoclease. "Stay here and guard the door, my friend," she told him. "I will be back before dawn."

Reluctantly, Iyoclease sat back down.

By this time Carl was sitting up and looking round at

them dizzily. Ian wound Carl's arm across his shoulders and said, "Come on, mate, time to move."

Carl, who was normally quite thin, felt relatively skeletal under Ian's arm. They'd attempted to get a small bit of cheese into him, but all he'd been able to do was sip some water.

"He'll eat later," Adria assured them.

At least Ian felt he could manage alone with Carl, which was a good thing, because Océanne would not step forward to help with him, and Theo and Madame Lafitte were busy carrying the bulk of their food while Adria and Jaaved were assisting the earl.

"Follow me and stay close," Adria said once she had inspected the street beyond their door. "You will need to step quickly," she added. Ian wondered if she fully understood how difficult it was moving quickly with a semiconscious person in tow.

Adria led them on a circuitous route through the streets and back alleys. Twice they barely escaped attention from German soldiers, but finally, after what felt like an interminable time, Adria led them to the end of a narrow alley and put her hand up for them to halt. When they were all clustered close to her, she motioned to a manhole cover in the center of a well-lit square and said, "There is the entrance to the tunnel."

"But there're guards posted just across the way!" Theo whispered.

Ian, who'd been struggling under the weight of his friend, bent and lowered Carl to a sitting position with his back against the wall. While catching his breath, he squinted into the dark and could clearly see three German soldiers, yawning and looking blearily out at the square.

"We'll need a distraction," Adria said before looking pointedly at Ian.

He nodded, still breathing hard. "Yes, I'll do it. Let me catch my breath first and I'll get them to chase me."

Theo placed a hand on his arm, looking worried. "Please be careful," she whispered.

Ian squeezed her arm. "I'll be all right," he said reassuringly.

Adria turned to him. "It's now or never, Ian Wigby."

Ian swallowed hard and gave Theo's hand one last gentle squeeze before pulling out of her grasp. "Watch after Carl," he told them all, then walked right out into the center of the square.

The soldiers did not react as he'd expected. At first they were so engrossed in their conversation they didn't seem to notice him. Ian stepped farther into the light of the square and cleared his throat. Immediately, they all stopped talking and turned to stare at him. "You there!" yelled one, raising his rifle at Ian. "What are you doing out past the curfew?"

Ian gulped and put up his hands in surrender. He hadn't counted on their aiming their rifles at him and he wondered, if he turned and fled, would the Germans really shoot him?

But he hardly had time to think about what to do next, because out of the shadows behind the soldiers rose a large figure draped in a cloak. Before the soldiers had even a moment to react, the newcomer brought his hands down in quick succession on the backs of their necks and they all dropped like stones.

The stranger then stepped over the soldiers and began to approach Ian, who still had his arms raised high in the air. "Lower your hands, Ian," said the man, pulling back his hood.

Ian opened his mouth to say the name of the approaching figure, but even before he could utter it, he heard Adria cry out, "Adrastus!"

The general of Lixus halted abruptly, his face a mixture of emotions. "Adria," he said softly when she too entered the light of the square. "I have missed you."

Adria's face had transformed. Her rather stern countenance had softened as she stared at her husband. "Don't go," she said to him when he began to turn away.

"You know I must."

"I've found the green door," she told him quickly. "And more importantly, I have found Iyoclease here, in this time. He is waiting inside the shop that marks the green door."

The general's eyes widened. "The Oracle's Iyoclease?" he asked. His wife nodded, and Adrastus appeared to consider this new twist. "He cannot remain in our time," he said.

"Yes, I know," she told him. "He will need you to send him back before you complete your quest."

The general looked from his wife to Ian and then over

to the rest of their group, waiting in the shadows. "What are they doing here?" he said.

"Completing part of the third prophecy," she told him. "I was just about to lead them to the outskirts of the city so they could escape the Germans. They have a boat waiting in La Havre to take them back to England."

"Tell me where the door is and I will send Iyoclease on; then I will hide the box and come back to you."

"Iyoclease will not know you," she told him. "I must come to make the introductions."

The general's lips pressed together to form a thin line. Ian didn't think he liked that idea very much. "I could show him," Ian said. He felt everyone's eyes shift to him, but Adria appeared angered by his suggestion. Ian gulped. "I know the way to the shop," he explained. "I could take the general there, introduce him to Iyoclease, and be back here before the clock strikes one."

Adria began to shake her head, but Adrastus readily agreed. "A good solution," he said, moving to the soldiers and pulling them over to a large tree. He then got out some rope from his satchel and wound it around them.

Meanwhile, Adria stepped to the manhole cover and waved her hand over the metal. It began to sag in the middle, and the edges bent up. Adria motioned to Ian, and the pair reached under the lid and slid it up onto the pavement. Ian was quite surprised when his fingers made indentations in the metal rim.

From the shadows the earl and Madame Lafitte

appeared, followed by Océanne and Theo with Carl walking between them. Carl looked better and better with each passing minute, and when Ian asked how he was feeling, his friend replied, "Almost back to normal."

Adrastus went over to their group and helped the injured earl down the ladder to the bottom of the tunnel, which was only about three meters from the surface of the street. Madame Lafitte and Océanne followed, then Theo, and then Carl, who managed the climb down all on his own.

When they were all safely at the entrance to the tunnel, Adria called up, "Show my husband to the door, Ian, then hurry back. We *must* be to the city's edge before dawn."

"Got it," Ian assured her, moving out of the way so that Adrastus could slide the manhole cover back into place except for a small gap.

"You should be able to move it aside far enough to let yourself down when you return, Ian," the general explained.

"Yes, sir."

The pair then raced out of the square, with Ian leading the way through the darkened streets. He had to slow his pace after a bit due to a stitch in his side, and the general didn't press him to hurry; he merely matched Ian's stride.

"General," Ian said when a thought occurred to him.

"Yes, Ian?"

"I wonder, if you gave me the box now instead of opening the portal to hide it somewhere else, might that alter

Laodamia's prophecy of the danger to you and your wife near the green door?"

Adrastus was silent for a moment, and Ian suspected he was thinking that through. With a tired sigh he said, "I cannot, Ian. I've sworn to follow the Oracle's directions to the letter. If I didn't open the portal, your way to the next of the United might be lost. No, it must proceed as planned, I'm afraid."

"I understand," Ian told him, although he wasn't happy about the answer.

They arrived at the shop and Ian could smell something cooking inside. He stepped to the door just as it opened. Iyoclease stood inside, eyeing the large man on his doorstep warily until he saw Ian. "What are you doing back here?" Iyoclease asked him.

"I've brought General Adrastus of Lixus," Ian told him proudly.

Iyoclease's brow lifted. "Are you the man that will help me get home?"

Adrastus smiled. "I am indeed," he said just as his stomach grumbled, and he peered past the soldier to the small stove across the shop, where a soup of potatoes and turnips simmered. "Before I send you home, however, might I have a bit of that soup? I haven't eaten since noon."

Ian left the general and the soldier to share some bread and soup and got under way back to the square and his friends. He would miss Iyoclease very much and found that now that he was alone with his thoughts, he had genuinely liked the soldier.

Ian also knew what fate awaited Laodamia's betrothed. He paused in the middle of the street and looked back. Should he warn the Phoenician?

Professor Nutley had told him what the records said: that Iyoclease would be killed in an ambush by the Oracle's enemies. Perhaps if Ian warned him about the ambush, Iyoclease would take more care and surround himself with more of his soldiers to protect him.

Several seconds passed while he thought about going back to say as much, but he hesitated, realizing the consequences of that action.

How would saving Iyoclease's life alter the future? Would Laodamia survive the attempt on her own life too? The professor had also mentioned that without Iyoclease to protect her, the great Oracle herself had been murdered not long after Iyoclease. Ian turned and stared down the street, his heart heavy with indecision. If he warned Iyoclease and saved his life, and then that of Laodamia, what would happen to the course of events unfolding now? Would it alter things for the better, or worse?

While he stood there, trying to figure it all out, he heard voices approaching. Startled by the noise, he darted into the shadows. He hoped that whoever was out walking about at this late hour didn't call the attention of more German guards.

He waited and watched while the clomp of footsteps echoed loudly on the cobblestones. "We don't even know if we can trust the baker!" said the approaching stranger.

"How do we know his shop was next to one with a green door, kept vacant for years?"

Ian sucked in a breath. He knew that voice.

"What would you have me do, Sister—resurrect the witch from the rubble of that building and have her tell us whether or not the man was lying?"

"If you hadn't made the witch attempt to retrieve the Guardian, she'd still be alive and able to tell us if this was the correct way to the door."

"Bah! So what if the witch is dead? The boy undoubtedly died in the explosion too, so she was worth the sacrifice."

"Still," moaned Atroposa, "we did not discover his body in the wreckage. We cannot rule out that he survived."

"Which is why we're still attempting to find the green door," Caphiera snapped. "Find the door, find the Keeper. Kill him, kill the quest."

Ian squished himself deeper into the shadows, ducking next to a smelly can of rubbish. The two sorceresses were nearly upon him now.

"How much farther?" asked Atroposa.

"According to this map, it's only a few streets."

Ian held his breath as the pair passed by his hiding place. He then counted to ten and quietly moved back into the street again. He could see them in the darkness, passing under a streetlamp, and to his relief they turned left when they should have gone right. Without another moment's hesitation he raced back to the shop, running as fast as he could until he reached the green door. Pounding on it until it opened, he cried out, "The sorceresses! They're coming!"

Adrastus stood in the doorway, holding a piece of bread, while Iyoclease moved into the space right behind the general. "Where are they now?" he asked.

"Right behind me!"

The general stepped out of the doorway, pushing Ian back. "Get back to the tunnels!" he ordered. "Flee this city tonight and do not tell my wife about the sorceresses' approach, do you hear me?"

"Y-y-y-yes, sir," Ian stammered. He was taken aback by the anger in Adrastus's voice and demeanor, but he didn't argue. Instead, he turned and hurried into the shadows again. Behind him he heard Adrastus say to Iyoclease, "It's time to send you home, my friend."

But before he could take another step, he also heard, "Well, well, well, what do we have here?"

Ian flattened himself against the side of the wall, hoping the darkness would conceal him.

"The Secret Keeper!" howled Atroposa.

"And another prize," said her sister. Ian risked looking back, and he could see that both Adrastus and Iyoclease had come out to face the two sorceresses. Iyoclease drew his short sword and Adrastus moved to raise his arms across his chest but Atroposa was quicker. She shot a blast of air at him that sent the general hurtling backward into the green door, smashing it right off its hinges.

Iyoclease raised his sword and ran toward Caphiera, but

with a flick of her wrist, he was stopped by a wall of ice. "Surrender your boxes, Keeper!"

Adrastus moaned on the ground where he lay; Ian suspected the wind had been knocked right out of both him and Iyoclease.

Ian knew their fates were lost unless he could do something to help them. He cast about for some type of weapon, anything he could use to defend himself, before stepping out into the open. He had to help, no matter what the consequences.

Finally, he spied a piece of metal pipe, but it was out a ways into the street. He turned his attention back to the sisters, trying to gauge his odds, when a hand came down hard on his shoulder, causing him to jump.

"Wait!" Carl whispered, holding fast to Ian's shoulder.

Ian was too stunned by Carl's sudden appearance to reply, and what was more, there was something odd about his friend—or rather, the air around him. It seemed to ripple with energy all about Carl's body.

Carl ducked low, darting out, and retrieved the pipe. "I had so many dreams about metal," he said, staring at the makeshift weapon in his hand. "I dreamt that I could do things with it. I felt I could bend it, shape it, force it into a new shape just by thinking. . . ." Carl's voice trailed off as the bar in his hand actually began to transform. Ian gasped, and so did Carl. "I'm doing it!" he whispered excitedly.

"Keep going!" Ian urged him, hoping that Carl would make the pipe into something useful to fight the sisters with.

Carl focused hard on the object in his hand, and before

their very eyes, the hollow tube collapsed in on itself, then elongated to something double in size. The tip of the pipe became sharply pointed, and when Carl looked up again, the metal tube had been remade into a thin but deadly spear.

Carl handed the weapon to Ian. "Aim for Atroposa!" he whispered. "Her back's to us and she'll never see it coming!"

Ian didn't hesitate. He took the spear, aiming for the sorceress, and let the deadly harpoon fly.

It struck her in the upper back, and with a great shriek of pain, the vile woman pitched forward, collapsing to the ground.

Adrastus jumped to his feet, drew his own sword, and charged at Caphiera, whose attention had turned to her sister. He would have dealt her a deadly blow had she not seen the movement and at the last second protected herself with another shield of ice. Still, the impact sent the sorceress reeling.

Iyoclease also got to his feet and hurried to aid Adrastus. The two of them hacked at Caphiera's icy shield until the sorceress was on her knees. "Get to the portal!" Iyoclease ordered. "Escape, Adrastus! Escape!"

"Not . . . without . . . you!" the general replied, striking again and again.

Iyoclease did the unexpected then: he shoved hard against the general, pushing him out of the way as he took over the battering of the sorceress's shield. "The quest is more important! I'll hold her here!"

Ian's hands were curled into fists. He wanted to race to Iyoclease's side, but he had no weapon. He looked about again for anything he could use when he noticed Carl bending low over a broken door. As Ian watched, his best friend pulled the handle cleanly off and began to melt it into a ball; then, using a brick, he mashed down the metal and formed it into two crude-looking daggers. Ian could hardly believe his own eyes. Carl stood and offered both of them to Ian.

"Your aim is better than mine," he said, pale and sweating with the effort.

Meanwhile, Adrastus had gone into the shop, and Ian knew he was opening the portal, attempting to escape. Iyoclease, however, was now in terrible trouble. Atroposa had gotten to her knees, the spear still protruding from her back. She raised one hand and sent Iyoclease hurtling away from Caphiera.

When the sorceress of ice could stand again, she threw aside her icy shield, growling low in her throat and approached the fallen soldier menacingly. "Look into my eyes, you despicable mortal!" she screeched.

Ian snatched the daggers from Carl and bolted into the street, mindless of the danger the sorceresses presented. He took three strides, raised one of the daggers, and threw it straight at Caphiera.

However, Atroposa cried out a warning, and in that instant her sister turned and raised her arm, catching the dagger above the wrist. With a screech the sorceress turned toward him. "Guardian!" she cried, raising her good hand

and preparing to strike. Ian took one more step and launched the other dagger, but just as he released it, something hit him hard in the chest and Ian was sent tumbling backward. He landed with a tremendous thud on the ground, dazed and struggling for air.

He was aware of bits and pieces of what happened immediately afterward. There was a horrible shriek, this one piercing and agonized, then a grating noise followed by an explosion so loud it rattled Ian's bones. He was showered with bits of brick and mortar and other debris, and he curled into a ball and lay still. A few heartbeats later, however, he was lifted under the arms and dragged over the rough cobblestones until he thought he couldn't take it anymore. "Stop," he finally managed to say. "Please, set me down!"

Ian's head was spinning and his back hurt fiercely. His ribs felt as if a horse were sitting on them. Mercifully, however, he was let down gently, and Carl's face appeared over his. "Mate," Carl said, his hair soaked with sweat and his features pale and sickly. "Can you stand?"

Ian blinked dully. "I'd rather lie here."

Iyoclease's face appeared next to Carl's. "Ian," he whispered urgently. "The sorceresses will recover and they'll be after us soon. You've got to move!"

Ian closed his eyes, took a deep breath, then opened them again and sat up. With help, he worked himself to his feet. Leaning heavily on Iyoclease, Ian limped along as quickly as he could, and the battered threesome made their way back to the square with the manhole.

Iyoclease used his sword to wedge the manhole cover aside, and with shaking limbs, Ian followed Carl down to the tunnel and waited for Iyoclease to move the cover back into place. When they were all at the bottom of the ladder, Ian asked, "Where are the others?"

"Down at the end of this corridor, waiting for us," Carl said.

"Why did you come back to the shop?" he asked next.

"It was Theo," Carl told him. "Or rather, it was her crystal. It started glowing red not long after you and Adrastus set off, and she whispered in my ear that she had a terrible feeling about you."

Ian rubbed his temples. He had a splitting headache. "Well, I'm awfully glad you came when you did," he said. "How did we get away?"

Iyoclease replied, "It was you. That last dagger you threw struck Caphiera in the eye and she fell to the street. Her sister made one last attempt to catch Adrastus, but he'd already opened the portal and stepped through. As he was closing it, Atroposa blew the shop to pieces, and as the dust was settling, we got away."

"So Adrastus is safe?" Ian asked. He was still terribly worried about the general.

"He is," Iyoclease answered. "But I am left here with no way back to my home."

Carl picked up the lantern he'd left at the bottom of the ladder and eyed the long tunnel. "Come on," he coaxed them. "We'd best get to the others and tell them what's happened."

Once Adria had heard their tale, she eyed Iyoclease, and seeing the woeful look in his eyes after he'd lost his chance at the portal, she said, "All is not lost, my friend. We need only return to England and the portal near the keep, and I will return you home."

At this, Iyoclease brightened. "Thank you, Adria."

"Now," said their guide. "Let us set off for England before all routes out of France are closed, shall we?"

THROUGH THE PORTAL

It took the group five long days to make their way to Le Havre. They kept to the tunnels all the way out of Paris and then to the side roads and less-traveled pathways, moving steadily north and only at night. Twice they had to take refuge in the barns of local farmers, who took pity on them and offered them food and drink.

As they neared the port city of Le Havre, however, it became increasingly dangerous for them to be out in the open. There were more Germans there, and fewer farms. They had a bit of luck when they happened along a farmer taking his harvest to port to trade, and for a few franks he agreed to help sneak them in under a tarp in his wagon.

After arriving at the port, they waited under the tarp until dusk, then set off for the docks, sneaking under a wire fence, which Carl enjoyed using his new talent to make a hole in so they could slip through.

"There!" said Jaaved, pointing out the unmistakable mast of the earl's yacht. "She's right where we left her, my lord."

The earl gripped Ian's shoulder tightly, preventing him from dashing out into the road to get to the vessel. "Wait, Ian," he commanded. "We must watch to make sure the guard doesn't detect us."

Sure enough, not a moment later a pair of civilian police wearing white armbands marched by. "They're not Germans," Ian whispered.

"No," the earl remarked, eyeing the men suspiciously. "But I believe they work for them and would turn us over if they caught us. We will stay here until after midnight, when darkness and the late hour will give us the most cover."

Ian sighed irritably. He was eager to get home, and it frustrated him to be so close and yet so far.

The earl seemed to understand. "A short wait, and then we'll be off."

"Yes, my lord," Ian said, although his mood remained foul.

Their wait was all the more irritating due to the weather. Clouds arrived at the port shortly after they did, and a sharp wind whipped out of the west, cutting through their coats and chilling them all to the bone.

Poor Océanne was blue with cold, and Ian huddled close to her, rubbing her hands in his own. "Thank you," she said shyly.

He forced himself to smile. "Only a bit longer to wait; then we'll have you below deck, where it's warm," he promised.

Theo moved close to them as well, huddling on Ian's

right and shivering from head to toe. "Rain's coming," she said to him.

Ian pulled his eyes reluctantly from Océanne to the sky. "Rain?"

Theo nodded. "Within the hour."

"Well, that's all we need," he grumbled.

He then inched over to the earl and told him what Theo had said about the rain. The earl frowned and motioned to Adria. She came near and the pair conferred for a moment before motioning to the whole group. "We'll wait until the rain starts, then make haste to the boat," the earl said.

"If it rains hard enough, it should give us some nice cover," Adria agreed.

Ian nodded, but he wasn't at all happy that they'd have to wait until the weather grew even worse to make a run for it.

Almost exactly an hour later, a deluge poured down on top of them. They were soaked through within moments.

The earl held up his hand, however, peering through the downpour for any signs of the port watchmen. After no such signs appeared, he motioned for all of them to hurry out of their hiding places and over to the boat. In just a few minutes, they were all safely down below.

Once everyone had found a blanket to warm up with, Ian, Carl, and Jaaved sprang into action, moving to the side of the boat and untying the lines from the pier. The earl and Iyoclease joined them, and before long they had the engine started and were inching out into the harbor.

The earl commanded the ship expertly, navigating the

rough waters until they were well away from the pier. It was rough going, because the farther from shore they got, the larger the waves, and the boat was soon pitching and lurching. "Get below!" the earl ordered above the sounds of the wind and the waves.

"What about you?" Ian asked.

"I'll be all right," the earl said with a smile. If Ian hadn't known better, he'd have sworn his patriarch was enjoying himself.

Ian scuttled below as he was told and found everyone there wide-eyed, clutching the sides of the boat. Within minutes most everyone on board—save Jaaved and Carl—was seasick.

The trip back to Dover was quite harrowing and took the rest of the night. Jaaved volunteered to stay above in the cold and the rain to help the earl with the navigation, and by dawn the White Cliffs were within sight.

Ian felt a surge of relief and happiness well up within him; despite his terribly upset stomach, his spirits soared at the sight of the magnificent cliffs he called home.

It was perhaps the final hours that made Ian the most anxious. He knew the channel was often patrolled by German U-boats, and he'd heard rumors that many a passenger ship was being targeted by their torpedoes. He had little doubt that if one of those U-boats happened to cross their path while they made their way steadily toward English soil, it'd sink them just for the sport of it.

But make it they did, and as they wound their way

closer to the much crowded Dover port, Ian thought he'd never leave his home again.

They were stopped by two patrol boats, and the earl had to identify himself to be allowed into port. Ian nearly laughed at the astonished looks on the soldiers' faces when they realized who was aboard the vessel.

A berth was cleared for them, and everyone aboard hurried to the dock, eager to get off the rocking boat. The rain was still drizzling down around them, and after an inquiry from the earl, two motorcars were sent for and the party was delivered to Castle Dover with much haste.

The earl's butler, Mr. Binsford, met them in the drive, and he took in the earl's haggard condition most anxiously. "My lord!" he said, moving quickly to the man's side and offering him some assistance. "You're injured!"

"I'm fine, Mr. Binsford," the earl lied.

Madame Lafitte stepped forward and smiled kindly at the butler. "He's not fine, Mr. Binsford. He needs rest and a doctor to look after those ribs immediately."

"I'll send for Dr. Lineberry," the butler promised.

"Some warm tea and a meal first, if you please?" the earl said. "For me and for all of my companions. And prepare a few of the guest rooms, Binsford. I feel the need to keep everyone close tonight."

The butler finally took note of the other members of the earl's party and nodded. "Of course, my lord."

Much later, after Ian was clean and rested and had had a bit of supper, he found the earl in his library, which was not at all where he'd expected him to be, given the late hour and the fact that he'd overheard Dr. Lineberry order him to bed for a week of rest.

"My lord?" Ian said when he spotted his patriarch staring out the window into the dark night.

The earl's shoulders sagged, but he did not turn around. "Ian," he said. "Come in, lad."

Ian moved into the library and noticed for the first time that the earl held a yellow piece of paper in his hand. He wondered what the telegram said, but it would have been impolite to ask directly, so he got around it by saying, "Is there news?"

The earl's reaction surprised him. He crinkled the paper into a small ball and squeezed it in his fist until his knuckles were tight. "I have a report from the man I hired within Belgium to find out what has happened to Monsieur Lafitte," he said, his voice tired and sad.

Ian felt the ominous sense of dread settle into his bones. He remembered what Theo had said about the fate of Monsieur Lafitte. "It's not good news, is it?"

"No, Ian. It isn't."

"Has he been taken somewhere else?"

"He's been shot. Murdered in cold blood."

Ian felt as if he'd been kicked in the stomach. "Poor Océanne!" he gasped. "And Madame Lafitte!"

The earl turned then, his eyes red and filled with sorrow. "Leo was one of my dearest friends, and I failed him," he confessed. "I failed to help him."

Ian recovered himself and shook his head vigorously.

"No!" he told the earl. "No, my lord! You didn't fail Monsieur Lafitte. The Nazis killed him and they would have killed his whole family had it not been for you. You saved Océanne and Madame Lafitte, my lord."

The earl closed his eyes and stood there, swaying slightly on his feet. He looked older than Ian could ever remember having seen him look, as if the news of Monsieur Lafitte's murder had taken years off his own life. "I should have done more," he said.

A knock on the door behind Ian caused him to turn. He saw that Theo was out of bed. "There you are!" she said when she saw him. "Ian, I've been looking all over for—" Theo stopped midsentence and stared at the earl, her forehead creasing with worry. "What's happened?"

The earl limped over to a nearby chaise and sat down heavily. He patted the cushion beside him and Theo moved to sit next to him. "I've received word regarding Océanne's father," he said gently.

Theo's hand flew to her mouth and she needed no further explanation. She flung her arms about the earl's neck and said, "Oh, my lord! I'm so terribly sorry!"

The earl appeared to struggle with his emotions for a moment and Ian looked away, feeling awkward and unsettled. "Thank you for your concern, Theo," the earl said after a moment, when he'd regained his voice. "Please don't say anything to Océanne or her mother until I've had a chance to explain."

Theo backed away from the earl and regarded him soberly. "I won't, my lord, I promise."

Ian remembered the late hour and what Theo had said when she came into the room. "You were looking for me?" he asked.

"Oh, yes! I almost forgot. Mistress Adria has asked if you would like to come say goodbye to Iyoclease in the morning. She's sending him back through the portal and then she'll go in search of her husband."

"Yes, of course," Ian quickly said. "When will they be setting off?"

"At dawn."

Ian looked to the earl as if to ask if he'd be joining them in the send-off, but the earl merely sighed and shook his head. "Please give my apologies to both Iyoclease and Mistress Adria," he said. "But I don't know that I'm up for any additional goodbyes at the moment."

Theo patted his hand knowingly. "Of course, my lord. Of course."

The earl seemed to think of something then. "I am informed that Mr. Perry Goodwyn is in residence here at my home, back from his envoy mission up the coast for the admiral. I'm quite certain that both Perry and Thatcher would like nothing better than to accompany you down to the portal and witness Adria's command over the portal door."

"That would be lovely," Theo quickly said. "Carl will be coming along too."

"Excellent," said the earl. "My flatware could use a bit of respite from Master Lawson's new talent."

Ian smiled. The last he'd seen his friend, he'd been turning all the earl's spoons into little charms for Eva. Carl had come home to a sizable stack of letters from her, and Ian knew his friend was most smitten.

Theo got up from the chaise and moved over to take Ian's hand. "Come along, Ian," she said. "You'll need to get some rest before tomorrow. Something tells me it will be another long day."

Ian, Theo, and Carl were able to catch only a few hours' rest before Adria woke them and said it was time to go. Ian rubbed his eyes and yawned loudly. Carl grumbled to himself as he put on his trousers and fumbled with the buttons on his shirt. "Tell me again why we need to go so early?"

"Adria wants to catch up with Adrastus," Ian replied, shivering in the cool morning air. "And she can't do that until she sends Iyoclease back to his own time."

"Let's hope we get a bit of breakfast before we give our farewells," Carl said with a yawn, and then he did something that caught Ian's attention. Carl subtly reached under his bed and pulled out the bronze sword they'd found next to the embedded skeleton in the wall of the portal. He normally kept it at the keep, tucked away in his trunk.

"When did you have time to retrieve that?" Ian asked him.

"Last night when you went to talk to the earl. I wanted to show it to Iyoclease and see if he recognizes it."

Ian had a moment when he didn't think that was an

255

especially good idea, because if Iyoclease did recognize the sword, he might also know the soldier who'd lost his life when the portal closed around him.

He considered saying as much to Carl, but his friend was already hurrying out the door on his way to see about breakfast.

Ian caught up to him at the bottom of the stairs, where Theo and Adria had already gathered. Both were watching with a mixture of humor and distaste as Carl stuffed his face with two muffins at the same time.

"My word, Carl," Adria said to him. "Attempt to chew that a bit before you swallow, lest you choke on it, all right?"

Carl nodded sheepishly and tried to wash it all down with a cup of tea.

Iyoclease arrived and so did Perry, looking chipper and excited. "I say," he said when he spotted them all in the hallway. "But you lot are a sight for sore eyes!"

Theo dashed over to him and gave him a hug. "We've missed you, Schoolmaster," she told him.

Perry smiled. "Yes, yes," he said. "Me too. Has anyone seen my brother?"

"I'm here," said Thatcher, coming down the hallway from the left side of the castle. The two brothers shook hands and patted each other on the shoulder. "Good to have you back, Perry," Thatcher told him.

"It's good to be back," Perry replied.

Introductions were then made and Perry took a particular interest in Iyoclease, who was dressed in the same attire he'd worn when he'd come through the portal. "What marvelous craftsmanship," Perry said to him when he took in the polished bronzed breastplate and gleaming helmet Iyoclease held tucked under one arm.

"We need to be off," Adria reminded them.

Ian was glad to set off. He longed to go back to his bed and planned to do just that the moment he'd given his farewells to Iyoclease and Adria.

It was still quite dark out, and Perry struck a match to light the lantern he'd brought along. He and his brother chatted about Perry's experience from the front lines and how happy he was to have a few weeks' leave before he'd be called up again.

When they reached the woods near the portal entrance, Ian and Carl led the way. Carl hadn't shown Iyoclease his sword yet; it was still tucked inside his coat. Ian suspected he intended to wait until they were near the skeleton to reveal it.

Walking down the stairs, he thought again about how the sword might belong to someone Iyoclease knew personally, and how showing it to him next to the skeleton embedded in the wall could prove unsettling to the already anxious soldier. Ian was about to say as much when he noticed something that stopped him in his tracks. He thrust out his arm to stop Carl from moving past him down the stairs.

"What?" Carl asked when he bumped sleepily into Ian's arm.

"Look," Ian said, pointing to the tunnel entrance.

Carl rubbed his eyes. "I don't see anything."

"You don't see the light coming from the tunnel?" Ian asked.

"Oh!" Carl said. "Yeah, now that you mention it. Is there someone down there, do you suppose?"

Ian moved quietly down the stairs. He could hear the others talking somewhere behind him and Carl, but no one else had reached the steps yet.

Making it to the bottom, he paused at the gate, and out of the corner of his eye, he saw that Carl had brought out his sword and was holding it in front of him.

Ian unlatched the catch and pulled the gate open, stepping into the dimness and staring with large astonished eyes at the end of the tunnel.

"It's open!" Carl nearly shouted. "The portal's open!"

Ian walked down the length of the tunnel to where the wall had once been. Piled into a heap were the skeletal remains of the soldier, but beyond them was something far more terrifying.

The portal opened up to the top of a bluff on a steep hillside overlooking a lush green valley. In the distance, structures were clearly distinguishable, and on all of them hung huge red flags with a white circle and a black swastika. "You've got to be bloomin' joking!" Carl whispered next to Ian.

"Ian?" he heard Theo call down the stairs.

Ian was nearly too stunned to reply. After Theo called to him a second time, he said, "Come quickly! And bring the others!"

He and Carl stood stock-still on their side of the tunnel, not daring to take an inch over the worn line of stone where the portal wall would reappear. There was a flurry of footsteps behind them; Perry and Thatcher were still chatting merrily until they entered the tunnel, and all conversation abruptly stopped.

"My heavens!" exclaimed one of them.

"It's open!" Theo said, and her footsteps hurried down the cavern floor. She came to stand next to Ian and took his hand. "Where is this place?"

"Austria or northern Germany, by the looks of that mountain range," Thatcher said, pointing to the beautiful snow-tipped mountains in the distance.

Adria stepped close too. "Who opened the portal?"

Ian tore his eyes away from the flags waving gently in the early morning breeze. "It was open when we got here," he told her.

Adria peered through the opening to the land beyond. "It has obviously opened for you."

"Me?" Ian gasped.

"Yes," she told him, an unreadable expression coming over her face. "I've not been here before," she said. "This must be the location that opened to my husband at the green door. If so, this would be the final location of his last box—but your fourth, if I'm not mistaken."

"Are you going to go find the general?" Ian asked, pointing to the beautiful land beyond the cavern.

Adria appeared tempted but shook her head. "Not

now," she said, looking at Iyoclease. "I must return our friend to his own time. Then I will come back and seek out my husband."

"Should we wait for you here?" Ian asked her, hoping her idea was to find Adrastus and bring him and the box back to England.

Adria smiled at him like he'd just said something funny. "No, Ian. You must venture through now and find the next Oracle and, hopefully, the silver box my husband is hiding too."

Ian's jaw fell open. "You can't expect me to go *there*!" he nearly shouted.

Carl, Thatcher, and Perry all jumped in with protests too. But Adria was firm in her resolve. "It is not my directive," she told them all. "It is Laodamia's. And go there you must. If you don't, then everything you have worked so hard for will be for naught, and all hope to stand against the four sorcerers will be lost."

Carl and Ian exchanged looks of outrage. "Bloody prophecy!" Carl growled.

Theo laid a gentle hand on Ian's shoulder. "Mistress Adria is right," she said. "We've got to step through and finish the third prophecy."

Ian stared at her with large eyes. "Theo," he said, "that's *Germany*! In case you hadn't noticed lately, they're trying to *kill* us. If we go there, we'll be shot before day's end!"

Theo pointed to the string around his neck holding the pouch with the Star of Lixus. "You'll speak perfect

German," she insisted. "And with our fair hair we shouldn't stand out. We can blend in until we find the Thinker."

"What's she going on about?" Carl demanded, clearly irritated by the prospect of venturing into enemy territory.

"The Thinker," Ian said glumly. "You're the Metal Master, which would make the next Oracle the Thinker."

"You can't seriously be thinking of going through the portal, can you?" Thatcher asked.

Ian cast a reluctant stare at his schoolmaster. "I'm afraid there's no help for it," he said, stepping over the line and turning to look back at them.

Theo promptly joined him but Ian took her by the shoulders, pivoted her around, and sent her back to the other side of the marker. "Absolutely not," he said to her. "I'll not risk your life too."

Theo glared at him and fought against his firm hands. "Stop it, Ian! You'll need me!"

Carl sighed heavily and took a large step forward. "I'll look after him, Theo," he said, reaching out to stop her when she tried to dart sideways across the line. "And please, don't tell Eva I've done something so stupid."

But Theo was ignoring Carl at the moment. "Let me come!" she demanded, her face red with determination.

"No," Ian said firmly. "Carl and I will manage on our own."

Thatcher reached over and held Theo by the shoulders. "Ian and Carl are right. It's far too dangerous this time."

Perry made a disgruntled sound, stepping over to stand beside Ian and Carl. "I've a feeling I'm going to regret this," he muttered when Ian smiled gratefully at him.

"Perry!" his brother snapped. "Get back here this instant! You're wearing your uniform, for heaven's sake!"

But Perry merely shrugged out of his coat and tossed it to Thatcher. "I'll steal something from one of the locals," he said. "Until then, no one's going to notice my trousers and boots as anything but fashionable."

Theo, who still appeared furious, reached up and took off the pouch containing her bit of the Star of Lixus. She tossed it to Perry and said, "Here, Schoolmaster. Please look after Ian and Carl."

"Thank you, my dear," Perry said. "I shall bring them back, I promise."

And then something unexpected happened. Iyoclease crossed the line and stood next to them too. "What are you doing?" Adria demanded.

"I can see that there is danger in this land," he said calmly. "They will need a soldier to protect them."

"No! It's too dangerous, Iyoclease! We must get you back home to your own time!" Adria insisted.

Iyoclease shook his head stubbornly. "I cannot believe that my only purpose within the prophecy was to helm a ship, Adria. There *must* be a larger reason why I'm here. And I believe that reason is to see these young men safely through this part of their quest."

Adria appeared completely astonished, as if she couldn't believe the man dared argue with her. "Iyoclease, I insist you come back over this line so that I can send you back to Laodamia at once!"

"You may send me back when I return," he said, and the last of his sentence was all but drowned out when there was a very loud grating noise and the wall appeared in front of them, sealing everyone on the other side out of view.

For several long seconds no one said a word. They all just stared at the stone, which held the skeleton again. After a moment or two, Perry cleared his throat. "Very well, then," he said. "Where did Laodamia say we must start?"

Ian pulled the prophecy from his pocket and began to scan the lines. "She said something about going where our hearts would fear to tread. . . ."

"We can check that one off," Carl said, turning to stare with distaste at the billowing flags below.

Ian ignored him and was about to suggest they form some sort of plan when a grating sound behind them made them turn back to the wall. Adria appeared with her arms crossed over her chest while Thatcher and Theo, somewhat astonished, stood in the background. With a determined look, Adria stepped over the line where the wall had been, then pivoted and thrust her hands down and out. The wall closed immediately.

"If Iyoclease will not cooperate, then I've no choice but to help you see this part of your quest through as well."

"Where should we begin?" Perry asked.

Adria squinted straight down the bluff to a cluster of buildings resembling an abbey or a church. "There," she said. "That's as good a place as any to start. We can approach the abbey through the woods, spy on it and the inhabitants from the cover of the trees, and hopefully glean some details about what part of Germany or Austria we're in."

Without further discussion Adria began walking purposefully down the steep hill. Ian didn't hesitate to follow her and was relieved when Carl came up beside him. "This is pure madness," Carl grumbled.

They had to cross a roadway at one point, and the five of them were nearly hit by a speeding motorcar that beeped rudely at them as it passed by. Ian's heart thundered as he scuttled across the road. He'd caught a glimpse of the red, white, and black flag painted on the side of the black sedan, and it sent a ripple of fear straight through him.

Adria hastened them into a clump of nearby woods for shelter, and luck seemed to be on their side, because the car didn't double back to take a better look at them.

Their good fortune held when they realized that the woods butted up to the side of the cluster of buildings and they were able to approach it under the cover of the forest.

Spreading out to use the trees to hide their advance, the five of them peeked out at the abbey. Carl didn't seem to like his tree, however, because he scooted over to sit next to Ian behind a large fir.

Once Carl had settled, Ian realized immediately that the car that had nearly run them down was just then pulling to a stop in front of the main entrance. Before the occupants of the car could exit, however, the door to the building flew open and out poured a huge crowd of young boys, rushing into the early-morning sun.

"It's a school!" Carl whispered.

Ian had a sudden dreadful thought. What if the Thinker was one of those boys? How would they ever discover him hidden so well amid such a large crowd?

Ian and Carl watched the swarm of boys and young men, clustered in small groups, talking and joking with each other just like Ian and the other orphans at Delphi Keep used to do before morning lessons began.

But there was one serious difference between the two scenes, and that was that these young boys were his sworn enemies.

With a jolt, Ian realized that the fifth Oracle was also certain to be an enemy. Carl seemed to come to the same conclusion. "Why do I think that our next Oracle's going to be a bloomin' Nazi?"

"Laodamia warned us that the fifth Oracle's heart would not be true to our cause," Ian said.

"I'm not bringing back a bloody *German* to join our ranks, Ian!" Carl hissed.

"We've no choice, Carl," Ian told him firmly. "If we don't add him, we can't complete the final prophecy."

Carl's face turned red with anger but he didn't argue further. Ian hoped he could contain his emotions until they'd managed to bring back the next Oracle.

A bell sounded from inside and the boys dashed back to the entrance. Within moments the grounds were still and peaceful again.

Ian's attention was then diverted to the black sedan parked near the front doors. He didn't remember seeing anyone exit the car, and sure enough, at that moment the door opened and out of it came a young lad of about eleven or so. From the driver's side came someone else, whom Ian and Carl recognized immediately.

"Wolfie!" snapped Dieter Van Schuft impatiently when the young boy slouched and hung his head. "Stand up straight, will you!"

From the door of the school, a priest appeared, stepping quickly to the pair.

"Laodamia better not have meant *him*!" Carl growled quietly.

Ian was silent. He stared, stunned, at the man he and Carl knew all too well—the man who had attempted to abduct and murder both Ian and Theo two years earlier, and whose wife had nearly shot Ian a year later while in Spain. And then Ian's attentions turned to the boy— clearly Dieter's son—as he darted away from his father, who was chasing him and working himself into a furious temper. "Papa, I don't want to stay here!" the boy shouted.

The priest stepped close to the boy and held out his hand. "Come with me, young man. I will show you to your room."

Wolfie stopped long enough to stare intently up at the priest. A moment later the man turned to Dieter and said, "He really shouldn't stay here. I suggest he go back home with you, Herr Van Schuft."

Ian blinked. What had caused the priest to change his mind so quickly?

"Wolfie!" Dieter snarled, catching hold of his son's arm roughly. "Stop that this instant!"

The priest seemed to wobble on his feet, and he shook his head as if to clear it. "Oh, my," he said, staring at Wolfie and his father as if seeing them for the first time. "Herr Van Schuft. It's so good to see you again. And this must be your son?"

Dieter forced a smile onto his face, his fingers turning white around the boy's arm from holding him so tightly. "Yes, Father Zeiler, this is my son, Wolfgang. Wolfie for short."

Father Zeiler offered Wolfie his hand, and the boy ignored it until his father smacked him hard on the back of the head. Ian winced. It looked to have been a hard blow.

Wolfie rubbed his head, then grudgingly took the priest's hand and shook it once before letting it go, pointing his eyes to the ground.

"He lost his mother last year," Dieter explained, and Ian's brow rose in surprise. He wondered if Frau Van Schuft had died in Spain after all.

"Oh, I'm terribly sorry, Herr Van Schuft," the priest said. "Illness, was it?"

Dieter let go of his son and appeared to hold himself rigidly. "Yes," he said. Shaking his head, clearly doubting the story, Carl looked at Ian.

"It was very abrupt and sudden," Dieter went on, his

hands trembling slightly. "She collapsed in the middle of the night and never woke up again."

"*That's a lie!*" Wolfie yelled, looking up with accusing eyes at his father. "She was murdered and you let it happen!"

"Wolfie!" Dieter gasped, his face turning red with embarrassment. "Keep silent!"

The priest appeared quite taken aback by the outburst and even more so by the accusation. "Well, it's true, isn't it?" Wolfie went on. "That hateful man, Magus, murdered my mother. And you stood by and let it happen!"

In the next instant Dieter slapped his son so hard the boy spun in a full circle and fell to the ground. Ian flinched again and felt renewed hatred for the despicable man. He wondered if there had been anyone else about—some of the other children or even another priest—whether Van Schuft would have openly struck his son.

Dieter stepped over to the now crouching form of his son, his hands curled into fists. Ian was certain he would rain down more violence on Wolfie, but instead, he continued to hover over him until finally the boy was brave enough to look up. When he did, Dieter spoke in the most threatening tone Ian could have imagined. "*Never* speak of that again!" he ordered.

The side of Wolfie's face where his father had struck him was bright red and his eyes looked to be brimming with tears, but he didn't flinch and he didn't cry. He merely nodded and stood up.

The priest still looked quite shocked by the violent outburst, and Dieter seemed to notice his expression for the first time. What he said next took Ian by surprise. "Fix the priest, Wolfie."

The priest's eyes darted to Dieter. "Excuse me?" he said.

Wolfie continued to stare rebelliously at the ground.

"Do it now!" Dieter demanded.

The priest turned his attention back to the boy, who had lifted his chin and was now looking at him intently. A moment later the priest seemed to wobble backward again, barely catching himself before shaking his head and staring at both Dieter and Wolfie as if he was surprised to see them. "Ah, Herr Van Schuft! It's so good to see you again! And this must be your son, Wolfgang is it?"

Carl turned to Ian. "We're in a load of bloody trouble, mate," he whispered.

MAGUS'S MISERY

Magus the Black stirred in the dark chamber that imprisoned him. Having no sense of time, he wondered how many months had passed since his sister Lachestia had entombed him. He could hear her rumbling through the earth now and then and wondered why she hadn't left him to pursue other entertainment. He considered that he might have caused her some harm in the last powerful exchange they'd had before she'd somehow gotten the better of him.

Leaning against the cold stone, he thought about what had become of his pets. He had left them to roam the mountains and await his return. Would the hellhounds eventually realize he was never coming back? Would they come in search of him?

Part of him hoped they would. Every day he grew just a bit weaker. In time, nothing would remain of him except a pile of ash.

The stone next to his head vibrated. Lachestia was on the move again.

Tired of the dark, he snapped his fingers, and a small flame grew from his fingertips. He stared forlornly at his surroundings: six stone slabs forming a solid box of doom. In the crevices between the slabs he could see small bits of dirt, seeping through and muddying the floor. Not only was he entombed, but he was buried too.

If only he had a bit of kindling to start a real fire, he could then call on his father to help him. He knew the great and mighty Demogorgon would never stand for this. But besides the dirt and an occasional bug, the box was empty. Well, empty except for Magus, of course.

With a sigh, the sorcerer allowed the flame from his fingertips to sputter out. What was the point? There was nothing to see, and the flame hardly gave him comfort anymore.

Magus lay down flat on his back and stared up at the dark. What he needed was for one of his other sisters to come looking for him. He knew that wouldn't happen unless either Caphiera and Atroposa angered their father and he ordered them to, or they required his help to carry out some evil plot. Atroposa would never come into Lachestia's territory on her own. His only hope was Caphiera, and she was nearly as dangerous and deadly to him as Lachestia.

Still, as long as he lived, there was hope. So the sorcerer of fire clung to that, especially since there was nothing else to do.

CHESS PIECES

Perry crept over to join Ian and Carl after Wolfie and the priest had disappeared into the church and Dieter had driven off. "Am I to understand that the boy who argued with his father is the fifth Oracle?"

Ian nodded while Carl cursed. "This is likely to get quite sticky," Perry said.

Adria and Iyoclease joined them too and motioned them a bit deeper into the woods, lest they be spotted from inside.

They arrived at a small clearing. Perry still appeared very worried by the prospect of their challenge. Carl continued to grumble and in general be completely disagreeable. "How do you suppose we go about snatching him, then?" Carl snapped. "I mean, we can't just walk in there and kidnap the bloody lout!"

"Master Lawson," Perry replied crisply. "Language."

"Sorry, sir," Carl said contritely. "But this is blo—suicide!"

"It is indeed," said Adria. "I recognized the boy's father. He is a servant of Magus the Black."

"Herr Van Schuft," Ian said. "We recognized him too."

Perry pulled his chin in. "Do you mean to say that the next Oracle is a *servant of the sorcerer?*"

"No," said Adria. "But his father clearly is. Still, the boy has all the markings of a Thinker. Able to read and control thoughts and even plant ideas in the minds of others. That priest was not weak minded. The boy shows extraordinary talent."

"This is a most dangerous quest, then," Iyoclease said. "If the boy can read thoughts, it would be difficult to lure him away from the abbey with a ruse. And surely five strangers approaching the abbey and inquiring about the boy would call unwanted attention."

"Especially in your attire," Adria remarked. Iyoclease looked down at himself and nodded.

"This is impossible," Carl grumbled. "There's no way to get him to come to us without him seeing the trick, and there's no way to sneak in unnoticed to entice him away where we can nab him and force him through the portal."

"Perhaps there is a way," Perry said. "Although I believe it might take some time to work it through—certainly longer than the morning."

"Do you have an idea, sir?" Ian asked.

Perry nodded. "With our pieces of the Star, we're able to speak flawless German. No one would suspect a man with two young sons inquiring about their admittance into the abbey's school, now, would they?"

Ian brightened. "Quite right!" he said. "Yes, sir, that does seem like a good idea!"

"Are you *mad?*" Carl gasped before he remembered to whom he was speaking. When Perry leveled a look at him, Carl amended himself by saying, "Er, what I mean, sir . . . with all due respect . . . you can't very well expect us to pretend to be *German!*"

"That's exactly what I expect, Mr. Lawson," Perry replied, and Ian could tell their schoolmaster was quickly losing patience with Carl's attitude.

"Carl," Ian said, knowing he might be able to talk some reason into him. "We'll be acting as spies, working not just to bring back Wolfie, but also gaining any valuable information we can give to the crown."

As he'd hoped, Carl pounced on the idea. "Spies, you say?" Ian nodded vigorously. Carl's face lit up with interest and he looked back again at the school. "I suppose some of those louts have parents who know what the German army is up to, eh?"

Again Ian nodded vigorously. "Some of their fathers might be high-ranking officers, in fact," Ian said. "You saw how Herr Van Schuft was dressed. He was wearing an SS uniform. I believe he's got himself a post in Hitler's personal army. So who knows what we could learn by posing as students and mingling with the others?"

"There's a flaw in your plans, though," Adria said to them. When they all turned to her, she said, "Mr. Goodwyn, however are you going to convince the headmaster at

274

the abbey that you have money to pay for Ian and Carl's attendance?"

"Has no one brought along any money?" Ian asked.

Perry dug into his trouser pocket and pulled up a few pound notes. "These won't do," he said.

Adria held her hands open. "I have a few gold coins left, but not enough. We'll need a considerable amount of German Reichsmarks."

Perry's face turned pensive, but Carl seemed to brighten even more. "Leave it to us," he said, pointing to himself and Ian.

"Leave what to us?" Ian asked. He had no idea what Carl had in mind, but he knew he probably wouldn't like it.

Instead of answering him, Carl simply motioned for Ian to follow him, and set off. Grudgingly, Ian followed Carl and soon caught up with him. "What're you planning?" Ian asked him.

"I saw a house from the bluff," Carl told him. "It looked to be a nice home where someone with a bit of money lives."

Ian had an unsettling feeling in the pit of his stomach. "Yes, and . . . ?"

"In a home like that, I bet they've got loads of valuables just lying about."

Ian stopped and caught Carl by the shoulder. "You want to *steal* from them?"

Carl looked at him frankly. "Yes, Ian. I want to steal from the same people who have bombed our cities, killed our countrymen, and murdered Madam Scargill, Monsieur Lafitte, and Eva's grandmother."

Ian felt the sobering truth of what Carl had just said sink into him. Still, he thought Carl's plan was far too risky, and he wanted to talk him out of it but Carl had already set off again. Ian decided to hold his tongue just long enough to find out what Carl intended to pinch.

Reaching the outskirts of the yard surrounding the stately home, the pair crouched down behind a row of trees to observe it before attempting to go inside. "Someone's home," Ian whispered, pointing to the back end of a motorcar partially hidden by a low wall.

Carl eyed the vehicle. "Let's hope they're not home for long," he said.

Luck seemed to be with them again, as not ten minutes later they heard a rear door open and saw a man in a long black leather coat and matching hat come out of the house and get into the motorcar.

They caught a better glimpse of the vehicle and the driver then, and Ian couldn't help sucking in a breath of surprise. "It's Van Schuft!"

Carl grinned wickedly again. "Oh, I think I'm going to enjoy this," he said, and when the motorcar was barely out of sight, he stood up and crept to the house.

Ian had no choice but to follow quickly. "Carl!" he whispered as he came close to his friend. "What if someone else is home?"

Carl paused, sliding his sword out of his coat. "We'll deal with them," he said.

Ian didn't like the venom in Carl's eyes, but he understood it nonetheless. And in a moment of anger he decided nicking a few of Van Schuft's valuables sounded like the right thing to do. The pair moved over to the rear door and Carl tried it but it was locked.

"Should we break a window?" Ian asked, looking around for a rock to use.

But Carl only laughed, and Ian noticed the air about Carl shimmering as the metal of the door handle seemed to soften for a moment and the door opened with a click. "I rather like being a Metal Master," he said.

The boys entered the home on tiptoe, listening intently for any sounds of other occupants. They heard nothing but the faint ticking of a clock in another room.

"There," Carl whispered, pointing to what was obviously the home's dining room. "I'd wager there's some good silver in there."

Ian frowned; once again he was having misgivings. He didn't like Carl's plan to steal from the home for several reasons: the first of which was that Van Schuft would surely see that his silver was missing and alert the authorities. And second, would they ever get away with presenting the forks and knives to the headmaster of the school?

He almost voiced this concern, but Carl was already opening the door to a large credenza and digging through the contents. "Aha! There's enough silver here to serve twenty people!"

"Do you really think the headmaster at the abbey will

take forks, knives, and spoons for our tuition?" Ian asked, knowing the idea was absurd.

But Carl was undeterred. "We can nick a few of these and sell them for Reichsmarks."

"Who are you going to sell them to?" Ian asked, still uncomfortable with the plan.

Carl paused. "Right," he said, considering the silver again. "We can have Mr. Goodwyn give the silver directly to the school's headmaster and tell him it's a family heirloom and he's exchanging it for his sons' education."

Ian moved over and placed a hand on Carl's arm. "Carl," Ian said. "We can't pinch something so obvious. Van Schuft's going to realize his silver's missing."

"So?"

"So," Ian said impatiently, "once he realizes he's been robbed, he'll alert the authorities, who will likely go first to the school, as it's so close to this home. And who's to say that one or two of the students didn't nick the silver between classes?"

Carl sat back on his heels, still holding on to the flatware. Reluctantly he began to put it back. "Well, we've got to find something valuable that he won't miss," he said. "I can change the shape of anything we find that has metal in it, but you're right. Van Schuft will likely spot his missing silver straightaway."

Ian let out a small sigh of relief, grateful that Carl was finally being reasonable. He then got to the business of opening drawers himself, searching for anything valuable that Dieter Van Schuft wouldn't immediately notice was gone.

In the back of the credenza, behind a silver serving bowl, Ian spotted a large box wrapped in velvet and bound with a cord. Something about the box unsettled him, almost as if he could sense there was something inside that nagged at him in a most disturbing way.

Curious, he reached for the box and brought it out to inspect it. It was heavy and the cord was tightly knotted. Ian had to work at it for a bit before he was able to undo the knot, but eventually he managed. He then removed the velvet wrapping and revealed a wooden box beautifully engraved. He pulled back the lid and saw that inside was a chessboard, folded in the middle and clasped together on the ends.

The moment Ian pulled out the chessboard, he felt his thoughts turning dark, and a ripple of anger coursed through him. "What's that you've got, Ian?" Carl said.

"Aren't you a nosy one?" Ian snapped.

Carl's eyes widened and he looked a bit hurt. "No need to bristle," he said. "I was just curious."

With great effort Ian set down the chessboard and moved away from it for a moment. Without even seeing the contents, he knew what was inside, and his body shook slightly with the struggle to leave it alone.

"It's a chessboard," Carl said, moving to pick it up.

"Don't!" Ian said, reaching out to grab him by the shoulder, and again Carl appeared injured by Ian's rather snappish tone.

"What's eating at you, anyway?" his friend asked, roughly pulling his arm out of Ian's grip.

"Carl," Ian said levelly, taking another step back from the chessboard. "Do you remember Jaaved's grandfather Jiffar?"

"What kind of question is that? Of course I remember him!"

"Do you remember the chess pieces he was working on the night he was murdered?"

Carl's eyes bulged. "In there?" he asked, pointing to the closed chessboard.

Ian nodded gravely.

Carl laughed. "Oh, but that's perfect!" he exclaimed. "Van Schuft's not going to miss those pieces! I mean, look at that box. It looks like it hasn't been opened in ages!"

"No, Carl," Ian said angrily. "We can't take the pieces. They'll turn us against each other just like they did the last time, or have you forgotten?"

The chess pieces in question were carved from an evil stone called Gorgonite, which had a most distressing and dangerous effect on anyone who handled them.

Carl's enthusiasm ebbed immediately. "Oh, right," he said. But then he added, "Still, if I remember correctly, the pieces had quite a bit of gold, silver, and precious gems attached to them."

Ian narrowed his eyes suspiciously. "What're you suggesting?"

"I could melt the metal right off the Gorgonite," he said. "I know I could."

Ian bent to put the chessboard back in the wooden box.

"No," he said, placing the lid on top quickly. "It's far too dangerous. We'll find something else to pinch."

Carl placed a hand on Ian's wrist to stop him from putting away the chessboard. "Anything else we find might be missed. This is our best chance to bring back a bit of gold without it being noticed."

Ian knew Carl was right, but the thought of him handling the pieces to melt the gold worried him.

"I'll be careful," Carl assured him. "And you can stand over there, if you'd like." Carl pointed to the far corner of the room, beyond the reach of the chess pieces' influence.

Ian felt his stomach flutter nervously. He didn't like being in this house, nicking Van Schuft's valuables, no matter how awful the man was. Stealing was stealing, and he felt ashamed for participating in it.

And then there was the chess set itself, which was a vile item not fit for humanity. He eyed the box critically. The one good thing about Carl's plan was that the chess pieces would be rendered useless once the gold and silver were removed. The box would simply be filled with lumpy pieces of awful black rock.

With a sigh, Ian said, "Very well, Carl." He then unwrapped the velvet again and handed over the wooden box. "Remove the gold, silver, and gems as quickly as you can. I'll be right over there, so if you begin to feel a bit wonky, tell me and I'll pull you away to help clear your head."

"Right," Carl said, bending eagerly to start the task.

281

Ian retreated to the far corner of the room, where he could watch his friend for signs of trouble.

Carl removed the chessboard and examined the catch for only a moment before opening it and exposing the pieces. Even from where he stood, Ian couldn't help admiring the chess pieces as a few of them spilled out onto the floor. Carl picked up the ruby-inlaid queen and got straight to work, melting away the silver into a round ball, then setting that aside along with the rubies and going for the next largest piece, the gold and emerald queen.

As Carl worked in silence, Ian watched him for any signs of aggression or anger. The air around Carl shimmered while he labored, and beads of sweat formed along his brow and ran down the sides of his face, but he worked diligently and quickly, moving through the pieces one at a time and setting to the side each new round ball of gold or silver and set of precious stones.

After ten minutes, Carl was halfway through the chess set when the shimmering air about him winked out, and instead of melting the metal around the rook in his hand, he regarded it thoughtfully, almost . . . lovingly. "Carl," Ian said, worried that he'd allowed his friend to work with the pieces for too long without a break.

"Yes, Ian?" Carl said easily.

"You all right?"

"Fine," Carl said, but when he turned his eyes to Ian and smiled, a chill ran right down Ian's spine. It was an evil smile.

"Why don't you come away from the pieces for a bit?"

Ian suggested, careful to keep his voice even. "We could go outside and get a bit of fresh air."

"No," said Carl. "I'd rather not."

Ian's heart beat faster. He took a few steps in Carl's direction, and that was when his best friend stood up, removing the sword from his belt to hold out defensively in front of him. "Carl!" Ian said sternly. "Put that away!"

"Oh, I don't think I will, Ian. And I don't think I'll give you this chess set after all. I think I'd like to keep it."

And then Carl did something Ian could hardly believe. His best friend lunged at him, and if the lid of the box hadn't been in Carl's way and caught his foot, causing him to stumble, Ian would have been run right through with the bronze sword.

Ian tackled him and jerked the sword free. After pulling Carl up roughly by the shoulders, he gripped him around the middle and lifted him off his feet.

Meanwhile, Carl thrashed and squirmed and hit him as hard as he could. Ian took an awful blow from Carl's elbow but somehow managed to maneuver him to the back door. He yanked it open quickly and shoved Carl out the door, then pulled a chair underneath the handle. He hurried back to the dining room, scooped all the melted metal and gemstones into his pockets, and dashed to the kitchen to find something to cover his hands with.

While he was looking, the pounding on the door subsided, and he heard the change in the sound of Carl's voice, calling to him that he was terribly sorry. He didn't know what had come over him.

Ian paid him no attention, focusing on cleaning up the mess and hurrying out of the home as quickly as possible.

He finally opened a drawer and found a pair of oven mitts. He used these to gingerly gather up the remaining chess pieces scattered about the floor where they'd fallen when he'd tackled Carl, and deposited them back in the box, then slammed the lid.

Before setting the box back into the credenza, Ian left the room to avoid falling under the Gorgonite's spell, and used his time to find some clothing for Iyoclease to wear.

He managed to find Dieter Van Schuft's bedroom on the first try, and made his way to the wardrobe. When he pulled it open, he discovered it filled with black SS uniforms. He thought that might be as good a disguise as any, so he selected a uniform from the back, reasoning that if Van Schuft could tell his uniforms apart, he might not miss the one at the back. He draped the hanger over his arm, then had to rummage around for an extra hat. He managed to locate one on a shelf at the top of the wardrobe.

Ian was about to leave the bedroom when he considered that Mr. Goodwyn and Mistress Adria might not take to the idea of Iyoclease wearing the uniform, so just in case, he added a wool sweater and a pair of trousers he found in the bureau to the pile.

He then hastily moved out of the bedroom, pausing in the dining room to tuck the box back into the credenza and pick up Carl's sword before hurrying out of the house.

Carl was sitting on the half wall when he came out. "Ian, I—" Carl began.

"Don't worry about it," Ian said, handing over a few clothes and half his bounty to Carl.

"I'm terribly sorry," Carl told him anyway, his face a mask of shame.

"I shouldn't have let you work on the chess pieces for so long," Ian told him. "I'm more to blame than you are."

For his part, Carl continued to stare guiltily at Ian. To show him that he still trusted him, Ian handed Carl back his sword and said, "Let's be off, then, shall we?"

Carl smiled gratefully and shifted the hanger with the uniform to his other hand so that he could take the sword. Something plopped to the ground, and Carl eyed it curiously. "Look," he said, bending over to pick up the shiny object.

"It's a whistle," Ian said. He wondered what on earth an SS officer would need a whistle for.

Carl put it to his lips and blew very lightly but no sound came out. He pulled it slightly away and stared at it curiously, then blew on it again, more vigorously, yet no sound could be heard. "It's broken," he said.

"Yes, well, bring it," Ian told him, motioning for them to be off. "I'm not going back inside to hang it up again."

Carl shrugged, putting the chain around his neck. "Maybe it'll be a good-luck charm," he said cheerfully. And with that, the pair set off.

SUSPICION

Dieter Van Schuft returned late that afternoon to his chalet, turning the key and entering his home with a tired sigh. For a moment he leaned against the door and closed his eyes, relishing the privacy and solitude. For once he could come into his residence without having to guard his thoughts against his son's probing mind. The relief he felt, however, was tinged with just a bit of guilt.

Wolfie had resisted the idea of the local boarding school ever since his mother's death, and Dieter had allowed him to stay at home all of the previous year, but the boy had been coddled for far too long, Dieter determined. It was time for him to step up like a good little soldier.

The situation would work out rather well, Dieter thought. Wolfie would need to be on his best behavior and avoid his little tricks if he was to get along with the rest of the boys. Just before admitting his son, Dieter had taken Wolfie to a facility just outside Berlin to show him exactly what the Third Reich was doing with those citizens it deemed not up to German standards. He remembered the fear in Wolfie's eyes and knew he'd be a good boy. He'd only pulled that trick with the priest that morning out of desperation, Dieter reasoned.

With a weary sigh, he pushed away from the door and walked through the halls of his beautiful country home. He smiled, realizing he could finally hire a few servants to take care of him while he was posted there. With Wolfie about, Dieter had worried that he'd use his mind tricks on the servants to get his way and one of them was bound to notice the odd little boy with the peculiar ability.

But now that Wolfie was at the boarding school, Dieter could hire a housekeeper and a cook. He planned to hold interviews the moment his schedule allowed him.

Dieter set his attaché on the dining room table and opened it. There was so much to do before the Führer's visit. Dieter was in charge of the festivities, and he was nearly overwhelmed with details.

Selecting several folders from his attaché, he turned to walk into the kitchen but stepped on something, causing it to crunch under his shoe. Dieter scowled, bending down to retrieve the object, thinking it was one of Wolfie's figurines. But as he held it up, he was so stunned he dropped it.

It fell to the floor with a loud clunk. Dieter hurried to pick it up again. "What is *this?*" he cried, recognizing the small pawn from the chess set hidden away in the credenza. Setting his folders back on the table, Dieter rushed over to the sideboard and immediately saw that the corner of the felt covering his silver was sticking out of the drawer.

Pulling it open violently and rattling the silver, he reached to the back and took out the felt-covered box. When he had it open, he sucked in a breath and felt nearly overcome with alarm. *"Wolfie, what have you done?!"* Dieter shouted.

And Dieter knew, without a doubt, that his son had destroyed the pieces and taken the gold, silver, and gems. He assumed his son would attempt to sell the bounty to run away from the boarding school.

Dieter was furious beyond reason. His eye caught sight of the oven mitts on top of the sideboard and he knew how Dieter had pried away the metal and gems, leaving only the horrible black rock.

If his master ever returned and discovered the ruined chess pieces, both he and Wolfie would pay with their lives. Dieter blinked rapidly and with mounting panic. What to do? *What to do?*

Suddenly, there was an urgent knock on the door. Dieter jumped and slammed the lid, then shoved the box back into the credenza. He stood, absently stuffing the pawn into his coat pocket, and hurried to the door.

"Heil Hitler!" said the man on his doorstep.

Dieter returned the salute, albeit not quite as enthusiastically. "Herr Bauer," he said impatiently. "What is it?"

The junior squad leader lowered his arm. "Sir, your presence is required by Oberführer Jager."

Dieter stared at the lower-ranking man, not quite understanding him. "Oberführer Jager?" he repeated. "But he is in Berlin."

"No, sir!" Bauer insisted. "He has come to inspect the preparations for the Führer's visit and to ensure that they are coming along according to schedule. He has just arrived by train, in fact, and ordered me to bring you to him immediately."

Dieter's lips pressed together in a thin line. The Oberführer was an overbearing brute of a man, whom Dieter privately detested. He would no doubt keep Dieter up late into the night poring over every detail and Dieter had bigger things to worry about.

Still, there was no way out of the command and he would have to oblige the Oberführer and deal with Wolfie later.

"Very well," Dieter said with a weary sigh. "Just let me get my hat and I'll be along."

Dieter closed the door in Bauer's face and moved to the dining room again to retrieve his hat and his attaché. He collected them before hurrying back out the door, completely forgetting the dark pawn in his pocket.

A NEW BOX

Later that night the five from the portal were tucked away in an inn on the outskirts of the town they'd learned was called Berchtesgaden, which sat in a valley at the base of the huge mountain range.

Perry had taken a rather keen interest in the town, and when they learned that the Führer himself would be arriving within a week's time to celebrate his victory in France, Ian's schoolmaster had appeared oddly pleased.

Perry's behavior overall was a bit odd, Ian thought. He'd leapt at the chance to don the SS uniform that Ian and Carl had brought back with them, leaving the trousers and sweater for Iyoclease.

The Phoenician soldier looked uncomfortable in his new clothes, but he'd voiced no complaint.

From the moment they'd settled into their rooms at the inn, Adria and Carl had worked furiously all afternoon to turn the lumps of gold and silver into antique-looking coins. "These were used in the last century," Adria told them when she'd completed the engraving on the first coin and showed it to Carl to copy.

Carl was a very good artist in his own right, and using her tools, he managed to create a duplicate with a bit of effort and careful attention.

Ian had watched the pair with wonder, amazed at their ability to turn any bit of metal into something as pliable as wet clay.

Carl's abilities were very advanced, according to Adria. "He has astonishing skill and ability for one so new to the talent of Metal Master. Laodamia would be most pleased."

Carl beamed. "It's easy," he said. "I just think of softening the metal and it happens."

Adria nodded knowingly. "You are quite the artisan too," she said, pointing to his growing stack of coins.

"How many more should we make?" he asked.

"A few," she told him. "And then you and I will have some fun with the silver."

Ian wasn't sure what she meant, but after a time, when all the gold balls had been transformed, Adria took up a small wooden rolling pin and began to smooth out the silver pieces one by one, much like Madame Dimbleby would roll out some dough for a pie crust. Before long, Adria had six flat rectangles, and with a wooden knife she made the edges of the rectangles clean and exactly the same size.

"You're making one of your boxes!" Ian said.

Adria smiled at him but said nothing as she continued with her project.

While she was crafting the feet, Perry and Iyoclease

came into the room with a large sack of delicious-smelling pastries filled with meat and potatoes.

After handing them out to everyone, Perry sat down in a nearby chair and stared thoughtfully out the window at the mountain.

Ian got up and moved over to talk quietly with him. "Mr. Goodwyn?" he said.

Without looking away from the window, Perry replied, "Did you know the Führer has a chalet at the top of that peak? It's a grand place, I hear, nicknamed the Eagle's Nest."

Ian squinted out the window. He could just make out what looked to be a roof on a summit that seemed impossibly high up. "How does anyone get up there?" he asked.

"There's a lift," Perry told him. "The chalet was presented to that despicable fellow on his fiftieth birthday. I hear he's afraid of heights too."

Perry's voice had an odd quality about it, and Ian didn't know if he liked the tone. He was about to say something when Adria spoke from her place at the table. Ian noticed she was letting Carl work on making hinges for the lid of the box. "What is your plan for tomorrow, Perry?"

"I will take the boys to the school and enroll them as my sons. This uniform should prevent too many unnecessary questions. After all, no one questions the SS." Perry laughed as if he'd just said something funny, but Ian saw no humor in it.

"And after?" Adria asked, staring pointedly at Ian.

Ian was a bit caught off guard but said, "Carl and I will

find Wolfie Van Schuft and somehow get him to come with us to the portal on the bluff."

Adria nodded. "Very good. But you should be very careful with this boy, Ian. He appears to be a talented Thinker, and Thinkers are very clever Oracles indeed. They can be manipulative and are very often dubious. The best of them can easily read thoughts and influence decisions. If you and Carl don't hide your intentions well, Wolfie will have you in the palm of his hand before you even know what's happened."

Ian could feel the anxiety in the pit of his stomach grow, and he stopped eating his pastry, lest he get a bellyache. "We'll be all right," Carl said confidently.

Adria eyed him shrewdly. "I hope so."

No one spoke much after that. Iyoclease ran a stone across the blade of his sword, which Carl promised to shrink for him right after he was through, to conceal it. Perry continued to stare at the Eagle's Nest and Adria finished the silver box, which Ian would have sworn was far more beautiful than any of the others, especially since she had thought to adorn it with a few of the precious sapphires and emeralds.

"It's quite fetching," Ian said when she caught him staring at her work.

The Phoenician woman smiled proudly. "It's a replica of a box that used to sit in Laodamia's chamber. I believe it was one of her most prized possessions, in fact."

Iyoclease looked up curiously. "Oh?" he said. "I don't recall her having something so exquisite."

Adria laughed. "Well, perhaps you haven't given it to her yet."

"I don't understand," he said, his brow furrowing.

"As I recall, you presented Mia with that box on the anniversary of your engagement, which was a few months after you returned from the portal, if I've worked out the timing correctly. I believe you said you'd acquired her gift from a master tradesman from the East. I adored that treasure box, and studied it carefully before I crafted my own for the prophecies, which were not nearly as elaborate as the one you gave her." Adria held the silver box up to catch the fading rays of sun slanting in through the window. With pride she said, "This one, however, just might do Mia's box justice."

Ian felt so drawn to Adria's creation that he was compelled to say, "If Laodamia's box was anything as grand as that one, I'm sure she would have treasured it."

Adria beamed at him and then did something most unexpected. She stretched out her hands, holding the box toward him, and said, "Here."

"*For me?*" he asked, incredulous that she would give away something so valuable.

Adria's expression softened into an amused smile. "Yes, Ian. For you."

"But," he said, staring at the beautiful treasure, "what am I supposed to do with it, mistress?"

"Perhaps you could give it to Océanne," she said easily. From his chair, Perry snorted.

Ian was almost too stunned to speak. "Thank you,"

he said, not knowing quite how to receive such a beautiful gift.

Adria smiled as if she was quite pleased with herself before gathering up her tools and handing them to Carl. "These are for you."

"Me?" he said, echoing Ian perfectly.

"Yes. Every Metal Master needs a set of tools to create their treasures with. I have had these specially crafted and they have served me well over the years."

"But what about you?" he asked. "What will you use?"

Adria's eyes turned melancholy. "I believe I am finished making treasures," she said. "I want only to find my husband and a nice little villa somewhere in time to live out the rest of my days with him."

Ian had almost forgotten about Adrastus. "Should we be looking for the general?" he asked.

Adria nodded. "Iyoclease and I will go in search of him while Mr. Goodwyn looks after you. We will meet back at the portal when you have the fifth Oracle."

"If you're off looking for Adrastus, how will you know when we've got the boy?" Perry asked.

"I'll know," she told him. "I know whenever a portal has opened."

"Yes, but how will *we* open it?" Ian asked.

"By bringing back the Thinker," she said easily. "The portal will open on its own when you are ready to take him back to Dover."

"But what if he won't come willingly?" Carl wondered.

"Oh," Adria said, laughing, "I've no doubt that he

won't come willingly, Carl. He'll put up a good fight. You'll have no choice but to force him through."

Ian was worried about that. He detested Dieter Van Schuft, thinking him intrinsically evil, but did that justify kidnapping his son? Ian had his doubts.

Iyoclease seemed to know what he was thinking, because he looked up from sharpening his sword and said, "You must force him, Ian. In fact, you must do whatever it requires to take the fifth Oracle back through the portal. Laodamia's prophecy insists upon it, and she would not have insisted if she were not certain that it was vital to the cause."

Ian gave the soldier a reluctant nod. "Very well," he said. "We'll do whatever it takes."

"Just don't do anything that would call attention to yourselves until you reach the woods," Perry warned. "I'll be waiting there to help you get the boy back through the portal."

Ian felt a bit better when he heard that. "Thank you, sir," he said. "I just hope we can keep our intentions from him until we're ready."

"You must, Ian," Adria insisted, her tone sharp. "If he suspects you and reads your thoughts, there will be little we can do to save you."

Ian gulped. What terrible mess were he and Carl about to get into? He could only imagine it was going to be a sticky one indeed.

TWO THINGS WICKED
THIS WAY COME....

C aphiera the Cold glared hard at her sister with her one remaining good eye. "Come along, Atroposa!" she snarled when her sibling fell behind yet again. They'd been moving nonstop across the countryside, working to avoid notice by mortals and intent on their destination.

They were traveling in great haste even though they'd been wounded in the disastrous encounter with the Keeper and the young Guardian. Caphiera had lost an eye and endured a deep puncture to her arm, while her sister had struggled to recover from the spear, which had lodged in her back. But none of their injuries would compare to the damage their sire, Demogorgon, would inflict if he learned that they had failed to capture the Secret Keeper before he'd fled through the portal.

"I must rest!" Atroposa moaned. "I can feel the tip of that spear still lodged in my back."

Caphiera stopped abruptly, turning in anger and spitting an icicle at her, but it hit the dirt by Atroposa's feet.

Atroposa waved her hand at the icy dart and it came up out of the ground and whirled back toward Caphiera.

Had the icicle been a little more to Caphiera's left, she never would have seen it now that she was missing her left eye, but she caught the movement just in time and put her hand up to absorb the icicle in her palm. Her temper was piqued, and Caphiera shouted at Atroposa, "You're slowing us down!"

Atroposa scowled and stretched out her arms as a strong breeze came rolling across the hills. The wind strengthened her. "I am wounded," she said flatly. "There is only so much ground I can traverse before I must regain my strength."

Caphiera pointed to the patch across her eye. "Am I not also wounded?" she shrieked.

Atroposa ignored her and moved away to a nearby boulder to sit down. She held out her arms again as another strong wind rolled over the hilly terrain. "Why must we make this detour?" she asked, as if she'd completely forgotten the argument.

Caphiera glared at her through her one good eye. "I told you," she said tartly. "Now that the Secret Keeper has escaped, we have no choice but to enlist the help of our brother and sister, and as Lachestia has obviously trapped Magus somewhere near her lair, we must make haste to free him and convince her to join us. In order to find Magus, we will need his beasts, and in order to command them, we will need Magus's servant, who is the only one besides Magus that they trust."

"Van Schuft," Atroposa said with disdain. "I never liked that mortal."

"He's a mortal," Caphiera said simply. "What's to like?"

"Demogorgon will require an audience with us soon," her sister warned, her voice even more mournful than normal.

"He is unlikely to punish us too severely when we tell him we have rescued our brother and tamed our sister," Caphiera replied.

But Atroposa only frowned more. Lachestia was the most powerful by far of her siblings and her madness only increased the danger she posed to them all. "You're assuming that we will be victorious in both those endeavors?"

"We have no choice," Caphiera said. "Without the Keeper or the box, we have nothing to present to our sire, and as you know, he doesn't suffer such failures lightly."

Atroposa shuddered, moving from the boulder, and appeared ready to get under way again. "Then let's be off," she said. "We'll not stop until we find Van Schuft and force him to fetch Magus's mutts."

With that the two wicked sisters set off again, determined to find Dieter Van Schuft and get on with recovering their brother before time and their sire's patience ran out.

TWO NEW BOARDERS

Ian and Carl stood, tentative and nervous, next to Perry just outside the headmaster's office in the Berchtesgaden School for Boys. It was midmorning and most of the students were in class and the hallways were relatively empty.

And even though only the occasional priest passed by the young men's post, Ian felt incredibly exposed, convinced that at any moment someone would point him out as a British spy and he'd be taken away and shot.

Also, his new uniform itched terribly; he wanted nothing more than to take it off and put on his own clothes. Still, as he looked up at Perry, he had to consider that at least he wasn't wearing the black uniform of the SS, posing as an officer in the private army of the Führer.

At half past nine, footsteps from the other side of the door sounded, and a stern-looking priest with a sharp, thin nose and a nearly lipless mouth abruptly opened the door. "Herr Goodwyn?" the priest asked.

"Yes," said Perry, snapping his heels together and offering a "Heil Hitler" salute.

Ian forced himself not to flinch. He hated that salute. He hated Hitler. Most of all, he hated being there and pretending to be a young German.

By the look on Carl's face, Ian guessed he hated it too.

"And these are the boys in question?" the priest asked, returning the salute with a bit of lackluster.

"Yes. These are my sons. Karl and Liam."

Carl had been lucky; he'd gotten to keep his name, although Perry had warned him to spell it with a K. Ian, however, had been told that he would have to use a more German-sounding first name, and Adria had suggested he take the name of the innkeeper's son, Liam. "It almost sounds like your name, doesn't it?" she'd told him.

Ian had agreed to use it, although it irked him that he couldn't simply use his own name, as no one would know him here.

"They are the same age?" the headmaster asked, motioning the three of them into his office.

Perry took a seat in a chair in front of the headmaster's ornately engraved desk, and Ian and Carl found spots on a small wooden bench at the back of the room. "Yes. They are twins," he said.

The priest squinted at Ian and Carl. "They are very different," he remarked.

"Fraternal," Perry told him, and left it at that.

The priest seemed to accept his explanation. "Tell me about their education in Berlin."

On the previous eve, just before dusk, Perry had dropped off two applications for their enrollment. He'd then come back and lectured the two young men about what he'd written on the applications: mainly that Carl and Ian had both been educated at a small school outside Hamburg, but as Perry's duties were now in Berchtesgaden, he thought it best to bring the boys with him.

The priest nodded, lacing his fingers together as he placed his elbows on his desk. "You appear quite young to have sons of fourteen," he remarked.

Ian tensed and felt Carl do the same. But Perry merely chuckled easily and said, "Yes, I've been told I look remarkable for my age, Father. I practice daily robust exercise and eat a healthy diet, as the Führer has advised all good German men should do!"

Both the priest and Perry laughed, and Ian and Carl forced a chuckle too. The headmaster and Perry spoke for another twenty minutes, and Ian marveled at his schoolmaster's calm and easy demeanor. He concluded that Perry was a natural spy at heart. As the clock on the wall crept toward quarter past ten, Perry ran his fingers along the inside of his officer's cap and said, "And now I believe I shall leave my sons in your most capable hands, Father. I must be off, you see. There is much to do for the Führer's visit next week."

The priest stood, which allowed them all to do the same. "Quite right," he said. "I would beg you for an introduction, Herr Goodwyn, except that I've already asked a colleague of yours, Herr Van Schuft, to grant me an audience with the Führer."

Perry's smile widened. "Oh, you know Dieter?" he said.

"His son attends our school," the headmaster told him.

"Ah!" Perry said enthusiastically. "I did not know Dieter had enrolled his son, Wolfgang. This is excellent, Father! My sons would welcome the chance to meet him, right, boys?"

Ian nodded enthusiastically, just like he knew he was expected to. Carl, he noticed, nodded a bit more reluctantly, but Ian could hardly blame him.

Perry turned his attention back to the priest. "They should room together!" he announced.

The priest appeared taken aback. "Oh," he said. "Wolfgang is a bit younger than your sons, Herr Goodwyn. And it is our tradition to arrange our students in rooms with others in their same class—"

"Change the arrangement," Perry interrupted, his voice hard and brokering no argument. When the priest stared at him in surprise, Perry added, "Father, my good friend Herr Van Schuft and I will be working closely together over the next several months. I am sure he would welcome a chance for our sons to become acquainted. In fact, I'm quite certain he would also *insist* on it."

The priest's expression grew uncertain, and perhaps even a bit afraid. Ian noticed that his eyes roved briefly to the red armband with the black swastika around Perry's right arm, and after only another second of hesitation, he said, "But of course, Herr Goodwyn. I will have the boys arranged all in one room."

Perry's smile flashed again. "Excellent, Father!" he said, taking out several of the gold coins Adria and Carl had crafted and handing these to the priest. "This should be enough to cover the cost of admission," he said.

The headmaster took the coins curiously. "These are quite valuable," he said, turning them over in his hands. "I believe they are collector's pieces."

Perry smiled winningly. "My wealthy uncle, who was a collector of such things, left them to me and I'm afraid I have no use for them other than to provide my sons with a proper German education."

The priest was also smiling, but Ian could tell he was still quite nervous with the SS officer in front of him and was anxious to be rid of him. "Very good, Herr Goodwyn," the priest said. "Your sons will be in the best of hands."

Perry swiveled sharply to Ian and Carl. Placing one hand on each of their shoulders, he said, "You two be good students and do your best to make friends with little Wolfie."

"Yes, sir," Ian said.

"Yes, sir," Carl repeated.

Without further ado, Perry strode out of the room, leaving them alone with their new headmaster. "Karl, Liam," the priest said sternly. "Let's get you two a schedule and your books so that you may join your next class."

Ian and Carl spent a tense day at the back of all their classes, doing their best to melt into the background. One or two of the boys nearby had smiled at them, but Carl had glared so hard in return that it wasn't long before they could hear whispers among their classmates about how un-friendly they were.

Ian did nothing to try to ingratiate himself with the other young men. He didn't want to like them, and he knew that if he got to know any of them by name or even engaged in a casual conversation, he'd probably change his view of them as the enemy, and he couldn't risk that.

So he and Carl kept to themselves, then, at day's end, reported as directed by the headmaster to the priest in charge of their dormitory.

This priest ordered them to follow, and they made their way outside and down a walkway to a large square structure that Ian assumed was the boys' dormitory. Here they were led up a large staircase to the second floor, down a long cor-ridor, and around a corner to a lone room with the door open.

Inside, two boys were busy packing their belongings, and one sat dejectedly in the corner on his bed, reading a book, ignoring everyone around him.

The two boys gathering up the last of their things made sure to glare angrily at Ian and Carl as they left, and Ian nearly felt bad for forcing them out, but then he reminded himself that he would be there only as long as it took to sneak Wolfie off into the woods.

The last boy out of the room closed the door with a bit more force than was necessary, and Carl raised his eyebrows at Ian as if to say, "See? All Germans are ill tempered."

Ian ignored him and turned to the boy reading his book. "Hello," he said. "I'm Liam and this is Karl."

The boy made no response; he just held the book up higher in front of him. Carl repeated the look he'd given Ian before.

Ian rolled his eyes and looked about for something to do. He moved to one of the beds, where the sheets had been removed by the previous occupant, and found that on the bureau between the two bare beds was fresh bedding. Not knowing what else to do, Ian got to work making his bed.

Behind him he could feel Carl's eyes on him, and was relieved when he saw Carl finally follow suit. As he worked, Ian couldn't help noting that the sheets were made from a coarse wool, scratchy to his fingers, not at all the quality of sheets he had back home.

"They do that on purpose," said the boy behind him.

Ian turned. "Sorry?"

"The sheets. They're horrid on purpose."

Ian froze. Wolfie had just read his thoughts, and Ian knew it. Wolfie seemed to realize he'd said the wrong thing, because he quickly added, "I could tell by the way you were handling them that you didn't approve."

"Right," Ian said, nervous that the younger boy had been rifling through his thoughts. Ian turned to face him and saw that Wolfie was blushing, but he quickly cast his eyes back to his book. Ian eyed Carl and saw that his friend was looking curiously at him. He wanted to tell Carl to guard his own thoughts very carefully, but at that moment Wolfie got up abruptly from his bed and moved to the door.

"I think I'll go out for a bit of air," he said, and with that he was gone.

"What was that about?" Carl asked.

Ian placed a finger to his lips and moved to the door. Carefully cracking it open, he peered into the hallway and saw the young Van Schuft dashing down the corridor, intent on putting some distance between them.

Ian closed the door and turned to face Carl. "He read my mind, Carl."

"When?"

"When we were making our beds."

Carl's eyes widened. "Does he know who we are?"

Ian frowned. "I don't think so. I wasn't thinking about anything at the time but the sheets."

"They're terrible," Carl said, eyeing his bed with distaste. "Who could sleep on such awful itchy things?"

Ian nodded. "That's exactly what I was thinking when he read my thoughts."

Carl sighed and sat down on his half-made bed. "If he can read our minds that easily, Ian, then how are we going to trick him into following us into the woods?"

Frustrated, Ian ran a hand through his hair. "I have no idea. But I believe the greater danger is in preventing him from figuring out who we are and where we're from."

Carl's eyes went wide again. "Gaw!" he said. "Ian, if he roots around in our heads and sees that we're British, he'll turn us both in and we'll be shot!"

"Exactly," Ian said, his hands trembling a little when he realized the terrible and precarious nature of their mission.

"What're we to do?"

Ian looked again at the door. "When we're around Wolfie, we'll have to keep our thoughts as innocent as possible. Think about what you'd like for lunch, or think about the weather, but don't think about home, or our quest or anything that might make him suspicious."

Carl looked at him as if he'd just said something outlandish. "*How* do you propose we persuade him over to the woods and kidnap him if we can't think about it beforehand?"

Ian sighed. "I have no idea, Carl. Perhaps we could offer Wolfie a distraction so that he's preoccupied and unable to rummage round in our minds while we work him close to the woods."

"What sort of preoccupation did you have in mind?"

Ian shrugged. "Dunno. But I'll think of something," he promised.

Carl frowned. "Yeah, all right. Let's have a go at him now, though, all right? Being surrounded by so many swastikas is making me twitchy."

They searched all about the dormitory for Wolfie but couldn't locate him anywhere. "Maybe he went back to the room?" Carl suggested when they had searched the library to no avail.

"Worth a look," Ian said.

The two young men trooped back up the stairs, crested the landing, and were about to turn down the corridor leading to their room when Carl reached out and caught

Ian by the arm. "Look!" he whispered, pointing below to the drive and a black sedan. Out of the car came Wolfie's father, looking as angry as any man Ian had ever seen. They watched from above as Dieter pointed to a priest, called him over, and spoke to him with rigid shoulders, his hands held in tight fists. For his part the priest shook his head and stepped back from Van Schuft, obviously unsettled by the encounter, and then, as if he'd known his father was nearby, Wolfie emerged from a door on the other side of the courtyard.

Dieter pointed to his son and ordered him over, and even from the upstairs landing Ian and Carl could see the fear in the boy's face. "That doesn't look good," Carl said.

Wolfie approached his father tentatively, which seemed only to make the elder Van Schuft angrier. He pointed again at Wolfie, then to the ground in front of him, and his son wisely quickened his step.

Meanwhile, the nearby priest was edging slowly away, as if the last thing he wanted to witness was the stern lecture that was sure to follow.

But when Wolfie arrived in front of his father, it was not a lecture that he received; it was a slap so hard that the boy went hurtling backward, landing flat on his back to stare up in surprise.

Dieter didn't leave him lying there for long; instead, he marched straight over to his son and lifted him roughly up, holding him by the shirt while he smacked him repeatedly.

"Oh, that's not right!" Carl cried, and Ian found himself

growing so angry about the abuse Wolfie was suffering that he thought seriously about dashing outside to pummel Van Schuft into leaving his son alone.

And then a small crowd of boys began to gather round, their faces horrified, and the poor priest who'd been called over by Dieter was attempting to pull him away from his son, but Dieter continued to strike his son again and again until poor Wolfie's nose and lip were bloody.

"Someone do something!" Carl growled, his hands gripping the banister until his knuckles were white. Just as Ian was about to bolt down the stairs to go help, however, three other priests, including the headmaster, went running outside and angrily shoved Dieter away from the poor boy.

Van Schuft was heaving and there was a crazed look to his eyes, but he threw off the hands of the priests, cursed at his son, and stomped away. A moment later the wheels of his car were spinning out of the drive, kicking up gravel as he fled.

While Ian and Carl watched, the courtyard below grew oddly quiet and all eyes fell on Wolfie. Two priests were now hovering over him and one of them picked him up and carried him away.

"Where do you think they're taking him?" Carl asked, his voice hoarse with rage.

"To the infirmary, I believe," Ian told him, radiating anger as well.

"We'll have to get word to Mr. Goodwyn," Carl whispered.

"Wait until the dinner bell has sounded," Ian told him.

"No one will be about then to see us sneaking off into the woods."

The bell for the evening meal was rung a short time later, and as Ian and Carl huddled in their rooms, they heard the sound of thunderous footsteps in the hall. Carl's stomach rumbled, and Ian couldn't help giving him a grin. "We'll eat after we speak with Mr. Goodwyn."

"Let's go now, then," Carl said.

The pair left their room and took the stairs down to the ground floor. Making sure no latecomers to the dinner hall were about, they snuck out the door and made their way cautiously to the woods.

They'd gone no more than a few yards beyond the tree line when they heard "Ian! Carl! Over here!"

Ian turned to his left and spotted their headmaster, still dressed in his black uniform and peeking up moodily at the sky. "I believe it's going to rain," he said when they'd approached and stopped in front of him.

"Wolfie's been taken to the infirmary," Ian told him, getting straight to the point just as he heard a *plop, plop, plop* sound and knew that the rain had already begun.

"What's happened?" Perry asked.

Ian and Carl told him all about the encounter between Wolfie and his father. "Good heavens," Perry said when they were through. "I wonder what the devil set him off."

Ian had a terrible thought. What if Dieter had discovered the chess box and the destroyed chess pieces? What if he'd assumed his son was the culprit? He turned to Carl and the look on his face suggested he might be thinking the same. Still, neither one of them spoke that theory out loud.

"We'll have to work quickly," Perry said. "You say he's been taken to the infirmary?"

"We think that's where they've taken him," said Carl. "I mean, he was a bloody mess, Mr. Goodwyn."

Perry frowned. "Language, Carl," he warned.

Carl shook his head. "No, sir! I meant he was actually bleeding and looked a mess."

"Oh," said Perry. "Right. Well then, you two must go to the infirmary and have a chat with the school nurse. See how badly he's injured and report back to me here."

Ian and Carl nodded, then sprinted back the way they'd come.

It took them a bit to find the infirmary, and when they finally did locate it, they discovered that Wolfie had already been released and was likely at supper. Carl and Ian hurried to the large dining hall, filled with laughing and chatty young men, but as they scoured the room with their eyes, they found no sign of the young Van Schuft.

"He's not here," Ian growled.

"Let's have a bite to eat, then," Carl said.

Ian frowned. "We've no time for that, Carl. We've got to find Wolfie."

"Aww, it'll just take a minute, Ian," Carl complained. "Come on, mate, I've had nothing since this afternoon!"

But Ian could feel a mounting tension inside him. "Nick a few rolls and leave the rest, Carl. We can't stay."

Carl grumbled under his breath but retrieved the rolls

all the same, and the pair went in search of Wolfie once again. "If I'd received such a beating from my father, I wouldn't show up for dinner either," Carl said as they left the dining hall.

Ian paused and turned to his friend. "You're right!" he said. "I' wouldn't either. I'd have gone straight back to my room."

Without further delay Ian and Carl ran back across the grounds to their dormitory and rushed up to their room. When Ian opened their door, however, he stopped short.

Poor Wolfie Van Schuft sat on the floor, shoveling clothes into a linen bag, his face puffed and swollen with bruises. "Get out!" he shouted when he saw them.

Ian was so surprised by his outburst that at first he couldn't think of a reply.

"I said get out!" Wolfie shouted again, glaring at Ian, and in a wink all Ian wanted to do was leave the room.

"We should go," he said, turning to Carl and moving to push him back from the open door.

"Hang on, mate," Carl said, pushing back against Ian. "We can't leave him."

Suddenly, Ian returned to his own senses and saw the expression on Carl's face change. "Oh, of course we should go!" said Carl. And instead of pushing against Ian, he took his arm and began to pull him from the doorframe.

But Ian realized instantly what was happening and he tugged out of Carl's grasp. Turning around, he spoke quickly and calmly. "Wolfie," he said, "I'm terribly sorry about what happened to you, but we'd like to help."

Wolfie glowered at him, and Ian could actually feel the young boy enter his mind again, but Ian pushed against the sensation with all his might, holding stubbornly to his own thoughts. After a moment the sensation eased and Wolfie rubbed at his temples as if he had a terrible headache, which Ian did not doubt he had.

"I'm leaving," Wolfie said, turning back to his sack. "Don't try and stop me!"

Carl pushed his way into the room. "We wouldn't dream of it," he said. "I saw what your father did to you, and I wouldn't wait around for another beating like that either."

The young lad paused his packing. "I didn't do it," he whispered, and Ian heard him sniffle.

"Do what?" Ian asked.

Wolfie looked up, his eyes almost pleading with Ian to believe him. "My papa accused me of taking something from our house, and I didn't do it."

Ian knew for certain then what the poor boy had been accused of. "I believe you," he said.

Again Wolfie rubbed his temples and looked away. "I have a terrible headache," he whispered.

"We can help, you know," Carl said.

"Help what?" asked Wolfie.

Carl pointed to the linen sack. "You to run away. We know a place where you can go. Somewhere out of this rain where no one will find you."

Wolfie eyed Carl, as if wondering if this was some sort

of a trick. Ian hoped that the boy wouldn't pry too far into Carl's thoughts and discover the truth.

"Would you like a roll?" Carl asked suddenly, offering one of the several buns he'd pinched from the dining hall.

Wolfie's face softened. "Thank you," he said, taking it from Carl.

Ian smiled. Good old Carl. "Come on," he said, reaching for the sack Wolfie had packed. "Let's be off before the other boys are through with dinner."

With no small amount of satisfaction, Ian was relieved when he saw Wolfie get up and follow them out of the room. Now, if only their luck would hold until they reached the portal, all would go as planned.

UNWELCOME GUESTS

D ieter Van Schuft returned to his home shaken and
sickened by the brutal beating he'd given his son.
With trembling fingers he pulled the small pawn out of his
pocket and set it on the top of his bureau.

He had never struck Wolfie with such unrestrained violence before, and Dieter cringed away from the chess piece
on his bureau as if it were a deadly serpent. He remembered
the rush of pleasure that had come from smacking his own
son, and now that he was away from the influence of the
Gorgonite, he found that memory disgusting.

Dieter closed his eyes and covered his face with his
hands. He'd knocked the boy senseless—of that he was certain. And for what? *What?*

Magus the Black was likely never coming back to claim
his precious chess set. His master had intended it for the
Führer, and Dieter likely would have offered it to him as a
present if it could have curried him favor. But even Dieter
knew that Adolf Hitler had the seeds of madness within

him, and he'd hidden the chess set for over a year without giving it to the Führer because he knew it could prove far more lethal than he'd intended.

So he'd debated what to do with it, never really deciding. And now his son had made the decision for him. He'd effectively dismantled the set and rendered it unusable.

After carrying the pawn in his pocket for a day and a half while he'd dealt with his superior, he had become more and more angry at his son. It had taken all his willpower, in fact, not to shout obscenities at the visiting Oberführer, which would have won him a court-martial. And the moment the Oberführer had allowed him to leave, Dieter had driven straight to the school, intent on having Wolfie give him back the precious metal and jewels.

But the moment he'd seen his son, Dieter had lost all control. And all over a chess set that no one but he and his former master knew of. When he thought of the dismantled pieces, Dieter had to admit that he was actually grateful to his son for doing exactly that. The chess set was far too dangerous an object.

Dieter moved unsteadily into the living room, where he rooted around in the side bar for his decanter of scotch. After pouring himself a stiff drink, he swallowed it in one gulp.

He felt no better.

He began pouring his second drink when the large oak tree outside his window rustled and groaned from a strong wind bending the branches. Dieter paused with the glass partway to his mouth as he looked outside and saw a most unusual sight. The rain had turned to snow.

Setting the glass down, Dieter moved to the kitchen door and stared out into the snowy yard. He saw two figures approaching the house, both of them tall and imposing.

He squinted through the pane and realized suddenly that he recognized one of them, and the breath caught in his throat. "Caphiera!"

Peering harder, he was certain that the second figure was none other than her frightful sister Atroposa. *Oh, no!* Dieter thought.

If they were here, was his master, Magus the Black, far behind? Dieter considered with a pounding heart what it would mean if Magus had indeed survived his encounter with his other sister, Lachestia. Dieter thought it unlikely he would live long enough to beg for his life if Magus had been rescued by these two and come in search of his loyal servant. Especially after Magus discovered what had become of his chess set.

And what would that mean for Wolfie? The boy would be hunted down like a dog and killed if Magus suspected that Wolfie was responsible for taking the metal off the chess pieces.

Still, Dieter didn't see his master. Only the two sisters, who had now stepped into his yard. He noticed that Caphiera wore some sort of patch over one eye, and Dieter made sure not to look directly into the other.

"Van Schuft!" Caphiera called.

At first, Dieter didn't move. He didn't know why the sisters had come to his home, and he wasn't at all certain that he wanted to know.

"Come out!" Atroposa ordered, her voice mournful and horrible.

Dieter gathered his courage and stepped out the door. Bowing low, he said, "Mistress Atroposa. Mistress Caphiera. To what do I owe the pleasure of your company?"

"We are in search of Magus the Black," said Caphiera.

Dieter stood up and was careful to avoid looking at her face. Instead, he focused his gaze on her long white coat, which was unusually unkempt and even torn in places. "He's not here, my mistress."

"Of course he's not here, you idiot!" Caphiera snapped.

"Forgive me," said Dieter, bowing low again. From experience he knew it was best to appear contrite when dealing with one of Demogorgon's brood. "I know only that my master has gone in search of his sister, the sorceress of earth. I have not heard what has become of him."

"He's been taken prisoner by Lachestia," Atroposa told him. "We're here to have you retrieve his mutts to help us track his location. We understand you know how to summon and command them?"

Dieter stiffened. He did indeed know how to call and control the hellhounds. In fact, he had a golden whistle hidden in the back of his wardrobe that allowed him to do just that. "I do," he said to them, thinking quickly. If he used the whistle and called the hellhounds, he would have complete control over them. Whoever blew the whistle controlled the beasts for at least a short time, so if he asked them to track their master, they would most certainly obey; however, the beasts were also the mortal enemies of

Caphiera, who had often tried to kill them. The hellhounds were as ferocious as lions, and like a lion needed the constant crack of a whip to remind it who was in control, so would the beasts need to hear the constant sound of the whistle to remain under Dieter's command.

The beasts would obey Dieter if he consistently used the whistle, but their instincts would be to attack or run away from Caphiera if Dieter did not assist.

That meant he would be required to go along with the sorceresses while the beasts hunted for their master, and with the beasts leading the way, the evil sisters would eventually discover their brother and liberate him. Dieter had little doubt about that. Once Magus was freed and discovered the condition of his chess set, Dieter's life would most certainly come to an abrupt end.

But, Dieter wondered, what if he used the whistle to his advantage? Perhaps there would be a moment when the sisters weren't looking that he could turn the beasts on them and escape with his life? Certainly the sorceresses would hunt for him, but he and Wolfie could go into hiding. Only his master knew how to track Dieter to the ends of the earth, a thought that made him shudder.

Dieter gulped while his thoughts whirred. "I have my master's whistle," he said finally. "But the beasts have been ordered to stay in the mountains, and if I call them, it will take at least a day if not longer for them to arrive."

"Get it," said Caphiera, her tone as cold as her heart. "And bring it here to summon them."

Dieter offered no further argument. He bowed out of

the yard and went back into the house, his fingers trembling along the wall as he walked to his bedroom and over to the wardrobe. He opened the door, reaching for one of his old uniforms at the very back—Dieter never threw anything out. After his master had set off to find the sorceress Lachestia, he had given Dieter the whistle and ordered him to keep it in a safe place. As Dieter had been promoted to the rank of storm command leader, he'd kept the whistle around the hanger of one of the uniforms of his previous rank, making sure it was well hidden at the back of his wardrobe next to a cluster of unused hangers, where no one was likely to find the whistle. Pulling out the last uniform on the rack, he was shocked to find the whistle missing.

"What is this?" he gasped, tearing the old uniform from the hanger and letting it drop carelessly to the floor. He then threw the hanger over his shoulder and poked his way into the back of the wardrobe, searching all the remaining hangers, tearing off each coat and casting it away as he searched desperately for the whistle. He then got down on hands and knees and searched the floor, but it wasn't there. No, the whistle was gone!

"*Wolfie!*" he growled, thinking it had to be his son, searching the house for items to steal along with the silver. And of course the whistle would appeal to him; it was made of gold, and what boy could resist a golden whistle? "Oh, my son, what *have* you done?"

Outside, another gust of wind rustled the trees and he knew the sorceresses were growing impatient. It was then that he had an idea. He hurried back through the house to the yard. "Mistresses," he said, bowing low again. "I had forgotten that I had hidden the whistle in my desk at work. If you will allow me to retrieve it, I promise that I shall not be long."

He could feel the impatience of the evil sisters wafting off them both. "Fine," said Atroposa after a lengthy pause. "But be quick about it. We shall wait for you here."

Dieter bowed again and backed out of the yard. A few moments later he was in his car, once more speeding toward the school.

FLIGHT AND FRIGHT

I an, Carl, and Wolfie got outside only to realize that it
was still pouring down rain. "Did you manage to pack an
umbrella in there?" Carl asked, hunching low into his coat
and pointing to the satchel Ian carried for Wolfie.

"I forgot it," the young boy said, his face sad and swollen.

"Well, come along," said Ian. "We know the perfect
hiding place not far from here."

To avoid being spotted by the boys returning from the
dining hall, Ian had led them out the back entrance, which
meant they had to circle around the abbey to reach
the woods on the far side.

With Ian in the lead, they edged carefully along the
building, ducking low under the windows so that no one
would see them sneaking about in the rain with a sack full
of clothing between them.

"Where is this place you know of?" Wolfie asked as the
woods came into view.

Ian was caught slightly off guard. He knew that Wolfie

might have resisted overusing his abilities upstairs due to his headache, but here he might force himself inside Ian's head if he became suspicious.

Keeping his thoughts as neutral as possible, Ian replied, "It's a cave, Wolfie. A place in the hills where no one will think to look for you, and inside it you'll be safe enough."

Ian then focused his thoughts on the view he'd first had of the valley below the portal gate and how beautiful it had been.

He couldn't be certain, but he had an odd little tickling sensation at the back of his thoughts, which suggested that Wolfie was rooting about for information. "Where will you go?" he asked the boy to distract him.

"My mother had a sister in Vienna," Wolfie said. "I met her once when I was little. She was nice to me."

"I'm sorry your father beat you," Ian said, and he honestly meant it.

Behind him Wolfie was silent a moment before he said, "Papa hasn't been the same since my mother died."

Ian looked behind him, Carl was frowning and Ian could read the complex mix of emotions there too. Frau Van Schuft had been an evil woman, but Wolfie probably didn't know that.

"There," said Ian, pointing to the tree he remembered hiding behind when he'd first seen the abbey up close. "That's where we'll need to go." He was about to dart across the short stretch of grass when he heard a rumbling sound from the drive. A motorcar was just pulling up to the abbey, and Ian recognized it and the driver immediately.

He heard Wolfie gasp in fear. "Back around the building!" Ian said, turning and waving Wolfie and Carl away.

"Why's he come back?" Carl said when they'd scuttled round the corner and peered back at the motorcar.

Dieter got out and slammed the door, eyeing the dormitory with malice.

"Don't let him find me!" Wolfie begged them, shivering pathetically beside Ian.

"Shhh!" Ian warned. "Wolfie, be quiet and wait until your father goes inside the building."

Dieter began to do just that when a priest stepped out of the abbey and right up to the elder man. "Herr Van Schuft," the priest said. Ian realized it was the headmaster himself.

"I must see my son," Dieter said curtly. "Immediately!"

The priest put up his arms as if to block him. "Your son has received quite enough of your attention for one evening," the priest said reasonably. "Now why don't you go home, Herr Van Schuft, and come back tomorrow for a visit?"

Other priests emerged from the abbey and gathered in the rain around the headmaster. Dieter looked at them as if he were a cornered rat. "You don't understand!" he said to them. "My son has stolen something from me, and I must retrieve it."

"What has he stolen?" the head priest asked, his tone changing to concern.

"A whistle," the desperate father said. "And I *must* have it back!"

325

Ian went rigid and out the corner of his eye he could see that Carl had too.

"I never took any whistle!" Wolfie said feebly, and then he too stiffened. Turning his head slowly, the young boy looked at Carl and at the shiny gold whistle dangling from his neck. "*You!*" he said accusingly.

"I can explain," said Carl, looking at Ian as if to ask for help.

Ian pressed his lips together and wrapped one hand around Wolfie's mouth and the other around his middle. "I'm terribly sorry," he said as the boy struggled against him. Almost immediately he felt Wolfie bolt into his thoughts and nearly convince him to let him go.

Desperate to fight off the feeling, Ian smacked his head against the wall, and in his arms he felt Wolfie flinch even as his own head erupted in pain. "Carl!" Ian commanded. "We've got to be off!"

Carl slapped his hand over the one covering Wolfie's mouth and grabbed Ian by the arm. "He can't get into both our heads," he said, and began to lead them to the edge of the woods.

Ian knew that at any moment they might be spotted, but they had to risk it now that Wolfie knew he and Carl had been in his house and had stolen his father's things.

His own ears were ringing with the smack he'd given himself, and he wished he hadn't done that quite so hard. Once Carl brought them into the trees, Ian sank to his knees to catch his breath. Wolfie was small for a boy, but he was still heavy.

"Ian!" Carl said, crouching down and keeping his hand firmly over Ian's. "We must move deeper into the trees! I believe Van Schuft saw us!"

Ian gulped down a lungful of air and struggled to stand up again. Wolfie kicked and squirmed but Ian wasn't about to let go. He had taken two steps when Carl paused, let go of Ian, and moved to a tree, which he thumped his own head against. Again, Wolfie flinched in Ian's arms, and Carl turned around, saying, "Do that again and I'll give myself such a wallop that you'll be sorry for a month!"

Ian would have smiled if the situation hadn't been so dire. "We must find Mr. Goodwyn!" Ian said desperately.

Carl appeared to waver between helping Ian with Wolfie and dashing off to retrieve their schoolmaster. "It's just a bit farther," he said, taking up Wolfie's feet, and Ian was glad he'd decided to stay with him.

The muddy forest floor dragged them down as they wound their way through the wet foliage, at last coming to the spot where a very wet Perry stood waiting miserably in the rain for them.

"Whatever took you lads so long?" he said when he'd spotted them.

Again, Ian sank to his knees, his arms ready to give way under the weight of the still struggling lad. Perry came forward quickly and helped Ian with Wolfie, but when Ian took his hand away from the boy's mouth, Wolfie let out a small shout before Ian could clamp it down again.

"Let me," Perry insisted, winding his own arms around Wolfie and being careful not to let him shout again.

"Thank you, sir," Ian said, letting go and sagging against a tree.

Perry smiled. "Of course," he said, then turned and set Wolfie down. Patting him on the head, he said, "Off with you now, young man. Back to your father you go."

The next moment, Wolfie jumped toward Carl, snapped the whistle from his neck, and dashed away back toward the abbey, blowing mightily on the whistle as he ran.

"No!" Ian shouted, bolting after him, but he was caught by the arm and held firmly in check by Perry.

Meanwhile, Carl, who'd been left a little stunned when the whistle had been torn from his neck, collected himself and dashed off after Wolfie. Ian watched helplessly as the pair quickly disappeared into the thick tangle of trees. The moment Wolfie was out of sight, Perry released Ian and wobbled backward. "I say, Ian, what just happened?"

Ian didn't wait to explain; instead, he took off running after Carl and Wolfie. He'd gone perhaps a hundred meters when he heard a sharp yelp and a desperate cry for help.

Ian ran straight for the noise and within seconds came upon a sight that pulled him up short. Adrastus of Lixus had hold of both Wolfie and Carl, although only Wolfie seemed to be fighting the restraint.

Looking up at Ian, the general smiled and said, "These two belong to you?"

"General!" Ian said, panting for air. "Thank you for catching the Thinker."

Adrastus turned Wolfie, who was dangling above the

328

ground, to face him. "Your mind games won't work on me, little one. Best to save your strength, eh?"

"Let me go!" Wolfie cried pitifully, but Adrastus clearly had no intention of doing that. He did release Carl, however, who seemed all too glad to set his feet back on the ground.

Carl brushed himself off, pocketed the whistle he'd recovered from Wolfie, and asked, "Where's Mistress Adria and Iyoclease?"

Adrastus appeared surprised. "They've come through the portal with you?"

Both Ian and Carl nodded. "They split up from us to go in search of you, sir," Ian told him.

The general pressed his lips together in irritation. "I have not seen them," he said. "And now that you have the Thinker, this is most unsettling. The portal will be opening soon, especially since I have the box with me."

"You'll give it to us?" Ian asked him. "Just like that?"

Adrastus nodded. "It appears that if you two found the fifth Oracle here, then that is what the prophecy wants me to do," he said. "I should not want my wife and Iyoclease to be in this dangerous place a moment longer than necessary. Come. I will see you to the portal and across, then go in search of my wife and Iyoclease."

"But what about Mr. Goodwyn?" Carl protested, his eyes searching the woods for any sign of their schoolmaster.

"There's one more with us, General," Ian said. "Our schoolmaster, who was waiting for us to coax Wolfie out of the school."

Adrastus growled, his impatience clearly expressed in his dark eyes, but at that moment, Perry appeared. Yet even when he waved to them, Ian saw the general put a hand on his sword. "He's our friend, General," Ian said quickly.

Adrastus's eyes slanted at Ian. "You are friends with the SS?"

"It's a costume," Carl told him. "We pinched it from Van Schuft's home."

The general's eyebrows rose. "Van Schuft? *He* is here?"

Ian nodded. "His house is just up this hill and to the left. You can see it from the entrance to the portal."

In Adrastus's arms, Wolfie squirmed and struggled with renewed vigor. "And that's Van Schuft's son," Carl said, a mean look in his eyes. "Can you believe that Laodamia actually wants us to bring him back through the portal?"

Adrastus appeared thoughtful, and he eyed the small boy curiously. "Van Schuft's son?" he said. "Well then, lads, by all means, let's send him through to Dover before his father can intercede."

Perry led them through the drizzle up the slippery slopes. When they all heard the sound of an approaching motorcar, they waited for it to pass. Ian saw with some satisfaction that behind the wheel was Dieter Van Schuft, but poor Wolfie saw his father too and he took up his battle to be released from the steel embrace of General Adrastus. "There, there, lad," Adrastus told him. "You'll not get loose from my grip, so it's better to stop your squirming."

Wolfie complied, rather abruptly, actually; however, in

the next moment, Perry had stepped into the roadway and was waving frantically after the motorcar.

Carl rounded immediately on Wolfie and struck him across the head. "Stop it!" he snarled.

Ian called to his schoolmaster, but it was too late. Van Schuft had seen Perry in the rearview mirror, and the motorcar screeched to a halt. Adrastus swore under his breath and silently edged back down the slope, taking Wolfie out of range.

Ian and Carl remained hidden in the shrubbery, watching with pounding hearts as the motorcar backed up and came to stop next to Perry.

Although Ian strained to hear what was said, he could hear nothing coherent, so he could only stare at his schoolmaster and attempt to read his body language. To his horror, Perry merely nodded and went round to the other side of the vehicle before glancing gravely in their direction and getting in. A moment later Van Schuft gunned the engine and he and Perry sped off.

"Oh, this is a bloody fine mess!" Carl snapped, stepping up to the roadway and peering after the motorcar. "Where do you think he's taken him?"

Ian didn't have a chance to answer. Behind him the foliage rustled and up came the general. "What's happened?" he asked.

"Van Schuft's taken Mr. Goodwyn."

"Taken him?" Adrastus repeated.

Ian nodded.

"Was it against his will?"

"No," Ian said. "I believe he went of his own accord."

Adrastus nodded. "Very well," he said. "Let's be on our way to the portal door."

Ian's jaw dropped. "But what about Mr. Goodwyn?" he cried. "We can't just *leave* him!"

The general leveled his eyes at Ian. "We can, and we must," he said. "Your friend has gained us a distraction and some valuable time, Ian. We should not waste the opportunity."

Carl brashly approached the general, however, his hands firmly placed on his hips. "No!" he yelled. "Mr. Goodwyn is our friend, and we'll not go back through the portal without him!"

Adrastus sighed as if he was terribly weary. "Carl," he said. "Would you have your friend Mr. Goodwyn's efforts go to waste? Further, would you place his life in even more jeopardy by attempting a rescue when he very well may not need one?"

"What are you talking about?" Ian shouted, his anger and fear for the well-being of his schoolmaster getting the better of him. "Van Schuft's taken him away! He'll probably shoot him before the evening is over!"

Adrastus stepped up to the road and began walking purposely across it. Over his shoulder he said, "Mr. Goodwyn went willingly, Ian. Dressed in that uniform, he's no doubt fooled Van Schuft, at least for now."

"But we can't leave him here!" Ian insisted, refusing to

walk after the general, and he was grateful that Carl stood next to him in silent objection.

With another audible sigh, Adrastus turned to face them. "All right," he said, relenting. "Allow me to get you three through the portal to safety and I give you my word that I will go after Mr. Goodwyn and send him back through as well. *Then* I will see to my wife and Iyoclease."

Ian winced at the particularly harsh tone to the general's speech. He seemed thoroughly out of patience with them all.

As if to confirm that, the general whirled around and barked, "Come! We must make haste and see this mission over and all of you to safety!"

Ian looked at Carl, who nodded. They would both co-operate now that the general had agreed to help their friend.

The pair trotted across the road and followed Adrastus up the slope to another set of trees. They had nearly caught up to him, in fact, when a piercing howl cut through the drizzling haze and sent goose pimples all along Ian's arms. "A hellhound!" he cried just before a second howl drowned out his voice.

When it ended, Carl turned his pale face to Ian and said, "Make that two."

THE RUSE IS UP

"Thank you for stopping," the drenched officer said, offering a small salute and a "Heil Hitler" as the motorcar came to a stop.

Dieter Van Schuft returned the salute impatiently. He'd thought about not stopping when he'd spotted the officer in his rearview mirror, but Berchtesgaden was a small town and word might travel among the rank and file that he'd left a fellow officer stranded. "Whatever are you doing out here in the rain?" Dieter demanded, noting that the storm leader was one rank below him.

The officer pointed down the road away from the school. "I was driving in from Berlin when my motorcar broke down," he explained. "A young boy walking along the road told me there was an abbey in this direction and that I might find assistance there."

Dieter focused on the man's words. When he'd insisted on seeing his son, a priest had been sent to bring Wolfie to him, and it was only then that they'd all learned that his

334

son had indeed run away. He'd even taken most of his clothes with him. "A young boy, you say?"

The officer nodded. "Yes." Holding his hand just above his waist, the officer said, "About this high and no older than eleven or twelve. Small for his age, I suspect, but most helpful."

Dieter peered at the long stretch of road in front of him. "I'm in search of a young boy of that description," he said. "Did he tell you his name?"

"He did indeed, sir, as I demanded he tell it to me. He said his name was Wolfgang Van Schuft. Do you know him?"

Dieter gripped the steering wheel with steely fingers. "I do indeed. I am Herr Van Schuft, Wolfgang's father, and you must show me where you discovered him," he said. "And in exchange, I will drive you to headquarters and ensure a guard is sent for your motorcar."

But the officer begged off. "Oh, Herr Van Schuft, that is most kind of you, but I am sure you will find your son by simply following this road a few kilometers. Wolfgang appears to be walking his way to Vienna."

Dieter clamped his jaws together and struggled to rein in his temper. Something about the young officer disturbed him, but he couldn't put his finger on it. "What is your name, Storm Leader?"

"Goodwyn, sir. I am Otto Goodwyn."

"Well, Herr Goodwyn," Dieter said, his voice only slightly better than a snarl. "I must insist that you get in. *Now.*"

The officer didn't answer him right away, but finally he said, "Yes, sir. As you wish."

After Herr Goodwyn was settled, Dieter drove away. He had to reach Wolfie and retrieve the whistle. The sorceresses were waiting, and he knew from experience that Demogorgon's brood were not long on patience.

They drove along in silence for a bit, Dieter scanning the sides of the road for any sign of his son, the man beside him watchful too.

After speeding along for at least two kilometers, Dieter slowed the car, his eyes darting left and right. "Where did you say you spotted my son?" he asked, slowing the car even more.

"There!" Herr Goodwyn said, pointing to a large crevice in the side of the rock to Dieter's right. "I remember I had just come upon that section there. I believe your son was not far from here."

Dieter pressed on the gas again, his heart racing. He had to find Wolfie, and do so quickly. Still there was no sign of him. Dieter pulled over and looked behind him, through the glass pane, at the rear of the car.

"Perhaps he's hiding," the officer said, and for the first time, Dieter detected the nervous undertones to his voice. He'd been specifically trained by his master to detect such signs in people, and he realized what he hadn't fully noticed at first: the man was jittery, as if he was trying very hard to conceal something.

Dieter turned his shrewd eyes on the officer. "Or," he

said easily, "perhaps this weather has got the better of him and he has sought shelter after all."

The officer seemed to jump at the conclusion. "Yes, yes!" he said. "As I recall, the boy did mention something about wanting to get out of the rain. In fact, now that I think on it, Herr Van Schuft, I believe the boy may have returned home. He lives nearby, am I right?"

Something inside Dieter shifted, and he knew, without a doubt, that this officer not only knew what had happened to his son, but had something to do with his disappearance. He was careful to keep his suspicions guarded. "Yes," he said. "Our home is not far from here. Back two kilometers and up the mountain a bit."

The officer smiled and seemed to relax. "Well, there you are!" he said. Moving to open his door, he added, "And I shall not keep you from your son a moment longer. I will find my own assistance, Herr Van Schuft, thank you very much." The man then turned away to step out of the car but was halted by the click of Dieter's Luger pistol.

"Not so fast," he ordered, and the officer complied, raising his hands above his head. "Where is my son?"

"Herr Van Schuft," the officer pleaded. "I have no idea where your son is. I told you, I saw him on the road and he directed me toward the abbey."

Dieter didn't believe him for a moment. He considered shooting him there and then, but someone might hear the noise and ask questions, and he wouldn't learn where his son was that way either. Instead, Dieter considered taking the man somewhere and torturing the truth out of him. He couldn't bring him home—the sorceresses were still hovering in his yard—but he thought of a bluff near his house with a cave built into the side. Dieter would take the man there and get the truth out.

Tucking the gun low in his lap, he shifted the car into drive and with some difficulty managed to turn it around. "I think we will have a chat about what you know and what you don't," Dieter told him. "I'm sure it will be quite revealing."

They'd gone no farther than a kilometer back the way they'd come, when the first howl rang out from the hilly terrain above them. Dieter's blood ran cold and he nearly lost his focus. Wolfie had somehow managed to blow the whistle, which meant that he was possibly still alive, but also now a primary target for the beasts. When he glanced sideways at the officer to make sure he wasn't trying any tricks, he noticed how starkly pale the man had turned, and his pallor became even more blanched when the second howl rang out. If Dieter hadn't known better, he'd have guessed that the man sitting next to him knew exactly what beast was creating the sound.

Dieter pressed the pedal all the way to the floor and drove as fast as he could, hoping only to reach his son ahead of the hellhounds.

THE SECRET KEEPER'S BETRAYAL

Adrastus moved like a panther through the woods, seemingly mindless of the hilly and difficult terrain. As Ian struggled alongside Carl to keep up with the general, he noted how much easier it had been to come down than it was to move up it. And this was the source of his mounting fear; the hellhounds would have no such difficulties. They were built to traverse such lands quickly and efficiently. The beasts were certain to catch up with them if they didn't reach the portal very, very soon.

"Hurry!" Adrastus called over his shoulder when he looked back and saw the young men lagging behind.

Beside Ian, Carl slipped and fell. His sides heaving, Ian reached back and gripped his friend by the arm, hauling him up and pushing Carl in front of him. It was then that he heard the sound again, that piercing cry and hollow howl lingering in the air like smoke above the bluff.

Carl grunted as he grabbed at the trees around him, pulling himself as much as pushing with his legs. Ian took his lead and did the same, using all his limbs to help keep ahead of them. "Not much farther!" Adrastus called, his lead up the slope even wider now. Ian watched his back with frustration. The man was impossible to keep up with. But then, after a few more meters, Adrastus came to an abrupt halt, ducked low, and edged back down toward Ian and Carl.

It took Ian a moment to realize that Adrastus was waving his free hand at them and mouthing, "Down!"

Ian grabbed hold of Carl, who was still hauling himself up the slope. "Wha . . . ?" Carl wheezed.

Ian pointed to the general, coming quickly to their side. When he was directly in front of Ian, he whispered, "The beasts are at the portal."

Ian could feel the blood drain from his face. How had they found it so quickly? "They're surveying the terrain from there," the general added. "We must seek shelter until they pass!"

Carl attempted to speak, but he was panting too strenuously. He settled for pointing down the slope and over to the right. "Van Schuft's house," Ian managed to say, knowing exactly what Carl was thinking.

Adrastus nodded. "Quickly and quietly," he ordered.

Ian nodded and saw Wolfie, white with fear, his eyes large and round as he gazed back up the slope toward where the beasts were waiting. He knew without a doubt that Wolfie had seen the beasts.

With great care the three of them made their way through the forest, edging closer and closer to the safety of

Van Schuft's home. Ian was certain that Carl would have no difficulties gaining entrance again. He only hoped they could find a suitable hiding place away from the monstrous curs.

Only as they closed in on the premises did it occur to Ian that Dieter Van Schuft might be home, but then, he knew that the brave and powerful general Adrastus was more than a match for him.

There was one other thought niggling at the back of Ian's mind, and that was that the appearance of the beasts might signal their master's return. When he'd last seen Magus the Black, he'd been with his sister Lachestia the Wicked. The pair had been so formidable and deadly that Ian had long wondered why they hadn't joined Caphiera and Atroposa in coming after the other Oracles.

And Dieter was the servant of Magus, so were they about to walk into a trap by entering Dieter's house?

He was about to voice his concerns when a howl from the slope above him made it clear that Ian and the others had little choice but to hurry into the home and hope for the best.

"They're coming!" Carl cried.

"There!" Adrastus said. "The house is there!"

The general began to run toward the house, and Ian and Carl ran too. Behind them they could hear foliage breaking and the sounds of large beasts tearing their way through the forest. Ian's legs felt rubbery and weak, but he willed himself forward with every ounce of remaining strength he had.

Several more strides brought them into Dieter's yard. They raced for the back door, but as they drew near it, a motorcar pulled up the winding drive and stopped sharply right in front of them.

Ian, Carl, and Adrastus stopped short when the door of the vehicle burst open and out leapt Dieter Van Schuft, a pistol in his hand and hatred in his eyes. "Unhand my son!" he shouted, leveling his weapon right at the general.

Adrastus stepped carefully in front of Ian and Carl, sweeping his arm back to block them from both Dieter and the approaching beasts. "Point that thing at the forest!" Adrastus demanded. "The beasts approach!"

And with that a thunderous noise filled the yard and two massive beasts stepped forward, their greasy black hackles raised. They snarled to expose wickedly sharp fangs.

Dieter paled when he saw them, and Ian watched him take several steps back, but up behind him came Perry, who snapped the gun out of his hands and pointed it directly at the approaching menaces. "Run!" he told them, but before Ian could even take a step, a great wind gusted through the yard and blew poor Perry straight into the trunk of a tree.

For a moment, Ian was too stunned to speak. A chilling voice called from behind him, which quickly brought him back to his senses. "Dieter Van Schuft!" said the voice. "I had perhaps underestimated your value! Not only have you summoned our brother's beasts for us, but you have also delivered us the Secret Keeper!"

Adrastus turned to face the new threat, his sword raised

high with one hand and Wolfie still clutched in his other. "Step back, Caphiera!" he shouted. "Or I shall kill the boy!"

Ian went rigid with shock. Would the general really kill an innocent boy?

"Oh, by all means," said another voice, hollow and cold, "kill the boy and provide us with a bit of sport too!"

The two sorceresses laughed evilly, and Ian felt sick to the core. "No!" shouted Dieter, running straight for his son, but another gust of wind blew him backward. He landed next to the unconscious Perry. "Ah, ah, ah," Caphiera warned. "Don't spoil the fun, Dieter. Now, go on, Keeper, kill the boy!"

Adrastus hesitated for only a moment before he lowered his sword and set Wolfie down. "I shall not kill an innocent," he said through gritted teeth.

Ian stared at Atroposa. He was afraid to look too closely at Caphiera, lest he be frozen by her stare, so he only heard her when she said, "Well then, Keeper. Allow me to do your dirty work for you. Young boy, come look into my eye, won't you?"

"No!" Ian shouted. Darting out from behind Adrastus, he dove on top of Wolfie, covering the boy's head with his arms.

A cackling of laughter filled the yard again. "Dieter," Caphiera called tauntingly. "It looks as if your son has befriended a . . . *Is that the Guardian?*"

Ian shuddered. Now they knew, and he could only imagine what they'd do next. "Why, Sister!" said Atroposa. "Dieter has indeed delivered more than he promised!"

"Shall we spare his son, then?" Caphiera asked.

Atroposa paused before answering. "It would spoil our fun, but I suppose we can allow one of them to live. Dieter, we will spare your son."

Ian eyed the dreadful man across the lawn as he got unsteadily to his feet. "Thank you, mistresses," he said, motioning to his son to come to him, but Wolfie did something unexpected: he refused to move away from Ian's side.

"Come here, my son," Dieter said.

Wolfie shook his head.

"Come here this instant!" Dieter snapped.

Again Wolfie shook his head. Meanwhile, the growling beasts, which had stayed at the edge of the yard, began to creep forward. Dieter seemed to sense the increasing danger and he begged his son: "Wolfie, if you won't come to me, then give me the whistle!"

"I don't have it!" Wolfie yelled at his father.

Dieter's voice was tinged with panic as the hellhounds took another step toward them. "Wolfie, you don't understand! I need that whistle!" But Wolfie shook his head earnestly, his eyes volleying back and forth between the approaching beasts and his father.

Dieter too watched them creeping forward, crouching low when Adrastus raised his sword. One of the hellhounds moved off from their group then and eyed Dieter while it edged menacingly forward. "Wolfie!" Dieter shouted at the top of his lungs. "I know you took the whistle and called the beasts! It gives you the power to command them! Blow it again and order them away!"

Carl and Ian exchanged looks and then Carl stepped boldly out from behind Adrastus, blew the whistle, and yelled, "Away from us!"

A shriek went out from both Caphiera and Atroposa, who covered their ears with their hands as if the sound caused them pain, but Ian could hear nothing. Still, he knew some kind of sound came out from the whistle, because the hounds laid down their own ears and growled, but both of them stopped their advance and even began to inch back. At the sight of the retreating hellhounds, everyone fell silent. Ian was stunned down to his toes, but perhaps even he wasn't as shocked as Carl. "Crikey!" Carl shouted when he realized what he could do. Blowing on the whistle again, he said, "Roll over and play dead!"

Ian gasped anew when he saw the two ferocious beasts drop down and roll over onto their backs. The scene was so horrible and so outrageous that he actually laughed. But his good humor didn't last long.

"Enough of these games!" shouted Atroposa, still covering one ear with her hand; but as her other arm made a sweeping motion, an arrow hit her in the side.

The sorceress screeched, crumpling to the earth, while a figure stepped out from the trees and came charging forward. As if in a dream, Ian watched Iyoclease raise his sword and swing it at the other sorceress's head.

Unfortunately, the Phoenician soldier had approached Caphiera on the side she could still see from, and at the last second she rushed forward and blocked the blow with a shield of ice, sending him hurtling backward. Adrastus charged Caphiera while her back was turned, but she must have sensed his approach, because she swung around and let loose the ice shield. It struck him in the chest and knocked the wind right out of him. He dropped to his knees, gasping for air.

Ian came to his senses then and grabbed Wolfie's arm, shouting to Carl, "Send the beasts after the sorceresses!"

Carl turned toward the beasts, blew on the whistle, and pointed at Caphiera and Atroposa. *"Attack them!"*

For good measure Carl blew on the whistle several more times, and each time, the beasts growled and whined and the sorceresses screeched, but the hellhounds did leap to their feet and lunge at the evil sisters. Reaching Caphiera first, the hounds darted and snapped at her while she used a new ice shield to deflect them.

Amid the chaos Adria appeared from out of the woods, a dagger in her hand; she adroitly skirted the hounds and Caphiera and ran straight for Atroposa.

But as Adria approached, Atroposa did something extraordinary: she whirled around in a tight circle, creating a thick cloud of dust, blinding everyone and everything in the yard. A moment later the dust cleared, and standing in the middle were Caphiera and Atroposa with Adria trapped between them. "Call off the beasts!" warned Caphiera, barely holding them at bay. "Call them off or Adria dies!"

"No!" Adria shouted, but Carl had already put the whistle to his lips, and with another fierce blow on it, he ordered the beasts to fall back; however, he blew it again and also ordered them to guard the sorceresses, lest they attempt to hurt Adria or flee.

Adrastus got to his feet, helping Iyoclease up too. Ian pulled Wolfie with him as he went to see to Perry, who was just coming back to consciousness.

"Give us the box!" Caphiera commanded. "Give it to us now or your wife will die!"

Adrastus eyed first his wife, then Carl. "We have control over the beasts, Caphiera," he said, avoiding the sorceress's gaze. "If you hurt one hair on my wife's head, Carl here will release the hellhounds and they'll tear you both to pieces!"

Had the sisters been uninjured, the hounds would have been a mere nuisance, but both of them were much worse for wear and everyone in the yard knew it. If the beasts were unleashed, the sorceresses would face a very real threat.

Atroposa turned her hollow eyes on Carl as if she wished she could send him away in a cyclone of fury.

While Ian was watching the scene warily, he was also trying to get his schoolmaster to his feet. He'd turned his back on Dieter, and that was all the opportunity the man needed to dart behind Carl, snatch the whistle from his hand, and shove him roughly to the ground. Then Van Schuft began to blow on the golden instrument in earnest.

Immediately the hellhounds turned their attention away from the sorceresses and over to Dieter. "Keeper," Dieter said menacingly. "Hand me the box or I shall have the hellhounds rip your wife to shreds."

The beasts turned their evil red eyes hungrily to Adria, who bravely stared back at them even though her face drained of color. "My husband," she said softly, her eyes never leaving the beasts, "do *not* betray the Oracle!"

Ian looked to Adrastus, and never a more sorrowful expression had he ever witnessed. The general reached into the folds of his cloak and took out the last silver box. "I swore on my life to Laodamia that I would never willingly give up the boxes to the enemy," he said. "And I meant every word of that oath sworn, but, Wife, my life holds little meaning without you." The general then tossed the treasure to Dieter, who caught it easily.

"Mistresses," Dieter said next. "If I'm to give you this box, which no doubt contains one of Laodamia's final prophecies, then I would like some assurances from you."

Caphiera laughed wickedly. "You do not tell *me* what to do, *mortal!*" she spat. And with a snap of her fingers, she pointed up to the tree Dieter's son was standing under. "See that?" she asked.

Ian raised his eyes and saw that a branch on the tree was bending low due to the weight of one very long and sharp icicle, which dangled dangerously right above Wolfie's head. Another snap, and another icicle appeared; then another and another until the whole tree was lined with them.

"Wolfie," Dieter said very quietly. "Come here, boy."

Wolfie's eyes were large and frightened. He had taken one step toward his father when an icicle dropped to within an inch of his foot. "If he moves even a hair," Caphiera warned, "I shall loose the whole lot upon him!"

Dieter was speechless, his eyes focused on all those deadly icicles. "Hand us the box," Atroposa demanded.

Van Schuft didn't even hesitate. He threw the box directly at Caphiera, who had to duck to avoid being struck. The moment Ian saw the sorceress crouch, he lunged for Wolfie, tackling him and rolling with him away from the tree. All around him he heard *thud, thud, thud,* and when they'd well cleared the branches, he looked back to see that the sorceress had released every one.

But Ian's attention quickly turned back to Caphiera and Atroposa, because he realized that Adria had leapt for the box too, had caught it, and was now holding it between her palms. In the next instant, the air about her shimmered just as the four walls of the silver treasure collapsed inward. In seconds, the beautiful box became a flattened glob of metal.

"*No!*" Caphiera roared when she saw what had become of the box. Adria smiled triumphantly at her and dropped the useless artifact to the ground. A moment later she was impaled by half a dozen icy spears, and she wilted to the earth.

Carl, Iyoclease, and Adrastus, seeing what had befallen Adria, all cried out, each reacting in the same manner as they raised their swords and lunged forward to attack. But then, so did the beasts!

It was as if the chaos released them from Dieter's

control, and they flew into the mix, snarling, growling, and lunging forward. One of them got hold of Atroposa, and Ian saw the sorceress raise another dust cloud, sending the beast hurtling through the air and striking a nearby sapling with such force that the tree broke in half. The beast dropped to the ground near Dieter and lay there for a moment, shaking its head while growling and snarling at its former master. Van Schuft was so startled that he dropped the whistle at the beast's feet. The hellhound's lip curled back menacingly, and Dieter let out a shriek and bolted straight into his home, leaving his son behind.

Perry, who had finally regained his senses, called out to Ian, "Help me get to Adria!"

Ian got to his feet, dragging Wolfie up with him, and the three ran to the side of the fallen woman while Carl, Adrastus, and Iyoclease fought the sorceresses and the other hellhound. Ian crouched next to Adria and looked at her wounds. There was a series of terrible punctures to her upper chest, and blood soaked the ground underneath her. "Ian . . . ," she whispered, clutching his arm.

"I'm here!" he said to her. "We're going to take you through the portal, mistress, and we'll send for our Healer! She'll put things right, don't you worry!"

"No," she gasped. "Too . . . late."

"Try not to talk," Perry told her, bending low and gently easing his arms underneath her.

"Ian . . . ," she repeated as Perry lifted her into the air. And she reached out to grip his arm feebly again, as if she had something terribly important to share with him.

350

"I'm here," Ian said. "But please, try not to talk, mistress."

Adria took a labored breath that sounded more like a gurgle. "Tell . . . Iyoclease . . ."

Ian bent close to her, barely able to hear. "Yes? Tell Iyoclease what?"

"Tell Iyoclease . . . Magus . . . kill . . . him."

Ian stepped back, stunned, and he and Perry shared a silent grim exchange.

"We must get to the portal now, Ian," said the schoolmaster. "Bring the boy and the others!" Perry then turned and hurried out of the yard.

Ian looked down at Wolfie, who was pale as a ghost and staring wide-eyed into space, obviously in shock from his near brush with death and all the awful sights taking place in his yard. Gripping him firmly by the hand, Ian shouted for Carl, who was barely holding his own with Iyoclease against Atroposa. The sorceress was whipping dirt and small cyclones at them while ducking away from the snapping jaws of the hellhound.

Meanwhile, the other beast was attacking both Adrastus and Caphiera, and they in turn were furiously going after each other while fending it off.

Ian had a sudden thought and he darted over to the whistle Dieter had dropped. Putting it to his lips, he blew it twice and shouted, "Beasts! Attack the sorceresses only! Leave the others alone! Attack Caphiera and Atroposa *only*!"

That was as much as he managed to shout before a gust

of air blew him backward and he fell over one of Caphiera's fallen icicles. The whistle flew out of his hand, and he left it in the dirt. The beasts were now focused only on the sorceresses, and Ian had to help Perry get Adria to the portal.

Ian grabbed Wolfie by the arm again and tugged him toward the slope while he shouted to Carl.

"You go on!" Carl said. "I'll be along soon!"

But Adrastus abruptly left off pummeling Caphiera and whirled away from the fight. Grabbing Carl by the collar and nudging Iyoclease up toward Ian and the others, he shouted, "To the portal!"

Ahead of them, Perry began to stumble on the steep slope, and Adrastus passed Ian and Wolfie, going quickly to Perry's side to take his wife from him.

Carl caught up with Ian then, his chest heaving with exertion. "The box," Ian said, motioning with his head toward the figure of Adrastus, carrying his wife quickly up the hill.

"I . . . saw," Carl said. "I don't . . . think . . . I can save it," he gasped. "She . . . destroyed it completely."

As the six of them hiked up the slope, the noise of the battle between the sorceresses and the hellhounds grew less intense and a horrible yelp was soon followed by a howl, long and low. The sound was especially mournful, and Ian suspected that one of the despicable brutes had finally perished.

He was glad about it, but he also knew that with one of the beasts out of the way, the sorceresses would team up and eventually dispense with the other; then they would focus their evil attentions on Ian and his group.

As he helped the despondent Wolfie up the slope, Ian looked behind him and saw Iyoclease, bringing up the rear. The soldier was bleeding from a nasty-looking wound on his arm, and he looked terribly pale, but he didn't complain; instead, he kept a guarded eye on the path behind them.

Ian was immensely relieved when he spotted the portal a few moments later and saw that it was indeed open. Adrastus reached it first and he knelt at the entrance to gently lay down his wife. It wasn't until Ian was a few steps closer that he realized Adria was dead.

The general was overcome with emotion, and his broad shoulders sagged and shook while he mourned the loss of the woman who had been with him from the start of his quest.

Iyoclease came up behind Ian, his breathing intense and labored. Ian squinted at the soldier and found him grimacing with pain and sweating heavily from the brow. What was worse, Ian now recognized the shape of the wound on Iyoclease's arm. "You've been bitten!" he said.

Iyoclease didn't answer him; instead, he sank to his knees, dropping his sword and groaning in pain. Carl and Wolfie looked to Ian, as if they didn't know what to do. "Schoolmaster!" Ian called to Perry.

Perry moved to Iyoclease's side to inspect the wound, which was turning black and angry. "Please, sir," he said desperately, placing a hand on the general's arm. "We must get Iyoclease through the portal. He's been bitten by the hellhound!"

Ian understood all too well what would happen if they didn't get help for Iyoclease quickly. He knew that Eva was in London, and he hoped the soldier could hold on long enough for her to arrive and save him.

Adrastus ran a loving hand over Adria's face, closing her eyes and whispering something softly in her ear. He then got up and moved over to Iyoclease. Rummaging through a leather pouch he carried under his cloak, he removed a small container of yellow powder. He sprinkled this on the wound and when the powder hit Iyoclease's skin, it sizzled and hissed. The soldier groaned through gritted teeth, but he didn't flinch or turn away.

With Perry's help, Adrastus then brought Iyoclease through the portal, into the familiar tunnel leading them back into Dover. Ian and Carl followed while Wolfie moved listlessly over to the wall well inside the cavern, sat down, and put his head into his hands, as if it was all simply too much for him.

After handing the yellow powder over to Perry, Adrastus turned his attention to Ian, taking him by the shoulders. "The powder will prevent the poison from spreading, but you must get Iyoclease to the Healer as quickly as possible."

"We'll send for her right away," Ian promised.

Adrastus nodded. He then took off the two bronze cuffs wrapped around his wrists and gave these to Ian. "Here," he said.

Ian hardly knew what to say or do, but he knew he couldn't accept the cuffs from Adrastus. "I can't take these!" he protested.

"You can and you will, Ian," Adrastus told him firmly. "I have failed you, lad. I have betrayed my oath and it has cost me my heart. If there is any redemption to be had, it may lie with you and these cuffs. Use them to find out what was in that box."

"But I don't even know how—"

"Put them on and cross your arms over your chest. The portal will connect with your mind. It will see your intentions and it will know how to achieve your goal. But know this, Ian: when Laodamia gave me these cuffs, she said they had once belonged to her husband, Iyoclease. I will leave you to work out the meaning of that."

With his piece said, the general stepped back and turned to go. Ian called out to him. "General! Where will you go?"

"Home, lad," he said without turning around. "I will use the portal to go home and bury my wife." Adrastus then stepped up to the body of Adria, bending down to retrieve her cuffs. He placed them onto his own wrists.

Distracted by Adrastus, Ian didn't immediately notice that Perry had given the yellow powder to Carl before he too stepped across the portal line, back to Berchtesgaden. "What are you doing?" Carl said sharply, which pulled Ian's attention to his schoolmaster.

"I have a plan," he said to them.

"What plan?" Ian said, already feeling dread.

"The Führer will be here in a week," Perry told them. He motioned to the SS uniform he still wore. "This will help me get close enough, lads. Dressed like this, I can get to the Führer and I can kill him. And if I can do that, then I can end the war."

Ian and Carl stared incredulously at him. "But that's suicide!" Ian shouted.

Perry offered him a sad smile. "Yes," he said. "Please tell my brother what took place here and let him know I was thinking of him in the end."

In the next instant, the portal wall closed.

DIETER'S REPLACEMENT

Dieter Van Schuft lay sprawled on the ground amid the rubble of his ruined home. He'd been knocked flat by a cyclone that had exploded into his home, sending shards of glass, wood, brick, and rock hurtling about, and catching Dieter in the chaos too.

Feebly he worked his way up to a sitting position and stared down at himself. He could see a dozen puncture wounds in his chest, none of them deep but all of them almost too painful to bear. Panting for air, Dieter looked at his upper right arm to inspect one of the wounds more closely. He could see something black embedded in his skin, and he could have sworn whatever it was, was digging its way deeper.

He searched about, looking for something to cut the thing out with, and he realized that he was sitting amid the dismantled pieces of his master's chess set. Clumps of Gorgonite were spread about him, and in a terrible moment of clarity, he realized that what had punctured him was the

357

Gorgonite and it was now working its way under his skin, as if it had a mind of its own—as if it was possessed by something dark and evil.

Dieter moaned as the pain intensified. He could feel his life slipping away from him. He tried to get to his feet, but his efforts were feeble, so he lay back against the wall and pulled open his shirt. A blackness was forming where the Gorgonite had penetrated his skin, and when he lifted his trembling hand, he could see that the blue hue to his veins was now turning an ugly black. The Gorgonite was poisoning him, and there was no antidote. He was a dead man.

Dieter closed his eyes. He thought of his late wife, and his son—who was surely dead by now too. Dieter's breathing became shallow, and he knew his time was at an end. But in his final moments he became aware of something other than the pain and the heaviness in his chest. Something seemed to join his consciousness and oozed into his body, as if it was replacing him. He didn't know what, but he did know it was something dark. Something evil. Something of extraordinary power. And in his final seconds of life, Dieter *knew* what had entered his body.

A few moments later Dieter's eyes opened, and he raised his chin to look around again. Only it wasn't Dieter who looked out at the world. The thing that took the form of Dieter Van Schuft got up and limped out of the wreckage to the yard. There he found Atroposa and Caphiera, bleeding and angry and muttering over a piece of melted metal. With amusement he realized the melted metal was the Secret Keeper's box.

"What do you laugh at, *mortal?*" Caphiera demanded when she spotted him laughing at her in the yard.

The thing inside Dieter didn't answer but bent low and picked up the whistle, which he'd found with no trouble at all. He stood again and observed the still form of one of the beasts, lying crumpled and broken nearby. The male, he knew, because he'd received the beast's spirit in the underworld, but the she-beast was still alive. Putting the whistle to his lips, the thing inside Dieter blew and heard the mournful wail of Medea, the hellhound, somewhere up the mountain.

"What do you think you're doing?" spat Atroposa.

"Calling my pets," he said—but not in Dieter's real voice; he used his own.

Atroposa and Caphiera reeled backward before dropping to their knees and prostrating themselves. "Sire!" they said as one. "You grace us with your presence!"

"I do indeed, my daughters," said the underworld god. Pointing to the box, he asked, "Is that from the Secret Keeper?"

They nodded hastily. "I destroyed it for you, Sire!" Atroposa said.

"*I* destroyed it!" Caphiera snapped.

"Enough!" Demogorgon roared. "As long as the box is demolished and the scroll with it, the prophecy cannot be fulfilled." He then looked down at himself and frowned. "This form will not hold my spirit for long without being consumed by my power. Before that happens, we must find your brother, tame your sister, and vanquish the United."

At that moment, the hellhound, crouched low with her tail tucked under her, appeared from the forest and approached warily. Demogorgon could see she was injured, but not mortally. "Lead us to my son, Medea," he said.

The hellhound licked Dieter's hand and turned to dash back into the woods. "Come!" commanded Demogorgon as he walked from the yard. "We have a world to conquer and limited time to do it in."

THE GARDENER'S GRAVE...
AGAIN

A week after returning from Berchtesgaden, Ian, Theo, Carl, Jaaved, Eva, and the earl stood with Iyoclease at the entrance to the portal. Ian wondered if he'd have a chance later to spend a little time with Wolfie, but he knew it was too dangerous. The poor boy was being kept in a room at the castle where only the earl, the earl's aunt the lady Arbuthnot and Mr. Binsford were allowed to see him. The earl had promised that as soon as Wolfie stopped trying to control the minds of everyone around him, he would be let out, but for now, no one could trust him. Lady Arbuthnot seemed able to thwart Wolfie's best efforts to control her mind, and her vigil with him was almost constant. Ian hoped she could win him over soon.

At present, however, Ian was jittery and nervous, feeling Adrastus's bronze cuffs fit loosely around his wrists. He knew the others were looking at him expectantly, which only added to his nerves.

"You can do it," Theo whispered, squeezing his hand. "Just do what Adrastus said and all will be well."

Ian smiled. He loved his sister for her faith in him. Turning to Iyoclease, he asked for the tenth time, "Are you ready?"

Iyoclease beamed at him, holding high the silver treasure box with Ian's copy of the map inside. "I am, Ian."

Ian had thought long and hard that week about how best to use the cuffs. He knew his first mission should be to send the recovering Iyoclease back home to his own time, but perhaps there was more that he should or could do to help set things straight.

He'd gotten the idea to send Iyoclease home with the treasure box Adria had crafted in their room at the inn, after receiving a note from the admiral that he was still waiting on the map that Ian had promised him. It had ignited a curious thought in Ian's mind, and to investigate it, he and Carl had taken the train to London to visit Professor Nutley.

Ian had asked the professor to show him the map that had come from the very first box he and Theo had discovered. That map—although aged and fragile—had been an exact replica of the one that Ian himself had created a full year before discovering the first silver box.

Theo had warned Ian not to have both maps in the same room with each other, and that had really sparked his theory. He wondered what would happen if he ignored her advice, and sure enough, when the professor had lifted the fragile piece of paper from his desk drawer and Ian had pulled out his original map at the same time, the older version had evaporated before their very eyes.

Poor Professor Nutley had been beside himself, but Ian hadn't felt bad at all. He now knew exactly how the map had gotten inside that first treasure box. It had been carried back to Laodamia by Iyoclease himself.

Also inside the box was the heart of the Star of Lixus. Ian had asked Jaaved for it, and when the young Moroccan had learned why, he'd been all too happy to give it up.

Ian knew that Laodamia would need the Star to create her prophecies in a language they could work out with the professor's help—a mix of English and ancient Greek. Ian also knew that sending the Star and the map tucked inside a small silver treasure box was essential, as Adria herself had admitted to being inspired to create the series of silver boxes by the very one owned by Laodamia—one the Oracle had received from her betrothed shortly after he returned from his mysterious disappearance.

But as useful and likely essential as all these things were to Laodamia and their quest, Ian still hesitated to send Iyoclease back without one more significant bit of knowledge. The reason he hesitated was that he didn't quite know how to tell a man that he would be murdered by the evil sorcerer named Magus the Black.

Ian, Carl, and Theo had long debated whether to tell Iyoclease. Carl reasoned that if Iyoclease knew of his destiny, he might take steps to alter it and irrevocably change history, with disastrous consequences.

Theo, however, was simply convinced that Ian *must* tell

the warrior his fate. Which was easy for her to say—she was a seer. She thought *everyone* should know their fate, if they could.

But Ian was torn. Even now, he didn't open the portal because he still hadn't made up his mind. "Master Wigby," the earl said. "The hour grows late."

Ian swallowed hard and raised his arms. Iyoclease smiled encouragingly at him, no doubt anxious to be off, and that look of exuberant happiness to be going home was what gave Ian pause. The poor man had no idea what he was going home to.

Lowering his arms, he said, "I can't."

"Why not?" asked Carl.

Without answering, Ian stepped up to Iyoclease and said, "If I knew something about your fate, Iyoclease, would you want me to tell you?"

The Phoenician soldier regarded Ian thoughtfully. "I have no doubt you know how I will perish, Ian," he said bluntly. "And by the look of all these sad faces just now, I'm assuming I do not die an old man?"

Ian stared hard at the ground. "Right before she died, Mistress Adria shared something with me. . . ."

"Yes?" Iyoclease said when Ian didn't continue.

Ian closed his eyes and spoke very quickly. "She said that Magus the Black killed you. She told me he was responsible for your murder."

The cavern they stood in was so silent Ian thought everyone might be able to detect his pounding heart. At last he heard Iyoclease speak. "Tell me word for word, what did my dear friend say?"

Ian tried to swallow the lump in his throat that formed every time he thought of the final moments of that brave woman. Wanting to quote her exactly, he said, "Her exact words were 'Tell Iyoclease, Magus kill him.'"

Ian looked up to gauge the noble man's reaction, but what he saw in Iyoclease's eyes surprised him. "You *know*?" he guessed.

Iyoclease smiled and squeezed Ian's shoulder. "Laodamia is my betrothed, Ian. Do you really believe she would not warn me of such a fate?"

Ian blinked. If Iyoclease knew who would kill him, why had he not altered history to strike first or take Laodamia out of Phoenicia and flee? Ian was about to ask that very thing when Iyoclease stopped him. "You know only a piece of the puzzle, Ian, but soon you will know more, that I promise you. Now, if you would oblige me, I would very much like to go home."

Ian looked at his cuffs again, terribly sad that he'd done nothing to help this man who'd done so much for him and his friends. He then remembered what Adrastus had told him: that the cuffs had once belonged to Iyoclease. Taking them off, he handed them to the soldier and said, "Here. These are yours now."

Iyoclease shook his head, but Ian wasn't having any of it. He knew he was possibly giving up his last chance to discover the truth about his origins. He'd had a chance to fantasize for a week about opening the portal up to the day that he'd been given to the gardener by his mother, but he hadn't done it. Now he was out of time, because clearly the only way the cuffs could ever be given to Adrastus in the first place was if Ian gave them to Iyoclease now.

But the soldier was still attempting to back away from Ian when he offered them. So Ian set his jaw with determination and pushed them onto each of the soldier's wrists. Once they were in place, Ian said, "Adrastus told me to cross my arms over my chest and allow the portal to enter my mind. Reading my intentions, it would open up to wherever I needed to go next."

Iyoclease frowned at him but did not protest further. Instead, he turned to face the stone wall and placed his arms across his chest before closing his eyes.

For a moment, nothing happened, and then, quite abruptly, there was a grinding noise and the wall disappeared. Beyond it were a bright blue sky and bleached sandstone. Iyoclease opened his eyes and stepped forward before turning around to wave at them.

Ian waved vigorously too, and just as the wall closed again, he thought he'd never seen a man look happier.

Three days later they received the news. On a dreary rainy day, the earl came to them at the keep, finding them holed up in the tower, where Ian and Carl were trying very hard to appear interested in the play put on by Theo, Eva, and Jaaved. Despite his best efforts, Ian knew he might lose the battle. The play was dreadfully dull. It was about a tea party, after all.

He'd have much preferred to be in the company of Océanne, but she and her mother were still in deep mourning over the loss of Monsieur Lafitte and were spending the afternoon with each other at Castle Dover.

So when the earl arrived, Ian felt relieved until he saw the expression on the man's face. In the earl's hand was a yellow telegram, but one look at the earl told him the news must be terrible. "I've received word, about Perry Goodwyn," he said, sitting down on Carl's cot.

"What is it?" asked Eva, setting down her teacup immediately.

The earl's lower lip trembled and it took a moment for him to collect himself. "Our sources in Germany report that a British spy was caught in Berchtesgaden, plotting an attempt on the Führer's life. He was shot at dawn, three days ago."

Ian felt as if he'd been punched in the stomach. Theo rushed into his arms and began sobbing in earnest, and Jaaved and Eva were overcome as well.

"His brother?" Ian asked, his voice hoarse and choked with emotion.

"I've just come from his cottage," said the earl. "I heard that he'd taken ill and was in bed since the day before yesterday. When I spoke with him, he said he knew the moment it happened. He'd felt a part of him die."

Ian cast his eyes to the floor. He felt terrible, not solely for the loss of a dear friend and his schoolmaster, but also because he'd done nothing to stop Perry from doing something so foolish. How had his schoolmaster ever thought he could get away with something so brazen?

The earl got to his feet and shuffled over to the steps. "We live in dark times, my children," he said to them. "Perry's brave sacrifice mustn't be for naught. Find the next box and the last Oracle, Ian."

Ian looked up then and he shook his head. *How* was he to find the next box without the cuffs or the one left in Germany to help him? He suddenly felt even more dreadful because he realized he'd likely given away any opportunity to find the next box when he'd given the cuffs to Iyoclease.

Stupid! he thought, hating himself for his impulsiveness.

Later that day Ian's mood was as foul as the weather. Shamefaced, he found himself leaving the comfort of the others, even though he knew he should be doing something to help ease all the terrible sorrow filling their lives.

But he found he didn't have it in him after hearing about Perry. He felt that he could barely take a full breath, in fact. The blow was more than physical; it had rocked him to the core.

He left the keep and began walking. The roads were choked with military traffic, which was why it took him most of the afternoon to reach his destination, but as he went into the quiet cemetery, he found a familiar comfort, especially when he approached the grave of the gardener.

He stood in front of it for a long, long time, his thoughts

tumbling around inside his head. The ache in his heart from Perry's loss filled his chest like mud; all the while the rain poured down around him, soaking him to the skin.

"Pardon me," said a soft voice behind him.

Ian jumped. He looked over his shoulder and found a feeble-looking old woman there, hunched down under her umbrella, staring at him curiously. "Yes?" he asked, not knowing what else to say.

"Did you know him?" she replied, pointing to the grave.

Ian blinked. "Yes," he said again. "We met once, but very briefly."

Again the woman stared curiously at him, and Ian wondered if she doubted his story. "He rescued me," he said, and as the words came out of his mouth, he knew them to be true.

"Rescued you?" she asked, stepping closer to him and lifting up her umbrella to kindly offer him a bit of shelter from the rain. "My brother rescued you?"

"Your brother?" Ian repeated.

The woman nodded. "Yes. Errol was my older brother."

Ian felt a tingle raise the hairs along the back of his neck. "You don't say?"

"It's true," she told him, nodding vigorously. "And he never said anything about rescuing a young lad. . . ." And then the woman seemed to catch herself, and her free hand came out to grip Ian's arm. "Are *you* the babe?" she asked. "The babe he was accused of stealing?"

Ian smiled. "I am the babe he rescued from a cavern near the Earl of Kent's castle, ma'am. I bear no grudge against your brother, and I know with certainty that he had no part in stealing me."

The woman's face filled with gratitude and she slid her hand down to Ian's and took a firm hold. "Come with me," she said. "You'll need a spot of tea, a warm fire, and a story to cheer your heart."

A bit later Ian sat huddled in a towel in the tiny kitchen of the dear old woman. "Name's Alice," she told him. "Mrs. Wallace, if you prefer."

Ian sipped his tea and smiled. He liked the old woman immensely, and his heart was eased by her kindly attentions. After setting a plate of biscuits in front of him, Alice shuffled off to her bedroom, only to reappear with some small object wrapped in velvet. Ian eyed the shape and size of the object keenly, his heart already quickening its beat. "This is for you," she said, placing the velvet-wrapped package on the table in front of him.

Ian stared at it without touching it. Could it be?

Alice sat down and pointed to the present. "The day my brother found you and your mother in that dark tunnel near the earl's property, he told me that after handing off her babe, the woman pushed this little treasure at him, insisting that he take it.

"He said that he didn't feel right about it, and he wondered why the woman wanted to pay him with treasure when he gladly would have seen you to safety. He took you to the earl and tried to explain it all, but poor Errol had a reputation as a drunkard, and the earl didn't believe him.

"Errol never blamed him, though. My brother had a good heart."

Alice looked at Ian hopefully, as if wishing he could see past her brother's foolish acts and find the way to his good nature. "Yes," he agreed, wanting nothing but to please her. "I'd long heard what a kind and gentle man your brother was, and the very best gardener in Dover too."

Alice sat back, beaming him a smile. "Yes, he most certainly was," she said. "But back to this treasure. You see, Errol wanted to explain to the earl that a strange woman had given him the treasure as payment for seeing the babe to safety, but after the earl accused him of stealing the child, Errol knew that he'd be further accused if he revealed this." For emphasis, Alice tapped the velvet covering. "So he kept it a secret, holding on to it all these years. I told him to sell it, as I knew he needed the money. Hard to find work after your reputation's been ruined. But he never did. No, Errol never sold it.

"Instead, he kept it carefully hidden, only bringing it out on special occasions and the like. No finer thing has ever graced our family's house, I tell you. On his deathbed he gave it to me, but not to keep, no. He made me promise not to keep it should its rightful owner ever turn up."

"Rightful owner?" Ian asked.

"Yes. You see, the more Errol thought on it, the more convinced he was that the box wasn't given to him as payment; it was given to him for safekeeping. He believed strongly that it belonged to the babe from the cavern and he made me swear that if you ever came round looking for it, I'd see you got it."

With trembling fingers Ian lifted the edge of the velvet and pulled away the cloth. He could hardly believe his eyes when he took in the sight. It was Adria's silver box, the very one she'd crafted at the inn in Berchtesgaden. The one he'd sent back with Iyoclease to give to Laodamia. A treasure box she herself had treasured.

"There's something inside," Alice said, coaxing him. "Errol tried for years to figure out how to open it, but he could never work out a way without damaging the box, so he left it alone and I did too."

Another lump formed in Ian's throat as his brain raced to connect the dots and a well of emotion so deep and so strong came up from inside him and this time he couldn't quite get past it. Alice seemed to see his distress and she got up from her chair and came over to wrap her arms about him. "There, there, lad," she said. "It's all right."

Ian clung to her, trying not to let himself fall to pieces, but that Alice would present him with *this* box and not one of the others slid so many puzzle pieces into place that the shock of it simply took his breath away.

"You're overcome because this box proves it, doesn't it?"

Ian blinked. He didn't know quite what she meant; after all, how could she possibly know all that the box's appearance signified?

When he didn't answer her, Alice backed away a bit to look down at him. "It's proof that your mum loved you very much, Ian. And whatever her reasons for giving you away, I'd wager, they were reasons born of desperation."

Ian ducked his chin and swallowed again and again, but try as he might, he could not hold back his emotion. He found he could barely breathe with the relief and the gratitude and the wonder of it all. In the back of his mind, he realized that he'd known all along who had come to the portal that day and given up her newborn babe. He also knew why Iyoclease had appeared so familiar to him at their first encounter. When he thought about it, they resembled each other very much.

So now he knew. Laodamia and Iyoclease were his parents, which meant that Theo really was related to him. She was Iyoclease's niece, and Ian's cousin. It astonished him that he'd taken so long to arrive at something so obvious. Perhaps he needed this box and this moment to confirm it. He had no doubt that was why Laodamia had made sure to bring her box to the portal that day. For him. She'd done it all for him.

Ian wiped his eyes and nose with his sleeve. Clearing his throat, he thanked Alice for her kindness and asked to be excused, promising to return to visit with her if she'd like.

"Oh, I'd like that very much, Ian," she said.

He left her then, cradling the box to him as if it held his very heart. He smiled when he thought about what he intended to do with the box. After opening it and removing the next scroll and whatever else his mother had hidden for him, he would give it to Océanne and tell her his true feelings. And then he would gather the members of the United, making plans to find the last Oracle, and together they would stand against the dreaded four. He no longer feared that encounter. His mother had seen him through to the end, and he vowed that he would not let her or his father down.

Ian thought on these things as he took his time making his way through the rain back to the keep, feeling not one drop because his spirit was now so light.

ACKNOWLEDGMENTS

If it's true that no man is an island, it is equally true that no book is written alone. Although we authors get to stamp our works with our own individual monikers, every book is in fact a compilation of efforts, and to those gifted and talented others who helped, I would like to offer my profound gratitude.

First and foremost, I sincerely thank my two fabulous editors, Krista Marino and Krista Vitola. Without these two amazingly talented ladies, many holes would have been left unfilled, loose ends would have dangled alarmingly, and great pockets of inconsistencies would have tripped up even the most ardent of readers. For the two Kristas' insight, advice, and wisdom, I can't thank them enough.

As I do in every novel I write, I would also like to give my most sincere thanks to my agent, one Mr. Jim McCarthy, without whom I'm quite positive I'd be sitting in an office cubicle working at some mundane job and feeling a little bit of my soul die each day. Thank you for this gift that is my life as a writer, Jim. I've never worked so hard and loved what I do so much.

Special thanks also to my publisher, Beverly Horowitz, for

her support and faith. And of course, special thanks to the fantastically gifted artist Antonio Javier Caparo. Antonio, I don't know how you manage to outdo yourself with each successive cover, but I love what you're doing, my friend!

Personal thanks also go to my friends and family, who consistently keep me from sinking into the back of my writing cave to glower over my computer, by offering support, enthusiasm, and wonderful levity. Love you all, very much.

ABOUT THE AUTHOR

When Victoria Laurie was eleven, her family moved from the United States to England for a year abroad. She attended the American Community School at Cobham, and one day, while on a class field trip, she first glimpsed the White Cliffs of Dover. Her trip to the cliffs, the year abroad, and her grandfather's stories of his childhood as an orphan left such an indelible impression on her that when she turned to a career as an author, she was compelled to write the Oracles of Delphi Keep series. *Quest for the Secret Keeper* is the third book in this series. The first two books, *Oracles of Delphi Keep* and *The Curse of Deadman's Forest,* are available from Delacorte Press.

You can visit Victoria at oraclesofdelphikeep.com.